Something Other than Pain
Shepard Security Book 2

By Kerry Taylor

ALEX

He'd left. I knew he had. I'd been sat in a wine bar, in the middle of downtown Chicago, waiting for my date to return from the men's room for over thirty minutes. He wasn't coming back. I was half expecting it if I was honest with myself. It was a blind date and I'd met him at a restaurant earlier in the evening. I'd arrived first. The meal went well considering it was a blind date, set up for me by a colleague from the office. He was good looking and funny and we'd laughed a lot. I had got the sense he was a little arrogant, but I'd pushed it aside and agreed to go to the wine bar for a drink with him when he offered. It was all going really well, which had surprised me because the very few dates I had been on since moving to Chicago just over four years ago, had been completely disastrous.

It wasn't until we stood to leave the restaurant that this one had taken a nosedive. I stood and slipped on my leather jacket then reached over to the wall for the crutch I used to support me when I walked. I had seen his face drop then, as though he just realised I was an alien or something.I smiled at him, but he just continued to stare and his face turned to one of deep annoyance. Great, here we go, I thought. I picked up the crutch and leant on it as I made my way to his side.

"Ready when you are." I said and he turned around to leave, but then stopped again.

"Is there something wrong….with your legs I mean? I didn't realise you…." He pointed to the crutch as though it were something truly terrifying.

"Is it a problem?" I asked bluntly. He looked at me then as though he was fighting between his desire to run away and how much of a prick it would make him.

"No" He finally settled on. "Of course not. Let's go." He walked out of the restaurant as quickly as he could then and the whole way, three blocks over, to the wine bar he had maintained a good couple of metres distance from me. I was starting to feel like a leper, not someone with a very slight limp and a crutch! I'd have stormed off and left him to his issues, except I was still clinging to hope. I was so desperately lonely, I just needed some human contact. I had arrived in the city, a long way from home, completely alone and suffering terrible side effects from a brain injury I had sustained almost a year before. Since then I had made myself a home, got a decent job and found ways to resolve some side effects of the injury, relieve some others and live with the rest. I had made a life for myself, but it was a very solitary existence. I had colleagues at the unemployment office I worked in, but nobody who ever wanted anything to do with me socially. In four years I hadn't made a single friend, not through lack of trying, and my family were deep in my miserable history where I wanted them to remain.

There was, therefore, no one in my life. The only time I spoke to a real person was at the office and other than that I was completely isolated and so desperately lonely.

I had continued to that wine bar, with that arrogant sonofabitch that night because I was holding out a pathetic wish that he would see past my issues and just come to like me. I just needed someone in my life.

I sat on the sofa, right in the centre of the crowded bar and began to tear up as I realised he was long gone. Once again I sat completely alone and embarrassed. I knew I needed to get out of there before I really broke down, so I threw back the last of my Cosmopolitan and signalled the waitress for the check. She returned with it a few moments later and I pulled out my wallet thinking I should just about be able to cover it with the twenty dollars I had left after already spending my entire weeks money on half the check at the fancy restaurant the guy had taken me to. I'd been fine about splitting it initially. I was a modern woman, willing to pay my way, but when the check had arrived after the meal, I found out the whiskey my crappy date had been throwing back like it was going out of fashion, all night, was 30 year aged malt whiskey at $18 a glass. Half the total balance had taken every penny I had for groceries, gas and my meds for that week. All I had left was the $20 which I was counting on to get a cab home, but now he had left and clearly not paid and I knew I was facing a very long, cold, painful walk home. It was my own fault. I'd been a damned fool.

I picked up the receipt and studied it. I couldn't believe my eyes when I saw the total, $65! We'd had one drink each! I looked down the list, a Cosmopolitan, a whiskey and at the bottom a $50 bottle of Burgundy. I called the waitress over and tried to suck up my tears.

"Excuse me, there's a bottle of red on this check that we didn't have?" I explained as she bent close to me. The music in the crowded bar was loud and I had to shout. "Oh yeah. I thought that was kinda strange. The guy you were with ordered it on his way out to take with him." She shouted back.

"Oh, I see." I nodded, not knowing what the hell to say or do. "That's ok then." I
added, not wanting to look foolish. She nodded and turned back to the table of rowdy guys in suits trying to get her attention.

I opened my wallet and frantically looked through it, even though I knew I only had the twenty dollar bill in there. My checking account had less than three dollars in and I knew I was screwed. I could leave the $20 and just run, but what if they realised and stopped me? It wasn't like I could make a quick getaway and if they called the police everything would unravel for me. I was beginning to lose it as the tears flowed faster and deep sobs tried to escape.

"Hi." I looked up and found a guy standing opposite me. He was tall, with very dark thick wavy hair and beautiful bright blue eyes. He was wearing grey suit pants and a crisp white shirt unbuttoned at the collar and the cuffs rolled up to his elbows, revealing well defined, muscular arms. He was a god, built, chiseled and amazingly handsome and there I was, a crying disaster area.
Perfect, just perfect!

"I don't mean to bother you," He went on when I just sat staring. He was British and, holy hell, that accent was sexy! "I just wanted to check you're ok? I'm over there with my mates and I couldn't help but notice how upset you look." I looked over to where he pointed and saw two other, huge, good looking guys sat at a table in the corner.

"I'm fine thanks." I called back. He moved around the table then and took a seat right next to me. I could smell his aftershave, spicy and masculine.

"No, you're not."He said right into my ear. I got goosebumps down both arms as I felt his warm breath on my face as he leant closer to be better heard.

"Maybe I can help?" He offered.

"Thanks, but it's nothing. Really I'm ok." I lied.

"Where's the guy you were with? Is he coming back?"

"No." The tears were threatening again and I fought to hold them back.

"He walked out with a bottle of red. Did he put it on that bill?" The stranger asked as he pointed to the receipt in my hand. *Great, why not? I was having a completely crappy night, why not humiliate myself with this gorgeous guy too?*

"Yeah ok, he did. He went on a date with me, screwed me out of $200 at dinner and then screwed me here too and walked out on me! You can go and have a good laugh about it all with your buddies now!" I shouted angrily. He met my eyes and his face was filled, not with the laughter I expected, but with concern and I instantly felt bad for being so harsh. "I'm sorry." I added when he just looked at me and didn't say anything. "It's just been a really bad night."

"It's ok. I get it, trust me. I've had my fair share of dates from hell." He said with a gentle smile. "Let me get this for you, ok?" He took the bill from my hand before I could stop him.

"No! You don't need to do that!" I protested.

"So you have money to cover it then?"He asked.

"Some of it." I replied sadly.

"So, I'm going to cover it then ok? Please? I can't stand to see someone so beautiful, so upset." I studied his handsome face. He was so kind and seemed so genuine. I wanted to break down in his arms so badly, just to have someone hold me for once, but I held as strong as I could.

"Thank you." I agreed. I had little choice really. "But if you give me your details I can pay you back next week."

"There's no need." He said as he pulled out his wallet and took out some dollar bills. I hurried to hand him the $20 dollars I had and again he was staring at me.

"You need that for a taxi, don't you?" He asked.

"No, it's ok. I can walk. It's not far."

"Where's not far?" He asked.

"It's just a few blocks. Please, just take it ok? This is embarrassing enough!" I cried.

"Fine, but I'm walking you home." He took the check from me and put it with the money from his wallet on the little tray.

"You don't need to. I'll be fine."

"No, sorry. There's no way I'm leaving you to walk several blocks alone. It's a sketchy area and I wouldn't feel right." He said firmly.

"I'll get a ride then." I bumbled huddiedly, not wanting him to realise I had lied about the distance or to go to any more trouble because of me.

"Look, I just want to make sure you're alright. I'm not a serial killer or anything. I just saw you were upset and I wanted to help if I could. If you don't feel comfortable with me walking you back then I'll put you in a taxi, but I'm not going to drop it until I know you're home safe, alright?"

"Why?" I retorted. "Why would you even care? You don't know me." I asked suspiciously.

"Just call me a good Samaritan." He said with a smile. "Or maybe I meant what I said before, that I can't stand to see someone so beautiful, so upset."

"Beautiful! Yeah right!" I scoffed. He shook his head and went to speak again, but I cut him off. "I'm grateful for your help, but you don't need to help me get home. I'm a big girl! If you just give me your address I'll be sure to send you the money back when I can next week." I said as firmly as I could, but he just smiled and I knew he wasn't going to give in.

"I'll just grab my coat then and I'll walk you back, ok?" He said, ignoring everything I'd said.

"Fine." I conceded. He was definitely persistent and I gave up. I'd just have to walk a few blocks and stop somewhere that looked like apartments. He was laughing as he walked back over to his table and I wondered what it was he found so amusing.

MATT
I couldn't help but chuckle to myself as I walked back over to where Jack and Cal were sat. I had never seen anyone fight so hard to reject a little help.

I had noticed her the second she had walked in with that prick. She was beautiful, her long wavy, bright blonde hair instantly catching my eye. Then I saw her wide, emerald green eyes, from across the bar and I was transfixed. A dainty little thing, I guessed barely five feet tall and slim, but with beautiful curves. When she smiled her entire face lit up and I had been desperate to go over and speak to her, but I couldn't with him there. I had kept an eye on her for the next hour. Her date had gone to the bar after about twenty minutes, I assumed to buy her another drink, but then he had walked straight past me with the bottle of wine in his hand.

I watched her get increasingly fidgety and upset as it seemed to dawn on her she had been abandoned and then when the waitress left the table and her lip was quivering I had to go to her.

I admired her fire as she tried everything she could to turn away my help. She was a feisty, stunning woman and I was determined to do whatever it took to get her number.

"Where did you go?"Jack asked as I returned to the table. Jack had been a good mate for over ten years. I worked with him at the same hospital and we were neighbours too. He was my sister's best friend and had helped us both through hell the year before. Cal was his fiance and we were all part of a very ramshackle family we had formed along the way along with our other mate, Rob.

"To help that girl out." I replied as I nodded to where she was hurriedly pulling on her jacket.

"Oh really?" Jack said suggestively.

"Not like that! Her dick of a date charged a $50 burgundy to her bill and walked out on her. She looked upset."

"And you want to make her feel all better?" Cal asked with a grin.

"Fuck off!" I said jovially. "I'm going to walk her home. She's in a bit of a state and I want to see she gets back alright." I explained as I shrugged on my heavy wool coat.

"She seems ok to me."Jack laughed as he looked behind me. I turned just in time to see her hurry out of the bar.

"Bloody woman!" I cursed as I grabbed my rucksack and hurried out after her.

"Good luck!" Jack called and I heard their laughter as I raced out to the snowy street. It was mid November and we'd had an early snow storm that week.

"Hey!" I called as I jogged the few metres to catch up with her. "I said I'd walk you home." She was struggling to walk quickly with what I guessed was a nerve damaged left leg and her crutch. She had on a ridiculous little jacket and she was already shivering.

"And I said you don't need to." She said defiantly.

"You don't give in do you?" I laughed.

"I could say the same of you!" She accused.

"You're right, I don't give in so you might as well stop trying to get away from me. I am walking you home."

"Do what you like." She sighed as she finally slowed down a little.

"I'm Matt by the way…..Matthew Simmons, but I prefer Matt," She turned to look at me as she walked and finally her face softened a little.

"Alex." She whispered.

"Nice to meet you Alex." I said with a smile. She shuddered and I knew she was frozen. I dropped my bag from my shoulder and took off my coat, which I wrapped around her shoulders. She stopped and turned to me.

"You'll freeze!" She said with yet more worry about putting me out.

"I have my suit jacket in here." I explained as i opened my bag and pulled out my grey blazer. I put it on and fell into step beside her again.

"Why are you being so nice to me?" She accused as though it were a crime.

"Because I'm a nice guy." I joked.

"Seriously, what do you want from me?" She asked and I got the feeling she really wasn't used to people taking care of her. She was trying to be so tough and guarded.

"Nothing, except maybe your telephone number."

"My number?"

"I'd like to take you out sometime if you'd be interested?" I asked nervously. She stopped again then and looked up at me with confusion. She thought for a minute, then turned away and started marching again.

"So you're not interested then?" I asked with disappointment as I walked faster to keep up.

"Just leave me alone!" She shouted and she was crying again. "It's a wager, isn't it? You and your friends having a good laugh about screwing the cripple!" She was almost screaming and I didn't know what to do. I stopped and tried to think what I had done to make her think I'd be so horrid. She was getting further away and I hurried to catch up, worried I would lose her in the maze of buildings.

"Hey!" I said as I stood in front of her and stopped her. She looked up and her eyes were filled with more pain than I had ever seen. "That is not true. I do like you and yeah, I admit, I wanted to help you out to maybe get a date, but if you're not interested then it's fine. I will happily see you home safe and leave you in peace. I would never, ever do that to a woman and neither would my mates. I'm sorry if I did something to make you feel otherwise." I tried to explain. She stared at me and I knew she was analysing everything I'd said and done. I could almost see her cogs turning as she fought an internal battle.

"You didn't." She finally whimpered. "I'm sorry i'm being such a bitch. I guess I'm just not used to guys being so…..so decent." She sighed.

"Well you're spending time with the wrong guys then."

"Yeah, I really am!" Finally she smiled. "Not that they're beating down my door or anything." She added.

"They should be." I said, more to myself.

"Yeah, ok!" She dismissed as she started walking again.

"I mean it! You're a beautiful….."

"Cripple!" She cut me off.

"Don't do that." I sighed. "So you walk with an aid. It doesn't make you any less."

"Tell my date that, and the last four before him. No one wants to date a young woman with a limp."

"I do. It makes no odds to me. All I see is a beautiful, feisty woman"

"Well there really is something wrong with you then!"

"Maybe, but don't tell me you'll judge me for it after what you just said to me about being judged." I said with a laugh. She gave me a hard stare that finally descended into a little laugh.

"You're even more beautiful when you smile." I said truthfully. When she smiled her entire face sparked to life and she almost glowed. She instantly looked away from me nervously. She looked around uncertainly and then pointed to a tall building across the street.

"That's me." She declared, "Thanks for walking me back," She moved to take my coat from her shoulders, but I put my hand on her shoulder to stop her.

"It's ok. I'll see that you get inside safely." I said firmly.

"You don't need to." She cried and I wondered what she was so worried about. I was only crossing the road with her and she'd be rid of me.

"And yet I am going to." I said as I took her elbow and led her across the busy street. She just stayed quiet and allowed me to hold her arm as we neared the building. I looked up the twenty storey or so building and realised it was completely dark, not a single light in one window. I looked a few metres ahead to the door and noticed a list of businesses next to the intercom.

"So, this is where you live is it?" I asked.

"Home sweet home." She said with a nervous smile.

"Which floor are you on?" I asked, trying to hold in my chuckle.

"Twelve."

"So you're in the accountants, or the surveyors office then?" I pointed to the sign and she turned to read it.

"Between them actually." And I knew, for sure, she was lying then.

"You don't actually live here, do you?" I asked. She began to worry her bottom lip between her teeth and it was the cutest thing I'd ever seen.

"No." She finally admitted.

"If you didn't want me to know where you live you could have just told me. I'd have got you a taxi." I sighed, wondering what had made her so distrustful.

"It's not that!" She said hurriedly. "It's just,,,,,,well I live in Gold coast and I didn't want you getting me a cab that far and I certainly wasn't going to make you walk it."

"Yet you were going to walk it yourself, alone in the middle of the night?"

"I'd have been fine."She pouted, looking down at the floor as she spoke. I longed to make her meet my eyes. Instead I looked down the street and hailed the taxi approaching us.

"What are you doing?" She asked.

"Getting you home as I said I would." The taxi pulled up and I opened the door. "Come on." I indicated she should get in, but she looked nervous.

"It's going to cost too much." She whispered.

"Alex, I live in Gold Coast too. I'll be getting a taxi there anyway. If you'd just been upfront with me..."

"I'm sorry," She said shakily.

"It's ok beautiful. Let's just get in now, ok?" I encouraged, bloody frozen myself and concerned about the way she shivered constantly. She smiled and then climbed into the backseat. I closed the door when she was safely inside and then dashed round to get in next to her. She really was a puzzling woman and I was hooked.

ALEX

I felt like a complete idiot once again. This poor guy had just wanted to look out for me and I'd lied to him, yelled at him, taken his money and his coat and dragged him around in the snow for no reason. What an absolute disaster! If by some miracle he was interested in me before, he wouldn't be now!

He told the driver Gold Coast and we set off through the city. I turned to him and watched as he settled his backpack between his feet on the floor. How had I messed everything up so badly? This guy may actually have wanted to date me and in return I had done everything I could to chase him away.

"I really am sorry about everything." I sighed, deciding honesty was my best option to not scare away this gorgeous man. "I'm not really so good with people."

"Why's that?"

"I don't know. I guess I probably spend way too much time alone."

"You live alone?" He asked.

"Just me, Charles Dickens and my orchid." I admitted.

"Charles Dickens?"

"I'm trying to get a collection together, original printings from back in the day. I've got quite a lot now." *Wow, that sounded pathetic Ali.*

"Sounds like fun." He said with a smile, making me laugh. "Are you from the city? I'm not good with American accents."

"No. I'm from LA. I came here about four years ago for a fresh start."

"Any family here?"

"No. No family period." I said curtly. "Like I said, just me, dickens and the orchid."

"Sounds lonely." He whispered and I dare not look in his eyes.

"I get by." I lied. "How about you. I'm no good with accents either, but I know you're not from here."

"I came over about twelve years ago from England. My sister lives in Chicago too, she moved out here just over a year ago."

"That must be nice." I was jealous, I so wished I had a sibling I actually cared about and who cared for me, who I could call and just chat to whenever I wanted or needed to.

"It is."

"What do you do? I'm guessing by the suit you must be some kind of lawyer?" I guessed.

"Lawyer? No bloody way! I'm too honest for that. I'm a surgeon at Chicago General, general surgeon."

"Oh." I whispered as I cursed in my head. I knew he was too good to be true! If there was one group of people I hated after everything I'd been through, it was doctors.

"I've done it now, haven't I? You're a doctor hater?" He asked as he studied my face.

"Well I've never met one as nice as you, let's put it that way."

"Seems like you need help choosing dates and doctors then." He laughed.

"Well, I don't really see doctors anymore so that doesn't matter and as for dates, I think I've let myself be burned for the last time tonight." I sighed.

"You shouldn't shut yourself off because a few idiots pissed you about. There are good blokes out there and you clearly deserve one."

"Well I wish they'd make themselves known."

"Erm, hello?" He called as he waved his hand at me.

"Why would you really be interested in me? You're.....well you're hot and I am not!" I said bluntly.

"Alex, you are beautiful and fiery and stubborn and I think it's all very attractive. I would do anything to get a date with you and I swear I would never hurt you like other guys you've been out with. I know I'm not supposed to say it myself, but I really am a good guy. I might be a little work obsessed and my sister says I'm the biggest neat freak she knows, but other than that I'm normal, I swear." I looked at him and believed every word he said. He was a good guy, you could see it in his face and from the respectful way he had treated me.

"You don't know what you'd be getting into with me." I sighed, knowing I was going to give in.

"I don't care." I took a deep breath and decided to be completely open. If he knew everything it was unlikely he'd be interested anyway.

"Look, you're a doctor, so I'm just going to put my cards on the table. I was in a nasty fall five years ago and I came away with a brain injury. My left leg is pretty crappy, as is my left arm. I have mood swings and occasionally seizures and I am constantly in pain. You really want to get into that?"

"Are you on medication?"

"Matt, I don't need a doctor." I sighed as I turned away.

"Sorry, old habits." He said as he took my hand. I turned and met his amazing blue eyes, as little electric shocks tingled where he touched. "Yes, I do want to get into whatever I have to, to get a date with you, ok?"

"That's just the tip of the iceberg. I'm a huge fucking mess and you should stay well away."

"I don't want to, so can I please just have your number. We're not getting married, it'll just be a date for now you know?" He said and I couldn't help but smile.

"Ok, but don't say you weren't warned." I sighed as I gave in and pulled out my cell. We exchanged numbers just as we drove into the area I lived in.

"You can let me out here, I live just around the corner." I said hurriedly.

"You're kidding. Where, not on East Rivera?" He asked.

"Yeah, why?"

"I live there too. We're neighbours." He directed the driver and stopped outside the apartment block almost directly opposite mine. He got out and paid the fare and I followed him.

"This is my building." He said as he pointed to the huge, tall state of the art modern apartment building.

"I'm over there." I said as I pointed across the street to my old dilapidated building.

"I can't believe we live that close and I've never noticed you before."

"It's a pretty busy street Matt."

"I suppose so. Come on, I'll walk you over. He took my hand this time as we crossed the street and I loved it. He made me feel so safe when he walked with me.

"Thank you so much for paying that bill and getting me home. I really do appreciate it." I said as we stopped out front of my building.

"You're very welcome. Am I going to get that date with you?" He asked.

"I would think so." I said with a smile.

"How about tomorrow afternoon?" He asked eagerly.

"I'm working until one, but I could meet you after if that's good for you?"

"Definitely. Shall I meet you here around three?"

"Sounds good." I agreed.

"Great. See you tomorrow then?"

"Tomorrow." He leant in and kissed my cheek and I couldn't help but blush. The arm, and hand holding and that kiss was the only touch I had received from another human for over four years and it felt magical. He turned to walk away and I panicked.

"Matt?" I called and he turned back to me.

"Yes beautiful?"

"If we're gonna go on a date, will you promise to just be straight with me. Please? If your not into me then just tell me, ok? I don't want to be hurt again." I said honestly.

"Alex, I will never hurt you. I promise. You don't have to worry, ok?" He was in front of me then, brushing his thumb over my tear stained cheek.

"Thank you." I whispered. He kissed my cheek again and this time I turned and walked inside. I prayed he meant what he said because I was at a very low point in my life and I truly felt that one more slap in the face would push me over the abyss.

***

"Crap, crap, crap!" I cursed loudly as I threw the very few items of clothing I owned from my closet. I was running late for the date with Matt following a crappy morning at the unemployment office. It had been crazy busy due to a technical error that had meant many payments, which should have been paid that morning, were not and I was faced with a huge queue of angry customers all morning. I had been yelled at, cried on and personally accused of withholding payments continually for five hours. By the time I arrived home I was ready to pour a glass of wine and curl up with Netflix and my bad mood, but I couldn't. I had a date and I needed to get in the right headspace. I couldn't turn up looking stressed and miserable, so I'd poured myself a glass of wine, cranked my playlist and tried to focus on the amazingly handsome man I would get to spend my afternoon with.

I had arrived home late, having left the office thirty minutes later than expected and then getting stuck in city traffic on the bus ride home. By the time I started getting ready I had a little over thirty minutes and It was not enough!

I had managed to style my hair half up so you couldn't see quite how wild it was. I needed to run the straightening iron over it, but there wasn't time. I had spent ten minutes applying make up as carefully as possible, but I really was useless. I had never even worn make up until I had arrived in the city and I had learnt the little I knew from Youtube videos, but I still struggled and so kept the coverage to a minimum, going more for a natural look.

Now I needed to pick an outfit and I realised I actually owned nothing! I had one date outfit, a pair of slim fit black trousers, a low cut white shirt and my leather jacket, all of which I had picked up at a thrift store months ago. It would have done, except I had worn it the night before and there was no way I could turn up to meet Matt in the same outfit I wore the night before!

My other clothes were all either cheap skinny jeans and T-shirts or boring black dresses for work, none of which were appropriate.

By the time I had thrown every item of clothing I owned across my bed, my phone was beeping, alerting me that the alarm I had set, to tell me to set off to meet Matt out front was up. I had five minutes to dress and get down to the entrance and I was ready to burst into tears. I knew it was pathetic, but since the brain injury I found it harder to control my emotions and I cried at the drop of a damned hat! I also lost track of time easily, which was why I had set the alarm and why I found myself late, again! I was always late.

"Come on Ali!" I told myself as I took a deep breath to hold back the stupid tears and silenced the alarm. It was no time to crumble. There was a kind, very handsome man waiting to take me out, downstairs. I needed to get my ass down there.

I pulled on my favourite dark wash skinny jeans and a simple, but well fitted dark green blouse. It was a little casual for a date, but it would have to do. I topped the outfit with my grey soft leather jacket and matching ballet flats, then grabbed my cell, purse and crutch and hurried out of the apartment.

As I walked through the small lobby of my building I saw Matt stood at the entrance waiting for me and he looked hot! He was wearing dark jeans, fancy brown boots and a heavy double breasted grey overcoat. He turned and smiled at me and my day instantly improved. His smile was intoxicating. He was just so unbelievably good looking and I once again wondered what the hell he saw in me?

"Hey. Sorry I'm late." I said nervously as we neared each other.

"No problem. You look beautiful. Are you ready to go?" He asked as he took my free hand. I nodded with a smile and he lead me from my building out to the snow covered street.

"Are you hungry? I thought we'd get an early dinner first?" Matt asked.

"Sounds good. I'm definitely hungry." I agreed realising I had skipped both breakfast and lunch in the chaos of the day so far.

"Do you like Italian?"

"It's my favourite" I agreed happily.

"Good. I know a great place. It's not fancy, but the food is amazing."

"Sounds good. I hate those stuffy, fancy places." Matt unlocked a fancy charcoal grey Range Rover which was parked just ahead and opened the passenger door for me. He took my hand and helped me as I struggled to climb up with my bum leg and tiny 5'2" height. I thanked him and then watched intently as he closed the door and jogged around the front of the huge car to jump in the driver's side.

The drive to the restaurant was short and when Matt placed a hand on my lower back and ushered me inside I instantly fell in love with the place. It was small, very intimate, cosy and welcoming. We were greeted by an actual italian man with the official accent and a friendly grin. He sat us at a small table tucked in the back corner, which looked so romantic with a single rose in a tiny vase and candles in the centre. It was the perfect place for a date, not too fancy, but really warm and comfortable. We took our seats and agreed on a half bottle of chardonnay to share since I wasn't a big drinker, and Matt was driving.

"Is this place ok? I know It's a bit simple, but the food really is the best I've found so far." Matt asked nervously. I looked around again at the small room, crammed with small bistro tables. The walls were covered in pictures of landscapes in Italy and classical music played quietly in the background. I compared it to the stuffy, fancy French restaurant I had been taken to the night before and smiled.

"I like it Matt. I'm not a fancy restaurant kinda girl. They just make me feel uncomfortable. This place is very cute." I assured him, making him smile again.

We ordered after receiving our drinks. I chose the carbonara while Matt opted for a risotto and then we were left to chat. It wasn't awkward as dates always had been in the past. It felt easy and natural to chat to Matt about the crappy morning I'd had at the office and to listen as he told me about his job and the crazy shifts he worked. He had a very laid back, relaxed air about him that instantly set me at ease too.

"So how long have you been in Chicago?" Matt asked as we started eating.

"Just over four years." I replied, hoping like hell he wouldn't ask for too many details about my past.

"What brought you across the country from LA?"

"Oh….erm, just a fresh start I guess." I bumbled, nervous all over again. "What brought you across the world?" I asked hoping to move the focus from my past.

"Adventure, excitement, all the usual dreams that a young, newly qualified graduate hopes for. I lived my whole life in a pretty boring, rural town in England. Don't get me wrong, I loved it. My parents were great, really loving and supportive and then Lucy, my sister, came along when I was twelve and we were inseparable. My parents were almost fifty when they found out she was on the way, unexpectedly of course. By the time she was toddling I was a teen and they were getting old. I took care of her a lot and we were so close. When I finished college I couldn't bare to move away and leave them all, so I studied close to home too and lived at home where I could still help out and be around for Lucy. I never regretted it, I was happy, but by the time I qualified I had itchy feet to see more of the world. By then Lucy was a teenager and I decided I needed to do something exciting, so I applied out here and actually got an internship at Chicago General. I've never really looked back. I've been here almost ten years now. I have a job I enjoy and some great friends."

"And you said your sister lives here too?" I asked.

"Yes, she moved out last year. We lost our parents a few years ago, car accident."

"I'm sorry." I whispered. It was puzzling to me, to see the pain in his face as he talked of the loss of his parents. It was an alien prospect to me to love your family the way Matt seemed to. Of course I knew loving families existed, but I'd only ever seen such things on TV shows. There was certainly no such love in the family I had come from.

"It was a shock and it hit Lucy hard, but at least they went together. They were always so in love, I think it's what they would have wanted." He smiled wistfully for a moment, then seemed to shake it away.. "Anyway, Lucy was a mess after their deaths. She refused to move here with me and wouldn't let me move home. She wanted her independence and I stupidly allowed it. She rushed into a marriage and it ended badly." There was a rush of anger in his eyes and it shocked me. I had seen nothing but kindness to that point.

"Did he cheat?" I asked, thinking that would explain the anger.

"I wish!" Matt laughed bitterly. "No. He was abusive. She hid it for over two years until things got so bad she had to leave him. She came here and she's doing better now."

"Good for her. She must be tough." I swallowed the lump forming in my throat. I had some idea of what

Matt's sister had gone through, having escaped my own hell.

"She is. I think you two would really hit it off." He said, the anger receding and the spectacular smile returning.

"I hope I get to meet her then. I haven't really made many friends since moving here, It'd be nice to meet some new people."

"You'll meet all of my friends beautiful, and they will all love you, but for now I'm keeping you all to myself." He said as he reached across the table and put his huge hand over my tiny one. I instantly felt the sparks I had felt when he touched me the night before and I shivered. I looked up and met his bright blue eyes, his stare intense. I stared for as long as I felt I could get away with, without looking crazy. Finally I had to break my gaze away, and looked around nervously. I felt so much for this man in such a short time of knowing him. What was happening?

"You...you were right, about the food I mean," I babbled randomly. "It was really good."

"I'm glad you liked it. Would you like dessert?" He asked, I knew it was an innocent question, but to my contact starved body, it lit a fire I thought had been permanently extinguished. Heat rushed over me and my heart pounded as I dared to look into those eyes once again. Hell. I wanted desert, a Matt shaped desert. I was needy and so hot as I zoned out imagining what he would look like stood naked before me, all muscle and strength. Desert sounded good and that shocked me something stupid, because it was the first time in my life

I had ever felt such a desire or even willingly considered ever getting close to a man in that way again.

"Alex, you ok love?" Matt asked, his face turning from a grin, to worry. I nipped my right thigh hard, something I did to try and refocus my mind. I managed to shake off my confusing thoughts and needy desires to get back to what was actually happening, the date.

"Sorry." I said guiltily. "I was miles away. What did you say?"

"That's ok." He grinned. "Dessert?"

"No I couldn't. I'm way too full, but thank you." I said hurriedly before my mind wondered once again at the thought of a whole different kind of dessert.

"Ok, I'll get the bill then. Do you want to head home or are you up to going somewhere else for a while?" I glanced down at my cell, which sat on the table and saw it was barely 5pm.

"I'm good to stay out. What did you have in mind?" I'd do anything to spend a little longer with him.

"There's a little cuban bar down the street that plays some great live music and serves all those fancy cocktails, like you were drinking last night. I thought we could have a few drinks, maybe dance a little and then catch a taxi home later. I can leave my car where it is until the morning. Sound ok?"

"Good music and cocktails? What's not to like? Let's go!" I said excitedly. Dancing! I had always wanted to go dancing, but I'd never had the opportunity and while I was nervous about how it would work with my left side as weak as it was, I didn't allow the worry to outweigh my excitement. I was having fun on the date with Matt and it seemed it could only get better.

MATT

Garcia's, the tiny cuban bar Jack had told me about that morning, was really busy when we walked in a short while later. I was surprised because it was really early, but that hadn't deterred the masses of bodies squeezed into the small space. Inside the walls were painted brightly and tiny tables were crushed together surrounding a large dancefloor and a stage where a band was playing lively music. I had never been in the place before, but feeling nervous about the date this morning I had turned to Jack for an idea of the perfect place to go. I had wanted the date to be fun for Alex after seeing how crushed she had been the previous night. She was a stunning, very intelligent, very fun woman who deserved to be shown that not all guys were complete wankers.

I was so drawn to her. I didn't really understand why, but I wasn't going to fight it. I had had girlfriends before, of course I had. I wasn't a monk, but they had never lasted longer than a few months because there was just never a real connection. They'd become bored of my working hours and not being given enough attention and I was never really invested enough to try and fix that, but Alex was different. From the moment she had walked in that bar the previous night I had been gripped by her. I needed to speak to her, to know her and after speaking to her I just needed more and more. She was special and I was not going to let her slip through my fingers.

"This place is amazing!" She called into my ear over the loud music as we walked through the crowded bar. I pulled her closer into my side, not wanting her to be jostled too much as we passed the crowds to get to the bar. I pushed her into a gap and surrounded her back, one hand either side of her on the bar. She felt so damned good pressed against me, the top of her head reaching only my chest. She smelled of something sweet, maybe vanilla? Whatever it was it was amazing and instantly had me wondering how it would feel to have her naked beneath me, surrounded by that scent as I kissed every part of her.

"What can I get you guys?" The server asked, snapping me from my fantasy.

"Can I get a mojito please?" Alex replied.

"And a beer." I added. We got our drinks and made our way over to an empty table right on the edge of the dance floor. It was crammed with people swaying and salsaing to the great live music. We watched on as we sipped out drinks, well Alex watched and I studied her. There was something so magical about the wonder and excitement in her eyes as she watched the dancing, as though it was the first time she'd seen such a thing. She seemed so innocent and naive in some ways, but in other she was tough and so strong. There was a worldliness in her eyes, something that told me she had seen tough times and had survived them to make her wiser. I hadn't missed the way she deflected any conversation that could even remotely lead to talk of her past. I'd just let it go, not wanting to push her, but I wondered what it was that brought her to a huge new city, alone and with health problems. What had she been through? Whatever it was I hoped I could be there for her, I hoped she would want me to be, because I was deeply under her spell.

"Would you like to dance Alex?" I asked after finishing my beer. I wasn't much of a dancer and wouldn't have had the courage without the wine and beer in my system, but she could barely sit still, her hand and foot tapping constantly and I knew she was eager to get out there. I wouldn't deny her that, I didn't think I could deny her anything.

"Really?" She said excitedly.

"I'm no Patrick Swayze, but I can move." I replied with a grin.

"I'm desperate to give it a go, but....I've never tried, with this...I'm not sure." She suddenly looked terrified as she pointed to her left leg. I stood and held out both hands. She took them and I pulled her up, noting as I did how weak her left hand was both when gripping and pulling. It made me wonder how she managed so well. Shaking away the medical thoughts I pulled her into my side and supported her weak side as we walked to a small clearing on the dance floor. I held her right hand and swung her so she landed pressed against my front with am 'oomph' and a giggle. I wrapped my arms tightly around her tiny waist and she moved her arms around my neck and that's how we stayed as we danced and laughed the evening away. There, with her wrapped securely in my arms, pressed against my body I felt happier that I had felt in a very long time. It was perfect, she was perfect.

ALEX

"Thank you Matt. I really have had an amazing time." I gushed as Matt and I climbed out of the cab outside my apartment building.

"Me too beautiful. Best date ever." We stopped before the steps up to my building and Matt pulled me into his front and encircled my waist with his strong arms, just like he had on the dance floor. It had been the greatest experience of my life dancing with him that night, feeling safe and supported in his arms as I just let free and had fun. "I hate for it to come to an end, but I have a shift at 6am tomorrow." He sighed.

"I have to work too. What time do you get off? Maybe I could cook?" I offered.

"I'll be done by seven, but you don't need to cook. I can get food on the way over."

"No. I'd like to cook for you. I only ever get to make meals for one. It'll make a change. Come over to mine, say seven thirty?" I knew I was being forward, especially for me, but with Matt I felt I could. He made me feel that comfortable.

"Ok baby, sounds good. I'll bring the wine. Which apartment?"

"724, top floor."

"I'll be there." Matt agreed. He reached up to move a stray tendril of hair that was blowing into my face, tucking it behind my ear, then he moved his thumb gently across my cheek and across my bottom lip. I was staring into his eyes and then suddenly, before I realised it was happening his lips were on mine. Did he move first or did I? I didn't care as I became lost in the soft kiss. His tongue touched my lips and it was all I needed to open to him. The kiss became a little harder then, almost possessive. I wanted to be his and I wanted him to be mine and the kiss said that. It was deep and sensual, so much more than I ever realised a simple kiss could mean. The way he held me in his arms, taking my weight as my legs began to tremble from the exertion of the evening and the overwhelming effect of the kiss, he made me feel that he really cared and that was a whole new experience to me. When he inevitably ended the kiss and pulled away he kept supportive hands on my waist until I got control of myself again.

"Wow." I whispered dreamily.

"Just what I was thinking." Matt said with a smile. "Will you be ok to get up to your apartment?"

"It was a damned good kiss Matt, but I can still walk!" I joked making him laugh. He bent down to kiss me again, this time just a brief kiss on the lips.

"Good night Alex." He said softly.

"Good night." With one more soft kiss Matt released me and I turned and walked into my building having had the greatest night of my life and my first real kiss at twenty six years old.

After one date I was completely wrapped up in Matt and just hoping like hell he wouldn't change his mind because I knew the hurt of feeling him ditch me would be the worst yet, a hurt I wasn't strong enough to handle.

MATT

I couldn't contain my happiness at the hospital the next morning. I had been on the greatest date of my life with the greatest woman I had ever met and I was seeing her again that night. No one could rain on my parade that day.

"Good date man?" Jack asked as he walked into the locker room later in the afternoon.

"Brilliant! Thanks for recommending that cuban place, she loved it."

"No problem. So will you be seeing her again then?"

"Yep. Tonight actually. She's making dinner when I get off." I tried, but failed to hide the goofy grin on my face.

"Really? That sounds promising. Lucy will be relieved, she's been going on and on about you being alone and how worried she is."

"Don't you dare go gossiping to Lucy about this yet." I said hurriedly.

"Oh man! You know I can't keep secrets from your sister. She's like a Jedi mind reader!" He whined.

"Just try Jack, please, for me. This is so new and Alex is shy. I don't want Lucy charging in and scaring her, at least not right away. I'll tell her if it keeps going well."

"Fine. I'll do my best to keep it quiet." Jack conceded.

"Thanks mate, appreciate it." I slapped his shoulder as I headed out.

"Matt?" Jack called. I turned back to him and he smiled. "I'm pleased for you man. You deserve some happiness."

"Cheers Jack." I left the locker room and headed for the OR for my next surgery, all the time the big, goofy smile remaining on my face.

***

I stepped up to Alex's apartment ten minutes earlier than we'd agreed, but I couldn't wait any longer. I'd been home, showered and changed. I just needed to see her again, feel her soft lips against mine once again. I knocked on the door with a bottle of Merlot in one hand and a small bunch of pink roses in the other. I had wanted to buy the biggest bunch I could find at first, but when I walked in the florist and studied the huge bouquets i realised it probably wouldn't be her choice. She was classier, more understated, so I chose the perfect pink roses, small and beautiful just like her.

I waited a few minutes after knocking, realising I was early and she could still be getting ready. When I didn't hear anything I knocked again. When there still wasn't a reply I decided to try the door incase she really was busy cooking or in her room. The door opened and I made a mental note to mention to her about keeping it locked as I stuck my head in and looked into a tiny lounge. While the space was small, it was perfectly ordered. There was a small cream leather sofa in the middle, facing a flat screen TV and a coffee table. One wall was lined with short bookcases, filled to bursting with books of all types. It was very Alex.

"Alex, you here Love?" I called loudly. I stepped inside and closed the door behind me, but i remained in the doorway, not wanting to intrude more than I already had. Off to the right of the lounge I could see a very compact kitchen, separated by a short breakfast bar. I could smell something amazing cooking and my stomach instantly rumbled in response.

"Alex?" I called again. I listened for her voice, but the place was silent except for something bubbling away on the hob in the kitchen.

I took another step inside and then I saw her, her hair anyway. She was on the kitchen floor. I ran over, dropping my gifts on the counter as I passed. My heart began to race as I neared her and got a proper look at her, laid unresponsive on the kitchen floor. Panic gripped me as I knelt in the tiny space near her head and moved her hair from her face.

"Alex?" I said as I listened for her airway. Relieved to hear her breathing I checked her over for injury and finding none I turned her into recovery position, on her side and started taking her pulse which was fast, but not alarmingly so. Thinking maybe she had just fainted I started trying to bring her round, lightly tapping her hand and calling her name. Finally her eyes fluttered open and she looked up at me with worry.

"Matt?" She whispered hoarsely.

"Hi beautiful." I was so relieved to see her beautiful emerald eyes.

"What happened?" She asked as she moved to sit up. I placed my hand on her shoulder and eased her back down.

"Just lie down for a moment until you fully come round baby. I don't know what happened. You were laid here when I walked in."

"I'm sorry." She whispered as she closed her eyes and laid back in defeat.

"Alex, there's nothing to be sorry for. Do you know what happened? Did you pass out?"

"This is so embarrassing. I told you I'm a mess." She cried.

"Alex, look at me," I ordered. Reluctantly she opened her eyes and looked at me. "There is nothing to be embarrassed about. Whatever has happened isn't going to change the way I already feel about you. I like you and nothing is changing that, You're stuck with me. I'm just worried. I need to know if we should call an ambulance or if you're just dehydrated, ok?" She studied me for a moment, as if trying to work out if I was being honest.

"I....I think I might have had a seizure." She eventually whispered nervously.

"Have you had them before?"

"Yes. I have a brain injury. They happen sometimes, but not for quite a while. I feel kind of cloudy though and that's how I usually feel after one."

"Does anything hurt? Did you hit anything when you went down?"

"No. I feel ok Matt."

"Come on then. Let's get you more comfortable." I said as I slid my hands under her and lifted her up.

"I can walk. I'm ok." She argued as I carried her into the lounge and laid her on the sofa.

"Seizures are hard on the body. You need to rest baby. Do you take meds for your seizures? To stop them?." She looked around sheepishly so I bent down in front of her and placed a hand on her forehead, hoping to soothe her so she would talk to me. Finally her wondering eyes met mine and I watched as they filled with tears. "What is it love? You can tell me."

"I….I kind of messed up with my pills this week." She admitted tearfully. "I….I don't have insurance and well….you know, meds are so expensive. I buy them weekly to break down the cost, but this week…..after that terrible date…"

"You couldn't afford your meds this week?" I asked.

"No."

"Oh Alex! You can't do that baby. They are too important." I reprimanded without considering how upset she already was.

"I know Matt. It's not like I went out and bought shoes with the money. He screwed me over that night and I had no choice!" She cried, tears running down her cheeks. "I had a few left over and I thought they'd get me through, but obviously not."

"It's ok." I soothed as I pulled her into my arms and held her close. "I shouldn't have snapped. I know how hard it must be to pay for meds all the time. I understand Alex, but you're not on your own anymore and I work in a hospital so if you're struggling to get the meds you tell me and I'll get them for you, ok?"

"You hardly know me Matt."

"I know enough to know me and you are heading somewhere great Alex." I admitted nervously, hoping she felt the same. She pulled away from my chest and studied my face for a moment, before lunging forward and kissing me, catching me completely off guard. Realising it meant she felt the same way I relaxed into the kiss and tangled my fingers in her beautiful blonde hair as we shared the wild, wanting kiss. When she pulled away after a few minutes she was flushed and smiling, but she looked tired and drained. I knew the seizure likely exhausted her and she still seemed a little dazed.

"Just have a nap baby. I'll sort dinner out and we'll have it later when you've had some rest."

"But you came by for a date Matt. I don't think this is what either of us had in mind." She sulked, making me smile. She was too damn cute.

"That kiss was exactly what I had in mind love." I said with a smile.

"So let's do more of that." She suggested.

"Later. One hour of sleep, ok? I'll wake you in one hour and then we can eat and do much more kissing, but you need to rest first. Deal?"

"Fine," She agreed as she stifled a yawn. She laid down and closed her eyes. I sat beside her and gently stroked her forehead and in moments she had completely relaxed and was fast asleep.

I covered her with a blanket which was sitting on the back of the sofa and then headed to the kitchen to shut off the oven and hob. I knew nothing about cooking, but there was a whole chicken in the oven and vegetables in pans on the hob so I hoped that switching it all off would stop it from over cooking.

Next I went in search of her bathroom. The first door I opened lead to a small double bedroom, filled almost completely by a double bed covered with a pink quilt and covered with cushions of various shades of pink too. I closed the door again, not wanting to snoop and moved to the next which was the bathroom. I looked through her medicine cabinet until I found her meds. Two to stop seizures and an antidepressant. All common meds used to treat the symptoms of a brain injury. I was surprised to find no pain meds. I had noticed she had trouble with her muscles, especially on her left side and with that bad leg, surely she needed pain meds at least some days?

I called Jack's cell, hoping he was just coming off shift as scheduled. He answered on the second ring.

"Matt? I thought you had a date?" He greeted.

"I do. I'm on it. Alex had a seizure. She was passed out when I got here."

"Is she ok? I'm still here if you want to bring her in?"

"No, she's ok. She was cognizant and her pulse was steady. She's resting now. She has a brain injury following some kind of accident five years ago. She controls the seizures with meds, but she's out. I was hoping..." Jack cut me off before I had to fully explain.

"No problem man. Text me the names and doses and I'll sort them out and bring them over right now on my way home. You said she lives across the street right?"

"Yeah, I'll text the address too. Thanks mate. I owe you one."

"No you don't. I'll be about thirty minutes." With that he hung up and I sent him a text with all of the information he needed.

I returned to the lounge and sat down on the floor in front of the sofa where Alex slept, just needing to be near her. She looked so peaceful, her blonde hair fanned out on the pillow around her beautiful face. She slept with her hand tucked underneath her cheek and she breathed so quietly. I knew I was a lucky man to have found her. I knew she had some issues with her injury and her past, but who didn't have issues? We were all flawed and I knew I had plenty of issues she'd have to accept if we were to be together. None of it mattered. I had known her for less than three days and I was falling hard for her. There was no stopping it and I loved it.

ALEX

I awoke from one of my usual heart stopping, terrifying nightmares, to the sounds of hushed voices and was instantly on alert, adrenaline still coursing through me from the nightmare. I never woke to voices, I lived alone and had for years. I opened my eyes slowly and tried hard to remember what had happened to lead me to fall asleep. I was laid on the sofa, which was also unusual. I always slept in my bed. I looked down at my favourite date outfit and remembered Matt was coming around. I had a vague memory of kissing him on the sofa, but everything else seemed fuzzy. I sat up slowly and looked around for the voices. Matt was stood with his back to me near the front door, looking sexy as hell in dark blue jeans and a fitted black polo t-shirt. He was talking to another very handsome man, this guy a little taller and broader than Matt with dark blond hair, a very chiselled jaw and also very heavily muscled, even more so than Matt. He looked over Matt's shoulder at me and smiled, but it didn't put me at ease. I barely knew Matt and to wake, no idea of what had happened, with a strange man in the room triggered my alarm bells. It was all too familiar and adrenaline hit me all over again, making me tremble uncontrollably, instantly, as though someone had flipped a switch. I suddenly became very hot and started to sweat as breathing became very difficult. I leapt to my feet and backed away into the corner of the room as Matt turned to me with a look of confusion.

"Alex, are you ok?" He asked. They both moved toward me and I completely freaked out, lost in images of being tackled to the ground by heavily muscled men, and sure history was about to repeat itself. I was such an idiot to trust Matt, if that was even his name.

"No, don't!" I cried breathlessly as I backed hard into the wall and held my hands out in front of me.

"Alex, it's me baby. You're safe." Matt soothed as he stopped his approach a few feet away from me.

"Just stay back…..please, just…..don't!" I was sobbing, making my frantic breathing even more erratic.

"Back up mate." Matt whispered to the blonde guy. He nodded and walked backwards until he hit the door of my apartment. He stopped there and watched closely. I maintained an eye on him in my peripheral, as I looked back to Matt.

"Alex. Listen to me. You're having a panic attack. You need to breathe baby, nice deep breaths." He encouraged calmly.

"Why are you here? Why was I passed out....what did you do to me......and who is he?" I demanded, fighting with everything I could muster to sound stronger than I was.

"I found you passed out when I arrived for our date. You were cooking for me tonight, remember?" He asked as he studied my face. "You came around and said you thought it was a seizure because your thoughts were cloudy. I think I agree, especially considering you said you went without meds and how confused you are right now."

"Him? Why is he here? Who i-is he?"

"That's Jack. I called him while you were asleep and asked him to bring you more meds. He works at the hospital with me. Remember me telling you about him and his fiance Cal?" I dared to take my eyes from Matt to look across at blondie. He smiled and waved a lanyard he wore around his neck to draw my attention. I could make out the logo of Chicago General printed on the ID card. When I looked back to his face, he held up a paper bag from a drug store and I allowed myself to relax my tense body.

"I'd never let anyone hurt you Alex, I swear. You're perfectly safe." Matt added softly. I looked back to his face and really focused on his eyes. They were filled with concern, for me. I wondered what had possessed me to think so badly of him.

"I-I'm sorry. I just saw a strange guy….and I was laid out. I'm sorry Matt." I whimpered as I slumped back, exhausted against the wall.

"It's ok baby, I completely understand. Can you let me hold you now?" He asked cautiously. *Way to go Ali! Only the second date and he's seen you unconscious and in a freaking clusterfuck of a freak out! Great work!* I nodded and Matt approached slowly as though I were a wild animal, liable to scarper at any moment. He very tentatively wrapped his arms around my whole body and after a moment I sank into his warmth and strength, feeling like a complete idiot!

"Deep breaths now baby. Try and calm down for me. Everything's alright." He soothed softly as he held me tight. I fought to slow my breathing and push back the flashbacks that were vying for viewing time in my mind. I clung to Matt as tight as I could, as though, if I didn't hang on the past would be able to drag me back in all over again.

"That's good love, You're doing so well." Matt encouraged as calm began to return to me little by little.

"I'm so sorry Matt."

"There's nothing to be sorry about baby."

"I ruined our date and you probably think I'm a crazy person now!" I cried as I stepped from his embrace and collapsed down on the sofa, my shaky legs refusing to work any longer.

"I do not think you're a crazy person Alex. You woke up, confused and dazed to find two men lurking in your place. You were right to freak out and our date isn't ruined. It's only half eight. There's time to enjoy our evening yet, but not until you've had a rest and taken your meds." With that Matt beckoned Jack over and took the bag of meds from him. As he did I remembered the conversation we'd had earlier when I told him I hadn't bought my meds that week and he'd said he thought we were headed somewhere, that we could have a real relationship, and the kiss, that amazing kiss! Now I had royally screwed that up!

"I'm sorry I freaked Jack. You must think I'm a nut case." I sighed as I looked over the back of the sofa to him. He beamed at me and it instantly set me at ease with him. His goodness shone through.

"Not at all sweet. Matt's right, you had every right to be wary. How about we start over?" He offered.

"Thank you." I said as I reached over the sofa and held out a hand. "Nice to finally meet you Jack. I've heard alot about you." Jack took my hand and squeezed it comfortingly. I was surprised by the comfort I felt from it, as opposed to the blinding panic I usually felt when men touched me in any way.

"Don't believe anything this guy tells you Alex. It's all lies." He laughed.

"Here love." Matt said as he handed me the bag of drugs. "Get your pills out and I'll get you some water." He walked off toward the kitchen and I looked in the bag. I almost cried with relief when I saw all of my pill bottles inside. I hated not taking them, Seizures were a bitch to deal with and I was more emotional without my meds too.

"How did you get these?" I asked Jack.

"We work in a hospital." He replied dryly.

"Well, thank you. I really appreciate it. Those seizures are no joke."

"Any time honey. You can always call me if you need anything. We all kind of come as a package deal with this guy here." Jack said as Matt returned with a glass of water. Jack handed me a card with his cell and pager numbers on. "I should get out of here and let you guys get to that date. Real nice to meet you Alex."

"You too. Thanks again for the pills." He gave me a wink and then turned to leave. Matt walked him to the door and showed him out while I took my handful of pills and then hurried through to the kitchen.

I looked in the oven and was relieved to find Matt had turned it off. I turned it back on to heat the chicken I was cooking. It would likely be pretty dry by the time it was warm again, but it'd be edible and I was hungry, plus I'd promised Matt dinner and it was the least I could offer him after what I'd put him through. I flicked on the burners under the various accompaniments too and hoped they wouldn't be too overcooked. I stood back lost in thought then. What a disaster I was! I really didn't understand why the hell Matt would be even remotely interested in me. I had met him on three separate nights and on two of those I was in some drama. Why would a man as wonderful as Matt want that hell brought into his life?

"Are you ok Alex?" Matt asked as he walked into the kitchen and wrapped his arms around me from behind.

"I just feel terrible. You come for a second date and find me passed out, then you have to deal with me in meltdown. I totally understand if this is too much for you Matt. You can walk away, no hard feelings." I didn't want to say it, and I really didn't want him to walk away, but after everything, I had to give the poor guy an out.

"I said it earlier and I'll say it again. You have nothing to feel bad about. You have an injury. You were upfront, you told me you have some issues and I accepted that the first night I met you.

"It doesn't change who you are, how gorgeous, funny and strong you are and it certainly doesn't change the feelings that I have developed for you in just three bloody days. I like you Alex, I want to get to know you, the good and the bad. I'm not going anywhere."

"You shouldn't have to deal with all of this Matt." I argued, my eyes filling with tears.

"Last year when my sister arrived here she was beaten almost to death. She had internal bleeding, a fractured wrist, broken ribs and her face was almost unrecognisable. She hadn't been eating and she was wasting away. I opened my apartment door one morning and there she was, in that state. We managed to get her strong again, she was happy with a job and a life here and then her ex, Phil, came after her. He kidnapped her and held her in a warehouse and beat her once again, near killed her, again! We went after her, me, Jack and my other mates. We found the warehouse and as we started searching it Lucy ran out, barely able to walk, her face swollen and bleeding and she screamed my name. I have nightmares about that Alex, about all of it. I wake up regularly, sometimes shouting. Sometimes when Lucy speaks to me I flashback to when she was pleading with us all, while Phil held a gun to her head. I've had some therapy for it, and it's less now, but it still happens. That's just one of my issues and it's going to be one you'll have to face if you're with me. Also the fact that I'm stupidly overprotective after what Lucy went through and I could probably drive you nuts with it. Is all of that going to make you walk away from me Alex?" He asked, his eyes filled with pain from having to recall what sounded like hell that he and his sister had been through.

"Of course not." I whispered through the tears now flooding down my face at the thought of what he had told me. His poor sister had suffered so much. "I'm so sorry Matt. It must have been unbearable for you to go through that, and your sister…..she really must be so special to have come out of the other end of all of that."

"The point is, we all have issues love, every single person. Mine are mental, some are physical. Jack has a leg injury from his last tour as a marine and he has some rough days with it, but he get's by and his fiance Cal doesn't just give up on him because of it.

"I don't look at you and see a girl with a nerve damaged leg and a crutch. I don't see the effects of your injury or the issues you seem to be trying to handle from your past. I look at you and I see beautiful emerald eyes, stunning blonde hair and a body to die for. I see a woman who is strong and not afraid to speak her mind. I see a woman who makes me feel more whole than I have ever felt in my entire life." He was right in front of me now, his hands on my shoulders, his eyes locked on mine, showing me with everything he was that he meant what he was saying. "Please Alex, I know there will be bumps in the road, but don't push me away. I want you exactly as you are, if you'll take me as I am too?"

I couldn't hold it in. A deep sob escaped and Matt pulled me close against him. I buried my face in his T-shirt and cried. No one had ever said anything so wonderful to me. No one had ever wanted to overlook my flaws in favour of the good. No one had ever wanted me and I was overwhelmed, completely overwhelmed. It took a few minutes, but eventually I managed to pull myself together and look up into those blue eyes. Matt smiled and I did too.

"I want you too Matt, exactly as you are." I whispered. I wanted him forever. I had never really felt love, not properly so it was a new feeling for me, but what I was starting to feel for the amazing man holding me in his arms had to be something pretty damn close.

***

We had a quiet night that night. I finished cooking the meal and we ate, even though it was terribly over cooked. Matt refused to admit how terrible it was and ate it happily, but I knew it was ruined. After dinner we curled up on my sofa together and chatted through a movie while finishing the bottle of wine Matt had brought, just getting to know each other and enjoying cuddling together.

Matt stayed with me all of that night and the next day. We slept the night cuddled up in my bed. Nothing more than a few kisses and some spooning. It was perfect.

The next day we vegged out together on my sofa mindlessly watching movies and chatting about nothing of importance. Matt ran out for breakfast for the both of us and we planned to order take out later in the evening. I had suggested we go out, but really I was exhausted from the seizure the previous night, my muscles all sore and aching and Matt seemed to know that and refused, saying he was enjoying having me to himself.

We got to know each other a lot more and I found that with every new thing I learned about this man, my feelings for him got stronger and stronger. He seemed too good to be true. I kept on waiting for him to realise what a mess I was and take off running as fast as he could, but he didn't. He genuinely seemed to like me and I could not understand why.

"What shall we watch next?" I asked as the last of the Die Hard movies ended. We had been having an action marathon and I was loving it, action being my favourite kind of movie.

"What do you fancy?" Matt asked with a smile.

"Are you bored of action yet?" I asked.

"Never! I can't believe I found a woman who loves action films! I've died and gone to heaven!" He joked, making me giggle. Before I could reply his cell rang and he groaned as he retrieved it from the coffee table.

"Sorry, it's my sister." He said as he answered. I stood and headed into the kitchen to give him some privacy. I busied myself making coffee.

"Alex, come and sit down. I'll do that." Matt called after a few minutes. I couldn't hold in the huge smile that filled my face, I had never had anyone care for me the way he did and it was such a wonderful feeling.

"It's fine." I called back as I carried on with finding mugs.

"Just a minute darling." I turned as Matt appeared in the kitchen still talking on his cell. I looked up into his eyes and he raised his eyebrows disapprovingly. "You need to rest." He rebuked.

"I'm fine Matt." I argued. "Go and finish your call."

"Actually, Lucy called to invite me to dinner."

"Oh, ok. No problem. I'll be fine now Matt. You go and see your family." I said encouragingly trying to hide my disappointment at the thought of him leaving.

"No….shit….I meant *us*, she invited *us* to dinner." Matt corrected himself with a shake of his head.

"Are you sure?" I asked, not wanting to intrude on their family dinner.

"Yes. She's desperate to meet you. If you're not up to it we can go another time though."

"Sure. We can go." I replied, trying to hide my terror at the idea of meeting the people that really mattered to the man I was coming to fall in love with.

"Brilliant. I'll let Lucy know. Why don't you go and get changed? Don't worry about dressing up. It's only family." Matt leant down and kissed the top of my head and the then walked back into the lounge.

Great. Yeah, it's only family. I thought to myself. *Just the people you love most in the world.* If they hated me it could be game over for Matt and I and that was a terrifying thought to me. I had been fine on my own for four years, but after knowing Matt for just four days I had no idea how I would ever cope without him in my life.

What the hell was wrong with me? Was it possible to fall for someone so completely, so damned quickly? I sure hoped so because it was definitely happening to me.

***

"Stop stressing. They are going to love you." Matt said as we headed down the hall to his sister and her fiance, one of Matt's best friends, apartment. My heart was pounding with nerves and worry. They were all going to see me for the freak I was, I knew it.

"I suck at meeting people Matt. No one likes me." I admitted, my voice slightly trembling with fear.

"I like you, a lot, and they will too." Matt said as he pulled me to a stop in front of him. I looked up into his eyes and forced myself to take a breath before I voiced my true fear.

"But what if they don't?"

"They will. But, if they don't then I don't care Alex. I am head over heels for you already woman, and nothing anyone says to me is going to change that, ok?"

"Ok," I agreed with a smile, feeling somewhat reassured. We continued down the hall and stopped at a door at the far end.

"Are you sure I look alright?" I asked, fidgeting with the black sheer blouse I had chosen with a pretty camisole under and paired with my black skinny jeans and low heeled boots. Matt looked me up and down and I panicked.

"Oh God, I knew it! It's too much black isn't it. I look like a freaking ninja.....or a funeral. Oh crap! I look like I'm going to a damned funeral don't I?" I cried. Matt leant in and stopped my rambling with a deep, passionate kiss.

When he pulled away I was silent, swept up in the beautiful moment.

"You look beautiful." He whispered with a grin, then he knocked on the door and I tried to take the goofy, just-been-kissed-school-girl look from my face.

I held my breath as I heard someone unlocking the apartment door and a second later it was thrown open by a huge chest, at least that's all I could see without straining my neck.

"Matt, come in man." The chest greeted. I looked up as far as I could and finally saw the owner of the chest. He was a good half a foot taller than Matt and therefore a whole lot taller than tiny me. He was good looking, in a very superhero-ish sort of way, with dark hair and very striking wide eyes. He smiled at me reassuringly as Matt tried to usher me inside.

"Alex, this is Rob, Lucy's fiance." Matt said as we passed the huge guy to enter the apartment. As we walked past I studied him further and decided he was absolutely the tallest, muscliest guy I had ever seen in real life. He looked like he could bench press a house!

"Nice to meet you sweetheart." Rob said after closing the door behind us. I was ready to fight the anxiety attack that always hit when I was in a small space with a man, but it never came. I was surprised because Rob was probably, in size at least, the most intimidating man I had ever met, but the panic never began.

"You too," I replied timidly as I looked up to his face once again and found it filled with a very kind smile. In that moment, seeing the softness and kindness in his face I knew why he was Matt's friend and why he hadn't scared me into my usual hysteria. He was a good man, just like Matt, it was in his eyes.

"You're here!" I turned to see a beautiful, female version of Matt at the other end of the room, hurrying towards us excitedly. She had all of Matt's colouring and their facial features were similar, except where Matt was tall and built, this girl was petite and very fragile looking. She leapt at Matt and wrapped her arms around his waist. He engulfed her with his own arms too and they briefly hugged. Their embrace was filled with love and emotion and I envied them. I had never known that feeling of family. Love was all new to me and I was learning through the feelings I had for Matt, but I would never have what Lucy and Matt had, sibling love, family. I wanted that, I had always wanted that, but it would never happen for me. My family were evil and there was no changing that.

"Darling, I want you meet Alex. Alex, this is my sister Lucy." Matt said as he pulled Lucy over to me. I snapped from my dark thoughts and plastered on a smile. I really needed to keep it together tonight. I could not freak out in front of these people!

"I'm so happy to finally meet you. I didn't think Matt would ever introduce you to us!" Lucy cried dramatically as she threw herself at me and wrapped me in a hug. The whole experience was so alien to me. Other than Matt, no one had ever hugged me. I stood awkwardly, one hand on my crutch, the other at my side, not knowing how the hell to react.

"We've known each other for four days Lucy." Matt commented dryly. "Back off a little Darling. You're scaring her." He added after another moment of me standing in her arms unmoving.

"It….it's ok Matt." I said nervously as Lucy, thankfully, released me. "It's nice to meet you too,"

"Let's take a seat." Rob suggested as he moved through to the middle of the lounge. Matt took my hand and led me over to the very large, grey leather L shaped sofa. I sat next to him and clung to his hand like a life line.

"Can I get you a beer Matt?" Rob offered as Lucy fluttered back through to the kitchen. She was so dainty and graceful, I felt like a total beast in comparison even though I was shorter than her. She was just so graceful where I was dumpy and klutzy.

"Yeah.Thanks mate." Matt replied.

"Alex, can I get you a drink?" Rob looked over to me and I felt nervous under his seemingly all-seeing gaze. I felt like he was looking deep into my thoughts.

"Erm…..a beer is fine for me too, thank you." I stuttered nervously. Rob nodded and hurried off the same way Lucy had gone. I sat mentally slapping my head. Why the hell did I just ask for a beer? I didn't drink in front of people because I transformed into a giggling idiot after even the smallest amount of alcohol. I only ever had one drink in public, on the very few occasions I had dared office nights out. I left the majority of my drinking for when I was alone at home, and yes, I knew how sad that was, but I had little choice.

I had panicked when Rob offered and couldn't think of a single damned drink other than the one Matt had just said, One beer, I could handle one beer, then I'd switch to water. It would be fine.

"Are you ok? I know my sister can be a little overwhelming." Matt whispered.

"She's really nice Matt, they both are. I'm ok. This is just all really new for me."

"I understand baby. Just tell me if it's getting too much and I'll make an excuse to get us out of here, ok?" I nodded my agreement as Rob returned with three beer bottles in hand. Matt and I each took one and I took a swig nervously as Rob sat in the armchair opposite us.

"How are you doing Alex? Jack told me you blacked out last night, when I spoke to him earlier." Rob said with seeming genuine concern. Why on earth would someone I just clapped eyes on give a single damn about me?

"I'm good thanks. It was nothing really, just a seizure. They happen occasionally."

"Just glad you're ok honey." Rob said with a genuine smile. He really seemed to care and it was so strange to me.

"What time can we expect Jack and Cal?" Matt asked. I was grateful for the change of subject.

"They were due about ten minutes ago. You know what they're like." Rob said with a laugh.

"Jack and Cal are not known for their time keeping skills." Matt clarified for me.

"Well I'm afraid to say I'm with them there. I'm never on time for anything." I admitted.

"Don't worry honey. You'll fit right in with this lot. I'm the only one who ever gets anywhere early. Matt's not too bad, but Lucy, Jack and Cal are always late for everything." At that moment the door to the apartment was thrown open and two men burst in, the two men Matt had been out with that night I met him and of course I knew Jack from the day before.

"Ok guys, stop bitching about how late we are. We're here now!" Jack called loudly as he entered the room. I had to grin at that, seeing as we had just been doing exactly what he insinuated.

"Hey guys." The other guy, who must be Cal, greeted. "Everyone ok?"

"Good man, You want a beer?" Rob offered as he stood once again.

"You read my mind." Cal replied with a nod.

"Alex." Jack said as he approached, "How are you feeling sweetie?"

"I'm ok now thanks Jack and thanks for yesterday."

"You're welcome. I'm glad to see you looking so much better. This is Cal, my fiance. Cal, this is Alex." Jack introduced as he pulled Cal into his side with a one armed hug.

"Very pleased to me you sweetheart." Cal said with a million dollar smile. He was a very handsome man, extremely well defined and heavily muscled, despite the fact he seemed quite a few years older than the other guys,

"You too." I said nervously. I had never been surrounded by so many huge, good looking guys. I was extremely overwhelmed and a little intimidated, but much to my surprise, I wasn't scared. Each and every one of them exuded kindness and it instantly set me at ease. Thankfully, just a few minutes later Lucy called us into the kitchen for dinner and I was spared having to make conversation in my anxious state. We all sat around a huge dining table in the middle of the expansive, modern kitchen and ate the most delicious meal. There was no doubting Lucy was an amazing cook. After dinner the guys shooed Lucy and I into the lounge while they all set to cleaning up, surprising me. Not one of them seemed like the domesticated type.

I sat on the sofa near Lucy, my third beer in my hand. I hadn't had a chance to ask for anything else. Everytime I finished a beer and told myself I needed to switch to water, Rob would hand me another opened beer bottle. I was really getting to the giggly, slightly out of it drunken state and I was worried I was going to make a huge fool of myself.

"So, Alex, tell me about yourself. I want to know all about you." Lucy said as she sat and sipped her wine. I knew she probably wanted to try and find out if I really was good enough for her brother. The problem was, I already knew I wasn't.

"Ok, well, there's not much to tell. I'm twenty six, moved here four years ago. I work at the unemployment office as a receptionist and that's about it really. I'm not a very exciting person I'm afraid."

"I don't believe that. Matt really likes you and he wouldn't if that was all there was to you." Lucy said with a smile. "What brought you to Chicago?"

"Oh.....I.....I needed a fresh start." I stuttered nervously. I did not want her to know the fucked up situation that had actually brought me to the city.

"I can understand that. I came here a year ago to escape a horrible marriage. I was looking to start fresh too and I did. I'm so happy with Rob now." I saw the happiness radiating from her. She practically glowed. I wanted that, I wanted the fresh start she had found for herself after only one year in the city. I had been there for four years and all I had succeeded in was moving from one form of isolation to another.

"Matt told me a little of what you went through. I'm sorry you had to deal with all of that." I said genuinely. I understood only too well the hell she had been through and I hated that anyone ever had to suffer like she had.

"I made it out, It was hell and I never thought it would end, but it did and I'm truly happy now. It made me stronger in the end and that's what I've chosen to take from it." I saw that strength in her. You could see the hell she had been through in her eyes, but she was right, she did get out and she had taken something positive from it all. Why couldn't I do that? Why couldn't I be that strong?

"How do you do that? How do you block out all of the bad stuff and focus only on the good it brought you?" I blurted without thinking.

"Alex, I'm going to be honest with you, because I think you need to know. I don't block out the bad. It's still there. The sight of some random object, or a sound or smell sometimes instantly throws me into a terrifying flashback and I have nightmares too, although not so many anymore. You can never truly let hell go once you have seen it for yourself, I think it will always be with you in some way, but I try to focus on the good in my life. I have an amazing fiance, the world's most supportive and loving brother and spectacular friends. I let them help me. I talk to them when I'm having a bad day and they try to help me make it better. It took time for me to fully let them in. I tried to protect them from my problems at first, but what I learnt is, you can't fight the past alone. You need help, you need support and you need the light of the ones who care about you to chase away the darkness." I listened to every word, feeling as though she could see my own personal hell somehow, as though she knew what had been done to me. Tears filled my eyes and I longed for what she described, people to care enough to want to help chase away the darkness inside me.

"I've always been alone. My family hated me and no one wants the cripple I am now. I only have myself to rely on." I whimpered tearfully, letting all of my miserable self pity show before I could shut my big mouth!

"Oh no darling." Lucy cried as she pulled me into a hug. I allowed myself to relax and rested my sobbing face on her shoulder. "You're not alone anymore, never again. Matt loves you and with him you get suckered with all of us. You have people you can rely on now. We will chase away your darkness too. We'll be there for you now." I couldn't say anything back. I was completely overawed by her words. Was it true? Did Matt love me and even if he did, why would that mean his family had to care about me?

"Thank you." I finally managed to whisper as I sat up and tried to wipe the tears from my face. "I'm sorry I lost it."

"Alex?" I looked up to find Matt in the doorway watching us. "What's wrong baby?"

"Nothing, I'm fine Matt." I said as calmly as I could, trying to wipe away the tears on my face,

"You're not, you were crying. What have you said to her Lucy?" He asked with a hint of anger.

"Matt stop!" I ordered loudly as I got to my feet. "Lucy was being nice to me and I got emotional. It's fine. I just need to clean up is all."

"Come on chick. I'll show you to the bathroom." Lucy offered as she got to her feet and wrapped a supportive arm around my back.

"I'm sorry Matt snapped at you. It's my fault." I apologised as we walked into a large white bathroom.

"It wasn't your fault. Matt's just over-protective and I'm afraid that is my fault. He cares about you Alex and I am so happy to know that. He deserves some happiness and I really do believe he can find it with you. You're perfect for each other, I already know it." She declared excitedly, making me smile.

She stood and chatted away to me about the guys while I washed my face of all my tear stained makeup. Her happiness was infectious and by the time we returned to the lounge she had me in hysterics with a story of the guys all coming into her apartment, totally wasted a few months back. I felt as though I had known her for years, not hours. She put me so at ease and I found I had the confidence to speak up with her. I saw the possibility of having a real girl friend in my life and I was so excited at the prospect.

"So anyway, Rob and Jack eventually passed out curled up together in my bed. Cal was snoring on the sofa, but Matt had disappeared so I started looking for him. The bathroom door was locked so I knew he was in there. I stood at the door and waited, but he wasn't coming out. Next thing I know there's a crash and…." Lucy stopped, laughing too much to carry on. "…..then I hear this noise…..this sort of squeak. I press my ear t-to the door and I heard it again, like a shuffling and some….some squeaks." Tears were streaming down her face and her words were pushed out between hysterical laughing. I was laughing just as heartily waiting to hear the end of the story. "So I stand at the door, my ear pressed against it and suddenly I realise what the noise is. He'd…..oh God!....he'd fallen in the bloody bath and the squeaks…..it was him trying to get his drunk arse out."

"No way!" I laughed, tears now running down my own face. "What did you do?"

"Apart from pee my pants laughing at him?" Lucy cried as she collapsed on the sofa and pulled me down beside her.

"What are you two laughing at?" Jack asked as he strolled in with a beer.

"Matt's drunk night in the bath!" Lucy replied with yet more laughter.

"I still can't believe I missed that shit!" Jack said with a mock pout. "You could have at least recorded the sounds Lucy!"

"Oh Bloody hell! Not this story again!" Matt sighed as he plopped down in the seat next to me and pulled me into his side. "One sodding drunken stumble and I'll never live it down!"

"So did you get out or not?" I asked him, still in fits of drunken giggles.

"Oh he got out, after forty-five minutes of struggling and squeaking! I was ready to either die of laughing or wake Rob to knock the door down for my poor brother!"

"Poor brother my arse! You left me there for your own entertainment Lucy simmons!" Matt sulked. I looked across to Lucy and we both burst into more laughter. We stayed at Rob and Lucy's for one more beer and then headed back to my place since we both had work the next morning. I really had enjoyed myself. All of Matt's family were kind, genuine people who had welcomed me with open arms. I felt as though I could really have some true friends in them and it meant a lot to me. We had all exchanged numbers and the guys had all taken the time to assure me I could call them anytime if I needed anything, which was very kind of them all and had me feeling quite emotional. I wasn't used to people caring, to people saying they would be there for me if I needed them. Those kinds of people had only ever existed in books in my personal experience, and so it was a real jolt to my system to realise that in actuality there really were kind people in the world. Lucy and I had also exchanged numbers and were already texting each other on the drive home that very night.

"You ok baby?" Matt asked as we pulled up to my apartment building.

"I'm great Matt. You were right, they were all so nice and I really like them. I had a lot of fun tonight."

"I'm glad. You deserve it and so much more. They all liked you too Alex, just as I knew they would." Matt said as he leant in and kissed my cheek gently. I was still sat revelling in the feel of his lips on my skin when he jumped out of the car and came around to my door.

"Come on love." He said as he gripped my waist and lifted me out.

"You know, I really shouldn't drink beer. It really doesn't like me." I explained, my words a little slurred.

"Then why did you drink it baby?"

"I panicked and then Rob was so nice.....he kept bringing me a new one. I didn't want to be rude."

"Oh Alex. You're so bloody cute." He laughed as he took my crutch from where I was uselessly holding it and instead supported my weak side as we went.

I fell asleep that night in Matt's arms, pretty drunk, but blissfully happy. Maybe things could get good for me, maybe there was a happily ever after in my future, I dared to think.

***

"No way Alex! Put that back now! I am not going anywhere in that dress!" Lucy barked playfully as I picked up a short, deep red halter dress. It had been three weeks since the night I met Matt's sister, but I felt like we had been friends forever. We talked almost every day on the phone and were always texting each other. We spent any time that our guys were busy working, doing things together. We'd been out for a few meals and had a few movie and wine binges at each other's apartments. We just seemed to click. We liked the same food, the same movies and we both shared dark pasts, which were never discussed, but always acknowledged. A best friend had been one of my biggest dreams when I was a little girl, just to have someone to laugh and gossip with, someone to turn to when everything became too much. I had never had that someone, but with Lucy I did and it was like a dream come true for me.

"You'd look amazing in this with your dark hair." I argued as I held the halter dress up to her slim body. We were on a shopping mission to get hot outfits. We had discovered that neither of us had ever been on a proper girls night out and we were determined to do it that night. Our plan was to buy the clothes, outfits that were a little braver than we'd usually dare be, then go back to Lucy's to get ready before heading out to a few bars before ending up in a club that I had heard from girls at the office, was good fun. We were both a little nervous about the idea, since we'd never done anything like it before, but we were more excited than anything to just have fun and let loose.

"Fine, I'll try it on, but I'm not buying anything that my arse or boobs hang out of." Lucy said firmly.

"We said we'd be brave with our outfits. We want to fit in at the club don't we? Plus think how hot Rob will think you look when he sees you." I coaxed as I grabbed a few more outfits on the way to the dressing rooms of the boutique we were shopping in. I watched as a huge smile spread across her face as she considered my argument.

"Give me the dress." She demanded before walking into a fitting room and closing the door behind her.

I walked into the one next door and locked the door. I tried two dresses, a very cute little black dress with spaghetti straps and a dark green fitted bodycon dress, but neither of them covered all of the ugly scars on my back and I wasn't ready for anyone to see them yet, so I rejected both and next pulled on a cute little skater skirt that stopped midway down my thigh, very short for me. It was black with a cute lace overlay. I pulled on the cream silk blouse that had been paired with it on a mannequin in the store, and tucked it into the high waisted skirt. The blouse had capped sleeves and completely covered my scarred back, but dropped very low in the front. I studied myself in the mirror and was surprised to see it looked pretty good. With the correct bra the blouse would show a little cleavage and the light colour made me look less pale.

"How's that dress Lucy?" I called, having not heard a peep from her since we walked in.

"I think it shows too much Alex." She replied and I heard the uncertainty in her voice.

"Well, I already chose and I am showing a lot of skin girl, so you have to too. Come out and show me." I called as I opened the door and stepped out in front of the huge mirror on the wall opposite. Slowly the door to Lucy's fitting room opened and she stepped out nervously with her arms crossed over her chest. She looked up at me and smiled.

"You look really cute in that Alex." She said with a smile.

"And you look freaking amazing it that dress!" I gasped. She really did. She had perfect sleek legs and the dress fitted her petite frame perfectly, showing how stunningly feminine her shape was. The halter lifted her breasts just enough to show a hint of cleavage and the colour was stunning on her. Finally she dropped her arms and looked at herself in the mirror.

"I don't know. I've never worn anything like this before." She hesitated.

"That was the plan wasn't it? Girls night with hot outfits? Let me tell you Lucy, that dress is smoking hot! Rob will be drooling when he sees you in it. This outfit isn't me either, but we wanted to step out of our comfort zone didn't we?"

"Yeah, you're right." She agreed, suddenly becoming more excited. "Sod it! It's girls night and I want to look good. Let's do this hun."

We bought the outfits, and then shoes from a shop next door to the clothing boutique. Lucy chose some pretty suede platforms which were the same shade red as the dress. I'd have loved to choose something similar, but my bum leg would never survive the night in such footwear. Instead I chose a low heeled black court shoe that would look pretty enough and which I would manage to walk and, more importantly, dance in.

When we got back to Lucy's she made us a quick meal, of some delicious rice dish and we ate in the lounge watching the latest episode of Greys, which we were both hooked on. We had decided it was a good idea to eat a proper meal before heading out so the alcohol wouldn't hit us so quickly. We were both pretty lightweight when it came to drinking and we didn't want the night to be over after two drinks.

Getting ready was the most fun. The guys were all out working, so Lucy cranked her playlist as loud as she could and we danced around with a glass of wine as we helped each other with hair and makeup. We both decided to go darker with our eye make-up and chose darker shades of lipstick than we usually would. It was a ritual most girls experienced in their teens, but for differing reasons Lucy and I had missed out. Doing it in our twenties was just as exciting though and we were having so much fun.

The completed look made a stark contrast to the natural look we both tended to favour. Lucy curled her long dark hair loosely and wore it down, while I pinned my wild locks in a neat updo. We both got dressed and I completed my outfit with a large pair of silver hoop earrings. Lucy chose a chunky gold bangle and matching drop earrings.

"Jesus. I look like a girl." Lucy joked when we both stood in front of the full length mirror in her room, both ready to go. I had to admit I was thinking something similar about myself. I couldn't remember ever having looked so feminine.

"I think we're ready for girls night Lucy, don't you?" I asked excitedly.

"Bring it on! I can't wait to dance!" She squealed. We both picked up our purses and I put mine across my body as I always did, then we walked out into the lounge where we found Rob sat on the sofa scrolling through his phone. Lucy walked over, seeming to become more confident in herself with each step. Rob, engrossed in his phone and not hearing her over the blaring music, didn't notice until she walked over and switched off the playlist and silence reigned. Rob's head snapped up and he froze when he saw his fiance.

"Fuck sweetheart. You look beautiful." He gasped breathlessly. He jumped to his feet and swept her into his arms. They moved into a kiss that seemed incredibly intimate. I turned around and tried to look busy studying the bookshelf instead of staring at them like some kind of voyeur.

"I'm going to have a whole lot of fun tearing that off you tonight when you get home." Rob almost growled.

"Rob! Alex is over there!" Lucy cried and I took that as my cue to turn around again. They were both looking at me and Rob smiled awkwardly.

"Sorry honey. Didn't see you there." He said. "You look great too."

"Thanks."

"Oh, we should get some photos Alex, come on!" Lucy called as she rifled through her purse for her cell. "Here Rob, take a load so we can pick out the best ones."

We posed together, some just smiling and some pulling ridiculous faces and poses. We all laughed as Rob snapped a ton of pictures and just as we were finishing up Matt burst into the apartment in shorts and a sexy tight fit t-shirt.

"Matt? What are you doing here? I thought you were just going to crash tonight?" I asked, unable to remove the smile from my face at seeing him.

"Rob text and said I should get over here and see you before you left. Glad he did now. You look stunning baby." He stalked over to me and wrapped his hands around my waist as he studied me intently. "Sexy as hell." He whispered in my ear as he pulled me close. His warm breath on my ear and his spicy aftershave set me alight and I felt that desperate need for him once again that I had been overwhelmed with more and more every time he was around. We had spent a few nights cuddled up together and there had been a lot of kissing, but nothing more. Matt seemed to sense I had issues around sex and he hadn't pushed, but I was certainly getting to the point where I was ready to give it a try. He awoke feelings within me that I didn't even know were possible.

He bent closer to me until our lips met and then we were tangled in a fiery kiss suggestive of what we were both ready to move onto, but couldn't give in to in his sister's lounge. I was embarrassed when we pulled apart, knowing Rob and Lucy were in the room with us, but when I looked around I found them in the corner doing the very same thing.

"Are you sure you're up to this tonight?" Matt asked quietly.

"I'm looking forward to it."

"And you've taken your pills? I hate to think of you collapsing on a filthy club floor."

"I've taken them Matt. I'll be fine." I assured him.

"I'll be at home, so just call me if you want picking up or if you need me for anything, ok?"

"I will Matt, but we'll be just fine. We're just going to have a few drinks, dance a little, then Rob's agreed to pick us up when we've had enough. You need to get some sleep." He had just worked an eighteen hour shift and he looked beat.

"We ready ro get this show on the road?" Lucy asked as she and Rob approached.

"Let's get this party started!" I agreed as we all headed out of the apartment and down to Rob's SUV which was parked on the street. Matt and I shared one more quick kiss before he headed to his car and we set off for our first big girls night.

***

"I'm sorry but I really need the loo again Alex!" Lucy shouted over the loud music in the club. We were finishing up our second bottle of wine and we were both well on our way, but Lucy was a little worse than I was. I was just relieved I seemed to have tolerated the alcohol better than I usually did. I could still stand and form words, that was progress!

"You need what?" I asked with confusion.

"I have to pee!"

"What did you call it? The loo? I love the weird way you and Matt talk!" I laughed as I finished my drink and got to my feet. "Come on, let's go and then we're hitting that dance floor."

"Ok, but I am warning you now, I am a really bad dancer!" Lucy called as she jumped up to follow me. I took her hand and led her through the busy club. I hated crowds and worse I hated to be touched by strangers, even if it was just brushing past them. It usually triggered wild perspiration and shortness of breath for me, but I had noticed during the last couple of hours that Lucy hated it all a lot more. Everytime she was knocked or brushed against, her whole body tensed and she took a deep breath, so I had strengthened my resolve and decided to be as strong as I could for her, at least for that night. It was our first girls night out ever, and I wanted it to be fun.

Of course, when we finally got to the ladies, the queue was about a mile long. We joined the back of it and I prayed it wouldn't take long because my leg killed when I was just stood still as we were, especially in heels, even the low ones I had chosen.

"It's so busy in here!" Lucy said over the music.

"Do you hate it? I should have picked somewhere quieter."

"No way! I wanted to experience a real night club and this is really cool! I don't hate it, it's just a lot to take in."

"We have to dance! I know I'll look like a freak trying to dance with my crutch, but I've always wanted to do it and I don't really care what anyone else thinks right now."

"Alex, you could never look like a freak. Don't talk about yourself like that. You are beautiful and smart and really.....I mean really *really* pretty." Lucy was sounding *really* wasted and I couldn't help but grin at the slight slur to her words.

"I think we might need some water before we drink any more." I laughed and Lucy nodded her agreement.

"To be honest, I think this may be the most I have ever drunk. I'm not feeling very well actually. Maybe I should just stick to water."

"Whatever you want hon. We can have fun without drinking anymore." Lucy just stared at me and I saw the colour of her face change before me, from her usual pale to a very odd grey colour. "Lucy, you ok?" I asked with concern.

"No, I feel really hot and sick all of a sudden. I'm sorry Alex."

"Don't be sorry. It's fine. Do you want to grab a cab and head home?"

"No. We didn't even dance yet!"

"There will be other nights to dance. You're not looking so good right now. I don't want you staying out if you're not up to it. Rob and Matt would kill me!"

"I hate to say it, bit I think maybe it might be best to call it a night. I'm so sorry Alex. I've ruined girls night!" She was almost in tears.

"You did not ruin it. We've had loads of fun and this is just the first of many nights out for us, right?" I asked hoping to cheer her mood.

"Right." She agreed.

"Good. Come on, let's go call Rob for a ride."

"Alright, but I really do need to pee first."

"Ok. It's nearly us, so you stay here and pee. I'll go and get you a bottle of water. It might help."

"Thank you. That sounds good."

"Pee and then wait in here for me, ok? Don't leave the restroom. I'll be like two minutes." Lucy nodded vehemently so I took that as her agreement and headed out to the bar. I would get her some water, so hopefully she would hold off throwing up in the car on the way home. She needed water, aspirin and sleep. We could try the night out another time.

I fought my way to the bar and waited several minutes until I could get the attention of the server. I got two bottles of water so Lucy could drink plenty and then hurried back to the ladies as fast as I could, conscious I had been longer than I had told Lucy I would be. It was a nightmare, trying to fight through the crowd with my crutch. People didn't in anyway try to make allowances for me and I had to really shove to get through, the whole time putting a lot more weight on my weak leg than I normally would.

I walked into the ladies to be greeted with an even longer queue than the one we had been met with before. I pushed past all of the glammed up, half dressed girls to get to the sinks. When I didn't find Lucy there I walked to the stalls, stood in the middle and called her name. There was no answer and I was immediately worried. Where was she? I pulled my cell out of my purse to call her, and found a text from her.

Needed air, Meet you at ent.

Terrified at the idea of her battling through the crowd and hanging around out in the dark street the club was on, on her own, drunk, ill and vulnerable, I hauled ass, as fast as I could make my bum leg go.

I practically threw myself out of the main entrance of the club and looked around frantically for Lucy, but she was nowhere in sight. I called out her name, but still she didn't appear. It was eerily quiet and dark out on the street and I was frantic. I started to walk further from the club as I called her cell. As I got near the end of the street I heard a scuffling and, having a very bad feeling, set off running as much as my injury would allow, ignoring the agony shooting up my leg.

As I began to round the corner onto an even darker, quieter street I heard a muffled cry and I ran faster than I ever knew I could. I called out Lucy's name and heard another muffled cry. Then I saw her, being dragged down the street by a monster of a man, dressed in all black. All I could see was Lucy's flailing arms and her legs being dragged between the strangers. They were a short distance ahead and I was sure, heading to the van parked a little further down the street.

"LUCY!" I screamed as I threw my crutch, the water and my purse to the ground and sprinted for her, not even considering the fact my injury had never let me get past a very slow jog before. Adrenaline overtook me. I would not let him take her. I would fight with everything I had to make sure Lucy never had to go through any more harm.

The huge guy turned to look at me as I screamed Lucy's name again and it was all I needed to gain on him. Lucy started fighting even harder and it slowed him down a lot. I managed to reach him and I threw myself on his back, digging my fingernails into any soft part of his face I could reach around to.

Six months after arriving in Chicago i had taken a short course of self-defense for women and I was so grateful for it in that moment. My attack worked. He dropped Lucy and she fell to the sidewalk as he turned and threw me off of his back. I managed to stay on my feet so I launched myself at him again before he could react, kneeing him straight in his junk. He doubled over with a loud cry of pain, while I stood firm and took a deep breath ready to keep fighting.

"Lucy, run!" I yelled, but she wasn't getting up. She was laid on the sidewalk, in a ball, sobbing and shaking. I had to get to her, but I wasn't going to turn my back on the kidnapper. I looked back to him and found him still trying to breathe through the agony of the hit to his privates. I decided to strike while he was still weak, and ran up and thrust my palm up into his nose as I'd been taught. He cried out and his nose was instantly bleeding, but he recovered and reacted quickly, jumping forward and throwing a punch at my face. I ducked on instinct, so luckily he only caught my right cheek, but it was enough to knock me off my feet amd make my vision fuzzy for a few seconds. I tried to shake off the fuzz and forced myself to stand, fists up, ready to hit again. I knew from experience, I was a harder target standing, but as I got to my feet all I could see was the guy retreating to his van. I watched him jump in the drivers side and then he sped off in the other direction.

"Oh thank fuck!" I gasped through the pain in my face. I dropped down to my knees beside Lucy and moved her hair from her face. She was sobbing quietly and her entire body was trembling, but she looked unharmed.

"Lucy, are you ok? He's gone. He drove off. Are you hurt?" I blurted all at once. I was trembling myself from the adrenaline and a butt load of pain. Lucy didn't respond and I really didn't know what to do. I looked around but there was no one near to help. I saw my cell on the sidewalk where I had dropped it when I leapt at the kidnapper, and reached for it. I scrolled down for the contact I knew would be best to help me make Lucy come around.

"It's ok hon, I'm calling Rob for you." I soothed as the call connected.

"Shepard!" Rob barked on answering on the second ring.

"Rob, it's Alex." My voice was trembling so badly and I knew I needed to get control so I wouldn't scare him more than he was already going to be.

"Alex? What's wrong?" He asked with worry.

"Lucy....some guy tried to take her Rob. I managed to stop him, he ran off, but Lucy....she's out of it, I can't get her to get up or speak. I....I don't know what to do." I was trying so hard to maintain control, but I was shaken and in pain and my terror showed through every word I spoke.

"Where are you?"

"Around the corner from Club 72, in the street."

"Is Lucy conscious?" He was terrified, I could hear it in his voice, despite the calm he tried to cover with.

"Yes. She's crying and shaking, but she won't answer me."

"I'm coming honey. Are you sure the guy left? Are you safe?"

"I watched him drive off."

"He could come back. You need to get somewhere safe Alex."

"I can't move Lucy and she's really not responding. I can't go anywhere. We're stuck here. Just hurry. If he comes back I won't let him take her Rob, I swear I won't."

"Just stay on the line. I'm only five minutes away. I'm going to conference in Jack and Matt to meet us there. Whatever you do don't hang up, ok honey?"

"Ok. Please hurry. Lucy's shaking even more. I'm worried Rob."

"She's probably having a panic attack. Just hold her tight Alex. It helps." Jesus, I was an idiot! Of course it was a panic attack! I'd had enough to be able to recognise one,

"I-I'm going to put my cell on the ground while I try to hold her closer….. just a minute." I didn't wait for his reply. I just put my cell on the ground and sat on the freezing sidewalk on my butt with my legs out in front of me. At least the snow had melted, small mercies and all. It took a huge effort, but I managed to drag Lucy onto my lap and I pressed her as close to my chest as I could, hoping my body heat would warm her too. Her whole body was tense and she didn't once move as I dragged her onto my lap, just kept her head down and her hands anxiously gripping her elbows around her middle.

I instantly started to tremble even more from the cold and the exertion, but Lucy seemed to relax a little after a moment and I was glad to know it had helped at least a little.

"Rob?" I whimpered as I put my cell to my ear once again.

"I'm here honey. Are you good?"

"Yeah. I managed to get Lucy in my arms. It helped….I think it helped." Before Rob could reply two more voices came on the line.

"Rob, what's going on?" Matt's voice.

"You do realise it's one AM right now?" Jack whined sleepily

"Matt?" I couldn't hold in my sob at the sound of his comforting voice.

"Alex, baby? Are you ok?" I tried to speak but all that came out was more sobs.

"Matt, they're on the street around the corner from Club 72. Someone tried to take Lucy." Rob barked down the line. I tried to calm my breathing and gain back control. If that guy did come back I'd be no use defending in the state that I was.

"What?!" Matt and Jack both roared at the same time. "Is she ok?"

"I don't think she's hurt…..but she's really upset, I can't get through to her." I whimpered as I reined in the sobs.

"Are you ok Alex?" Matt asked.

"Yeah….just worried about Lucy, and terrified that psycho will come back."

"I'm getting in my car now. I'll be there in a few minutes." Matt said.

"Me too. Cal's with me." Jack added.

"Can't you get off the street?" Matt asked,

"Alex can't move Lucy and she's not responding. I'm there now. I'm coming around the corner Alex." As soon as Rob finished speaking blinding lights came around the corner and I could barely breathe. It was Rob, he said it was, but what if it wasn't?

"Please tell me that's you Rob?" I whimpered tearfully.

"It's me." As he spoke the car screeched to a halt and Rob leapt out. I wanted to cry in relief, but I made myself hold it in. I hung up the call and dropped my phone so I could hold Lucy better with both hands.

"Lucy. I'm here sweetheart." Rob soothed as he got down on his knees and leant down to see her face.

"She's not trembling as much now Rob. You should get her in the car. She's freezing." I whispered weakly. I knew because I was frozen myself, colder than I ever remembered being in my life. The hot, daring outfits didn't seem like a good idea anymore!

Rob nodded and scooped Lucy up from my arms. It was a relief to get her weight off of my freezing, very painful legs. Rob turned toward the car, but then stopped and looked down at me.

"Come on honey, you too, in the car." He said with a reassuring smile.

"I need a minute Rob. Just take care of Lucy. I'm good."

"You're hurt. Your face is swollen and you're bleeding." Rob pointed to my arm and I noticed for the first time he was right, I was bleeding from my elbow a little.

"I'm fine. Lucy's not. Go Rob. I'm right behind you." I said firmly. I knew it was wasting time to argue and I should just get up and follow him, but I couldn't. My nerve damaged leg was more painful than I had ever known and my other was painful from the cold. My head was also still throbbing from the punch I'd taken and my body trembled violently from the adrenaline and the cold. I needed a few minutes to get the strength to stand and to take control of the panic attack I knew was waiting to rear its ugly head.

Rob finally nodded and carried Lucy to the back seat of the car. He placed her inside and spoke to her, but I could see he kept an eye on me the entire time too and I was grateful to know he cared. I just hoped Lucy would be alright. It was all my fault. I should never have left her in the bathroom, then none of this would have happened.

I felt my chest becoming tighter and I knew that the panic was trying to seize me now my mission to protect Lucy was done. Being hit and feeling the terror of the whole thing brought back flashes of my past, one after the other. I pressed my eyes closed and took several deep breaths to push it all back where it belonged, in the dark depths of my memory. I managed to calm myself and my chest became lighter. Knowing I had to get my ass off the cold sidewalk, I took one more deep breath to ready myself for the pain I knew would hit when making myself stand, but as I did so, there were more headlights and before I had time to worry, Matt was out of the car and running towards me.

"Jesus Alex! What the hell happened?" He demanded as he bent down in front of me. He pulled off the heavy wool coat he wore and wrapped it hurriedly around my trembling shoulders.

"I'm ok." I whispered.

"Where's Lucy?" I pointed behind him to Rob's SUV.

"Rob?" Matt called.

"She's good. She's coming round. She doesn't look hurt physically. Just stay with Alex. I have a feeling we owe her a whole fucking lot of thanks tonight." Rob called back.

"No….it's my fault. I left her…..if I hadn't have left her Matt." I sobbed nonsensically.

"Sshh baby. You're safe, you're both safe and that's all that matters now." Matt soothed as he reached down to pick me up. He lifted me from the sidewalk and I winced in pain.

"Where are you hurt Alex?" Matt tried to loosen his hold on me, but it didn't ease the agony in my leg.

"Put me back down Matt, please put me down!" I cried. Matt lowered me back down to the sidewalk and knelt in front of me, his face filled with concern.

"Matt, is she ok?" We both looked up to find Cal running toward us. Jack was leant in the back of the SUV beside Rob, checking on Lucy.

"No. I'm going to call an ambulance." Matt said as he stood again.

"Please don't Matt. I'm ok. I only took one hit and it wasn't even that hard. It's just my leg, I ran on it, a lot....and then it's been on the freezing concrete......I-I just need to get home and soak it in the tub and I'll be fine."

"Baby, you can't even get up. How are we going to get you home?"

"I just need a minute to let the pain pass, then I'll get up. Just give me a minute." I so wanted to fall apart, but it wasn't the time and the middle of the street certainly wasn't the place either. I had to keep it together until I got home. Matt was considering what I said when suddenly Lucy screamed his name from the back of the SUV. It was a terror filled scream and it instantly put me on alert, so I couldn't imagine how it hit Matt. He looked between the car and me and it was obvious he didn't know what to do.

"Matt, Go. She needs you. I'm ok." I said hurriedly.

"I've got Alex man." Cal assured Matt, as he knelt on the sidewalk beside me.

"I'll be right back!" Matt called as he hurried away.

"Some first girls night out this turned out to be for us!" I said dryly.

"Let's get you warmer, ok sweetie?" Cal said as he pulled off his own thick winter coat. He wrapped it tightly around my legs, very carefully tucking it underneath so they no longer touched the sidewalk.

"Thanks Cal. I really am ok. It's Lucy I'm worried about. That guy….he was dragging her down the street. He was going to throw her in the back of a van. I was so fucking worried I wouldn't…..wouldn't get to her in time." I was tearing up again and I knew more sobs were on the way.

"But you did. You stopped him and you're both here. Lucy's strong. It sounds like she was hit with a panic attack, not for the first time either. She'll be just fine in a few hours"

"I hope so." I whispered.

"I'm back." Matt declared as he approached. "Lucy's ok. She was trapped in a flashback of when her ex kidnapped her. Rob brought her round. She's asking for you baby."

"Oh thank god!" I cried with relief.

"Rob's going to take her home. We'll follow them back to theirs for tonight until Rob gets a chance to look into who was behind this. He wants us all together and safe for tonight. Is that ok Alex?"

"As long as there's a tub to soak my leg Matt. I'd like to be near Lucy tonight anyway. She may need you."

"It's you she was worried about. She screamed for me because she thought you'd been taken. I assured her you're ok."

"I think you can try lifting me again now Matt. The throbbing is less and I really want to get back so I can see Lucy for myself."

"Ok beautiful, but if it's bad, just tell me to put you down again, ok?" I nodded and Matt bent to pick me up again. He gathered me in his arms and while my leg still screamed in pain, it was less and I was able to bear it. Matt carried me over to his car and placed me down across the back seat with my legs laid out in front of me.

"I'll ride in the back and try to stop her being jostled too much." Cal offered.

"That ok with you Alex?" Matt asked. I nodded and Cal climbed into the back of Matt's Range Rover with me. He buckled a seatbelt over me as best he could and then he pulled me back so I leant my back against his solid front. I instantly relaxed into him, grateful for the comfort he provided. Matt jumped in and started the car.

"I'm so tired." I admitted as my eyes became very heavy in the comfort of the warm car.

"It's the come down from the adrenaline. Just rest Sweetie. We'll wake you when we get there." Cal soothed. He placed a gentle kiss on my forehead and for the first time in my life I got a taste of how it must feel to have a loving brother or father figure in your life. Feeling relieved Lucy would be ok and knowing I was incredibly safe with Cal and Matt I allowed sleep to overtake me and I stopped fighting my heavy eyelids.

MATT

"Holy fuck! Matt, come look at this!" Rob gasped from where he leant over his laptop at the coffee table in his lounge. The ladies were both fast asleep in the bedrooms. They'd both been deeply asleep when we carried them in and we decided to just let them rest as long as they could. Rob and I both knew the nightmares would be coming soon. Alex had suffered with them every single night I had stayed with her and while I didn't know what the root of them was, I was sure what Alex had been through that night would amplify them.

I quietly closed the door to the room Alex slept in. I had checked on her again for about the hundredth time in the last couple of hours. She was still sleeping soundly. I crossed the lounge to where Rob had been on his laptop for the last thirty minutes tracking down surveillance footage of where we found Alex and Lucy. He had one of his guys stationed outside his apartment building and another outside the apartment. He was worried whoever had tried to take Lucy was targeting him and he was taking no chances with her safety. Jack and Cal were already bent down watching the screen and I joined them, crowding in around Rob. The image on the screen was surprisingly clear. It was an image of the street Alex and Lucy were found on and on the sidewalk was a guy in a black hooded sweatshirt, dragging my sister roughly away. She was fighting, but the guy was at least twice her size and her fights were useless.

"Who the hell is that?" I asked angrily.

"Don't know, Fucker never shows his face to the camera. Keep watching." Rob said, clearly filled with rage at seeing the woman he loved being hurt.

I continued watching as the guy dragged Lucy further down the street and then suddenly out of nowhere Alex appeared. She flew down the street at such a pace and I suddenly knew why her leg had been so painful.

"What the fuck?" Jack gasped. "How is she running on that leg?"

"Adrenaline." I said, unable to hide my proud smile as I watched Alex leap onto the guys back and lay into his face. We all watched silently as the guy let Lucy drop and threw Alex off of his back. She remained standing and barely took a second to catch her breath before she launched herself at him again. We all gasped as Alex kneed him in the nuts with crazy force.

"She is badass, Matt." Rob said with shock. The guy seemed to flounder for a minute as he nursed his sore groin, but Alex didn't let up. She approached him with a brilliant upward thrust into his nose, making it explode.

"Fucking bastard!" I raged as I watched the guy punch her back so hard she fell to the ground.

"Sonofabitch!" Jack gasped at the same time.

We watched as the fucker ran off out of the angle of the camera. Alex stumbled to her feet again, fists raised, ready to fight, but the guy was gone. She fell down beside Lucy and Rob paused the footage.

"She saved Lucy's life. She was fucking brilliant." Rob said with what I knew was gratitude.

"She's an amazing woman, but he hurt her and Lucy. He needs to be dealt with Rob." I hissed angrily.

"I'm on it man. I got the plate for the van on another camera down the street. I have guys running it now. We'll get the fucker!"

"Matt?" At that moment Alex stumbled out of the bedroom. She still looked half asleep and she was really struggling to stand. I ran across the room and she practically fell into my arms.

"Sorry....my leg. It's bad." She whispered, her voice still trembling.

"What can we do to help Matt?" Rob asked as he appeared beside me.

"I have my vicodin in the car, the ones I take when my leg plays up." Jack offered.

"Thanks Jack. I'll help her into the bath to soak it if you can grab those. That should help. Can you set the bath running for me Cal please?" I asked as I gathered Alex up and settled her in my arms. Cal nodded and hurried off toward the main bathroom.

"I'm sorry I'm causing all this trouble Matt."

"It's no trouble baby. Don't you dare apologise."

"We saw the surveillance footage Alex, we saw what you did to save Lucy. I will never be able to repay you for protecting her like that." Rob said reverently.

"It was all my fault Rob, don't say that please. If I hadn't left her in the bathroom she'd never have been out there alone in the first place!" Alex cried almost hysterically. I went to calm her, but Lucy burst out of her room before I could speak.

"That is crap Alex! You left me in a safe place to get me water to make me feel better. I'm the idiot who thought it would be wise to wander off outside, all alone!" Lucy raged.

"Lucy, are you ok?" Alex asked as she struggled to get out of my arms.

"Baby, you can't put weight on that leg." I cautioned as I gripped her tighter.

"I'll manage Matt, put me down. I need to get to Lucy….please." I wanted to refuse, but I saw the desperation in her eyes and I couldn't. I slowly lowered her legs to the ground and she took a moment to right herself before she stepped out of my hold and embraced Lucy tightly.

"I'm so sorry I left you. I was so scared he was going to take you." Alex whimpered. They were both sobbing and holding each other tightly.

"I'm ok, thanks to you. You really kicked his arse….I mean I was only half there, but i heard him scream."

"That would have been the knee to the balls, that Alex gave him sweetheart." Rob laughed. Alex and Lucy remained where they were, embracing and sobbing for a few minutes, until I knew by the way her body tensed, that Alex was in real pain.

"Alex, at least sit down now love." I suggested. She pulled away from Lucy and reached out for my hand when she began to sway shakily. I grabbed her and carried her over to the sofa, where I gently set her on my knee.

"Oh Alex, what did he do to you?" Lucy asked as she sat beside us.

"This wasn't him. I just went a little hard on my bad leg. It will settle down eventually."

"And your face?" Lucy brushed her hand over Alex's deeply bruised and slightly swollen cheek.

"I'm fine. Don't worry about me. Are you ok?"

"I am. I'm sorry I freaked out on you, i just got sucked into a flashback and I froze. Did you find out who it was Rob?" Lucy asked.

"Not yet sweetheart, but I will and until then I won't be taking any chances with your safety."

"He....he said something to me. He said 'Time to pay his debt bitch!' What does that mean Rob? Do you owe someone?" Lucy asked hesitantly.

"No, of course not! Matt? Could it be anything to do with you?"

"Who the hell would I owe? I spend all my time asleep or working." I snapped. I would never ever do anything that could bring risk to my sister, not after everything she had been through.

"I'll figure it all out. I don't want you worrying about it Lucy, but at the same time you need to be cautious. I don't want you going anywhere without one of us, or my security staff until this is all cleared up, ok?" Rob said firmly.

"No arguments from me. One kidnapping and one attempted kidnapping is enough for one lifetime." Lucy replied with an eye roll.

"You scared the shit out of me." Rob said as he wrapped Lucy in his arms. I gathered Alex closer to me and got to my feet, carrying her into the bathroom to leave Rob and Lucy to have their moment. They needed it. What had happened had been far too close to the time only a year ago when Lucy had been kidnapped by her husband

and been beaten almost to death. It was still so raw for all of us and we really didn't need this terrifying near miss to set us all on high alert again. I just prayed it would all be resolved quickly because we were not all fully over what Lucy had been through before I wasn't sure there was one of us strong enough to go through something like that again.

ALEX

Cal filled Rob and Lucy's huge free-standing, roll top, tub for me, then he left Matt to help me get in. I felt awkward. Matt and I had slept side by side, clothed a couple of nights and we'd kissed a lot, but that was as close as we had gotten. He hadn't seen me naked yet and while I wasn't particularly self conscious of my body, I had scars, a lot of really nasty scars and I knew as soon as Matt saw them, he would want to know where they came from and I really wasn't ready to go into my Pandora's box of bad memories with him yet.

"I want to be a gentleman about this baby, but I don't think you'll manage on your own right now." Matt said softly. "I could probably close my eyes and manage to help."

"There's no need Matt. We both know you're going to see my body eventually. No point making this harder trying to be modest, and you're right, I need help right now. It's just.....well....." I couldn't get the words I wanted to say, out.

"It's ok. Just tell me."

"I have some scars Matt....quite a lot actually and I know you'll need an explanation, but i can't....I'm not ready to go back to the memories right now....I'm sorry." I admitted, knowing how weak that made me, but not knowing how to get the strength I needed to be braver.

"I understand Alex. I know you have things to tell me and I have accepted that you won't be able to tell me until you're ready. It's ok."

"You might not even want me when you've seen them Matt. They're so ugly."

"No part of you could ever be ugly. I love you Alex Harrison. I love every single part of you, even the scars. Don't ever doubt that." My eyes filled with tears at his words. He loved me. He'd mentioned love before, but he'd never really come out and told me he loved me and the fact that he was the only person to ever say those words to me had a huge impact.

"I love you too." I whispered tearfully. It had been less than a month since I met the man, but I knew how I felt. Matt's face lit with a huge smile and it was infectious, I smiled too through my tears. We didn't say anything else as Matt helped me remove the skirt I had put on excitedly so many hours ago. I tried to unbutton my shirt, but my hands trembled too much so Matt took over and did the remainder. I heard the slight increase in the speed of his breathing when he saw the scars on my abdomen, numerous long lines filling almost the entire space. I studied his face, but his expression gave nothing away. He removed my shirt and dropped it to the ground as he moved around to my back to unclasp my bra. He couldn't hide the intake of breath when he saw the hundreds of lines criss crossing my back. I heard it clearly and I turned despite the pain it caused, to look at his face. A tear was running down his face and he hurried to wipe it away.

"I'm sorry baby. It was a shock….I hate to think of anyone hurting you this way." He said as he pulled me into his arms again.

"It's the past Matt. You're my future, you're my happiness now." I whispered.

"I'll never let anyone hurt you again Alex. I'll do everything in my power to always keep you safe." He pledged emotionally.

"I know. I love you."

"I love you too baby, so much."

"Please never stop saying that. I love the way it makes me feel. No one has ever said those words but you Matt. It means everything to me."

"I'll never stop saying them and I'll never stop meaning them either. You are everything to me Alex, everything."

We remained in a peaceful silence as Matt helped me remove the last of my clothes and lowered me down into the soothing water. I laid back and took some deep breaths. The heat of the water eased the pain in my leg and Matt's words eased the pain in my heart and I was, maybe for the first time in my life, feeling peaceful. Matt knelt on the floor beside me and soothingly rubbed a warm washcloth over my arms and chest.

"This is heaven." I eventually sighed.

"Maybe we should get a bath at my place. Before you I only needed a shower, but now I'm thinking baths could be fun too." Matt said cheekily, making me smile.

"I won't argue. Girls enjoy a good soak and I can tell you I'd enjoy it a whole lot more if you were in with me."

"I'll be on the phone first thing, one large bathtub please." Matt joked.

"Do you really think Lucy is ok Matt? She seemed so relaxed when Rob said she might be in danger. Shouldn't she be more worried?"

"She's a lot tougher than she looks. She will be worried, but she's good at hiding it. Plus, nothing will be scarier to Lucy than her ex being after her last year. I guess if she got through that, she knows she can get through this too."

"I guess. Do you think, whoever they were, they'll try to take her again?"

"Probably, but they won't get near. We messed up last year with Phil. He got to Lucy because we weren't cautious enough. We won't make that mistake again. Rob won't take a single bloody risk this time. He'll have a team of his guys following Lucy everywhere. Try not to worry too much, my little brawler. She'll be safe." Matt assured me as he ran a comforting hand through my hair.

"You guys are all so lucky to have each other. If you need them, there they are, ready to do whatever it takes to support you. I think it's rare to have that, you know?"

"It is rare and I agree, we are lucky, but by we, I mean you too beautiful. You are a part of this family now. You were the minute they all met you and saw how much I was already in love with you. It helped that they all fell in love with you right away too, but you cemented it tonight Alex. The way you saved my sister makes you a part of us and when Rob says he will never be able to repay you, he means it. My family is your family now and if you need something they will be there, no matter what, no matter when. You only need ask and they'll come."

"I've never had a real family Matt." I admitted tearfully. "What you said means so much to me and I love them all too. They're all really great, kind people. Thank you for bringing them all into my life, thank you for rescuing me from drowning in loneliness."

"That's it. I can't hold back anymore. I have to hold you." Matt declared and before I could react he was lifting me gently from the water and holding me in his arms tightly.

"Matt! You're going to be all wet!" I cried, half laughing and half crying.

"Don't care." He held me as though he feared I may float up and away if not gripped tight enough and I loved it. I had never felt so loved in my life and It was all I had spent my entire 26 years of life so far, wishing for.

***

When we exited the bathroom some time later Matt helped me back to the bedroom I had slept in earlier. On the bed clothes were laid out for both of us, which was good since Matt's trousers and shirt were soaked through. I sat on the edge of the bed, the worst of the pain in my leg having faded to more of a bad ache. I pulled on the jeans and hooded sweater Lucy must have laid out for me. They fitted pretty well, except I had to turn the jeans up a couple of inches. Matt dressed in jeans and a polo t-shirt and then we made our way back into the lounge.

"How are you feeling sweetie?" Cal asked as I sat beside him on the sofa.

"A lot better thanks."

"Jack got the pain pills if you need them?"

"Oh, I'm not sure. I don't really take pain meds other than over the counter. Are they strong?"

"Maybe just take one baby. It'll help ease the pain in that leg." Matt suggested. I nodded and Jack instantly handed me a glass of water and shook a pill from the bottle he held. I thanked him and took it, hoping it didn't make me as loopy as alcohol did.

"Ok, who wants food? I made breakfast!" Lucy declared excitedly from the kitchen. It was very early the next morning and none of us had really slept much. I couldn't believe the way Lucy had managed to shake away the terror that was clearly consuming her only a matter of hours earlier and the fatigue. She really was an incredibly tough woman.

Cal and Jack moved faster than I had ever seen them after Lucy's call, obviously starving as always.

"Come on. You need to eat." Matt prompted as he too stood.

"I don't suppose anyone grabbed my crutch and my purse in the chaos last night. I dropped them in the street."

"We'll ask. If not I'll help you cancel your cards and we might have to get your locks changed if your keys were in there?"

"Oh no, they were." I sighed.

"I'll help you sort it out, don't worry. First food." He pulled me up and wrapped a supportive arm around my back as I hobbled into the kitchen.

"Alex! Oh good the clothes fit!" Lucy said cheerily as we entered and took a seat. "Hurry up and fill your plate. The men in this family are like bloody savages around food!" I couldn't help but giggle at what seemed to be quite an accurate description of the four men shovelling food down like it may disappear at any moment. I couldn't believe how fast Matt had sat and piled a plate with eggs and bacon!

I filled my plate and we all ate in a comfortable silence. Lucy made everyone coffee, except her and Matt who, of course, wanted tea. It was nice, it really felt like a family meal and I loved every second of it, despite the horrible events of the night before that had brought us all there.

"Oh, anyone find Alex's stuff on the street last night before we left?"

"Yeah, they're in my trunk, a purse and your crutch honey?" Jack replied, much to my relief.

"Yes. Thank you. At least I don't have to cancel everything and change my locks."

"You should stay with Matt until all of this is cleared up Alex." Rob said, more of an order than a suggestion.

"Why? He wasn't after me? He probably doesn't even know I exist."

"He'll know you exist after that knee to the balls last night." Jack declared laughing.

"I agree. It's better to be safe baby." Matt added.

"Matt, you're never even there and as much as I love your place, I'd be happier in my own when you're working. I'm more comfortable there alone than I am at yours."

"Ok. I understand that. My place is still new to you. At least stay with me on nights I'm not working though, ok?"

"Ok. That's a deal." I agreed, grateful for any time I got to spend with him.

"I'm coming to assess your building and apartment security if you're staying there alone some nights. Today. You don't stay there alone until I say it's secure, ok?" Rob said firmly. I dare not argue with his tone of voice, but I couldn't afford new security.

"The building has cameras and you need a key to get in the main entrance. I have two locks on my apartment door too so I'm good Rob, thanks though."

"I'll be there this afternoon. You don't stay there alone until I say, ok?" Rob simply said again.

"Fine. Ok then." I conceded, knowing I couldn't win.

Lucy flashed me a sympathetic smile and I guessed she knew better than anyone it was easier to just give in to Rob.

I had to admit, it was nice to know he cared, that they all cared that I was safe. Matt was right. They had seemed to have taken me as a part of their freeform family and cared about me as much as they cared for each other. I had no idea what I had done to deserve such a gift in my life, but I was sure as heck grabbing it with both hands and never letting it go. I meant what I had told Matt. I cared about them all too and I would be sure to return the care they had shown me. I had never been a part of a proper family and I really didn't know what it entailed, but I would learn, for these kind people and for myself, I would learn.

ALEX

The next two weeks passed blissfully for me. Matt and I fell into a rhythm of me staying at his place when he was there for the night and him coming to crash at mine whenever he could inbetween the odd hours he kept. If we couldn't see each other we talked on the phone and texted each other constantly. Matt took me on dates whenever he had time off and we had some amazing days and nights out together, but it was the times we spent snuggled together on the sofa at one of our places or cuddled up together in bed that I loved most. In those quiet, relaxed moments I felt so at ease and so very loved by Matt. He was always honest with me about everything and he always looked to take care of me and ensure I was happy and comfortable. Those were such huge things to me and they made me feel so complete, in a way I had never thought possible.

Matt's family also made me feel even more welcome in those weeks. Rob had, as he had told me, come to my apartment that afternoon after the night of the attack and installed two more locks on my apartment door and had a crew install a state of the art security system, which he refused to let me pay for. It monitored my front door and all of the windows in the apartment and would send an alarm straight to Rob's company, to him and to Matt if triggered. I had to admit it made me feel a lot safer, even though I knew no one would be coming for me. Lucy was fast becoming my first ever best friend. She was constantly inviting me over to hers or out to restaurants or shopping when she knew Matt was working. Of course she had an entourage of two of Robs security guards everywhere we went, but she never seemed worried so I took her lead. We also spoke on the phone nearly everyday and we just continued to get closer and closer. It was so incredibly special to have a friend to chat to and laugh with. I was starting to feel like a real person, with a normal life and I loved it.

Jack and Cal were also regularly checking up on me with texts and phone calls over those weeks, checking if I needed anything, asking if I was doing ok and always making me laugh at their stupid jokes . They called in a couple of evenings when Matt was working to have a coffee and just chat with me and I knew it was probably because they were all on high alert after what happened and they wanted to check on me, but it showed they cared and that really mattered to me. They were all amazing friends to have in my life and I was grateful for them every damned day.

"You ready baby?" I was in Matt's bedroom, at his place getting dressed up to go over to Rob and Lucy's for thanksgiving dinner. Even though Matt and Lucy didn't technically celebrate the holiday, Lucy had wanted to do the whole family dinner for all of us. It was to be my first real thanksgiving celebration and I was excited about it, especially since it also happened to be my twenty seventh birthday. Of course I was the only one who knew that, but I loved the fact we were all getting together. I could almost pretend the gathering was to celebrate my birthday, another thing I had never celebrated before.

"I'll be there in a second." I replied as I pulled on my low heeled ankle boots. I stood and looked at myself in the full length mirror. I was surprised myself with how cute I looked in slim fit black slacks and a loose dark green chiffon blouse. I pulled on my little black leather jacket and fluffed up my hair which I had loosely curled. It was unlike me to put so much effort into my appearance and I was pleased with the results that afternoon.

***

I held Matt's hand as we headed down the hall to Rob and Lucy's apartment thirty minutes later.

"You really do look amazing Alex. I mean you always do, but today you're truly stunning." Matt said as he kissed the back of my hand which was clasped in his.

"You're looking pretty hot yourself." I replied as I looked him up and down in his dark blue jeans, pristine white shirt and grey blazer. He was every part the GQ model I had fallen for instantly that first night.

"Why thank you kind lady." He joked as we reached Rob and Lucy's apartment. He turned the handle to walk straight in, which surprised me. He always knocked usually.

"Matt, we shouldn't just….." I was cut off by shouting and popping. I turned quickly, wondering what the hell was going on and found a room beautifully decorated with Rose Gold and cream balloons and birthday decorations.

"Surprise!" was shouted loudly and party poppers banged. I almost jumped clean out of my skin in shock. I looked around and found Lucy, Rob, Jack and Cal jumping out from hiding places around the lounge.

"Is it your birthday?" I asked Matt. Were our birthdays on the same date?

"No. it's yours isn't it?" Matt asked with a huge grin.

"How did you know?" I asked as I tried to contain my smile.

"I have my ways." Matt replied with a smile. He bent down to kiss me and I held him tight, completely overcome with surprise. "Happy birthday baby" He whispered into my ear. We moved into the apartment and I didn't miss how Rob hurried over to close the door and set the alarm behind us. He never ever relaxed. He was always on high alert.

"Happy birthday chick!" Lucy said excitedly as she hurried over to hug me.

"Thank you. I know this must be your handiwork." I said as I held her tight. "What about thanksgiving?" I asked.

"Oh, who cares about thanksgiving when it's your birthday?" Lucy laughed.

"Thank you so much."

"You're very welcome."

Jack and cal came up next to hug me and wish me a happy birthday and then Rob stood in front of me wearing a little card cone hat and looking pained in it.

"Happy birthday sweetheart." He wished as he finally gave me a genuine smile and kissed my cheek.

"Thanks Rob. Nice hat. Very manly." I said with a giggle. "Lucy said I had to get in the party spirit. I gotta say the hat's not doing it." I reached up and took it from him, putting it on myself instead.

"I owe you big time." He said with a smile, making me laugh.

We all sat down to an amazing lunch then, a beautiful selection of italian dishes including a caprese salad,

bruschetta, three different pasta dishes and a huge selection and anti-pasti. The guys didn't let us down as they tucked in like they hadn't eaten for weeks. I stuffed myself silly too and I laughed and enjoyed myself completely uninhibited. I was so happy and comfortable with them all and able to just relax and be myself.
Lucy brought a beautiful pink birthday cake out after lunch was finished. It was decorated with delicate little sugar paste flowers and I was amazed by the work that must have gone into it. They sang 'happy birthday' to me and I couldn't hold in my tears then. I was so overcome by it all. I blew out the candles and wished with everything I had I could continue to be as happy as I was at that moment.

"Thank you." I whispered. "All of you. I'm sorry I'm getting all soppy. It's just this is the first time in my entire life i've celebrated a birthday. I used to dream about it when I was a kid, like cake and balloons, the whole birthday shabang, but I never thought.....It's amazing." I finally made myself stop babbling. They all looked at each other and I knew I should have kept my mouth shut, It was the wine!

"We go big on birthdays in this family sweetie. You'll never get a birthday to yourself again!" Jack said happily and I was grateful to him for picking the atmosphere back up.

"That's fine by me." I said with a smile as I pulled back the tears.

"Are we getting some of that cake Lucy, or is it just ornamental?" Matt asked. He put his hand on mine on the table and squeezed it reassuringly.

"Did you make that Lucy?" I asked.

"Yeah." She said reluctantly. " I am really not a baker, but I thought I'd have a go. Our mum would turn in her grave if I ever bought a birthday cake. She used to make the most amazing cakes for our birthdays. Do you remember Matt?"

"I do darling, especially the pink unicorn she made for your tenth. You loved that."

"Oh yeah, I'd forgotten that one." She said with a little sadness. "Anyway, I'm not as good as her and it's not the prettiest, but I think it'll taste nice."

"It's amazing Lucy. I love it!"

Lucy shrugged off my compliment and sliced the cake, which did taste really good. It was the first birthday cake I had ever been given and it was far more special to me than I thought any of them could possibly realise.

After cake we went to sit in the lounge and they all gave me presents. I had to try hard not to let more tears escape as I looked across the pile of brightly wrapped gifts. I was so overwhelmed by their kindness.

I opened the one from Rob and Lucy first and could hardly believe when I pulled out a beautiful, soft black leather Michael Kors handbag. It was a little messenger. just the type I loved to wear across my body so my hands were free for my crutch, and I knew it must have cost a fortune.

"Do you like it? We can go and swap it if not." Lucy asked nervously.

"I absolutely love it." I said very emotionally. I put it down carefully and hurried to my feet to approach them. Lucy stood up and hugged me tight.

"Thank you so much." I whispered "It's the nicest thing I have ever had." Lucy pulled back and wiped a stray tear from my cheek. I turned to Rob then who was sat watching us and smiled.

"Come on Rob, your turn." I said. He stood up and hugged me for a moment.

"Thank you."

"You're very welcome sweetheart." He said as he pulled away and sat back down beside Lucy.

I opened another then, from Jack and Cal. I could tell it was a book as I picked it up and I was so excited. There was nothing, in the world that I loved more than books. I tore it open and gasped when I realised it was a Dickens book I was missing, from a collection I had been building up since I arrived in Chicago four years ago. It was the last one and completed my set. They were my most prized possessions. I had bought the first one at a thrift store on my second day in the city. I had been lost, alone and in terrible pain, but that book got me through those first few days and I had made it my mission to collect them ever since. Of course I had quickly realised I was extremely lucky to find the first in a thrift shop. The books were a rare collection, over a hundred years old, highly sought after and extremely expensive,

"How did you know?" I asked as I looked at them both.

"Cal noticed when we were at yours last week. He's been on a mission, searching the internet and calling book stores all week." Jack explained.

"It's the last one. I've been building that collection for four years. I can't believe it's actually complete. I was tearing up once again, completely overawed by the thoughtfulness and kindness of these amazing people. "I'm going to treasure this. Thank you guys, so very much." I began to move to them, but they stood and came to me. Cal pulled me in tight and I tried to find the words to explain how very grateful I was.

"Thank you Cal. I don't know what to say.....just thank you. Those books are very precious to me." I babbled, words completely failing me.

"You're so welcome sweetheart."

I hugged and thanked Jack as well and as they both sat down again I dare not open the last one from Matt. I was a crying, emotional wreck and I was struggling to suck it up.

"I hope you guys realise you are giving me the greatest day of my life right here." I said with a smile as I picked up a slim square box from Matt.

"That was the plan, wasn't it Matt?" Lucy asked.

"Yep. It was." Matt agreed.

I was grinning from ear to ear, my eyes filled with tears of joy, as I opened Matt's gift. Inside the wrapping was a black velvet box and I had to force myself to take a calming breath before I opened it.

"You can be honest if it's not your style." Matt said and I knew he was nervous. Excited to know what he had chosen I quickly opened the box and instantly fell in love with what I found. It was a bangle, with diamonds dotted intermittently all of the way around. It was simple and yet so amazingly beautiful at the same time. It was so me. He knew me so well, they all did. They had all chosen the most wonderful gifts for me.

"It's platinum and I was told should be hard wearing so it's suitable to wear whenever. I had it engraved inside." Matt explained. I tipped it up in the light and studied the inside.

My past, My present, My future, My forever. Love always, Matt xxx

"Oh Matt!" I cried through big ugly sobs. "It's perfect. Thank you. I love you." I leapt to my feet and onto his lap where he wrapped me tightly in his arms.

"I love you too beautiful. Forever." Matt whispered. He held me like that until I managed to calm my emotions enough to compose myself, then he helped me clip on the beautiful bracelet.

"It's beautiful." I said happily.

"Just like you baby." Matt said with a grin.

"Ok, enough of this soppy stuff. Is this a party or not? It's definitely time for cocktails!" Lucy said, making me laugh.

"Oh yeah! I've been practising my mixology. I'm going to show you all a thing or two!" Jack said, making the room erupt into laughter.

"Mixology? You sure about that Jack? I haven't seen any practising going on at home?" Cal asked dryly.

"Just you wait! I have skills,"

It turned out to be the best afternoon and evening of my life. We all laughed until it hurt at Jack's 'skills' which turned out to be nonexistent and he instead ended up covering Rob and Lucy's kitchen in various liquors. We all drank cocktails and laughed, just having fun as day turned into night. Lucy and I finally got to dance as we had longed to, but instead of a club, it was in the middle of her lounge with the stereo blasting. The guys were all laughing at our expense, but we didn't care.

Around midnight Matt woke me where I had fallen asleep with Lucy on the sofa a while before.

"Let's get you home beautiful." He whispered.

"Ok." I agreed, too tired to argue. Matt pulled me up and the movement woke Lucy.

"What's going on?" She slurred drunkenly.

"Alex and Matt are going home and you are going to bed." Rob said with amusement.

"Oh yeah, I like the sound of that, sexy man." Lucy purred suggestively making Matt groan painfully and the rest of us burst out laughing.

"I'm standing here you know Lucy?" Matt cried.

"Oh yeah, sorry bro." Lucy giggled.

"Thank you everyone. I had such....such a great day.....and night. And the presents! Thank you so much for the presents! They are all so special to me." I gushed, knowing I sounded drunk, but unable to stop myself. "I love all you guys."

"You are so welcome A-Alex. It's so nice to see you so ha-happy." Lucy slurred as she stood and almost fell on me. I stumbled back as I grabbed her so she wouldn't hurt herself. Matt steadied us as Rob stepped forward to support Lucy. "Ooops." She giggled. "Might have had a little bit too much booze."

"Gee, you think darling?" Matt said sarcastically. "Sleep it off and you'll be fine. I'll ring you tomorrow." He added as he placed a kiss on her forehead and then wrapped his arm around me. I really was as happy as I had ever been. I had family, and a man who loved me, really loved me and who I loved just as much right back. I had never imagined I could ever be that happy, but it was happening and I was determined nothing would ruin it for me.

MATT

I couldn't contain my smile at work the next day. Alex had been so very happy the previous day and that was everything to me. I had seen her birth date on her meds and made a note of it, wanting to make it special for her. I had pledged to do whatever it took to replace at least some of her horrifying memories from the past with good ones. I still had no idea really of what she had been through, but I had seen the scars and they were clearly the result of multiple horrendous attacks. I recognised the ones on her abdomen as cuts made with a sharp blade of some kind. They were jagged and very puckered suggesting she never received proper care for the cuts. The lines were placed very deliberately and I knew whoever had done that to her had done so for no other reason than they enjoyed it. Who the hell would do that to an innocent girl? The scars were old, maybe seven or eight years making Alex a teenager at the time. And her back? I had never seen so many scars in one place, all of varying ages. Someone had beaten the shit out of her back with a cane or something equally as sadistic. It filled me with rage just trying to comprehend what exactly she had been put through and I longed to get my hands on the monster who had done that and Christ knew what else to her. While we hadn't discussed her past, the scars and the nightmares she woke screaming from most nights were enough to warn me that whatever had happened to her, was bad and a part of me wasn't sure if I was ready to know the details at that point either.

Seeing her the previous night, so carefree, dancing away with my sister and enjoying herself was a real joy. I wanted to give her that and so much more, always, and I would do everything in my power to make her life that way.

"Matt. How was Alex this morning?" I snapped out of my thoughts and looked up to find Jack approaching. He had on his coat and I knew he was just coming on shift as I was finishing up.

"How do you think? I left her in a very dark room with water and two aspirin." I laughed. "She really had a great birthday though. Thanks for being there for her mate."

"No thanks needed Matt. She's one of us now. She's a really entertaining drunk though."

"Yeah, I don't think she drinks much. Bless her." She had been fairly tipsy after two small glasses of wine and it had gone on from there. I couldn't help but smile again as I remembered how cute she was, slightly slurring her words and pretty unsteady on her feet.

"She'll fit right in with your sister then!" Jack chuckled. "You just finishing up?"

"I am. I can't wait to go and see how Alex has survived her raging hangover."

"What she said about never celebrating a birthday before? She seems to have missed out on a lot Matt. Do you know anything about her past before you met her?"

"She's not ready to tell me yet. I think it must be really painful. She has a lot of nightmares and the odd panic attack, though she seems to be good at stopping those before they really start. There are scars too, a lot of scars on her body. Someone hurt her. Whatever happened, it was bad and I'm pretty sure it involves her family."

"Her family? That's tough Matt." Jack sighed. "You know if she needs anything Cal and I are on board, no matter what."

"I appreciate that mate. I think she will need support along the way. I don't think she's ever had people she can count on, but just knowing she has us all in her corner now, that we're there for her, helps a lot. She seems to have dealt with it all really well on her own thus far to be honest, I'm just glad she has a choice now, she's not alone anymore."

"She's such a sweet person. I really don't know how anyone could ever do anything to hurt her. You're a lucky guy to have found her man."

"I bloody know. I won't do anything to mess this up Jack. I love her, I really do."

"I know man. Go on, get your shit and get back to her. I've got things here now."

I thanked Jack and took his advice, handing over my patients then getting my coat and bag and driving back to Alex's place as quick as I safely could. I couldn't wait to have her in my arms again.

I unlocked her apartment door with the keys she had given me the week before and reset the alarm as I entered.

"Alex? You ok beautiful?" I called as I headed through the lounge and into the bedroom. I smiled when I saw the blinds were still shut and the bed rumpled as though she'd only just gotten out. I heard the shower being turned off and the tell tale squeak of the cubicle door opening and closing. I made my way through to the bathroom and leant on the doorjamb watching her wrap herself in a towel.

"Hi beautiful." I said, causing her to squeal and jump around ready to fight.

"Fuck Matt! You scared the shit out of me!" She gasped with a half smile.

"Sorry baby. I thought you heard me call for you. How's the head?"

"I am never drinking that much again! My head has been pounding all day. I only just dragged my sorry ass out of bed. Luckily the shower seemed to help some."

"Have you eaten?"

"Oh hell No! Please don't talk about food Matt." She cried dramatically while clutching her stomach.

"You need food for a hangover baby."

"No, I don't. Not yet anyway. I just need to lie back down with your arms around me. I think that sounds like the best hangover cure in the world right now." She said as she stepped into my arms. I picked her up and carried her through to her room where I placed her down on the bed. I then stripped down to my boxers and climbed in beside her to hold her just as she had wanted. I laid listening to her steady breathing, her body pressed to mine and tried hard to keep my thoughts clean, but it was so damn hard with her soft body, warm and naked, pressed into my front. It had been six weeks since we met and while we'd done plenty of 'fooling around', we hadn't had sex yet. I was waiting for her cue, since I was pretty sure from some of the things she'd screamed during nightmares she had experienced some form of sexual abuse. I wouldn't push her. I could wait until she was ready, however long that may take. I loved the woman and there was no need to rush things, she was mine and we had all of the time in the world, I was happy to wait for her to make a move, I'd just take plenty of cold showers in the meantime.

We were both asleep in minutes and there, with the beautiful woman who owned my heart curled up in my arms, I had never felt more content in my life.

ALEX

I woke up early the next morning pressed firmly into Matt's front. He held me tightly and I had never felt safer. He was snoring quietly and I thought it was the cutest sound I had ever heard. I knew I should feel conscious that I was completely naked, but I wasn't. Matt had already seen me naked several times and I was comfortable with it. I was even getting comfortable with the idea of us doing more.

So far we had only kissed and some fairly heavy touching, but nothing more. I was scared if I was honest. For me sex had only ever meant darkness and pain, and I was terrified that would all come flashing back to me if I tried to get intimate with Matt and then he wouldn't want me after I freaked out on him. If I couldn't give him sex, surely he wouldn't want me? I knew Matt would never hurt me, but what if I was damaged after everything and it hurt me? I would lose my shit and I would never be able to let him touch me again.

But lately desire was winning out over fear. When Matt was near me, especially pressed against me in bed, I had feelings I had never really experienced before, feelings of want and desire. I wanted him to touch me. He had been every bit the gentleman, seeming to know I was nervous about the whole thing and waiting for my cues along the way.

"What are you thinking so hard about?" Matt asked sleepily, making me jump.

"How did you know I'm awake?"

"You're breathing is slower when you're asleep." He replied with a smile. I reached up and kissed his jaw.

"I love you." I whispered as I kissed my way up his jaw to his lips.

"I love you too Alex." Matt's lips met mine and then we were locked into a fast, hungry kiss. Matt moved his arm that I wasn't laid on, up and buried his hand in my hair, cupping the back of my head. The need to touch him was stronger than ever and I crawled up onto my knees, the whole time never breaking our passionate kiss. I straddled Matts waist and rubbed my hands up and down his tightly muscled chest. He moved a hand to the small of my back and stroked gently up and down as we continued to kiss and touch, our breathing becoming hot and heavy,

I was nervous and desperate all at the same time. I needed him to touch me, I needed him to make my experience of sex good and loving, instead of the pain and terror I had only ever known.

Eventually Matt pulled away from the kiss and instead began to kiss my neck and up behind my ear. Those kisses awakened the desire in me even more and I squirmed on top of him just needing something, but not understanding what.

"Matt!" I cried desperately.

"It's ok baby. I know." Matt whispered as he flipped us so I lay beneath him on the bed. He ran a hand up from my stomach so slowly and then suddenly his hand was cupping my left breast, so gently, so lovingly.

"Are you sure you're ready for this Alex?" He whispered cautiously as he continued to kiss around my neck and my jaw.

"Yes. I need this Matt....please." I wrapped my arms around him and rubbed my hands up and down his back, loving the strength and firmness of his deliciously toned body.

"Just tell me if you need to stop. Promise? We can go as slow as you need." Matt said seriously.

"I promise." Oh God, this was it. Six weeks of bliss together and this was the clincher. We were going to have sex. Could I handle this? Would it be as good as I felt at that moment or was I really some freak who couldn't enjoy it? My heart pounded, part terror, but mostly desire. I wanted this with Matt, I wanted to try. He would never hurt me. I was safe and I was wanted. This was love, not force.

Before Matt could move onto whatever he was about to do, his cell interrupted the perfect moment with a loud, shrill ring.

"Ignore it beautiful." He whispered as he moved his kisses down my body toward my breasts.

"Are you on call?" I asked as I tried to make my lust fuelled brain think.

"No" Finally the ringing stopped and I relaxed into Matt's painfully slow journey down my neck and chest.

"You're so beautiful Alex." Matt whispered. And then the ringing started again.

"Fuck!" Matt swore as he sat up and looked over at the nightstand. "It's Rob."

"You should get it. It must be important." I said reluctantly. I didn't want Matt to stop what he had been doing to make me feel so amazing, but Lucy might need him. It must be important for Rob to keep ringing so early in the morning.

"Sorry baby" He apologised as he stood from the bed and picked up the call. I pulled the sheet over my naked body and curled up, longing for Matt to continue. It had felt so good, every touch of his hands and his lips had felt amazing and my body was practically vibrating with need. Maybe sex with him could be the magical experience I had heard so much about.

"Right now?" I heard Matt snap with annoyance. "Yeah, ok. I'll be there in the next half an hour." With that he hung up and threw his phone down on the bed beside me.

"You have to go?" I asked with a pout.

"Rob found something on the guy who attacked you and Lucy. He wants me at his office."

"It's ok. I have work anyway."

"It is definitely not ok." Matt sighed. "We *will* pick this up later. I'm not working today. I want a 'to be continued' on this, ok?"

"Absolutely. I'll be counting down the day to get back to this bed and to you Matt." I whispered as I got up on my knees and kissed him briefly. "Now go get dressed. I'll make you coffee to go."

"I think a cold shower is in order first." He laughed as he headed for the bathroom. I got up, threw on my short white cotton robe and hurried out to make him coffee in a travel mug to take with him. Realising I had failed, in my fragile state, to provide him any dinner after work the night before, I also made him a quick snack to take with him. My brain was still lost to the pleasure I had felt in the bedroom and I struggled to focus, but when Matt appeared, dressed immaculately, as always, and looking sexy as hell with his hair still wet from the shower, the coffee and turkey sub were ready. He took them, thanking me with a long slow kiss and then left the apartment. I stood and stared at the closed door for several minutes after he closed it, feeling as giddy as a school girl following her first kiss. It had been an eye opening morning for me and I was excited to see what would happen that night.

MATT

"Right, I'm here!" I declared as I walked into Rob's office ten minutes after leaving Alex's apartment. "This better be bloody important. I was in the middle of something." So close, I'd been so bloody close to getting my hands on that sexy woman that I loved. She had been ready, so very ready and the moment I had spent weeks waiting for was mine to take, until Rob called. I was raging, but he sounded so stressed and he said it was important, so I'd walked away, very reluctantly. Tonight,

I decided, would be the night. If Alex was still ready we would finally have sex tonight. I couldn't wait to feel her gorgeous body writhing against mine.

"Sorry man." Rob said from where he sat behind his desk. "It's important though. Take a seat." I nodded and took a seat opposite him, realising he was in no mood to make pleasantries. His clothes were rumpled and his hair a mess. He was obviously stressed out.

"Have you slept?" I asked.

"No. I got some files from a contact in the FBI yesterday and I've been working on them all night. I know who tried to grab Lucy."

"Who was it?" I asked eagerly. Whoever it was I would help Rob get rid of them. No way was I allowing Lucy to be taken again. I wasn't a violent man by nature and my profession was to save lives, not take them, but this was different. This was my little sister and never again would I sit back and let anyone hurt her. I had messed up leaving her alone to fall into Phil, her ex-husband's, trap. I had failed her then and I would never, ever let that happen again. I would always do whatever was required to keep her safe from harm.

Rob shook his head as he gathered his cell and several files and came to sit on the chair beside me. He opened one and showed me a fuzzy photo of a tattoo on a forearm.

"This was enhanced from footage of the guy who tried to take Lucy, recorded earlier in the evening. Do you recognise it?"

"No. Should I?"

"I thought you could have seen it at the hospital. It's a gang tattoo, the 43rd street Vipers, they're called. They're a small but efficient gang run out of Chicago. They do muscle for hire jobs." Rob explained.

"What the hell do any of them have to do with us and Lucy?"

"Nothing. That's why last night I sent a couple of my team to find the guy who grabbed Lucy. The FBI had files on their most recent hangouts and my team checked them all out until they found our guy, Troy Pratt. They found him downtown, strung out on something, so were able to pretty easily get answers from him before handing him to the cops."

"And?"

"He said he was hired by some rich guy from California to grab Lucy and drive her to San Diego where he would be met to make the exchange, $100,000 for her, alive."

"What the fuck?" I snapped as I stood, just needing to pace the room. "Why the hell would some rich guy in California want Lucy? It doesn't make sense. Did you get a name for this guy?"

"Yeah Marcus Dalton. He's a trust fund kid from Long Beach. He's mixed up in some shady dealings. The FBI has been keeping tabs on him after discovering his involvement in some gun running shipments out of LA. They have a tap on his cell and he's under surveillance, but so far they haven't got anything concrete on him. I've been digging into his dealings all night, but come up with nothing that links him to me or you. Do you recognise him?" Rob asked as he held out a colour photo. I stopped and took it from him, studying it closely.

The guy was on his mobile, leant against a black car in the picture. He had dark hair, shifty looking eyes and he wore a flashy suit. His face was pinched and he looked like a real hard faced prick .

"No. I'd remember a guy like that if I met him. I don't recognise him." I said as I handed the photo back.

"My contact is going to send me a recording from their tap on his phone. He says it's the call of this guy arranging for Lucy to be taken. Hopefully that will give us some idea what the hell this is all about."

"Where's Lucy?" I asked with worry.

"Safe at home with five of my guys stationed in and around the apartment and building. No one is getting near her." Rob explained, though I wasn't sure if it was me or himself he was reassuring.

"We need to get this sorted mate. She can't handle this shit a second time. She's only just back to full strength from Phils last attack." I sighed as I flopped back into the chair beside Rob.

"We will. No one's getting near her again Matt. I won't let it happen." Rob pledged, just as his mobile beeped with a message. "It's the recording." He said as he went back to the other side of his desk and brought up and email with the recording attached. I sat forward and listened as it started.

"She's fucking tiny, You'll only need one guy!" A voice growled angrily.

"Fine. One guy. We take her alive and get her to San Diego and I want $100,000 Dalton. You try to fuck me over and you're dead!"

"Yeah, fine. $100,000, but she can't be all messed up. I need her to complete a transaction. She needs to look presentable. You need to control her, you keep bruises where they can be hidden, clear?"

"Whatever. You sure she lives alone?" Rob and I shared a confused glance.

"Positive. No one would want the stupid bitch except the loser I'm selling her to!" Rage was surging through my veins and making my blood boil at the thought of anyone talking about my sister that way. I couldn't even comprehend what would have happened if Alex hadn't been able to stop the kidnapping. I looked across to Rob and saw he was equally as angry.

"We good to have some fun en route to San Diego then?"

"Do what you want with the whore as long as you get her here in a saleable condition." The voice spat. Rob slammed his hand hard on the desk and his face turned red with rage.

"Of course. Give me the name and address and I'll have her to you as soon as."

"Name's Alicia Dalton. I'll text you the address. Keep me updated and do not fuck this up!" The voice barked and then the recording ended.

"Alicia Dalton?" I said with confusion.

"I know, I'm on it now." Rob replied as he started furiously typing on his laptop.

"You think they took the wrong girl?" I asked hopefully. If they did that meant they weren't even after Lucy. It was all a mistake!

"It's possible. A club full of similarly dressed young girls, could be Lucy just looked similar to the target. I'm looking into Alicia Dalton now."

"Find a picture, see if she looks like Lucy." I suggested. Rob nodded and continued typing. After a couple of minutes the curses started.

"Sonofabitch!" He hissed. "Alicia Dalton is the fucking younger sister of Marcus Dalton." Rob looked up at me as I considered that.

"But I thought one of the voices on the recording was him?" I asked.

"It was, that cocksucker just arranged the kidnapping of his own sister so he can sell her."

"Jesus Rob. We need to find her and warn her." The poor woman needed to get somewhere safe before they tried to take her again.

"I'm working on it, but she has no drivers license, no ID of any kind. No social media, not even an email account that I can see. It's like she hasn't existed since the day her birth was registered."

"Sounds like she's a smart woman. She obviously had some idea what her brother had in mind and ran."

"Let's hope so. I'm trying to get the text with her address that Dalton sent following that call." I waited silently, letting Rob work until finally he said, "Got it."

"Let's go." I was already on my feet, wanting to check on this poor Alicia and warn her as quickly as possible, whoever she was,

"Shit!" Rob cursed again, making me stop and turn back to him. He was staring at me, worry on his face.

"What?" I asked.

"Where the fuck is Alex right now?" He asked.

"At work, why?" The look on Rob's face already had me feeling nauseous with worry.

"This address Matt, It's Alex's apartment. They did take the wrong girl. They wanted Alex. She must be Alicia." My blood ran cold as what he said hit me like a ten ton weight. Her family were involved in her hellish history, I'd worked that out myself. Marcus Dalton was looking for his sister. It all fitted.

"Jesus fucking Christ!" I gasped and then I was running for my car, my mobile pressed to my ear, desperately needing her to answer my call. I had to get to her before they did. I couldn't let another person I loved be taken by monsters. *Please be safe Alex, please!*

ALEX

That morning I was on cloud nine as I got dressed for work and boarded the bus, lost in happy thoughts as it wove through the crazy city traffic to the office. Nothing could dampen my happiness at the amazing things I had felt with the small amount Matt had touched my body that morning. I had hope that I could really have a normal relationship, with sex and intimacy, that was actually loving and enjoyable. I had hope that there wasn't something wrong with me, as I had so often been told in the past by the monsters who didn't get the responses they wanted as they forced themselves on me. I had hope that Matt could really love me for me. So much hope for happiness.

When I arrived at the office my mood was tested a little by the usual line of stony faced clients which awaited me, but I tried hard to maintain my high. As they flooded in throughout the day with their usual complaints about late or missed payments or all other manner of issues, I was faced with the usual - individuals crying at me, plenty of screaming in my face and a small amount of verbal abuse. Nothing new, but still incredibly stressful and my happiness was gradually chipped away piece by piece.

By my morning break a couple of hours in, I was more in need of an entire bottle of wine than a sandwich, but deciding manning the desk drunk probably wasn't my best idea for the remainder of my shift, I decided a sandwich, and maybe a treat of a huge donut, would get me through instead. I grabbed my coat and purse and hurried out of the office, headed to the diner across the street where I always ate on my break.

I was almost to the front door when a body slammed me from behind and shoved me into the alley between the diner and the printers store next door. I moved to scream, but a leather gloved hand clamped down over my mouth before I could make a sound.

"Shut the fuck up!" A male voice hissed in my ear. I was pressed face forward into the brick wall, the attacker pressed against my back, one of his hands clamping my mouth, the other gripping my waist so tightly that no matter how I struggled, I couldn't get free.

"He was right." He carried on in my ear. "You're a pretty little bitch."

I tried harder to scream, but it was useless. He had too firm a grip on me and I couldn't get loose. He lifted me clean off the ground and before I realised what was happening a car had screeched to a stop on the street and I was being thrown into the trunk. Before I could make a sound the trunk was slammed shut and the car sped off.

I stopped for a second to try and process what had happened. Had I just been kidnapped? I started to feel my way around the trunk. It was empty except for me. I remembered reading a novel once where a woman was kidnapped and thrown in a trunk and she had escaped by pulling a lever which opened the hatch from the inside, so I felt for that, but of course there was nothing. I tried kicking it open with my good leg, but I wasn't strong enough.

Realising after a few minutes I'd never escape I started to really panic and the tears began. I had been kidnapped and I had no idea by who or what they wanted from me. No one knew I'd been taken. Matt, would have no idea what had happened. I might die without ever getting to spend enough time with that amazing man and that was my biggest regret in that moment. I had just found the love of my life and it was most likely all over for me.

After about ten minutes the car came to a stop and I immediately started screaming and kicking the top of the trunk in the hope we were stopped at a gas station or some other public place and someone would hear me. I screamed 'HELP!' until my throat was raw, and then I screamed some more, but there was only silence outside. Refusing to give up I gave my voice a rest and kicked my foot harder until, eventually the trunk was thrown open and a slimy looking guy, with lank, greasy hair reached in and grabbed me by my ponytail.

"Shut the fuck up, you stupid bitch!" He hissed as he dragged me from the trunk by my hair and threw me to the ground of what looked like an abandoned auto repair shop.

My scalp throbbed with the pain of my pulled hair as I landed with a thud. I looked up at my kidnapper and studied him. He was maybe a few years younger than me and had tattoos up both arms. He was looking at me lecherously, the tent in the front of his filthy, ripped jeans making me feel nauseous.

"Who are you and what the hell do you want?" I dared to ask. I couldn't show weakness. It was something I'd learned years ago in the hell my family forced me into. You had to seem strong no matter how scared you were.

"You've got a big fucking mouth bitch! Better learn to keep it shut or I'll find a better use for it." He sneered as he palmed his growing erection.

Breathe Ali, just breathe, I told myself as I swallowed down the bile fighting to rise in my throat. Having a panic attack was not an option. I needed to do something while he was the only guy there. I needed to escape during what could be my only chance. It was obvious by the way he was pacing back and forth and checking his phone that he was waiting for someone and I knew once there was more of them I'd have no chance, but one guy, maybe I could take down one guy.

I was damned well gonna fight with every ounce of strength I had,, that was for sure.

"It's a good job you're getting me a good fucking payday bitch. I ain't got time to be waiting around like this. That fucker better get here soon!" He ranted, and I realised he was probably eager to get back for a fix, judging by the needle marks up his bare arms.

"I think I should at least know who you're handing me to." I demanded as I forced myself to get to my feet. My crutch had been abandoned in the street when I'd been taken and I wished like hell I had it as a weapon.

"You don't get to know shit bitch!" He raged as he ran at me and backhanded me hard across my right cheek. I stumbled back losing my balance and landed with a thud on my back, hitting my head on the way down. "I told you to keep your fucking mouth shut!" He raged as he laid two hard kicks into my ribs. They knocked the air clean out of my lungs and the pain was unbearable, but I forced myself not to cry out. *Don't show weakness*, I chanted over and over in my head.

He walked around me, the whole time studying me with an evil look in his eyes I knew only too well. He kicked me twice on the other side of my ribs and again the pain and the inability to breathe was all consuming, but I didn't cry out or allow the tears that threatened to fall. He was over me then and I knew what was coming. I had been in that awful position, trapped beneath a man twice my size. too many times to count, only this time I wasn't tied down and I refused to let it happen again. When he straddled my hips with his weight it put pressure on my already agonising sides and I found it even harder to breathe.

"We've got some time. Let's see what you've got bitch." He hissed as he tore open the few buttons at the top of the shift dress I wore. The buttons flew off and fired around me as he tore further until the dress was split down to my navel and my black lace bra was on display. Adrenaline, my old friend, had made a return and I was trembling violently as flashbacks of so many attacks, just like what was happening, fought their way in.

"NO!" I yelled, both to him and those flashbacks. I needed to be focussed. I didn't have time to be haunted by the past. He pulled out a knife from his back pocket, and slowly pulled it open and presented me with the sharp blade. Pictures of the beast who had used a very similar knife to make the cuts on my abdomen rushed in, but I pushed them back. *Focus Ali. Stay strong and find a way to escape.* I chanted those words over and over to focus my thoughts as he used the sharp knife to cut the piece between the cups of my bra exposing my breasts.

"Come on bitch! I want to hear some fucking screaming before I fuck you." He spat as he pressed the sharp blade into the skin just above my left breast. It was agony and I felt nauseous as I watched blood trickle down my chest, but I refused to scream. This wasn't new to me. I'd been through this kind of torture before. Hell, I'd been through much worse.

He was pissed by my silence and he started ranting and cursing as he sat back to undo his belt and jeans. I watched as he put the knife down beside his right leg to

free both hands and I knew that was my chance. I
waited until both of his hands were busy and he was mid
rant, calling me every name under the sun, and then I
struck. In one lunge I sat up as much as possible,
grabbed the knife and slammed it down hard into his
thigh. He screamed as he leapt up, the knife still in his
leg and I took my opportunity to stand too.
"You're fucking dead bitch!" He raged as he pulled the
knife out and staggered around, blood pouring from the
wound. Terrified one knife wound wasn't enough to
incapacitate him I looked around for another weapon
and then saw it. Just behind where he stood there was a
large well in the ground, the kind used for mechanics to
get under cars. Before I could talk myself out of it I ran
at him with my left shoulder. He wasn't expecting it and
with the knife wound in his leg he was unsteady. He
stumbled back and then things seemed to move in slow
motion as he fell backwards into the deep well in the
ground, He dropped and landed with a sickening
cracking sound I knew I would never forget. I looked
down at him and saw blood pouring from the back of his
head. There was no way he was coming after me
anytime soon. I pushed back the thought that I may
have just killed a man and raced over to the car he had
brought me in. I knew more men were coming and I
needed to get away before they arrived. Thankfully the
keys were in the ignition, so I hustled over and slid open
the heavily rusted, rolling doors of the auto shop. I
blinked through the invading sunlight and looked around
for any approaching cars. Seeing none I wrapped my
coat around my torn dress and bra and climbed into the

driver's seat, choosing to ignore the blood still pouring from where he had cut me and the agony and shortness of breath my injured ribs were causing. *Focus Ali. Stay strong and find a way to escape.* I continued my chant as I started the car and raced out of the auto shop, down a dirt road. I eventually hit a highway, though I had no idea which. I just needed to get as far away as possible. When I felt it was safe I would stop and call Matt. My cell sat in the centre console where the kidnapper must have put it after taking it from my coat pocket on the street.

After ten minutes I was really struggling to breathe with the adrenaline and panic making my breaths gasping and heavy, which only aggravated my agonising, battered ribs. Finally I reached some a service stop and pulled up right near a diner, where all of the patrons would see me through the windows if anyone tried to take me again. I cut the engine and just allowed myself a moment to breathe. I had fought and for once, I'd won. With shaky hands I grabbed my cell and unlocked the screen. I had never needed anyone as desperately as I needed Matt at the that moment. I found his contact and hit dial, putting it on to loudspeaker because the idea of holding it to my ear seemed impossible.

"Alex!" Matt yelled on answering.

"Matt." I gasped with a sense of relief at hearing his voice.

"Alex? Baby, where are you?" Matt asked and the panic in his voice surprised me. Did he know I'd been taken?

"I….I don't know. He took me….this guy, he grabbed me and put me in a trunk. I got away…..I think I got away Matt." I said weakly.

"You got away? That's good Alex….. Are you safe? Are you hurt?" He asked.

"I….I th-think I killed him." I whispered.

"Alex, it's Rob. Listen to me honey. I'm trying to track your cell, but it'll be quicker if you can tell me where you are." Rob said so calmly.

"I took his car and I'm on a highway…..a-at a service stop." I looked around for a sign.

"Is there a diner or something?" Rob asked.

"Yeah, it's called Rusty's"

"I know it honey. We're coming for you. We'll be about twenty minutes. Can you go and wait in the diner for us?" Rob asked.

"No. I'm bleeding and I look like shit. I'll draw way too much attention."

"What do you mean you're bleeding? From where?" Matt demanded, his trademark cool, long gone.

"Matt, I'm ok. Calm down. It's a cut, but not deep. It's just bleeding a lot, but it'll stop. I'll stay in the car and wait. I'll be fine." I said as calmly as I could.

"Try and put pressure on it baby, to slow the bleeding. We're coming for you and Rob's just called a friend in CPD to meet us. Everything will be alright."

"I know. I love you Matt. I'm going to go because my cell is almost dead and I want to save the battery in case, ok?"

"Ok. I love you too baby."

"Sit tight Alex. Call us if you need to. We're close." Rob said.

"Ok" I agreed and then hung up before I got upset and scared Matt any more. I put my cell on the passenger seat where I could grab it easily if necessary and then looked for something to press on the cut on my chest. It was still pouring with blood down my right breast and I was getting worried that it wasn't stopping. I found some napkins in the glove compartment and opened my coat just enough to get to the cut. It was deeper than I thought, which was probably why it wouldn't stop bleeding. I pressed the napkins down hard and couldn't help the small cry that escaped at the pain of pressing on the very tender area. I kept the pressure firm as I lay my head back on the seat and tried hard to slow my breaths. The desperate, frantic breathing was not helping my battered ribs and I really needed to find a way to lessen the pain at least a little.

I closed my eyes and tried to focus. I'd been kidnapped and apparently was to be sold on, to who knew which monster, but I'd escaped. I had stayed strong and managed to get free for the first time and that felt damned good, even if I was beaten and bleeding. He didn't get to touch me and that was a huge result in my book. I had sworn the day I arrived in Chicago no man would ever touch me without my permission ever again and that had been tested in that old auto shop, but I managed to stop it, I had fought back and won and it felt damned good!

MATT

"Hurry the fuck up Rob!" I barked for the millionth time. Rob and I had already discovered Alex had been taken after going to her office and finding her missing. We searched the area and I found her crutch in an alley across the street from the office. Rob checked the surveillance footage on the street and we both watched in horror as Alex was thrown into the trunk of a beaten up old Chevy. We had been back at Rob's office trying to get a lead on the car's location when Alex had called me. I had never been so relieved to hear her beautiful voice, but she was hurt and I had terrible images of what that monster had time to do to her in the time he had her. I needed to get to her. I needed to feel her in my arms.

"I'm already flooring it man. Just calm down. We'll be there in two minutes." Rob said calmly, pissing me off even more. He wasn't so calm when we were racing to get Lucy last year, then again neither was I, but she's my sister and Alex is my girlfriend. I was allowed to freak out over both of them.

"If that bastard has touched her Rob…" I said angrily.

"I know man, I do, but try to keep your calm. Alex obviously needs medical attention and right now you're it." I knew he was right, so I tried to calm my breathing and settle my rage as we rounded the corner into the service station. Rob pulled up right behind the black Chevy we'd seen on the footage and we both leapt out. I grabbed my backpack, which I'd thankfully thought to bring just in case. It held emergency medical supplies which I knew I would need.

"Alex?" I gasped as I opened the driver's side door of the car. She was laid back on the seat, her eyes closed and her hand held inside her coat to her chest.

"Oh Matt!" She cried as she sat up and I wrapped her trembling body in my arms.

"I'm here." I whispered. I could instantly hear how short her breaths were and I knew something wasn't right. Never wanting to let her go, but knowing I needed to look at her injuries I pulled back and studied her.

"Matt, can we get her in my car? It'd be safer if anything arises?" Rob suggested.

"Think you can move to Rob's SUV baby?" I asked.

"Yeah, I'm ok Matt. Let's go." She agreed. She grabbed her phone from the seat beside her and then turned and swung both feet out of the door. I held her hands and helped her out, noting her sharp intake of breath when she stood.

"Is it your ribs?" I asked as I wrapped an arm around her shoulders to help her stand. Rob was instantly at the other side taking the rest if her weight and we started to half carry her to the back of the SUV. She nodded tearfully.

"Hey honey." Rob greeted and I saw the worry I felt, reflected in his face. There was no missing the scraps of torn fabric hanging from the opening at the collar of her coat. I could barely breathe at the thought of that prick from the footage raping her.

"Be careful, she has injured ribs." I cautioned Rob through the lump lodged in my throat as we gently lifted Alex into the back seat.

"I'm ok guys." She tried to assure us with a forced smile.

"You will be love. You will be." I said, unsure who I was trying to convince.

"Rob. He took me to an old auto shop about ten kilometres down the highway. He….I…I stabbed him in the leg and pushed him down a deep ditch in the ground. I think he's dead." She said shakily. "You'll need to tell the police."

"I'll see to it all honey. Just let Matt take care of you and we'll get you back to the city as soon as I've spoken to CPD." Rob explained as a cruiser pulled up beside the SUV. He nodded to me and then closed the door, leaving us in the quiet of the car.

"Let me see this cut first." I said as I placed my hand over the napkins she held there. She let her hand drop and I pulled her coat open. Her dress was torn open right down the top half and her bra hung open, clearly having been sliced apart in the centre, leaving her exposed and me feeling sure the worst had happened and the woman I loved had been raped, all because I'd been too stupid to connect the dots. I swallowed down my anger and tended to the deep cut on her chest. It had clearly been made with a sharp knife and was deep. It had stopped bleeding, but would definitely require stitches. I'd make sure they were done by plastics to avoid any more scars on her beautiful body.

"This has stopped bleeding, so I'll just secure it with some butterflies for now and dress it and we'll get it stitched at the hospital." I explained. She was so quiet and distant and I was terrified for her.

Next I checked her ribs and was relieved to find they were most likely just bruised, but I'd get x-rays to be sure at the hospital.

"Alex, are you hurt anywhere else?" I asked, too scared to ask what I really needed to.

"No. I'm ok Matt." She whispered distantly. I wanted to question her further, but I knew she was fighting hard not to lose it and I didn't want to push her too hard.

"Hold me Matt, please just hold me." She pleaded. I sat next to her and pulled her into my side, holding her as tight as I dare without hurting her injured ribs. She buried her face in my shirt and sat there, silent. I expected her to break down, but she didn't and I admired her strength.

"Are we good to go to the ER?" Rob asked as he climbed in the driver's side and closed his door. I reached for Alex's seat belt and buckled her in as best I could without her moving from my chest. Then nodded to Rob. He looked at me with a question and I simply shook my head, telling him I didn't know what we were both worried about yet. He nodded and then started the car.

Alex remained in exactly the same position for the entire fifteen minute journey to Chicago General where Rob had arranged for Jack to be ready for us. She never spoke, never cried and I was more terrified than I had ever felt in my life. I couldn't lose Alex, she really was everything to me. Whatever that bastard had put her through, I needed to find a way to get her through it. I loved her and I would be there for her no matter what.

ALEX

"Alex? Can you come with me now sweet?" Jack's voice cut in to the loop of terror filled flashbacks racing through my mind. It seemed once the panic of escaping was over, the flashbacks I had pushed back returned with a vengeance. I forced myself to move from where I had been pressed against Matt for the entire journey and looked up to meet Jack's friendly, but obviously worried face.

"Hi." I whispered.

"Hey. So glad to see you safe honey." He said as he reached into the car and gently lifted me out. He laid me down on a gurney waiting right beside him, two nurses holding it steady.

"Matt!" I cried in a panic.

"I'm here baby. I'm staying with you. Don't worry." Matt soothed as he appeared beside the gurney. He held my hand as he walked beside me while I was pushed inside and down a corridor into a private room.

"She has a deep lac on her chest, a minor head injury and severe bruising down both sides. Pulse was steady and she's been cognizant throughout." Matt said. I closed my eyes again and just focused on gripping his hand tightly to try and push back the flashbacks still playing on a loop. Voices continued around me in a blur as I focused only on the feel of Matt's hand in mine.

"Alex?" I opened my eyes at the sound of my name and once again found Jack stood before me. "Honey, I know this is so hard, but I need to know what happened. Your dress is torn and your bra. I need all of the information to be able to take care of you in the best way possible, so I need to know…..Did he raped you Alex?" Just the word rape was enough to open the floodgates I had fought to keep closed since I had been taken hours ago. "Baby, it's ok. You're safe now. No one will get near you again. Whatever happened, we can deal with it together." Matt soothed and I felt his hand gently stroking my forehead. I forced myself to open my eyes and put an end to his misery. He thought I had been raped and me crying was making the whole thing worse. "No. He didn't. He wanted to….he was getting to it, but I managed to get away." I explained as calmly as I could. "You're sure honey? He didn't touch you in any way below the waist? I can get a female doctor if you'd prefer to talk to a woman." Jack offered.

"I'm sure Jack," I said firmly. "He slapped my face, kicked my sides, tore my dress, cut my bra…...then h-he cut my chest, but then while he was undoing his pants I….I got the knife and fought back. He didn't touch me other than what you see."

"Thank fucking God!" Matt sighed as he placed a kiss on my forehead.

"You did so good getting away sweet. We're all so proud of you." Jack said as he held my hand and squeezed it reassuringly.

"Rob, get out of my way right fucking now!" We heard from outside the room and I couldn't help but smile a little at the rage in Lucy's voice as she yelled at her husband.

"Let her in Matt, I'm ok." I whispered, tired, but in less pain thanks to whatever Jack had given me through an

IV in my right arm. Matt nodded and stood to walk to the door.

"Come in darling." Matt said softly and seconds later Lucy ran in, her cheeks stained with tears and her face pale.

"Jesus Alex. I was so bloody worried about you." She cried as she took Matt's place at my side and gave me a hug as best she could with me laid down.

"Mind her chest and ribs darling." Matt warned. Lucy lifted the blanket which was covering me and studied the cut on my chest. I still wore the tatters of my dress and they covered enough of my chest for me me not to be embarrassed by Lucy's peek.

"Oh hun. I'm so sorry. Are your ribs broken?" Lucy asked as tears filled her eyes again.

"Just bruised. I'm ok, I was lucky really. Just really tired now." I whispered, my throat sore from screaming in the trunk.

"Can't she get some rest Jack?" Lucy demanded as she angrily stared down the man who was easily ten inches taller and wider than her.

"We need to get x-rays and stitch that cut first sweet. Then she can rest."

"Fine. Get something she can change into and I'll help her out of that dress. It's covered in blood."

"Yes ma'am!" Jack joked with a mock salute as he walked from the room and returned a moment later with a blue hospital gown.

"Thank you. Now everyone out and give her some privacy while she changes." Lucy demanded as she grabbed the gown. Jack and the nurse left, but Matt stood staring his sister down.

"Matt." Lucy said as if in warning.

"I can help." He said firmly.

"Please." I whispered. "Just give me a few minutes Matt. Lucy and I will manage." I loved him being near me, it was the only time I felt safe when he was there, but I didn't want him seeing me in the state I was. I knew Lucy had personally experienced a lot worse than she would see on my body. She could handle it. I wasn't so sure Matt could. He cared too much, it would hurt him to see my torn clothes and bruised body.

"I'll be right outside the door. Just call and I'll come." He said, then turned and left, closing the door behind him. The second the door clicked shut the first sob escaped and Lucy was on the bed beside me, pulling me up into her arms. I leant against her, my face buried in her shoulder and just let the sobs run free.

"It's ok chick. You just let it all out. I know exactly how you feel. I've got you." She whispered as she held me and rubbed my back soothingly.

"I'm sorry. I'm being such a baby. He didn't even really touch me, it's just….it brought back so many…..so much…."

"I know Alex. It just brought back every horrible memory of every terrifying experience you ever had and they won't go back to that box you keep them in now. I know how it goes. Just let it out, it will help." She was right, she did know exactly what was happening in my fucked up brain and I was so grateful to have someone who understood. I cried for a few minutes until I felt better able to pull myself together more. I took some deep breaths and sat up, worried I was crushing poor Lucy. "Let's get these clothes off and get you cleaned up a little. You'll feel better then." She suggested and I nodded my agreement. She stood first and held my hands as I got shakily to my feet. She led me through to the adjoining ensuite and helped me to sit on the closed toilet seat. There she removed all of my clothes except my panties and wiped all of the blood from my chest with a warm washcloth. She was right, I did feel better when I was cleaner. Next she put on the gown Jack had given her and I stood clutching the wall as she tied it in the back.

"With all of the developments in the last century, you'd think they could design a bloody hospital gown that covers you arse wouldn't you?" She joked, making me laugh a little through my still flowing tears. She carefully released my dishevelled ponytail and gently redid it, gathering all of the stray hair that was hanging in my face, then she helped me back to the bed and tucked me in like I had wished my parents would so many times when I was a little girl.

"Are you sure he didn't....you know?" Lucy asked quietly. "You can tell me. I've been through it too many times hun. I completely understand it's not something you'd want to talk about."

"I've been through it far too many times too Lucy, but not today. I got away today before he could do any real damage."

"Ok darling." She whispered as she bent down and placed a gentle kiss on my forehead, just like Matt often did. It was such a loving gesture and it instantly made me feel that little bit more secure. "Rest. I'll call Jack back in and see about that x-ray."

"Lucy." I called as she turned to walk away. She turned back to me and smiled. "Thank you, for understanding." It had helped, the knowledge that she knew exactly what was going through my mind and how I felt. It had made the last fifteen minutes a lot easier to handle and I could already feel my darkness very slowly sliding neatly back into it's little box.

"That's what besties are for." She smiled and then walked to the door and called Jack and Matt back in.

***

It took almost two hours for my ribs to be x-rayed and the plastic surgeon, Matt and Jack insisted on, to come and stitch the cut on my chest. I was grateful that they were doing their best to spare me another scar, but by the time he arrived I really didn't care. I just needed to sleep. Finally, as the sun began to set outside the window, Jack gave me a mild sedative and told me to rest. They were keeping me over night as a precaution because of underlying health issues with my brain injury and the fact I'd had a knock to the head. Again, I didn't care as long as I had a bed to sleep in and Matt by my side. He held my hand and gently brushed my forehead as I finally drifted off.

***

I couldn't believe my eyes when I woke up the next morning. The sun was streaming through the large window and illuminating the room full of snoozing bodies. Matt was where I left him. In a chair on my right hand side, his chin resting on his chest and quietly snoring away. Lucy was in a chair beside him, her head on his shoulder, also fast asleep. On my right hand side Jack sat closest to me with Cal in a chair right beside him and they both slept with their heads pressed together, Cal snoring pretty loudly. Last was Rob, sat in a chair directly in the doorway and I knew he'd positioned himself there so no one could get past him to come in. His head was leant against the doorjamb and he slept with his arms crossed on his chest. They were all there, for me and it was overwhelming. They made me feel stronger and I realised Lucy had been right the first day I met her. It was so much easier to face your dark past with the help of amazing people like those who surrounded me.

I was deep in thought when the sound of the door handle startled me. I looked up and watched as Rob instantly stood as though he had been wide awake, not even a little dazed and opened the door to see who was daring to enter.

"Cops want to speak to her, boss." A male voice said.

"She's exhausted. Can't they wait?" Rob asked.

"Rob, it's ok." I whispered, loud enough to get his attention, but hoping not to wake everyone. Rob turned to me and smiled before turning back to the open door.

"Wait!" He barked to the guy outside the room, then he closed the door and walked to the foot of my bed.

"How you feeling honey?" He asked quietly.

"Sore, but a little better. I can talk to the police. I'd rather just get it over with Rob." I explained.

"Are you sure. I can hold them off a couple of days, no problem."

"Is he dead….that guy, did I kill him?" I asked nervously.

"No Alex. The knife missed the artery, and the fall gave him a nasty crack to the head and a concussion, but he was fine. They stitched him up and took him into custody last night." I couldn't hide my sigh of relief. I never wanted to kill him, just stop him.

"Am I going to be in trouble for what I did?" I asked, my voice trembling.

"No Alex. It was self-defense and no one is going to argue that based on your injuries and the surveillance footage we have of him taking you. Don't worry sweetheart. The police will just want your statement." Rob assured me. He gently held my foot over the blanket and he made me feel a little better about the whole thing.

"Thanks for being here." I whispered.

"You never need to thank any of us for that honey. We love you. We wouldn't want to be anywhere else." He said kindly. "I have two of my team outside the room and they'll be switching out to make sure you always have two guys wherever you are. You're going back to Matt's and there will be two personal protection guards with you, one at the door, and one patrolling the building at all times until this is over. No one is getting near you again Alex."

"You think they'll come for me again?" I asked nervously.

"We need to discuss everything when we get you home, but let's just get your statement out of the way with the cops first, ok?"

"Ok. Thank you for keeping me safe Rob. I feel safe knowing you're all looking out for me."

"Damn right you're safe sweet. We got you now." Jack piped up loudly, making everyone jump awake.

"Fuck Jack! We talked about morning voices!" Cal grumbled as he sat up and stretched.

"How are you feeling baby?" Matt asked as he leant in and kissed my cheek.

"A lot better. Just sore down my sides."

"You look better hun, not so pale." Lucy agreed with an encouraging smile.

"CPD are here for a statement. They'll want us to clear out Matt since we found her and will be making statements too."

"Fuck that! I'm not leaving Alex to go through what happened without me here." Matt snapped.

"Will Lucy be able to stay?" I asked nervously, dreading Matt not being with me.

"Sure honey and Jack and Cal if you want. It's just a conflict if Matt and I are here because we're witnesses too."

"I don't care what it is. I'm staying." Matt ranted.

"Matt." I whispered, drawing his angry glare from Rob and down to me. "I'll be fine. I've lived through ten times worse than what happened yesterday. I can make the statement just fine, especially if Lucy, Jack and Cal are willing to sit with me. Stop stressing. I got away and I'm fine." I said firmly. I watched as his face finally relaxed a little and he forced a smile.

"Sorry love. I'll try to reign it in a bit. I just love you so much and I was so scared yesterday."

"I know. I love you too. Go get a coffee with Rob and bring us all back some breakfast please, I'm famished." I ordered.

"Ok baby." He agreed as he leant in to gently kiss my lips. He gave me one more award winning smile and then turned to Rob.

"Cam and Evan are right outside the door, but one of you guys stay in here at all times too, agreed?" Rob ordered in a very sergeant-major type tone. Jack and Cal both nodded in agreement and Rob turned to Lucy.

"Stay with Jack or Cal. I won't be long sweetheart." Lucy nodded too and they briefly kissed before Rob and Matt left the room.

"You sure you're ready for this honey?" Cal asked.

"Not really, but it needs doing and there's no time like the present. I just hope they don't arrest me and haul me off." I said, only half joking. I was terrified.

"No one is hauling you off anywhere with us here sweet. Don't worry. You're not going to be in any trouble." Jack promised just as the door opened and two men walked in. They both looked to be in their forties, dressed in cheap suits, one fat and one thin, and both of them looking stern and miserable as all get out.

"Alex Harrison?" The tallest of them asked in a gruff voice.

"Present." I joked, hoping they'd crack a smile and stop scaring me, but evidently jokes were lost on them. While

Jack, Cal and Lucy cracked up a little, they both just scowled harder. Lucy moved into the chair Matt had vacated and gripped my hand supportively.

"I'm detective Wyatt and this is detective Briggs. We're here about an alleged kidnapping."

"Alleged?" Cal snapped, clearly annoyed.

"And you are?" Detective Wyatt asked with a look of disgust.

"Ex NYPD sergeant Calvin Warren." Cal said sternly. "Now, back to that 'alleged' part?"

"Miss Harrison was found under no duress, not bound or restrained in anyway at a service stop. There was no evidence of her being held in the auto shop we found Troy Pratt stabbed and bleeding to death in. The whole case is still open and we have several questions before we can further label this a kidnapping." Heat rushed over me and I instantly felt panicked. I reached for Jack and thankfully he grabbed my hand and held it tightly.

"What about the footage of this Troy grabbing Alex in the street and throwing her in a trunk? And what about the pool of her blood in the auto shop? That's not enough evidence for you?" Jack barked.

"We are yet to see any such footage and the auto shop is still being processed by forensics"

"This is a fucking joke!" Jack snapped as he looked angrily to Cal.

"Miss Harrison?" The tall detective looked to me and I instantly felt nauseous and short of breath.

"Yes." I said as calmly as I could.

"That's your name, Alex Harrison?" *Oh God, here we go.* I gripped the hands of my friends tighter and they squeezed back reassuringly. "Because it seems to us that is a false identity. We have reason to believe your name is Alicia Dalton, isn't it?" He sneered as though he'd really caught me out and I began to tremble more as a panic attack increased it's hold on me. "Your family has been looking for you for some time Alicia. They have evidence to show you as mentally incompetent. They have a court order in motion for you to be returned to their care immediately." The room started to spin and I felt like I was truly losing it. Could they do that? Could they get some court order to make me go back to that prison, to that hell?

"Not a fucking chance!" Cal raged. "There is no way that's happening Alex, don't listen to that shit." He was on his feet now and stood between me and them, as though he could protect me. I took a deep breath and tried to take control back, This didn't make sense. Rob had told me there wouldn't be any trouble from what I did to my kidnapper and I trusted his word. The detectives were also supposed to be there to take a statement, but instead they were trying to intimidate me. Then it clicked and I realised with a sense of doom.

"Where are you from?" I asked, my voice timid and weak through the trembling and difficulty I was having catching my breath.

"What was that Alex?" Cal asked as he turned to me.

"They didn't say which police division they were with. I just wondered, are they CPD?" I asked.

"That has no relevance right now." the taller, thinner detective snapped.

"ID's." Cal demanded.

"What?" The detective bumbled.

"I have every right to see your ID. Hand it over now." Cal demanded. The two detectives reluctantly produced their police shields and Cal studied them.

"My, my, you're a long way from home boys." He said, then turned to me. "LAPD" he said and I relaxed a little knowing anything they said would be just threats paid for by my family.

"They sent them Cal. My family. They must be on the Dalton payroll." I explained, knowing only too well the power my family's wealth could command. I felt physically sick at the realisation that my family were involved in me being taken. What the hell could they possibly want from me?

"Jack, get Rob's security in here to hold these guys. I think the feds might be interested in their little game." Cal said with delight.

"You have no right to detain us," The fatter detective finally spoke up nervously, but before any more could be said two huge guys dressed entirely in black walked in and cuffed the two detectives, then searched them and removed their guns.

"Find somewhere secure to hold them. I'm sure Rob can have someone come pick them up." Cal ordered and then the detectives were gone.

"Oh God!" I cried as I finally gave in and crumbled. The fear, even only for those few minutes, that my family would find a way to drag me back to the hell that had near killed me, had terrified me more than anything I had ever suffered.

"It's ok. You're safe sweet. I told you no one was taking you and I meant it." Jack said as he perched on the bad and pulled me into his hold.

"I'll be right outside. I need to call Rob and get him back up here." I heard Cal say and then the door opened and closed.

"You never have to go back Alex, never." Lucy whispered as I felt her sit on the bed beside me and join the hug, her arms wrapped around me above Jack's. She knew. She always knew what was going on in my head.

"She's right sweet. You're where you belong now, with us and you're here to stay." I continued to sob as the terror of the whole situation washed over me and then I managed to gradually calm myself as I took in the kind words Jack and Lucy uttered to me softly, assuring me I was loved and safe and going nowhere. Finally, feeling composed I sat up and looked into two worried faces.

"Hey!" Jack whined. "I was enjoying the group hug." He joked making both Lucy and I smile.

"Please can you bust me out of here Jack? I really do hate hospitals." I admitted. It was true, following the fall that caused my brain injury I had been forced to spend almost five months in hospital and during all of that time my family had been forced to visit, in order to keep up appearances. I paid dearly during each visit they were forced to endure, as soon as they were sure the coast was clear. I pushed back the painful memories and looked pleadingly to Jack.

"Once the guys get back I'll review your notes and see what I can do, ok?"

"Thank you."

"You are going to stay at Matt's aren't you?" Lucy asked nervously. "You can't stay by yourself after what happened. If you're not comfortable living with Matt then you're staying with Rob and I. There's no way you're going back to your place." There was a fire in her eyes and I knew there was no use arguing with her, not that I wanted to anyway.

"It's ok Lucy. I'm happy to stay with Matt as long as he doesn't mind. After yesterday and then my family sending those idiot detectives, I really don't want to be alone."

Matt burst into the room a moment later, looking tired and stressed out. He locked eyes with me and smiled reassuringly.

"Are you ok Alex? Cal told us what happened."

"I'm fine. They had me panicking for a few minutes, but then Cal and I got to the bottom of it."

"Rob's calling a few contacts to make sure those idiot detectives are investigated by the right people." I nodded, but really I knew two detectives was a drop in the ocean compared to the hordes of people my family had in their pocket. There would be many more police where those two had come from, along with judges, lawyers, politicians and many other powerful people across California.

"I'll see about getting you released sweet." Jack interjected as he stood and left the room. Lucy climbed down from the bed and went to sit in the chair Rob had been sleeping in earlier. She pulled out her kindle and busied herself reading.

Matt stalked over to the bed and kissed me as though it had been days since we'd seen one another. The kiss was claiming and possessive, just what I needed to remind me I was free from the Dalton family hold, no matter what they tried to pull.

"My family arranged the kidnapping, didn't they?" I asked, already sure of the answer, but needing to hear it anyway.

"Yeah love, your brother. I'm so sorry." Matt whispered. I slumped into him, burying my face in his shirt, hoping I could just hide there forever.

"How did you work out he's my brother?" I asked, realising they didn't even know my real name.

"Rob pieced it together with some help from some FBI files. He stumbled on to it all while he was trying to work out who grabbed Lucy that night." As he spoke Matt held me tight to his body and laid us both down on the bed, wrapped tightly together.

"They didn't want Lucy, they wanted me?" Suddenly it all fell into place.

"We think so." Matt confirmed.

"Do you know what they want from me?" I whimpered as I fought to hide the terror causing my heart to pound and my throat to constrict with the threat of a huge crying fit.

"We should talk about this later Alex, when you're feeling stronger."

"Please, just tell me." I pushed.

"The FBI has had your brother's cell tapped because they're investigating him. Rob and I heard the recording of the call he made to arrange your kidnapping. He made it clear that he needed you taken so he could sell you to someone." I could hear the strain in Matt's voice as he spoke and I knew he was worried about telling me something so terrible. The thing was, the idea of being sold by Marcus really wasn't anything new. It was basically what he had done to me, on a smaller scale, for years.

"They must have run out of money." I said as I thought about why they would suddenly need me back after four years of no contact. If they were desperate enough to have me kidnapped they were obviously in dire straits and I was once again a casualty of their quest for continued wealth.

"They won't get that close again baby. Rob has security all around us and that's where they'll be until we find a way to put an end to this. I won't let anyone hurt you ever again." He promised as he placed a loving kiss on the top of my head.

"You all need to be careful Matt." I said firmly as I looked up to meet his gaze. I needed him to understand what I was saying was serious. "Marcus is a psychopath and he and my father will do whatever it takes to keep them in the lifestyle they want. If they need me to make a deal and you guys get in the way…..I can't be the reason any of you are hurt."

"Alex, no one is getting hurt. Rob knows what he's doing and trust me, we got the message about how unstable your brother is just from listening to that one phone conversation." Matt said firmly.

"I can only imagine how that went." My brother was unhinged. A phone call to arrange a kidnapping was child's play to him. There was no end to the evil Marcus Dalton was capable of.

"You should try to rest love. You've had a tough morning." Matt whispered, redirecting the conversation.

"I want to get out of here Matt." I pleaded.

"Soon. Just rest for now. I promise I'll have you out of here and settled at my place before dinner tonight, ok?"

"Ok." I agreed. "Will you stay and hold me until I fall asleep?"

"I'm not going anywhere."

I laid in his arms, relishing the feeling of safety his hold provided. He gently rubbed a soothing hand up and down my back and before I knew it the terror of what lay ahead for me was pushed aside and sleep consumed me.

***

I was discharged from the hospital later that afternoon. Jack and Cal had been to my place and packed a small suitcase with some clothes, toiletries, books and my cell charger and meds. Lucy helped me dress and then we all headed out to the parking lot. I didn't miss the way all four guys surrounded Lucy and I, as we walked to where Matt's Range Rover was parked. There were the two 'men in black', as I had coined Rob's security guys, the two I had seen that morning, walking just ahead of us and also two other 'men in black' waiting at the far end of the parking lot, leant against a huge black SUV. It was overwhelming to realise they were all there because, once again, the Daltons wanted my body to use for their profit.

"We'll follow you guys back." Jack said, as he and Cal forked off toward Cal's truck.

"I'll get Lucy home and then I'm headed to the office to get a jump on this. Cam and Evan will be outside the apartment until midnight, then they'll switch out. I'll text you all my teams details so you know who's who. They'll always be at least one guy outside the apartment and one patrolling the building." Rob explained again, for at least the third time.

"Thanks mate." Matt said gratefully.

"Call me if anything new comes up." Rob added as he looked pointedly to me and I knew he meant if I gave Matt any extra details of my past. I knew I would need to give them at least something, but it didn't make the prospect of dredging it all up any less terrifying. "Stay safe honey." Rob added as he leant in and placed a gently kiss on my cheek.

"Thank you for doing all of this Rob." I whispered, once again exhausted. Matt wrapped his arm tighter around me and led me over to his car, then helped me climb up into the passenger seat.

The drive to his place was quiet. I was exhausted, mostly because of the pain meds I'd been given before leaving the hospital, but also because of all of the drama swirling through my mind nonstop.

When we walked into Matt's apartment I managed to relax a little. The building he lived in was very secure and there were at least two of Rob's team close by. I felt safe as I listened to Matt arm his security alarm.

I loved Matt's apartment. It was at least three times the size of my own and much newer. It was open plan and had a really nice airy feel to it. It was always immaculately neat because Matt was a little crazy about tidiness, but the place was still very warm and welcoming.

"Do you want to get some more rest?" Matt asked as I stood staring out of the huge panoramic windows which overlooked the crowded streets below.

"Maybe later. There's some things I need to talk to you about." I said hesitantly. No time like the present.

"We don't need to do that now baby. You're tired."

"Rob needs more information and there may be a few things that could help him, hidden in my past. You already know who I am Matt. Might as well tell you everything now." I sighed.

"Are you even up to going into it all right now?" Matt asked with concern.

"No. I'll never be up to it Matt. I just have to do it now while I can." I leant back against the window and ran my hands nervously through my wild hair.

"Come sit down." Matt beckoned. I nodded and walked over to curl up beside him on the large, black leather sofa. I sat with my back against Matt's front, knowing it would be easier to tell him everything if I didn't have to see the reactions on his face. "Just take your time Alex." He whispered as he wrapped both his arms around my waist and pulled me into his lap. The movement hurt my sides, but it felt good to be surrounded by his warmth and safety. I laid my head back against his chest and tried to find a way to begin.

"I guess you already know my family is pretty wealthy. The money was inherited on my dad's side, though my mother was from a pretty well off background too. I was born five years after Marcus and as far back as I can remember I was always treated very differently to him. He went to fancy boarding schools for his entire childhood. He came home for holidays and when he was home he was spoiled with anything he wanted. He was loved and doted on by my parents and they were always so proud of him, despite the fact he used to get into all kinds of trouble.

"My life was very different. I had a suite in the huge house we lived in. It was nice, comfortable and I had the basics of what was needed, a bed and clothing. I was allowed to read and books were brought to me each week, but I was so isolated. I was never allowed to leave my suite unless I was told to. I spent the first sixteen years of my life in those three rooms. The staff in the house brought me food and took care of me to some extent, although they weren't permitted to talk to me more than absolutely necessary. I had a tutor who taught me for several hours each day, though again he was cautioned not to engage me more than he needed to. It was lonely and I was always desperate to get outside and feel the freedom I watched Marcus enjoy, but it wasn't so bad because it was all I had ever known. I read a lot of books and got a pretty good education. I was always hungry because my mother rationed the food I was allowed, but I had enough to survive.

"When I was almost seventeen things changed. Marcus came home from college and got a job working in banking. He started to take an interest in me and came to chat with me in my room at night. At first it was nice to have someone really talk to me. He seemed to care about me and even explained to me why my parents treated me so coldly. He told me my mother, wasn't actually my mother. Turned out I was the result of an affair my father had with a staff member, some young girl who really didn't want a baby. She dumped me with my father and he ordered my mother to claim me as hers to save his reputation. That made me understand why they had treated me so differently. It was pretty clear I had not been wanted. Marcus was kind at first though, made me feel as though he really liked me and I was so desperate for real human interaction." Matt pulled me even tighter against him, as though he knew what was coming. I swallowed the huge lump in my throat and went on.

"After a few weeks of getting to know him he came to me late one night and started touching me. I tried to push him off, but he's a big guy. He….he forced himself on me and I cried and screamed throughout. No one came though, no one ever came." Tears were streaming down my face as I recalled that first soul destroying night.

"I'm so sorry baby." Matt whispered, his voice hoarse.

"He came every night after that. I used to try everything to stop him. First pretending I was asleep, but he didn't care if I was asleep or awake. I started hiding then, but he always found me. After a few weeks I summed up the courage to leave my suite, which I never did before, and I hid in the house. It took him two hours to find me that night, but when he did he dragged me back to my room by my hair and took what he wanted even more viciously. After that I was locked in my suite and never allowed to leave it again. It went on for a couple of years like that. I always fought him, but never won. I told the staff what he was doing in the hope they'd tell my parents and he'd have to stop, but nothing ever changed.

"When I was about nineteen the door opened late one night and it wasn't just Marcus who walked in. He was followed by two huge guys, with heavy accents. He told them they had two hours and they could use me however they wanted as long as they didn't kill me. That was the worst night." A sob escaped, but I pulled back any that tried to follow, just needing to get it out. "I had thought Marcus was cruel, but what I went through with those guys and several others, not just that night, but many more after, was far worse."

"Your scars?" Matt whispered.

"Yeah. They liked pain….my pain and they got off on hurting me. Sometimes Marcus would be in the room watching and touching himself while I screamed and begged for it to stop. He never stopped them. He enjoyed it. I later discovered he was using me to sweeten drug deals he was making with the Russian mob." I paused for a moment and took a deep breath, telling myself I could get through the whole story, I had to get it out.

"For years, either he abused me, or he allowed the criminals he was doing business with to abuse me. I'd have given up and ended it all, but I couldn't bring myself to do it. I wasn't strong enough. I hoped one day Marcus would just do it for me, but deep down I knew that would never happen. I was earning him some good money.

"I guess I was around twenty-two when I finally got a chance to escape. One of the russian guys who was regularly brought to my room had left me laid on the floor. He'd had his hands around my neck while he…..." I couldn't bring myself to say more. It hurt too much to go there. "Anyway, he seemed to think I was passed out, but I'd just pretended so he would stop. He walked out of the room, to get Marcus I guess, and left the door to my room open. I took my opportunity. I pulled on my clothes and then ran as fast as I could, just needing to get out of there. Marcus was chasing me before I got more than ten feet. I fled down the staircase, but he caught up with me half way down. He grabbed my arms and smiled at me….this really cold, evil look on his face." I swallowed the lump in my throat as the images played out in my mind, clear as the day it had happened. "I was terrified and rightly so. He….he threw me Matt, down the remainder of the long marble staircase. I think he was hoping to kill me, but I survived, although I came away with the brain injury."

"Jesus Alex. I'm so fucking sorry." Matt uttered again, his voice strained and pained.

"The recovery was slow, although I had good doctors because my parents needed to keep up their wholesome, loving family image. It took me five months to learn to do everything again. When my family visited to maintain their caring image, they'd hurt me and suffocate me to punish me for what I was putting then through. I was too messed up to tell anyone. It slowed my progress, but I got back on my feet. I planned to escape from the hospital as soon as I could, but before that was possible Marcus arrived to take me home and things went back to how they were, except I was in agony from the side effects of the brain injury. They refused to allow me any of the meds I had been given at the hospital, telling me I wasn't worth the cost and it made things ten times harder than they had been before for me.

"After about six months Marcus brought this new guy to my room. He was older and american, not Russian. He started to talk to me, instead of hurting me. He asked me about my limp and I told him about the brain injury. Max.....that was his name, he told me he had a sister who had been in a bad accident a few years earlier. She was in a long term care facility, unable to communicate or take care of herself in any way. I think I reminded him of her. Before he left he told me he would find a way to help me. I didn't really believe him, but I was glad he hadn't hurt me that night.

"About a week later Max broke into the house in the middle of the night and carried me out of there. I was too weak from the effects of the brain injury and the beatings I had taken to be scared, I just had to trust him. It wasn't like things could get much worse. He took me to his home and had a nurse there ready to care for me. I finally received pain meds and muscle relaxants and all the other meds I should have been taking and over a couple of weeks I got stronger. I didn't see a lot of Max, but he checked in on me sometimes and always reassured me my family had no idea where I was. He was kind to me and we had several conversations where he made me realise I was worthy of a better life, that there was something more out there for me, something other than pain.

"After a month recovering in his home he told me he wanted to get me out of LA and far away so I would be safe. I agreed happily and he brought me here. He gave me a new identity, and the documents to back it up. He bought my apartment for me and left me with an account with ten thousand dollars. I never heard from him again after that, but he saved my life Matt. They'd have killed me eventually." I was relieved to have unloaded it all, even though I was trembling and tears streamed down my face.

"I know love. Thank God for him, whoever he was." Matt whispered as he reined kisses on the top of my head.

"Do….do you feel different now you know?" I asked very reluctantly. "I mean, I-I'd understand if you did. I get it."

"Alex, I don't know what you mean."

"If you don't want me anymore after….well you know."

"Hey, look at me." He ordered. I turned in his arms and slowly moved my head up to meet his gaze. "What you went through was not your fault. Your family are animals. What they did to you was unthinkable. The fact you survived it is a miracle and that's what I see when I look at you Alex, a miracle. You came out of that hell, strong and positive. There aren't many people who could have done that. I love you baby and what you just told me only strengthens my feelings. I'm not going anywhere, ever. You and me, forever." He said firmly.

"Forever." I whispered as our lips met in a desperate claiming kiss. Matt's hands were tangled in my hair, gently pulling me into him as close as possible. He needed to feel me, to know I was his and I needed the same thing. I needed his kiss to remind me of who I was and not who I had been all those years ago.

"I love you so much Alex." Matt rasped when we were forced to come up for air, breathless and flushed.

"I love you too, more than I can ever say."

"I just realised, I keep calling you Alex, but that's not your name. Would you prefer I call you Alicia?"He asked and I flinched at the sound of that name.

"I never want to be Alicia again Matt. That name brings too much back. Alex Harrison is more than a cover. It was my fresh start and I'd like to keep it if I can. I never want to be a Dalton again. Alex is good, or Ali, which is what Max called me."

"You'll always be my Alex then love." He whispered as he kissed me again.

"You should call Rob and tell him anything you think is relevant."

"Are you ok with that?"

"Yes. I trust Rob and the others. I have no problem with them knowing what happened, though I'm not sure I could tell them like I just told you." I admitted.

"That won't be necessary. Do you know the name of the Russians your family was in business with?"

"Yeah, the Sokolovs. I don't know many first names though. There was a Yuri and a Dimitri, but there were alot more who's name I never knew."

"Rob will figure it out. Do you want to get some rest now love?" I nodded and Matt scooped me up and carried me through to his room where he tightly tucked me into his bed. He turned on the TV mounted on the wall opposite and loaded up Netflix for me.

"Will you be ok while I talk to Rob?" He asked as he handed me the TV control.

"Sure. I'm pretty tired after all of that, I'll just watch some TV and end up fast asleep."

"Ok. I'll come cuddle with you as soon as I can." He promised and then with a brief kiss he was gone.

I found an episode of an old sitcom to watch and collapsed back against Matt's luxuriously soft pillows, trying to block out the hell I had just unleashed on my tired brain.

MATT

I closed my bedroom door and stalked into the lounge, fighting with the rage that was overcoming me and telling me to hit something, anything, just punch the crap out of something! What Alex had been through was far worse than anything I had imagined when I'd seen her scars. She had been abused for years, first by her own damn brother and then by criminals brought in by her fucking family! She had been raped again and again, beaten and cut and then her bastard brother had almost killed her and left her with a brain injury. How could anyone do that to their flesh and blood? Suddenly my need to hit something changed in to a desperate urge to speak to Lucy, to know that my little sister was safe.

I pulled my mobile from my pocket and hit her contact. It barely rang before I heard her voice and felt instantly relieved.

"Hi Matt." She greeted.

"Hi Darling."

"How's Alex?"

"Resting." I replied, too torn up to say more.

"Are you ok?" She asked with concern in her voice.

"Not really darling. I just needed to hear your voice." I admitted.

"She told you everything didn't she?"

"Yeah."

"I'm sorry Matt. I'm guessing it was worse than we expected?"

"A lot worse. Her brother.....the things he put her through Lucy. I don't know how he could do that to someone he should have loved and protected." I was almost crying and it took me a lot of deep breaths to pull it back.

"We're so lucky Matt. The relationship we have, the way Mum and Dad loved us. We were so bloody lucky."

"We were and I never take for granted the fact I have you in my life darling. I love you and I hope you know I will always do my best to protect you and care for you."

"I do Matt. I love you too." Lucy said tearfully.

"I should go. I need to call Rob. I just had to hear your voice after...."

"I know, I understand. I'm glad you rang. Come to ours for dinner tomorrow, ok?"

"Ok, we will. Thanks darling. See you tomorrow." We said goodbye and I hung up, feeling a little lighter to know my sister was safe and having been slightly soothed by her voice.

I moved through to the kitchen, further away from my room so Alex wouldn't overhear my next conversation. Rob answered after a few rings and he sounded tired. I knew he had slept even less than the rest of us in Alex's hospital room the previous night. As always he had wanted to maintain vigilance and that did not allow decent sleep.

"Hey man. How's Alex feeling?" He asked upon answering.

"She's tired and emotional, but doing well all things considered. She's resting now."

"That's good. She's a tough little thing. She'll get through this Matt."

"She told me Rob, all of it. It's bad....what they subjected her to, really bad."

"You want to talk it through with me?" He offered and I was so damn relieved. I needed to talk to someone and I knew Rob would understand the way I was feeling. He had been forced to deal with the knowledge of the way Lucy had been abused by her husband for years before she found the courage to leave. Rob understood better than anyone what it was to try and handle the fact the woman you loved had been hurt again and again.

For the next ten minutes I recalled everything Alex had told me, from her miserable childhood, through all of the abuse and the attempted murder, right up until that guy took pity and helped her escape. Rob was quiet throughout and when I finally finished I heard him take a deep breath.

"Fucking hell Matt. I knew Alex had a dark past. It's in her eyes even though she tries so hard to push it away with that happy face she wears all the time. I knew it was going to be bad, but not that bad, not years of abuse and murder attempts. It's a fucking miracle she even survived. No wonder she's such a tough cookie."

"I know. She really is the strongest person I have ever met. It explains why her and Lucy are such kindred spirits. They've both seen true evil and lived to tell the tale."

"We need to find a way to bring that family down. Alex needs to know it's over, for good. She needs to be able to live without looking over her shoulder."

"I agree and I want her brother dead, fucking piece of shit that he is, doesn't deserve to be allowed to survive another day. Even prison would be too good for that scumbag!"

"If he's involved with the LA Sokolov's there's a good chance he'll wind up dead anyway. They're a real nasty bunch to get mixed up with."

"Do you think we can find a way to get the Daltons?" I asked.

"I have a few ideas, but I need to do some more research into their dealings with the Russians first. You're just going to have to leave this with me for a while Matt. Just focus on taking care of Alex and keeping her safe. I'll work this end and see what I can come up with."

"Sounds good mate. Keep me updated please and let me know if you need any help with anything."

***

Alex was sleeping peacefully when I walked into my room. She was burrowed down under the duvet, her hand tucked under her right cheek and the other clutched tightly against her chest. She looked so small and vulnerable and again I was consumed with rage at the thought of what those monsters had done to her. She was so good and kind and pure. They had tried to take all of that from her and maybe for a while they had even succeeded, but eventually she'd escaped and she'd rebuilt who she really was, gifting me with the beautiful, strong willed, fiery woman I loved unreservedly.

In six weeks she had captured my heart and I was head over heels for her. There was nothing I wouldn't do to protect her and make her happy. She had made me feel truly whole for the first time in my life. She was a part I had never known my heart was missing. I knew as I watched her sleep, that nothing short of death would stop me from protecting her from anything that may come along. I would fight with every fibre of my being to ensure she never had to suffer, ever again.

ALEX

"Are you sure you're up to this?" Matt asked. We were in the elevator climbing up to Rob and Lucy's apartment for dinner. I was exhausted, having slept fitfully the night before. I had been hit by one nightmare after another, all images of my terrifying past. I had woken up three times screaming, in a cold sweat, and each time Matt had been there to hold me and assure me I was safe. In the end I had given up on sleep and just lay awake, watching Matt sleep.

If I was honest I wasn't really up to the meal, but I knew Matt needed to feel the support of his family after the truths I had unleashed on him the day before. He'd been quiet and fidgety all day and I quickly realised he was struggling to process it all. I was hoping the guys would be able to help him make peace with it all. So I sucked up the exhaustion, anxiety and raging throbbing down both of my sides and painted on a smile.

"I'm fine. I'm looking forward to doing something normal instead of brooding over what's coming next. Let's just have some fun tonight Matt, ok?"

"Ok baby." He agreed.

We walked hand in hand to Rob and Lucy's apartment and were greeted at the door by, a very tired looking, Lucy.

"Hi guys. Come in." She smiled, but it didn't seem to reach her eyes. I looked to Matt as we entered and saw he was studying his sister closely too.

"Are you ok darling?" He asked, once we were inside.

"Fine, just a little tired. Can I get you both a drink? I just opened a bottle of shiraz?" She didn't hug either of us as she normally did, just walked off into the lounge looking exhausted.

"Just water for me please, I'm driving." Matt replied, though I saw he wasn't convinced by the answer she had given to his question. Lucy was trying her hardest to avoid eye contact, busying herself straightening already straight sofa cushions.

"Alex?"

"A glass of that wine sounds good please."

"At least I'm not drinking alone then." She said as she finally looked up and met my eyes with a hint of a genuine smile.

"I heard somewhere that friends, don't let friends drink alone so I guess I'll just have to take one for the team." I joked, making her smile further. She disappeared into the kitchen just as Rob emerged from his home office.

"Hey guys." He greeted, lowering his broad frame into the huge armchair opposite where we sat on the sofa. "How are you feeling Alex?"

"A lot better thanks."

"Is Lucy ok?" Matt asked in a more hushed tone.

"Really bad night. She woke up twice screaming and was tossing and turning non stop. It's the worst she's been in months. I think what happened to Alex must have brought it all back." Rob explained.

"She should have cancelled the meal. She should be resting."

"I suggested it Matt, but she didn't want to. She said seeing everyone would put her more at ease so I dropped it." Matt nodded and the conversation ended because Lucy was back with a bottle of water and two, very large, glasses of wine.

"You can stop whispering about me now guys." She said knowingly as she handed out the drinks and plonked down beside me.

"We weren't!" Matt defended.

"Alex? What were they talking about?" She asked with a roll of her eyes.

"To be fair to them, they weren't whispering, more talking in hushed tones." I said, hoping to keep it light and not upset her. It worked, because she laughed and I was relieved.

"Are Jack and Cal coming?" Matt asked, obviously hoping for a subject change.

"Jack's on his way. Cal has some big open day at the gym tomorrow and he's still prepping the place for it. He'll be here before we eat." Rob explained.

"Open day?"

"He needs to boost his membership numbers and so he's hoping an open day, letting people come and try it out for free for a day, will get him some more contracts." Lucy perked up as she spoke and seemed suddenly more animated. "I'm looking forward to it."

"Sounds like a good idea. I might call in and check it out." Matt pondered.

"I thought you were working?" I asked. He started four days of fifteen hour shifts tomorrow, I clearly remembered him telling me before all of the drama.

"I was, but I'm going to speak to the chief tomorrow and arrange some personal days. I want to take care of you, at least for the next week or so."

"There's no need for that Matt. I've only got a few stitches and some bruising. I feel fine. I don't want our lives to be turned upside down by all of this. I have the security and I'm staying with you. That's enough disruption for now." I said firmly. I loved the fact he wanted to stay home and care for me, but I didn't want to feel like we were hiding ourselves away because my twisted family had decided they wanted me to suffer some more. I wouldn't let them win.

"It's a bit more than a few stitches and some bruising Alex. You can barely get up and down without help." Matt retorted with concern.

"It's nothing Matt. Trust me, I've managed with much worse." I said, knowing it was harsh to bring up the past, but wanting him to understand more than anything I needed to feel strong and not be babied.

"You can spend the day with me tomorrow!" Lucy cut in excitedly. "Matt can drop you off in the morning and you can come to the gym with me. It'll be fun and Cal will be glad for an extra pair of hands."

"I'm working a fifteen hour shift, in fact four in a row." Matt said.

"Even better. Alex can stay with us for the next four days then. She's right. You guys can't let what happened take over. You need to go on as normally as possible." Lucy said firmly and I knew she understood what I had been trying to say. "Alex can stay here and you can come and crash with her at night Matt. That all ok with you Alex?"

"As long as Rob is good with it all?" I asked as I looked to the man himself.

"You're always welcome here sweetheart and I think if Matt's going to be working so many hours we'd all feel better if you were here rather than at Matt's alone."

"Matt?" I looked to him and knew he wasn't happy.

"I want to take care of you." He sulked.

"Matt, you said you love me because I'm strong. Please let me keep on being that woman you love. I need this. I can't let my family destroy me again, I won't. You can take care of me without being glued to my side."

"Ok baby." He relented as he pulled me into a tight hug. I sank into his side and relished his arms around me.

"As long as the security stays with you at all times and you listen to Rob."

"I will Matt. I'm not going to take any chances, I promise."

"I love you Alex." He whispered and before I could reciprocate he had me locked against his body, in the grip of an all consuming kiss that swept me away from all reality until all that was left was Matt.

"Oh good. I'm just in time to watch you two drooling all over each other!" Jacks loud words pulled us back to the room and we sat back from one another. Jack shut the front door and walked in, dressed impeccably in his navy suit and pale blue button down shirt, the top two buttons open being the only indication he'd been working a long shift before arriving.

"Please, don't let me interrupt!" He joked with a grin.

"Hi Jack." I said, trying not to show how embarrassed I was at having lost control with Matt right in front of them all.

"Hey sweet. How are you doing?" He asked in a softer voice as he took the last armchair in the room.

"Better thanks."

"Thank fuck you're finally here. My stomach thinks my throat's been cut." Rob whined as he looked pleadingly to Lucy.

"We still need to wait for Cal. I told you to eat lunch!" She said in a very motherly tone.

"Cal could be hours!"

"Actually he called me on my way up here. He's leaving now. He'll be about thirty minutes." Jack said, making Rob groan again.

"Ok, ok! I'll go and get it all ready so we can eat as soon as Cal gets here. That suit you grumpy?" Lucy asked.

Rob nodded with a mock pout. It was strange to see the always very serious man, being more playful. "Come on Alex, come keep me company in the kitchen."

Lucy pulled me to my feet and barely gave me time to grab my crutch before she was dragging me behind her. "Let them talk." Lucy said as she ushered me to sit at a stool opposite where she was working at the counter. She refilled our wine glasses and then started chopping salad items.

"He called you didn't he, last night?" I asked. He must have. She seemed to have this knowing look in her eyes and I knew she had purposely left the guys to talk.

"Yeah, he did, but he didn't really tell me anything. I think he was just upset because it was your brother. It made him think about his relationship with me."

"It was hard to tell him, but I needed to get it out there. He's been quiet today. I think I really upset him."

"I don't know exactly what you told him hun, but I have a few ideas. If what happened is even close to what I suspect, I know Matt will be angry. Not with you, but with the people who hurt you. He loves you and it must be so hard for him to know everything that you've been through, to think of others hurting you.

"It'll take some time, but he'll come to terms with it all. Talking to the guys will help him. Don't worry too much.

Matt's tough." I dared a look up from where I'd been studying my wine glass and met eyes filled with sympathy and understanding.

"I'm so scared Lucy." I whimpered tearfully. "I can't go back....I'd never survive it again." She was beside me instantly, wrapping her arms around me and holding me close.

"That's never going to happen. You never have to go back. The guys will protect you, I know they will." She soothed. I allowed the tears to flow for a few minutes, feeling I didn't need to be strong with Lucy, that it was alright to just let out my fears. "I promise it will all be ok." She whispered over and over.

"Well aren't I the lucky guy? Just in time for another of those group hugs?" Jack's voice cut into my misery. Lucy and I both looked up and found him approaching. He engulfed us both in his huge arms and held us as we sank against his warmth and strength. I continued to sob into his pristine shirt, unable to stop no matter how I tried. I heard Lucy's muffled sniffles and knew she was crying too, but Jack didn't comment, just held us until we both managed to get it together a little.

"I'm sorry Jack." I whispered when I felt calm enough to look up and meet his eyes.

"Don't be sorry sweet. These group hugs are quickly becoming my favourite moments, though don't tell Cal that. It may hurt his ego." He joked, making me smile.

"Your secret's safe with me." I agreed as Lucy took a huge deep breath and then looked up at us both.

"Well that was therapeutic." She sighed.

"Feeling better ladies?" Jack asked.

"Much. Thanks Jack." Lucy replied while I just nodded. He placed a kiss on the top of each of our heads and then stepped back and walked over to get a bottle of water from the refrigerator.

"Cal will be here in ten sweet," He said.

"Oh crap! I better get on with dinner or Rob's going to go all incredible hulk."

"You need a hand?" Jack offered.

"No, it's all under control. You go back through." Lucy ordered as she started bustling around the kitchen. I walked over to wash my hands and then set to chopping the salad she had already started. It felt good to have a task to concentrate on and within minutes Lucy and I were back to laughing and joking, spurred on by several refills of our wine glasses. It was just what I needed. I just hoped whatever the guys were talking about was helping Matt too.

***

Matt reluctantly dropped me off at Rob and Lucy's early the next morning. He had been better since the meal the night before. He seemed to be more his relaxed self and I was relieved. The meal had been fun and loud as usual and it had definitely been cathartic for both me and Matt. He still wasn't happy about working instead of being with me, but he seemed relieved I would be with Lucy and Cal all day, as well as my new shadow, my security detail.

Lucy had shooed him away after our goodbyes and helped me get settled in their guest room, unpacking my small bag and showing me where everything I may need was.

Once that was done and we'd both had a quick coffee, we were in her jeep on our way to Cals gym, Rob's two security guys in an SUV right behind us. It felt good as we drove through the city, music blasting, both singing stupidly. I almost managed to forget about Marcus and the kidnapping, almost.

"Excellent. The workforce has arrived." Cal joked as we walked through the doors of his place. I was surprised. His gym wasn't what I had expected at all. I thought it would be all grimy mats and sweaty bodies, but the place was bright and smelt clean. There was a ton of equipment and a boxing ring in the back. There were a few guys working out in one corner and music pumped in the background. All in all it was a nice place and it had me itching to try some of the machines. Working out wasn't easy for me with my weak left side and my bum leg, but since I arrived in Chicago I had tried hard to stay fit, never again wanting to feel as weak as I had felt those long months I spent in the hospital. I'd never been to a gym because my pathetic salary wouldn't stretch to the cost after bills and my meds, but I jogged (very slowly) and I had a DVD of yoga that I enjoyed to attempt several times a week.

"Where do you want us?" Lucy asked.

"I'm going to put a sign and some balloons out front to advertise. Can you watch the desk and just do a general tidy round. I had a rush early this morning and it's a bit messy on the floor, especially near the free weights." Cal directed. "Are Rob's guys here with you hon?" He asked me.

"Yeah. Rob told them they could stay out in the parking lot while you're here with me."

"Ok hon. I'll get sorted, then take them some coffee." He said, and then he was gone.

Lucy directed me into a huge staff room where she hung our coats and purses and poured us each a coffee. She showed me the desk and how to swipe the members gym cards when they arrived and left then we both set to walking around the expansive gym space, picking up used towels and tidying equipment. When we were sure the place was tidy we returned to the desk and chatted while we drank coffee. As work went, it was pretty relaxed.

The morning passed quickly. The gym was pretty quiet so Lucy and I were basically just chatting and drinking coffee for the most part. Cal would come and go as he manned the gym floor and kept a close eye on the people working out, since they weren't all regulars.

At lunchtime Lucy was escorted by one of my security entourage to the diner across the street and all three of us had delicious club sandwiches and fries. It was a great morning and I so wished I could have a job that was as much fun, rather than the daily misery of the unemployment office. Matt had spoken to my boss after the kidnapping and arranged for me to have two weeks sick leave, but soon I would have to go back and that was a depressing thought.

"Right ladies. We're going to become pretty busy this afternoon. I have fifteen potential new members booked in for trials and wednesdays are busy with regulars too so if you're both happy I was thinking Lucy can stay on the desk and Alex, I was hoping you'd be ok to man the floor with me. I don't expect you to get involved too much. Just try to help out where possible, answer questions if you can, watch out for idiots and grab me if you see anyone doing anything dangerous."

"Sounds good." I agreed happily. It felt good to know Cal trusted me to do that and wasn't worrying about handling me with kid gloves, as everyone had since the attack.

"Great. Don't do anything you're not comfortable with and call me if you need me. I'll be close by." Cal was right, the gym got very busy, very quickly after lunch. There was a huge influx of people and we each took our posts. Cal was over by the free weights so he could keep an eye on what the guys were lifting and spot them where necessary. Lucy was crazy busy at the desk and so I took the other side of the gym, near the machines. I walked around greeting people and just generally watching what they were doing. A few people stopped to ask me questions about the equipment, mainly women, and thankfully I managed to help each of them out. I got chatting to a few people about how nice the gym was compared to others and I even got two women to sign up to twelve month memberships.

"You doing ok over here honey?" Cal asked as he approached in a lull late in the afternoon.

"I'm loving it Cal, really enjoying myself." I said excitedly. It was the most fun I had ever had at work and I loved the buzz of the gym.

"Glad to hear it. You're doing great. I've had four people tell me they signed up for memberships because of your enthusiasm for the place. You're a natural."

"I'm not sure I'd go that far. It's kind of strange for all these people to be working their asses off while I can't even stand without help." I said, nodding to my crutch.

"The fact you have an injury doesn't affect the way you interact with people Alex. You're a great people person and you seem to know what you're doing instructing on the equipment. Have you worked in a gym before?"

"No, but I read a lot about physiotherapy after my accident and it was part of the programme." I explained.

"Did you have physiotherapy on your leg?" He asked.

"Some, to get me walking again, but it stopped once I left the hospital. I do some exercises on my own when I can."

"I have a qualification in physio. I completed it last year in hopes of starting a program here. I'd like to try doing some work with you if you're up for it? I really think I could help you with your balance issues and maybe strengthen your left side." He offered, rendering me speechless.

"Really?" I gasped eventually. Cal nodded and I couldn't hide my smile. "I'd love that Cal. I can't pay much though."

"I'm not going to charge you Alex, you're family. Plus you'll be my first subject and I might be useless." He joked.

"I doubt that."

"We'll need to work everyday, for around an hour. It'll take time to get results."

"I understand that Cal, but I'm totally game. I'd love to improve my mobility if it's possible. I could do it before or after work?"

"Well, that's the other thing. I've been looking for someone to help out around here when Lucy's not here. She only works two days a week now, and I need help. Would you be interested? It would mainly be manning the desk and a bit of what you did today."

"Oh my god!" I squealed, unable to hold it in. "Are you serious?"

"Definitely. You're a natural around here and I know you can handle the shit the guys sometimes give. You're a tough lady."

"When can I start?" I asked excitedly. Working there felt like a dream compared to the office I worked in.

"Work out your notice with the other place and think about how many days you want to work. I cover the late nights most of the time and CJ does those I can't, so I won't need you here then, and Lucy does Tuesdays and Thursdays so it's the other days I need."

"Ok Cal. I'll talk it over with Matt and give my notice at the office."

"Sure thing. Just let me know when you've decided. I'm so pleased Alex. You and Lucy will brighten this place up no end."

"Thank you Cal. When do you think we could start the physio?"

"Anytime hon."

"Tomorrow morning, early?" I asked excitedly.

"Eager. I like it." Cal grinned. "I'll pick you up from Rob and Lucy's on my way in, seven AM?"

"Perfect. I can't wait!"

"You won't be saying that when I'm done with you. We're going to have to work hard Alex."

"Bring it on." I replied, making him chuckle as he walked back to his post. I couldn't stop smiling, a new, much better job and physio on my crappy body, on top of having Matt and his family. Life really did seem to be falling into place for me and I was overjoyed. Now just to evade my evil family and all could be well. *Yeah right*, I thought. That was not how my life ever went. *Come on Ali, a girl can hope.*

"I really hope he's not your boyfriend!" I turned at the sound of a deep, mocking voice and was faced with a tall, lean guy grinning at me. He had slicked back dark hair and a long, very angular face. His eyes were roaming my body lecherously and I instantly felt on alert. "He's old enough to be your father!" He added as he took a step toward me.

"I think that's a bit of an exaggeration." I said, determined not to be intimidated.

"Trust me sugar, you're not his type. An arrogant prick like him'd never go for damaged goods." He said, nodding to my leg. The words were like a slap to the face, but I stood my ground. I'd faced far worse.

"But you're different right? You would?" I asked.

"I don't give a shit what you look like stood. Makes no odds when you're on your knees for me." He leered, making my stomach roll and bile rise. I took a step back and looked around nervously for Cal. He was deep in conversation across the room, his back to me. I looked to the desk and was glad to see Lucy watching. I looked from her to Cal and back to her. She nodded, getting my plea and I watched her jump up.

"Come on. Don't play with me bitch. I know what you need. Bet a man ain't touched you in years. There aren't many men who'd touch a cripple, but what can I say? I'm feeling real charitable today.." He hissed, right in my ear. When I turned back to him he was right in front of me, leant forward far too much in my personal space. "Pussy's pussy, makes no odds to me." He said as he placed his hand on my ass and grabbed. That was all it took for me to snap. I wouldn't let anyone touch me ever again without my permission. I raised my left leg and kneed him in the crotch with everything I had. He cried out and dropped to the ground, rolling around and clutching his junk.

"How's that for damaged goods, you prick?!" I yelled as I tried to calm myself.

"Alex!" I looked up and saw Cal and Lucy approaching hurriedly. "Are you ok?" Cal asked as he reached me and wrapped me in his arms tightly. I allowed myself to relax in his hold, noticing for the first time that I was shaking so much my teeth were chattering.

"I'm sorry Cal." I whispered, realising I'd probably just lost all chance of getting that job.

"No, don't be sorry. Tell me what happened honey." He coaxed as he continued to hold me.

"It doesn't matter now."

"Alex. Tell me." He demanded and I knew he wasn't going to drop it. I figured I really did owe him an explanation.

"He was propositioning me, telling me no one would touch a cripple, but he didn't mind. Apparently it makes no difference if I'm on my knees." I whispered awkwardly. "He called me bitch and said 'pussy's pussy', then grabbed my ass and I snapped Cal. I'm so sorry."

"You did good sweetie, really good. Nothing to be sorry for." Cal said. He kissed my forehead and then turned to where Lucy stood behind him. "Take her to get some coffee honey. I've got some rubbish to take out." Lucy nodded and wrapped her arm around my shoulders. She led me around the slime ball still laid on the floor nursing his junk, and into the staff room. I went to sit at the table in the middle of the room, but Lucy stopped me, grabbing my wrist and pulling me back to the doorway.

"You need to watch this. It'll make you feel better," She said with a huge smile. I stood beside her and we watched as Cal dragged the guy up from the ground by the scruff of his t-shirt. By the time Cal had him against a wall, three huge guys had abandoned the weight lifting benches and stood strategically surrounding them.

"This guy seems to have some trouble with understanding how to respect women. What do you think we should do with him guys?" Cal asked, his voice nothing like the tone I was familiar with. Gone was the soft, kind Cal I knew and instead I saw the ruthless, intimidating cop he must have once been.

"I think we could probably teach him some manners." One guy surrounding Cal offered.

"Yeah, with our fists." Another added.

"Much as I like that idea guys, I'm having an open day and I just don't think blood on the mats is the image I was aiming for."

"Please, just let me go. I won't come back. I swear." The slimeball pleaded desperately, not looking so cocky anymore. Cal put his free hand on the slimeballs throat, though he didn't squeeze. The guy cried out in fear, making Cal and his three amigos laugh.

"Get your shit and get the fuck out of my gym. I see you around here or anywhere near any of my staff again and I'll let my guys teach you that lesson. Got it cocksucker?" Cal raged in his face. At the wimps vehement nod, Cal released him and he landed on the floor in a heap.

He only half stood before beginning his headlong run for the locker room, stumbling the entire way. The three regulars who'd backed Cal up were following him, only making him run faster. He tripped on the last mat he passed and was propelled face first into the wall a few yards from where Lucy and I stood watching. As he righted himself and flew through the swing door into the locker room, Lucy and I were in fits of giggles.

"Told you it would cheer you up." She said through her laughter. "I thought the stupid wanker was going to piss himself. Did you see his face?"

"I would feel bad, except he totally deserved that." I laughed as I gripped the wall. I was laughing so hard I could barely stand.

"Cal's very good at handling the dickheads that come in here. Don't you worry chick. You'll be just fine working here. Next time knee them twice though!" She said as the laughing finally died down a little. We watched slimeball be escorted out of the door with a shove from Cal a few minutes later and then returned to the desk. "You ok Alex?" Cal asked with concern when he returned.

"Feeling a lot better after watching you guys scare the shit out of him." I said with a smile.

"I'm sorry you had to put up with that crap hon. I promise we don't get many like that sonofabitch. He was just here for the open day. My members know better than to disrespect you ladies. They are cheeky and love to flirt, but they'd never say what he said."

"It's fine Cal. It's not like I haven't heard worse. I'm just sorry I made such a scene."

"Don't worry about that. Everyone here was cheering you on," Cal chuckled. "Please tell me you haven't changed your mind about the job?"

"No, not at all. I want to work here Cal. I can handle whatever comes with that, I know I can."

"I think you just proved that honey." He laughed as he turned and headed back to the guys lifting weights. I smiled to myself, realising I had managed to stand up for myself once again. I was getting good at being strong, I realised. Maybe I'd actually be ready for Marcus when he inevitably caught up with me. Maybe this time *I'd* win.

***

"Good day ladies?" Rob asked as we all sat down to dinner later that evening.

"Great. Cal got twelve new memberships from the open day. He's thinking of doing it every few months."

"Did you enjoy it Alex?" Rob asked as he tucked into the delicious salmon Lucy had cooked for us.

"Yeah. It was fun. Cal offered me a job."

"That's great honey. You'll be safer and I'm sure happier too with Cal than in that office you work at. Matt will be pleased."

"Thanks Rob."

"What have you both got planned for tomorrow?"

"Shopping and lunch in the city." Lucy declared excitedly.

"I have physio with Cal first." I added. "Cal's picking me up at seven."

"Oh that's brilliant Alex. I bet Cal will be great at Physio. He'll be just the right amount of scary to motivate you."

"I hope so. I'll need plenty of motivation at seven AM." I joked. "Seriously though, I've wanted to do physio for years, but it's just so expensive. I've tried on my own, but it hasn't really worked. I'm sure with the right exercises I could get this leg a lot better than it is." I explained.

"Physio worked wonders for Jack. His leg went from hanging on by a thread to walking perfectly again in just over a year. It was amazing really." Rob said and I was surprised.

"Jack? What happened to his leg?" I asked. I remembered Matt once mentioning something, but I'd forgotten all about it.

"His last tour in Iraq, he was injured when the humvee he was in, hit an IED. His right leg was almost completely severed. We managed to get him airlifted fast and they were able to fix and save his leg, but it was a very long recovery and it ended his career with the military. It took months of physio to get him walking again and for a while he used a stick for support. Eventually though, he was able to walk without it. Now he works his crazy shifts at the hospital, works out like no one else I know and pushes himself as hard as he ever did."

"That's amazing. I didn't even realise."

"He still has some pain when he pushes himself too hard. Cal's always on at him for it, but if the physio helped him, I'm sure it can help you too Alex." Lucy said enthusiastically.

"I'm going to remain positively optimistic."

"Good for you honey." Rob agreed. We all went back to our meals while dreams of walking without the crutch swirled around my head. I'd work my ass off with Cal and maybe one day I could throw the damned stick in lake Michigan.

"Make sure you stay with Cam and Evan while you shop tomorrow, won't you?" Rob asked, dragging me from my thoughts.

"We will Rob, but I hope you know all of this security is unnecessary."

"Why's that sweet heart?" Rob said with a smirk.

"Because Alex is a total badass." I couldn't hide my giggle at the word 'badass' in Lucy's gentle accent." She took another guy down today at the gym."

"What do you mean?" Rob demanded, his face turning from amusement to concern. He dropped his knife and fork to his plate with a clang and looked to me. "Did someone approach you today Alex? Cam didn't report anything." I knew he was worried it was something to do with the kidnapping.

"No, no. It was nothing like that. There was just this guy there for a trial and he started saying some pretty sick stuff, while also propositioning me. He grabbed my ass and I may have kneed him in his soft bits." I admitted. Rob instantly relaxed and started to laugh.

"You should have seen it Rob!" Lucy said excitedly. "The knob went down like a sack of potatoes! It was bloody brilliant!"

"Jesus Alex. You don't take any shit do you?" He laughed.

"I figure I failed to fight back for a really long time with my family. I'm done being a victim now. So yeah Rob, you're right. I'm not taking any shit ever again." I said firmly, then hurriedly looked down at my plate, embarrassed for my little outburst. Suddenly a huge paw engulfed my hand which was tapping nervously on the table. I tentatively looked up to Rob and found nothing but understanding.

"Good for you Alex." He said softly, then pulled his hand back. I looked across to Lucy who was beaming at me and then got back to dinner. They got me, all of Matt's family got me and the way my past affected me. They didn't hold it against me or judge me for it, they just quietly supported me and it meant everything.

After dinner Lucy and I both washed up and slipped into pyjamas, then laid out on the sofa, top to toe, with a heavy blanket and a romcom. Rob was, as always, working in his office, but he popped out every so often to check if we needed anything. It was so sweet the way he always kissed Lucy before returning to his office. Such a small gesture, that showed so much about the way they felt for each other.

We finished the romcom, both finding it a little nauseatingly sweet. Deciding we couldn't take anymore niceness, we settled on an action movie, which suited us both a lot more. Plenty of violence, car chases and a few hot men was much more interesting.

"Still doing ok in here ladies?" Rob asked quietly as he walked in about half way through the action movie.

"Lucy's asleep. She nodded off about ten minutes ago." I whispered.

"She rarely finishes a movie, bless her." He walked over and crouched down in front of her. He reached down and pressed the softest kiss on her cheek. "I'll put her in our bed. She'll be a lot comfier there." He said as he effortlessly gathered her into his arms.

"I should get some sleep too. I have to be up early tomorrow."

"Can I get you anything before you go honey?" Rob asked.

"No thanks. I think I'm good."

"Ok sweetheart. Just yell if you change your mind during the night. I'm a light sleeper, I'll hear you. Matt said he'd be here around midnight" I nodded.I knew what time Matt would arrive because I was counting down the hours until I could feel his arms around me. I had missed him so much that day.

"Thanks Rob. Good night." I whispered as I got to my feet.

"Night honey." I watched as Rob carried Lucy toward their room and once again longed to see Matt.

I hurried through my nighttime rituals and then climbed into the incredibly comfy bed. If I could just get to sleep then the two hours until Matt arrived wouldn't seem so long. With thoughts of being enveloped in his arms I managed to nod off eventually.

MATT

Fifteen hours! It had been over fifteen hours since I dropped Alex at Rob's apartment that morning and I was beyond desperate to see her. It had killed me to be away from her for so long knowing she was injured, scared for her life and in danger, but she wanted to go on as normal and not give into fear and I was so proud of her strength that there was no way I could argue. So I'd left her, after Rob assuring me for at least the fifth time he would keep her safe. Now the damn shift was over and I got to hold her for the rest of the night.

I practically sprinted from the lift to Rob and Lucy's apartment, just needing to get eyes on her and know she was alright.

I let myself in quietly, then locked the door and reset the alarm behind me. When I turned around Rob was stood in the lounge in sleep shorts and a scruffy t-shirt. He might have startled me, except I was used to it with Rob. He was always creeping up on me.

"Hi mate. Sorry if I woke you." I said as I dumped my bag beside the door and pulled my coat off.

"I was listening for you." I nodded and walked past him to sit and unlace my boots.

"How's Alex?" I asked.

"She's good. She enjoyed it at the gym. Cal offered her a job which she's excited about."

"That's great. I fucking hate her working with some of the scumbags who come in that unemployment office." I admitted.

"Yeah, she'll be safer with Cal. I agree it's a good idea. She's starting physio with Cal tomorrow too. That your doing?"

"I may have mentioned that I thought she could benefit from further physio, to Cal. I'm glad she agreed to give it a try. She still suffers a lot with that leg. I think it could be improved."

"She seemed excited to get started so fingers crossed."

"So everything's good?" I asked, the tenseness in his face making me uneasy.

"She's been calling out in her sleep for the last hour." He said with worry. "I've been in a couple of times to try and settle her, but as soon as I leave it starts again. Some guy said something to her at the gym today and grabbed her ass. Lucy said she handled it and Cal threw the guy out, but I think maybe it's set her nightmares off. That's why I was listening for you, to warn you."

"What guy at the gym?" I asked angrily.

"Some prick there for the open day. He won't be back. Lucy told me Cal and a bunch of regulars scared the shit out of him."

"I'll have to talk to Cal if she's going to be working there."

"Don't underestimate her Matt. She doesn't need you to step in to every battle. She's tough as they come. She kneed the prick in the balls today,had him rolling round on the floor. Let her be strong, she needs that." Rob cautioned. I buried my head in my hands and thought about his words. I knew he was right. Alex was tough. She didn't need me to always be jumping in on her behalf, but that was what I did. It was what I had always done for Lucy and for my patients. Now I loved Alex and I wanted to fight all of her battles for her, no matter how big or small. But Rob was right. She didn't need that. She'd been on her own a long time and she'd survived hell. She liked to be able to fight her own battles and I needed to accept that part of her if we were ever going to work. I needed to wait until she asked for me to step in before I took over. All I could do was be there to show her I loved and supported her and be there whenever she needed me, I could do that. It would be hard for me. I was protective by nature, but for her, I could learn to step back. Before I could tell Rob he was right Alex started crying out nonsensically and I leapt to my feet and ran to her.

This was when she needed me, when there was no battle to fight and it was just us. This was when she allowed herself to be vulnerable and needed someone to be there to hold her together. That I could do.

"Baby, it's ok. I'm here. It's just a dream." I whispered as I lay down and pulled her tightly against me.

"Matt?" She whimpered into my chest.

"I'm here love. Everything's ok now." I soothed and she finally relaxed in my arms.

"I missed you today." She whispered, muffled against my chest.

"I missed you too, so bloody much. This is all that's got me through, knowing I'd have you in my arms tonight."

"I'm so glad you're here." She whispered sleepily and then in seconds she was asleep again. I laid for a while, just enjoying knowing she was safe in my arms, taking in her heavenly vanilla scent and running my hand through her soft hair. I knew I was a lucky bastard to have her. She was an incredibly special woman and she was mine. I'd never take that for granted, never doubt the honour that it was to have her come into my life.

ALEX

It's been three weeks since that first day I helped out at Cal's gym and since then things have only gotten better and better. I called the unemployment office the very next day and gave my notice. They didn't even grumble when I said I wouldn't be working any notice, which was a bonus. I couldn't stand another day in that place that I truly loathed.

I started working at the gym two days after that. At first Cal had me on what he called 'light duties' because of my ribs, but after the first week they were healing nicely and I was able to get better stuck into the job. I loved being there. Cal was so funny, especially with the cocky assholes who were regulars there. He was epic when putting them in their place and bringing their monstrous egos down a peg or two. None of them ever took it badly, just shrugging it off and carrying on as always. I helped out on the floor, mainly with the equipment, and manned the front desk. I worked mondays, wednesdays and Fridays, all day which was more than I'd worked at the office, but it didn't feel like work at the gym. It was fun and I felt safe with Cal.

I still had my security detail shadow, even though we hadn't heard a peep from Marcus or any other criminals since the kidnapping. Rob was still closely monitoring the Daltons, but all had gone suspiciously quiet on that front. I tried to convince Rob he could at least drop the detail to one guy, but he flat out refused saying my family could just be waiting for us to lower our guard and since he was the expert I dropped it.

During those weeks I had also started the physio sessions with Cal. We did them first thing in the morning while Cal's other employee, CJ, monitored the gym floor. It had been hell at first. Cal had me stretching muscles I didn't even know I still had. He pushed me harder than I ever realised I'd be able to go and after just two weeks I was able to do squats leant against the wall and my left arm was a lot stronger. The grip in my left hand was massively improved, as was my balance. Cal was sure if we continued working at it every day I would see improvement in my leg and be less reliant on the crutch, which was what I desperately wanted.

Matt seemed so pleased with my progress in the physio and with how much happier I was at work. We too had become a lot closer. One week after the kidnapping attempt, Matt asked me to move in permanently with him and sell my place. I argued that it was fast, but Matt rightfully pointed out there was no way I could go back to my apartment when Marcus knew it was where I lived. He also pointed out that we loved each other and nothing would change that no matter how far the distance between then and when we took our next step forward together. He wanted us to go to bed together every single night possible and so did I. I couldn't argue in the end, so I agreed and that weekend Jack, Cal, Rob and Lucy helped us clear out my place. We gave most of the furniture to a local charity because Matt already had everything, much better quality than the stuff I owned.

Lucy helped me pack up all of my belongings that I had accumulated since moving to Chicago, including three huge boxes of my most beloved items, my books. In total I had seven boxes and a large suitcase, all of which the guys kindly trudged over to Matt's for me. The furniture was collected by the charity and we all gave the place a quick clean, then Matt arranged a realtor for me and within the week I accepted an offer much higher than I had expected.

So Matt and I had moved in together and with every day we grew closer and were always professing our love to each other which regularly earned us plenty of teasing and mocking from the others, but we didn't care.

We slept beside each other every night even fooled around a little, but Matt was holding back on sex and I knew it was because of what I had told him about my past. I understood how he felt, I knew he would be terrified of hurting me, either physically or mentally, but he needed to get over it. I trusted him and I knew he would never hurt me. More than that I needed him. With every minute I spent next to him I became more and more desperate for him to touch me, to claim me. I needed to know what it felt like to have his hands roam every inch of my body. I needed him to show me what sex should be, needed him to prove to me that sex was intimacy, trust and love, instead of the pain, fear and cruelty I had only ever known.

Matt and I had been together three months and I knew it was time. The bruises and cut on my body were healed, almost completely. My past seemed to have returned where it belonged and we were in a good place. I was more than ready, well past that actually, more to the point of desperation and I refused to be put off any longer.

That night was the night, I had decided. It was exactly three months since the night Matt and I met and I had gone all out, calling at the store on the way home to get ingredients for a fancy meal, along with candles for the table and a huge box of condoms, just incase. There was no way I was getting to that point to find out Matt didn't have any.

When I got home, after Cam had cleared the apartment, which of course the security did every time I entered, I got started on Matt's favourite meal, roast beef and all the accompaniments. While that was cooking I showered, groomed everywhere and covered my body in my favourite vanilla scented lotion. I slipped into a black, lacy lingerie set I had special ordered on the internet, complete with suspenders and black stockings. I carefully put on my makeup and styled my hair up, in a fancy knot I'd learned to do from Youtube. Finally I pulled on a cute little black dress I had bought the week before when shopping with Lucy. It was very form fitting, with a sweetheart neckline that along with my sexy new strapless bra, gave me a generous cleavage considering what I had to work with. Lucy had assured me Matt would find my bare shoulders sexy and I had trusted her opinion. I had wanted to wear heels, but it just wasn't an option yet. *Soon*, I kept on telling myself, *keep working with Cal and soon it will be an option.* I tried on some kitten heels, but I preferred to go without, so I did. Also, without shoes, and because of all of the work Cal had done with me, I felt confident around the house for a short time without my crutch, and really, who wants to walk with a crutch when trying to seduce someone? I knew it would affect how sexy I felt, even if it didn't bother Matt.

I sprayed on some perfume and touched up my lipstick, then studied myself in the full length mirror. I looked so different! But in a good way. I looked curvy and feminine and probably as sexy as I would ever get, so I shrugged, deciding I had done all I could, and headed out to check on the meal.

The sound of Matt's key in the door and his voice chatting to Cam, who was outside the apartment, had my heart racing and my hands sweating with nerves a short while later. *Breathe Ali*, I cautioned myself. I knew I could do this. I had to if I wanted to push Matt into taking that big step with me. I knew he would never initiate after everything I had told him. If I wanted this, I had to woman up and take it.

"Honey I'm home!" Matt joked as he came in and reset the alarm behind him. I took a deep breath and then walked as sultry as I could from the kitchen and around the corner.

"Hey there handsome." I said in my sexiest voice. Matt's head snapped up from where he was untying his boots and he smiled.

"Alex, jesus! You look fucking gorgeous baby." He whispered. He was surprised and it was just the effect I was hoping for. He pulled off his boots and stalked toward me. "What's all this in aid of?" He asked as his hands landed on my hips.

"It is our three month anniversary today. Three months since I met you, the best damned thing that ever happened to me. I wanted to mark that occasion."

"It's me who should be marking that date love. I'm the lucky bastard who gets to be with the most amazing woman on this earth. I love you so much." He moved his hands from my hips and gently cupped my face, his thumbs softly brushing my cheeks.

"I love you too Matt. My life began that night three months ago. All of my life before that was just a terrifying nightmare that you, somehow, managed to wake me from. Being with you makes me happier than I ever even dreamt I could be."

"I know baby. I know because you make me feel the same way. You make me feel complete, like before you there was always something missing, but now, with you in my life. I'm whole. Me and you Alex, forever." He whispered, his lips drawing closer to mine.

"Forever." My voice was husky and heavy, weighty with lust and a desperate need. Matts lips met mine and we were instantly tangled in the most intense kiss we had ever shared. While one of Matt's hands roamed to tangle in my hair, pulling my lips harder to his, the other hand cupped my ass and lifted me until we were eye level and able to deepen the kiss further. I wrapped my legs around his slim waist and my arms around his shoulders, clinging to him as my body was set alight with arousal.

Matt backed us up to the wall furthest from the door, until my back was against the cool plaster. He stopped the attack on my mouth and moved down to my neck, nipping with his teeth and then soothing with kisses. I pushed a hand into his hair and clutched the soft waves frantically, loving what he was doing, but urgently needing more.

"Matt," I gasped. "take me to bed." I was relieved when he started moving toward our room as he continued to reign kisses down my neck and right shoulder. He kicked the door to our room open and walked in. It was dark out, but the lights of the city were coming through the windows, creating just enough brightness to illuminate the room.

Matt stopped his burning path of kisses and looked to me with hooded eyes. I saw doubt there and I knew he felt torn.

"What is it honey?" I asked breathlessly.

"Are you sure you're ready for this?"

"More sure than I have ever been about anything. I want you, I need you. Show me Matt, show me how it should be." I was almost pleading with him because I needed him to understand how very sure I was.

"Ok baby." He agreed hoarsely and I was relieved to realise he was as desperate for this as I was. Without another word he lowered me down and lay me in the centre of the bed. He started, very slowly, to peel off his clothes, first his suit jacket, followed by his shirt. I laid back and enjoyed the show, my need only becoming more desperate with every bit of his firm, sexy body that was revealed. As he removed his bottom half, all except his boxers, his eyes stayed locked on mine, not once looking away as he undressed painfully slow.

By the time I realised maybe I should be undressing too and not just laid staring at him, he was climbing up the bed, over me in only his boxers. His lips met mine in a gentle touch, then his tongue swiped across the seam of my mouth, demanding entry. I opened for him and this time the kiss was deep and seductive, while also slow and claiming.

"You're so beautiful Alex." He whispered as he pulled back and brushed the wild strands of hair from my face. "I want to spend the rest of my life proving how much I love you, starting right now, right here." He kissed behind my right ear and then moved slowly down my neck, each kiss increasing the raging need building in my core.

"Matt!" I panted, not knowing what I needed him to do, but needing something.

"It's ok love, I know." He whispered as he pulled the tight black dress down over my bra and clean off my body in one quick move. He threw it behind him, then remained knelt up over me, studying the underwear and stockings I lay in.

"So bloody sexy!" He growled as he bent and was over me again, kissing more urgently down my chest, between my breasts and down to my stomach. His hands roamed up and released the front clasp of my bra, freeing my aching breasts. He massaged both with his hands as he continued to place gentle kisses on my stomach. I moaned in delight and then squeaked in shock as he clamped my right nipple in his hot mouth. He kneaded the other with his hand as he sucked and nibbled at the right, sending shocks of pleasure through my body that I had never experienced before. After a while he swapped out, giving my left breast the attention of his skilled mouth. I continued to moan and keen at the wonderful sensations he was giving.

At some point he moved from leaning over me, to his knees between mine. I only realised when I felt the unmistakable pressure of his erection against my core, which only added to my wanton desires.

"Matt, please….I need you." I whimpered between moans of pleasure. I needed him inside me, needed him to claim me as his, forever. He moved up to kiss my lips gently and I saw him studying my face, checking I was still with him, still good with what was happening. He obviously saw what he needed, because he moved from the bed and slowly peeled away my stockings, closely followed by my panties until I lay completely naked and unable to stop writhing with need for him.

"I'll go slow love, If you need to stop, you just tell me. Promise?" He asked as he discarded the last of my underwear to the floor.

"I promise. I trust you Matt." I replied. He nodded and quickly shucked his boxers revealing what I already knew from our nights cuddling together, my man was very well endowed. He climbed the bed on his knees, stalking over my body like a jungle cat, with a look of wildness in his eyes. He kissed my neck as he reached up to the nightstand to pull a condom from the drawer. He placed the foil packet on the bed beside me and then reigned more smoldering kisses down my torso, while at the same time his hand wandered down until his fingers found my centre. His fingers worked me deftly, touching everywhere I needed and so much more. I was lost to pleasure as he skillfully brought me to the brink.

"Matt, I want you.....please. I want you inside me the first time." I panted. I was breathless and dizzy with pleasure and want.

"Jesus Alex! You're so fucking perfect baby." Matt whispered as he rose on his haunches to roll on the condom. His eyes locked with mine as he lined up with my core and then slid into me gently. He moved slowly and cautiously, pushing forward little by little, his eyes never once leaving mine, constantly checking my state of mind for panic or fear. I knew he would find none though. All I felt with him inside me was pleasure. He was big and stretched me to my limits, but it felt mind blowingly good and there was nothing going through my head but my need for more!

I studied his face as he slowly began to move in and out, and saw pure emotion there. With every movement he was showing me that I belonged to him, that he loved me and would never hurt me. He was at his most raw, opening himself to me completely, baring his body, heart and soul, showing me he was mine just as much as I was his. We claimed each other as our bodies slowly moved together.

His slow movements were building immense feelings with in me. I needed him closer, so I wrapped my legs tight around his waist, locking my feet, drawing him deeper inside me. He leant down to kiss my neck and I pushed my hands through his wild hair, pulling and grabbing as the most intense, wonderful feeling built inside me.

"Matt!" I cried, desperate for just that little more to push me over the abyss. He moved his kisses down my collarbone and to my right nipple. When he bit down gently on the aching bud it was just what I needed and I screamed out his name as pleasure began to consume me completely. I was lost to all rational thought. All I could do was feel. Spots marred my vision as I fought to keep my eyes locked with Matts. He sped up, pushing into me harder, drawing out the pleasure until I was sure I couldn't take anymore, but at the same time I never wanted it to end. Matt cried out my name as my pleasure reached its crescendo and fireworks erupted in my head as euphoria overcame me.

We both crashed over the edge together. Matt dropped his weight down, but lifted enough not to crush me. I remained wrapped around his body, him still inside me, our sweaty bodies tangled together as we both panted breathlessly. Slowly I came back to earth from wherever Matt had just taken me. His eyes met mine again and he smiled.

"Are you ok?" He asked cautiously.

"Blissfully happy is more like it." I whispered with a huge grin I couldn't contain if I tried. "That was amazing."

"Amazing doesn't even cover it baby." He gently kissed my forehead before pulling out of me and standing.

"Won't be a minute." He said as he headed for the ensuite, presumably to deal with the condom. I stretched out, basking in the ecstasy running through my body. Matt returned a minute later, laying on his back and pulling me tight into his side. I curled into him, my head on his chest.

"You sure you're ok Alex? I wasn't too rough was I?" He asked as he rubbed a soft hand up and down my thigh his arm wrapped around my back beneath me.

"It was perfect Matt. I've read about sex like that in romance books, but that's the first time...I......well, I never thought I could enjoy making love like that."

"It's never been that good for me either baby. It's you, us. We just fit together and sparks fly. You're mine Alex and I'm yours, forever."

"Forever. I like the sound of that Matt, being yours and you being mine."

"Good, because you're stuck with me now baby." He pulled me tighter against him and we just held each other in a blissful silence. I had never felt so happy and relaxed in my entire life and within minutes I was drifting into sleep, safe in the arms of the man I loved beyond all measure.

MATT

Alex drifted off in my arms and I just lay holding her, perfectly content. It had been terrifying at first making love to her. I was so worried I would do something to hurt her or trigger memories of her past and I couldn't bare the thought of ever upsetting her like that. I had gone as slowly as my raging hard-on would allow, wanting to maintain a watch on Alex's face to check for signs of distress and also wanting to make it good for her. It had been hard to go slow when I had wanted to be inside her for so long. I had been like a teenager, ready to blow in my pants at just the sight of her fantastic, sexy curves in that delicious, lacy underwear, but I had managed to hold off and not make an idiot of myself, and make it good for Alex. She deserved special, she deserved for someone to love her with care and attention to her needs. She needed to see that sex could be bliss and love and I was so fucking grateful I was the one to show her.

After a while my eyes became heavy too and I was drifting into probably the greatest snooze of my life, following the greatest sex of my life. I was just getting into dreams of Alex when a piercing alarm caused me to wake urgently. My eyes snapped open and my first thought was it was the house alarm, someone was trying to break in.

"Matt!" Alex cried with panic from where she still lay on my chest. "It's the alarm!" She sat up and I leapt from the bed, grabbing my boxers from the floor and pulling them on hurriedly. There was pounding on my apartment door and I knew it would be Rob's guys. Alex was sat in the middle of the bed, her face filled with terror. I ran to her and hurriedly wrapped her naked body in the sheet.

"Come on baby. We need to move." I said as calmly as I could. No way was I leaving her if someone had breached my place. I reached into the top drawer of my dresser and pulled out the loaded gun I kept there. Rob had taught me to shoot at the range years ago and I was a damned good shot. I checked it was loaded and the safety was off, then tucked it at the small of my back. I turned back to where Alex still sat frozen in place and saw her eyeing me fearfully.

"Just in case love. It's ok." I assured as I pulled her up by her hands. "Stay right next to me." I cautioned as I wrapped her sheet clad body against my side and headed out of the bedroom.

It wasn't until we entered the lounge that I realised what was actually going on. There was smoke billowing from a pan on the hob and the acrid stench of burning. Alex looked around too.

"Oh hell, dinner!" She wailed as she fled my hold and ran for the kitchen. I followed her in, relieved it was the smoke alarm blaring and not the security alarm.

"Baby, stay back." I called as I ran after her. There was a saucepan on the hob, the contents long blackened and smoke erupting wildly. I reached Alex and pulled her behind me as I grabbed a dish towel and used it to pick the smoking pan up. I dumped it in the sink and turned the cold water on full, dousing the heat with a sizzle.

"I'm so sorry Matt!" Alex cried. "I forgot all about it."

"It's ok baby. Are you alright?" I asked, checking her hands as I spoke, afraid she had touched the hot pan.

"I'm fine. Can we shut that alarm off?" She asked. I reached up to turn on the extractor hood and then walked across the room and opened the doors to the balcony as wide as possible.

"Matt!" Cam called from where he still frantically banged on the door. I hurried over and entered the alarm code to disable before opening the door. Cam and Evan burst in looking as rattled as I had ever seen them.

"Where's Alex?" Cam asked urgently.

"In the kitchen. It's the smoke alarm. We burnt dinner."

"What took you so long to open the door?" He demanded as Evan walked past us toward the kitchen.

"We were asleep and I had to deal with the pan before it burst into flames." Finally the deafening alarm stopped.

"Are you ok Alex?" I heard Evan ask.

"Apart from being slightly deaf you mean?" She joked, making me smile. Heavy footsteps in the hall had both Cam and I turning to the door on high alert. Cam had a hand on the weapon he wore under his jacket and I was ready to reach for my own if necessary, but we both relaxed when Cal burst through the open door a little out of breath.

"Matt, what's going on? I got the 911 text from Rob on my way home from the gym." He asked as he surveyed the room. I looked to Cam questioningly.

"I had to alert Rob something was going on. It's protocol." Cam replied with a shrug.

"Is Alex alright?" Cal asked more urgently.

"I'm here Cal, I'm good." Alex called as she popped her head out from the kitchen. "I just burnt the asparagus and it set the smoke alarm blaring."

"Sorry mate, false alarm." I added with a slap on his shoulder.

"Thank fuck for that." Cal sighed as he flopped down on my sofa. "I'll call Rob and let him know."

"We'll return to our posts." And before I could reply Cam and Evan left the apartment, closing the door behind them. I locked the door and went in search of Alex as Cal tried to settle Rob down.

"Well, this was embarrassing." Alex laughed as I locked eyes with her across the kitchen counter.

"A night we'll definitely never forget." I walked around the counter and pulled her tight into my arms. The adrenaline that had surged when I awoke and thought someone had come for her, was now receding and I wanted nothing other than to return to bed and worship her beautiful body again and again.

"Rob was half way here. I told him to go back to bed. I text Jack too so he doesn't come flying over here when he gets the 911 text." Cal called. I placed a kiss on the top of Alex's head and then left her to go back to Cal.

"I'll go and put some clothes on." Alex called as she hurried into the hall. I watched her go and then turned to Cal.

"Thanks for coming mate. I near had a bloody heart attack when that alarm went off. I thought they'd come for her." I admitted. I pulled the small handgun from the small of my back and ensured the safety was on before putting it on the coffee table and falling back into an armchair.

"Me too Matt. Thank fuck it was just a ruined dinner." Cal chuckled. "I should go, I'm beat and Jack finishes his shift in ten minutes, as long as you're both alright?"

"We're fine thanks Cal. Sorry for the drama."

"No problem." Cal dismissed as he got to his feet. He called goodnight to Alex and then left as quickly as he'd arrived. I locked the door behind him and reset the alarm for the night.

Alex walked into the lounge in bright pink sleep shorts and a white tank top. She had tied her wild hair up in a ponytail high on her head and she looked incredibly cute.

"Are you ok love?" I asked as I stalked over and pulled her back against my front. I held her close and basked in her perfect vanilla smell,

"Sure. I can't believe I ruined dinner though. It was roast beef, your favourite. It's frazzled now." She pouted.

"It doesn't matter. I had the best night of my life with you tonight baby. Nothing can change that." I leaned in and gently kissed her pouting lips, until they morphed into a beautiful smile.

"I completely agree." She purred as she pressed her body tighter into mine, her hard nipples pressing through her top and against my torso.

"Baby, you're killing me here." I growled.

"So, let's go back to bed then?" She whispered, her voice and body too bloody sexy to refuse.

"You want to go again?" I asked, wanting to be sure she was ready.

"What's wrong? Can't keep up old man?" She teased, shocking me.

"Old man?!" I shouted playfully. "I'll show you old man, you cheeky little minx!" I bent and hauled her up over my shoulder. She squealed excitedly as I marched back to our bedroom to show her over and over just how young and fit I still was.

ALEX

"Well you're very bloody happy this morning!" Lucy pointed out as we made our way through the packed out mall. It was one week until Christmas and it seemed every person in Chicago was out to shop along with me and Lucy and my security shadow.

I took a sip of the iced frappe Lucy and I had called for on our way in, to delay my answer. Matt was her brother and it definitely made it awkward to talk to her about the earth shattering night I had spent with him the night before. It had been so incredible though and I was bursting to talk about it. Matt and I had been up almost the entire night discovering each others bodies while Matt showed me what 'making love' really meant.

"Come on, tell me!" Lucy demanded.

"Last night, Matt and I…..we…...you know." I hedged.

"You did? That's great Alex…..really great, but please, no details. Ew, I can't hear about my brother…..No way! No details!" She squeaked.

"Ok, I'll spare you. It's just…..I didn't think, after everything, I never thought I could go there again and I never imagined it would be so freaking amazing!"

"I know chick. Trust me, I've been there. After what Phil did to me, I bloody hated sex. I told myself I'd never be forced to endure that hell ever again, but then there was Rob and let me tell you, sex with that man is not something you have to endure. It's bloody magic and after he showed me what I was missing I never looked back."

"Ew, I'm not sure I want to think of Rob like that to be honest!" I cried as I gave her a playful shove. She laughed too as she righted herself.

"I'm just so happy Lucy. Matt makes me feel so good and right. I forget about all of the bad stuff with him and I get to actually look forward. I never thought I'd get to such a good place in my life."

"You deserve it Alex. This is the way life should be. Some people get to spend their whole lives in this happy, contented place. We just took the harder route to it."

"Well I wish someone had told me there was a short cut!" I joked, trying to keep the mood upbeat.

"We made it. That's all that matters. We bloody made it and we're happy now." Lucy sighed. "Come on, I have a great idea for Rob for a present!" She dragged me into a photography store where we spent almost an hour being shown fancy digital cameras. Apparently Rob took a lot of photos with his cell and fancied himself a bit of an ametuer photographer, so Lucy had decided he needed some good equipment for Christmas.

When that was all bought, we went to a large jewellers where I chose Matt a sporty, yet dressy Tag watch for his present, something Lucy had told me he had always wanted.. I knew it would be good for him to wear on a daily basis and hoped he would like the modern design we chose. Lucy had assured me she thought he would. We picked up gifts for everyone else on our way through the chaos that was the mall. Buying each other gifts was more tricky because security didn't want us splitting up, so we decided instead that when all of the drama was over we would go on a girls road trip and stay at a fancy spa for a night. I loved the idea and hoped we could do it soon.

When we were finished shopping we stopped at a little restaurant in the food court and ordered pasta dishes and a glass of wine each. We were beat and glad to rest our aching feet.

"I cannot believe how busy this place is!" Lucy sighed as our food was delivered to the table.

"It is the week before Christmas." I pointed out as I tucked into my spaghetti.

"Why does everyone always have to leave it to the last minute though? It's not like they don't know Christmas is coming."

"Erm, hate to point this out hon, but we left it to the last minute." I laughed, making her smile."Come on, eat up and we'll head back to get wrapping." Lucy was about to reply when suddenly Cam and Evan approached from where they had been sat a few feet away at a seperate table.

"Sorry ladies, we need to move now!" Cam barked as Evan started grabbing all of the bags that sat on the floor by our feet.

"Why?" Lucy asked. "What's going on?"

"There's a serious threat in the vicinity." Cam said shortly, He pulled a hundred dollar bill from his pocket and slammed in on the table, then pulled me to my feet and Evan grabbed Lucy.

"What threat? Is it Marcus? Is he here?" I asked as I tried to keep up with Cam. He was holding my right hand and dragging me so fast I couldn't use my crutch for the support I needed.

"Talk later, move now!" Cam barked as he kept a good watch around us while we marched. I fought to keep up, but stumbled and ended up on my ass.

"Alex!" Lucy cried as she wriggled from Evan's hold and rushed over to me. "Are you ok?"

"Ladies, we have to move, right now!" Cam barked.

"I....I'm ok. Just give me a hand." I said to Lucy and she helped me to my feet again. Before either of us could react Cam grabbed me and started marching even faster.

"Cam, stop! You're dragging her! She has an injured leg you arsehole!" Lucy raged from where Evan was dragging her behind me.

"I'm sorry Alex, but we don't have time right now." Cam said as he continued to drag me through the mall. I had no idea who we were running from or why, but the urgency from the guys had me terrified. I dared a look behind me as we neared the exit from the mall into the parking lot, but I didn't see anyone I recognised. I heard Lucy ranting behind me, calling the guys all of the names under the sun as they just dragged us along like misbehaving dogs.

By the time we got close to Lucy's jeep my left leg was cramping painfully from being pushed too hard and I was shaking all over thanks to adrenaline.

"Ladies, you're in the SUV with me. Lucy, give Evan the keys to your Jeep and he'll drive it back." Cam barked. Lucy started looking through her purse for the keys and we turned in the direction of the Suv which was parked two rows from the jeep.

"Good lord Alicia!" The voice instantly sent ice through my veins. I looked around frantically and found Marcus leant against a fancy looking red sports car, two spaces over from the SUV we were headed for. He was dressed in a sharp black suit with a grey shirt beneath. He had barely changed in the four years since I'd last seen him. He still made every hair on my body raise in fear.

"You've certainly filled out. I'd certainly get a better price for you nowadays." He sneered. Just the sound of his voice had my heart pounding.

"Go with Evan, get in Lucy's Jeep, now!" Cam whispered in my ear, but I was frozen to the spot, paralysed with fear at the the sight of my own personal torturer. For four years he had plagued my nightmares and there he stood in the flesh. Marcus pushed off of the car and moved toward me. Still I dare not move. I couldn't make my brain or any of my muscles function. I was literally paralyzed by fear.

"Stay back or I will use force." Cam shouted, causing Marcus to grin that sadistic smile he was so damned good at.

"Yuri is waiting for you Alicia. He is willing to pay good money for your whore ass. You think these idiots or your cocksucker boyfriend can protect you? Not going to happen bitch. You know where you belong and you'll be there soon enough."

"Fuck you Marcus! I'm never going back!" I cried desperately, unable to stop the words from spilling out.

"Alex, come on. Don't let him see you scared." Lucy urged quietly, as she took my trembling hand. I looked up into her eyes and that was what I needed to make my legs move. I wouldn't let Marcus hurt her. I wanted to get as far away from him as possible. Evan led the way to Lucy's bright red Jeep and they helped me get my terrified, trembling ass into the back seat. Lucy jumped in beside me and Evan got into the driver's seat and then we were speeding out of the parking lot. Moment's later I turned to see Cam racing in the SUV behind us.

"Alex, you need to breathe chick." Lucy whispered as she took my hand and squeezed it tightly. I had no idea what she was talking about, I couldn't even process her words. Marcus had been a few feet from me. He'd sold me to Yuri. He said no one could protect me. He was still trying to get to me. Fear was not a strong enough word for what I felt.

"Evan, she's not taking deep enough breaths, she's going to pass out!" I heard Lucy cry, but still it meant

nothing. I heard Evan calling my name from the front, but I couldn't make myself react. It was like I was trapped in my head, unable to respond or even move.
"Take us to Matt's." Lucy called.
"Matt." His name felt like safety.
"It's ok hun. I'm ringing him now. He'll meet us there. You'll see him soon."
Matt. I needed his arms around me more than I needed air to breathe. I knew his strength surrounding me would be the only thing that would make me feel safe after seeing the monster that haunted my nightmares.

MATT
The previous night Alex and I had been up almost all night making love. It had been the most incredible night of my life and I was desperate for her to get home from shopping with Lucy so I could get my hands on her again.
I had plans for the evening. First we were headed to buy a christmas tree and decorations for the apartment. I had never bothered with a tree before because there was only me there and it seemed a pointless effort for just me, but now that Alex lived with me, I wanted to ensure our first Christmas together was special, so I was determined to go all out. We'd bring the tree back, decorate it and then curl up together with a Christmas movie and Thai food, before I took her back to bed and continued where we left off that morning. I could barely contain my excitement as I started to get ready, anticipating Alex's return in the next couple of hours.

I took a quick shower, following my workout for the day, then dressed in dark jeans and a black shirt, sleeves rolled to my elbows. It was smarter than my usual t-shirts, but not over the top. I rubbed a little wax through my hair, then went to make coffee while I waited eagerly for Alex to get home.

I had just sat down with the newspaper and a coffee when my phone lit up with Lucy's face. I answered eagerly, hoping they were headed back.

"Hi darling." I greeted.

"Matt, where are you?" Lucy blurted and I instantly jumped to my feet, knowing from her tone something was wrong.

"At home. Why? Where's Alex?"

"She's here Matt, but we saw her brother. He scared the crap out of her. She's freaking out and I can't get her to calm down."

"Where are you?" I asked, as I tucked the phone between my shoulder and ear so I could pull my boots on. I needed to get to Alex right away.

"We're coming to you now. Evan is driving us in my car. We'll be about five minutes."

"I'll meet you in the car park darling."

"Just hurry Matt." Lucy said and then hung up.

I shoved my mobile in my back pocket and hurriedly pulled a coat on. I couldn't believe her fucking brother had found her. Why the fuck did he have to keep torturing her? Hadn't he taken enough from her already? If he dared come near me he'd be sorry. I'd flatten the bastard.

I grabbed a blanket, knowing the way Alex trembled and shivered following a panic attack, then bolted from the apartment, sure to lock the door behind myself. I ran to the lift and beat the button until it arrived at my floor. By the time I got to the underground carpark of my building, Lucy's red Jeep was pulling in, followed by a large black SUV.

"Matt, over here!" Lucy cried as she threw the back door open. I ran over and looked in. Alex was worse than I'd ever seen her. She was completely pale and her body was vibrating in the seat she shook so badly. Her breathing was the biggest concern. She was taking frantic, very tiny short gasps, nowhere near deep enough to take in enough oxygen. Lucy jumped out of the car so I could get in.

"Hey beautiful." I whispered softly when I sat in the seat beside Alex. She didn't move her stare from the headrest of the seat in front. "Alex, can you hear me baby?"

"Marcus….he….he.." She couldn't get what she wanted to say out between her fight for air.

"I know love. I know, but he's gone now. I'm here and no one will ever hurt you while I'm here." I tried to reassure her. She moved her very shaky hand onto my knee and it was all the signal I needed that she knew it was me beside her. No longer worried I would spook her further, I grabbed her from the seat and cradled her tightly in my lap. I wrapped the blanket I had brought out, tightly about her and just held her, rocking back and forth as I encouraged her to take deep breaths.

"Come on now beautiful. Nice deep breaths for me. You can do it, I know you can." I whispered as I continued to rock her. Gradually her breathing became slower and slower until she started to regain a little colour to her face.

"Are you with me baby?" I asked after a while.

"He.....he sold me Matt.....to Yuri..... sold me to the guy who....the one who scarred my back. I can't.....I can't go back." She whimpered tearfully.

"Alex, you're never going back baby. You're with me now, where you belong. I'll never let Marcus, or Yuri, or anyone do those awful things to you ever again. He wanted to scare you today love, but that's all he could do, because Cam and Evan were there to protect you and that's the way it will be until we know for sure you're safe. He will never get his hands on you ever again." I said firmly.

"I was so scared. I couldn't move....couldn't even think.....I froze Matt."

"It's over now. Everything's ok. You're home, safe and sound."

"I love you Matt." She whispered and I knew she was exhausted.

"I love you too baby. Shall we go up and you can rest for a while?" I offered. Alex nodded, tears still streaming down her face. I gathered her tighter to me and then climbed out of the car. I wasn't surprised to find Lucy wrapped protectively in Rob's arms. I knew his guys would have called him and he would have wanted to check on the ladies.

"Is she ok Matt?" Lucy asked with worry.

"Better for now. I'm taking her up to rest. Are you coming up?"

"If it's ok?"

"Of course darling. Come on. We could probably all do with a drink."

"You can put me down Matt. I can walk." Alex said as we made our way to the lifts.

"I've got you love. I like having you in my arms." I placed a kiss on her head and smiled as she just relaxed into me and closed her eyes. It soothed me to know I gave her safety. After the hell her life had been I was happy to be that for her.

When we got into the apartment Alex just wanted to rest, so I took her to our room and got her settled with the TV on quietly in the background, then laid with her for ten minutes until she was sound asleep, exhausted both physically and emotionally. When I was sure she was fast asleep and settled I crept from the room to talk to Rob and find out what the hell had happened.

"How is she?" Lucy asked from where she and Rob sat at the breakfast bar in the kitchen, as soon as I stepped out of the hall.

"She's ok. Just shattered. She's asleep." I walked into the kitchen and leant against the worktop opposite them. "What happened?"

"I just went through everything with the guys. While the ladies were stopped for lunch Cam spotted Marcus watching them from the floor above. They moved toward the vehicles as quick as possible, but Marcus was waiting by the SUV. Alex froze up and it took a while to get her to Lucy's car. In that time he threatened her, scared her, but didn't get near her. He didn't follow, Cam checked the whole way back. They're checking the cars for trackers, but I don't think this guy is that clever." Rob surmised.

"So he just wanted to scare her then?"

"Seems like it. He made no move to grab her."

"What did he say to her?"

"He looks like a real fucking psycho Matt. He told her she had filled out and he'd be able to get more for her now. What does that mean?" Lucy asked.

"Her brother…..he used to let criminals he dealt with use her. He kept her locked up and gave her no option. They forced themselves on her and hurt her and he profited from it." I explained, knowing Alex wouldn't mind Lucy knowing.

"Oh God Matt! That's…...poor Alex. If I'd known I'd have given the bastard a slap for what he said to her. How could he? His own sister?"

"He's an animal Lucy. Did he say anything else?" I asked.

"He said some guy was willing to pay a lot of money for her and he was waiting, told Alex no one could protect her, that she'd be where she belongs soon. He mentioned you too Matt, said her boyfriend couldn't protect her."

"We'll see about that! Fucking prick!" I hissed angrily.

"Did he give the guys name? The one he said would pay for her?" Rob asked.

"Yuri. That was the name."

"Sokolov?" I looked to Rob.

"I'd guess so. Alex said there was a Yuri before didn't she?" Rob asked.

"Yeah, and earlier in the car Alex said Marcus was going to sell her to someone who used to hurt her. It had to be him. Can you do some digging?"

"Already on it." Rob said, holding up his mobile, which he was clicking away on. I nodded and moved to get glasses down. I needed a drink and Lucy still looked shaken too. I pulled half a bottle of red from the fridge and held it up to Lucy.

"Oh jesus yes, please Matt." She sighed. I poured us both a glass and grabbed Rob a water, knowing he wouldn't drink while working.

"Are you alright darling?" I asked as I handed her the glass of wine.

"Yeah, it was just hard to see Alex so terrified. She's always so tough. I didn't know what to do."

"I think she's tough when she needs to be because of what that dick put her through. She refuses to let anyone have power over her like he did, but when it's actually him she's faced with, it's just too terrifying for her. You did well darling, getting her away and bringing her here. It was the best thing you could have done for her."

"You calm her Matt, make her feel safe. I knew you'd bring her round." Lucy said with a gentle smile.

"She'll be ok once she's had some rest. Like you said she's tough. That bastard was wrong. I can and will protect her."

"She knows that. The only time she plucked up the courage to speak was when he mentioned you. Just the mention of you made her braver." I nodded and took a drink of wine to settle my anger at what that bastard had said to Alex. He needed taking care of. I needed to find a way to get him out of Alex's life as soon as possible.

"Right, I've got a couple of guys looking into Yuri Sokolov. Cam and Evan are headed to the office to fill out an incident report on today and Alec and Gareth are now on duty here."

"Thanks mate. Let me know if you turn anything up on that Russian."

"You need to talk to your team about Alex, Rob. They really dragged her around today and she ended up falling."

"What?" I snapped, angry at the thought of the men there to protect her, hurting her.

"They have a job to do sweetheart. They had to get both of you to the cars as quickly as possible." Rob explained.

"Yeah, I get that Rob, but Cam grabbed Alex's hand and literally dragged her through the mall. He went so quick she had no chance of using her crutch and she couldn't keep up because of her leg injury. She stumbled and fell and they didn't even check she was ok, just pulled her up and again with the dragging. I even tried to tell Cam he needed to slow down, but he just ignored me. By the time we got to the carpark and were faced with her brother, she was so exhausted and in pain she stood no chance of standing up to anyone. It wasn't right Rob."

"That's not on mate. Allowances need to be made where possible. She gets alot of pain in that leg and there's only so fast she can move."

"I'll talk to them all, make sure they're aware and take it into account when working with Alex." Rob said, then turned to Lucy. "I'm sorry sweetheart. You're right, that wasn't right. I'll talk to Cam about it." He placed a kiss on her forehead and she melted in his arms. "I'm going to head to the office for a few hours. Shall I give you a ride home?"

"No, it's ok. I'll drive. I'll walk down with you though." Lucy said, as she finished the last of her wine and shrugged on her coat. "Have Alex ring me later." She said as she reached up to kiss my cheek.

"I will darling. Drive safe." I gave her a brief hug and then showed them both out. Rob assured me he would call later with news on the Russian and hopefully Marcus' whereabouts, then they headed for the lift and I closed the door. I set the alarm and went through to lie with the woman I loved.

ALEX

I woke up later that afternoon, feeling more energised, but still shaken. Waking to find Matt laid beside me, watching over me had helped to ease my anxiety some though and once I had eaten the soup Matt warmed for me and changed into clean clothes, I felt much more like myself.

Matt wanted to go Christmas tree shopping and after a little coaxing and promises he would keep me safe I agreed and even felt pretty excited about it as we climbed into Matt's Range Rover. I had never had a Christmas tree. As a child my family celebrated the holiday, but I was never included. Then, since moving to Chicago I had spent Christmases in my apartment, alone. I never saw the need to waste money on a tree or decorations when it would only be for me, so I never bothered.

So as Matt and I pulled into a large yard filled with fresh cut Christmas pines I was really excited. First we went into the little store and Matt dutifully pushed a cart as I filled it with all of the decorations I wanted for the tree. We ended up with a lot of glass tree ornaments and baubles, all sticking to the red and gold colour theme I had settled on. I also bought lights, stockings for Matt and I and a huge holly wreath for the apartment door. I was determined if we were doing it, we were going all out. When we had bought out almost the entire store, Matt loaded everything into his back seat and we went to pick out a tree.

"Which one should we pick?" I asked with the wonder of a small child as we walked through the rows and rows of pine trees.

"Whichever one you want baby." Matt said as he leant down to kiss me briefly.

"How big do you think?"

"Well, considering we need to get it either inside, or on the roof of my car, I'd say six foot is probably about our limit."

"Six foot? That's gonna be huge!" I couldn't hide my excitement even if I'd have tried. I was having too much fun.

I dragged Matt around the whole lot to make sure we picked the absolute best tree. He didn't complain or get bored of my constant chatter on the merits of each tree. He just held my hand and smiled as we went, entering his own opinion when I requested it. Eventually I picked a very full, beautiful six foot tall spruce and we waited while it was loaded onto the roof of Matt's car, then we were on our way home to decorate it. I bounced up and down excitedly the whole way home, the events that had frozen me with fear earlier that afternoon, long since forgotten.

I was in hysterics as Matt fought to carry the huge tree into the elevator and then out again and into our apartment. Alec and Gareth, who had shadowed us the whole trip, followed with the bags of decorations. Everything was dumped in the lounge and I collapsed down on the sofa, still laughing so hard I cried as the guys cleared the apartment room by room. I watched Alec and Gareth leave as I fought to reign in my laughter, then turned to Matt.

"That was so much fun Matt. Thank you." I said as I got up and approached him. I locked my hands behind his head, my arms rested on his shoulders and snaked around his neck. He pulled me in closer and then our lips met. Matt kissed me in that magic way only he could, claiming me, letting me know with every touch the love he felt. I kissed him back, hoping he felt my love for him in just the same way.

"Come on baby. Let's get this tree up before I drag you back to bed and have my wicked way with you."

"I'm sure the tree will wait." I whispered, feeling needy at even the mention of Matt having his way with me.

"Later baby, I promise." One more chaste kiss to my lips and then Matt was freeing the tree from it's net and fixing it into the base we had bought to hold it up.

The next hour was spent with stringing baubles and ornaments and lovingly hanging then on our first ever Christmas tree. Matt wrapped the lights evenly around the tree and I followed with the decorations. I got a strange look from Alec when I popped out of the apartment to hang the wreath, but ignored him and carried on.

"You want to do the star love?" Matt asked when the star at the top of the tree was all we had left to do.

"Definitely." I said with a huge smile I couldn't contain. Matt nodded and before I knew what was happening he had me lifted in his arms so I could reach the top. I laughed happily as I carefully placed the glittering gold star we had picked out, as the crowning glory of our tree.

Matt put me down and moved over to the socket where the lights were plugged in.

"Ready?" He asked.

"No! Wait. We need to shut the lights off!" I cried as I hurried to flip all the lights in the apartment off. When darkness descended I moved back in front of the tree.

"Ok, now," I told Matt and suddenly the tree was lit up with hundreds of twinkling LED lights. It was so pretty and I was instantly emotional.

"You like it beautiful?" Matt asked as his arms encircled my waist from behind.

"It's perfect Matt. I love it." I replied tearfully.

"Me too baby." He whispered. "You did a great job."

"We both did. This is going to be such an amazing holiday Matt. I just know it."

"It is baby. I'll make sure of it, this Christmas and every single one that follows. We're going to be so happy you and I Alex."

"Forever." I whispered, as I stared adoringly at the tree, feeling safe and loved pressed against Matt with his arms holding me close. It was one of many perfect moments Matt had given me in the time I had known him, moment's I had waited my whole miserable life to experience, but never expected to actually happen. He was right, we would be happy if I could ever escape the darkness that followed me.

"Forever." He said with a carefully placed kiss behind my ear.

That night we made love beneath that beautiful Christmas tree and Matt showed me over and over what a 'merry Christmas' really was.

***

We woke the day before Christmas eve to over 12 inches of snow which had dropped overnight. I walked into the lounge that morning and almost cried at the sight of the beautiful christmas tree sat in front of the windows, overlooking the white blanketed city. It was a magical sight and just how I had dreamt a Christmas should be.

"Very festive, isn't it love?" Matt asked as he strolled toward me from the kitchen, a mug of black coffee in hand.

"I can't believe we are actually going to have a white Christmas! Can it get any more perfect?"

"It can. The guys and I have plans for today. I'm not working until six, Jack's off and Cal and Rob are bunking off. We're all going to have some fun."

"Really?" I asked excitedly.

"Really baby. Go get dressed and wrap up as warm as possible. I'll make us a quick breakfast, then we're meeting the others at ten."

"I'm so excited right now!" I squealed as I launched myself the few feet to Matt. I reached up and kissed him a little wildly, hoping to show him how blissfully happy he made me. "Love you sexy." I said as I turned toward the bedroom.

"Love you too beautiful."

MATT

Alex really was like a kid hopped up on sugar as we drove out of the city and toward the national park we'd all agreed to meet at. The roads were sketchy with the snow, but there wasn't really any ice and my range rover was well equipped to handle it.

As soon as I woke that morning and saw the snow, I knew Alex would love it and I wanted to do something special for her. She was seriously in love with Christmas and everything that came with it and I wanted to continue that for her, so I'd rung Jack who was always my ideas man. He suggested Alex had probably never really just got to play in the snow, like kids do. She grew up in LA and since she'd been in the city she had probably never been steady enough on her feet to go out into the snow.

Jack had arranged it all for me, checked the roads to the national park were clear and been out to buy sledges. Rob and Cal had liked the idea of letting loose and having some fun, so everyone was on board and I knew Alex was going to love it.

"Are we here?" Alex asked as I pulled into the car park and saw Rob's SUV ahead.

"Yeah baby. We're here." I parked up and Alex was out of the car before I even had the hand brake on.

"Matt, this place is breathtaking." Alex gasped as I got out of the car and made my way around to her. I looked around and had to agree. All you could see for miles around was beautiful landscapes framed by mountains in the background. The snow was deeper and untouched, making everything sparkle in the morning sunlight. Jack had picked well.

"It is. We're spending the day here love. There's apparently a very good hill for sledging and Jack bought sledges. You up for that?" I asked.

"Damn right I am! I've never done that before."

"Hey guys." We both looked up to find Rob climbing out of his SUV, dressed in jeans, huge snow boots and a heavy puffer coat.

"Hi mate." I greeted. Cal and Jack jumped out next, dressed very similarly to Rob. They were both grinning like idiots and I knew the day of child's play we had planned was right up their street.

"Where's Lucy?" Alex asked after greeting them all.

"In the car. She says she's not leaving the heat until she has to." Rob laughed as he started unloading bags and sledges from his boot.

"Lucy isn't a big fan of the cold." I explained further, making everyone laugh.

"Understatement of the decade." Jack added.

"I'll get her ass out here." I watched as Alex trudged through the snow. I had been worried about how well she would manage. Walking in foot deep snow was hard for anyone, but her weak leg would really struggle. She was getting stronger every day she worked with Cal and she barely used her crutch in the apartment any more. I'd told her she wouldn't be able to use it today, it would have been too difficult for her in the conditions, so she'd left it at home. Watching her walk the few feet to Rob's passenger door I saw she was managing pretty well, but she'd be exhausted if she had to go far. Good job I had a plan.

"Lucy! Get your ass out here right now. It's not that cold!" Alex chided playfully as she ripped the passenger door open.

"Are you joking? It's bloody freezing!" Lucy ranted. We all laughed as Alex grabbed Lucy and hauled her out of the car. Lucy sulked as she pulled on a wooly hat and thick padded gloves, but within minutes Alex had her in stitches with something she'd whispered to her.

Jack and Cal pulled on large rucksacks, filled with snacks and drinks and some supplies just in case anything arose and carried four brightly coloured plastic sledges.

I walked over to Alex and bent down in front of her.

"Come on baby. Hop up." I instructed. Alex beamed at me, before running a little and leaping onto my back. I stood and jostled her until I had a good grip on her thighs. She wrapped her arms around my neck and laughed, sounding so carefree that it warmed my heart.

"Your ride awaits too sweetheart." Rob offered as he bent down in front of Lucy. She laughed and climbed on his back, holding on around his neck tightly as he lifted her with a lot more ease than I'd managed. He was however a lot bigger than me.

"Cal?" Jack piped up. "Where's my damn ride?"

"Dream on lover." Cal replied, making us all laugh as we set out into the park. The walk to the sledging hill was about half a mile and we got about half of that before Alex decided I had carried her far enough and should put her down. I just laughed off her protests and continued on following Jack and Cal.

"Right, who's up first?" Cal asked when we reached the top of the steep hill. All around us everything was still and silent and the view from where we stood was outstanding. It really was the most amazing place to spend the day.

"Maybe Jack should go first." Lucy suggested. "Then if he's killed I'll give it a miss."

"So it's like that is it sweet?" Jack mock pouted.

"I'll go first!" Alex volunteered. I could tell she was bursting to have a go. I put her down and took a red sledge from Cal.

"Do you know what you're doing?" I asked.

"Sliding down a snowy hill on a piece of plastic. Not much to it really, is there?" She quipped, making me smile.

"Smart arse." I muttered as I held the sledge and helped her climb in.

"Give me one. We'll go together." Lucy said as she stepped forward. Jack put down a blue sledge and helped Lucy into it.

"Ready?" Alex asked as they looked to each other, their eyes aglow with excitement.

"Let's go!" Lucy cried and Jack and I both pushed the sledges off. The silent park was filled with overjoyed squeals as they sped down the hill and landed on their backs in the deep snow at the bottom.

"That was freaking amazing!" Alex yelled as she got to her feet.

"Bloody terrifying, more like." Lucy quipped with a grin. As they both scaled back up the hill, Jack and Cal took the other two sledges and had a turn, laughing heartily the entire way down.

We spent a couple of hours just like that, up and down that steep hill over and over. Alex loved it and screamed excitedly each time she flew down on the sledge. We went down together on one sledge several times and I loved seeing her excitement and enjoyment up close as we landed in a tangled heap, laughing joyfully at the bottom.

Before long the big kids in Jack and Cal came out in full force and they started rolling around, launching snowballs at each other. Rob soon joined in while Lucy, Alex and I just watched on, laughing at the way he and Jack had turned it into a military operation.

As Cal passed in front of where we stood, Jack threw a huge snowball, missing Cal who ducked and hitting Alex square in the face. Everyone stopped dead as she brushed the snow from her face.

"Jack, you idiot!" I shouted as I hurried over to help her and make sure it hadn't caused injury. It had been thrown with some force.

"Alex, I'm so sorry sweet. Are you ok?" Jack asked with real regret. Alex swiped the last of the snow from her face and looked directly across to him.

"You are going down soldier boy!" She wailed and then started gathering a snowball. Before Jack realised what was coming, she hit the top of his head with her snowball and Cal burst out laughing.

"Oh, it's on right now!" Jack said and then everyone was launching balls of snow at one another, even Lucy who had teamed up with Alex to focus solely on getting Jack. Before long the ladies were bored of Jack evading their hits and just launched themselves at him when he wasn't expecting it. They landed on top of him, shoving him face first into the snow.

"Say we win!" Alex demanded as they fought to hold him down.

"Never!" Jack cried, so Lucy started stuffing snow inside his coat and up his shirt until he finally admitted defeat and told them they won.

"Thanks for all the help there babe." Jack joked to Cal when he was finally allowed up.

"I thought an ex-marine would be able to handle two five foot nothing girls. You're losing your edge Jack." Cal retorted, making us all laugh.

"Come on. Much as I enjoy watching Jack get his ass kicked, we should head back and stop for some lunch on the way." Rob declared. Alex and Lucy looked frozen and I agreed it was time to get them warmed up.

"I did not get my ass kicked!" Jack pouted as he started gathering everything up. "I had to let them win or they'd have sulked all afternoon."

"Whatever you say man." Rob chuckled.

ALEX

We stopped about half way back to the city at a cute little 1950's style diner. I was swept up in the wonderful fun we had all had out on that hill all morning. I had felt more alive than ever before with the man I loved and family I adored. I was free of my crutch and had forgotten all about my injury amidst all of the excitement. It truly had been a magical day and I was so grateful to all of them for giving it to me.

"That's so good." I sighed as I took a long drink of the warm hot cocoa I'd ordered. It was just what I needed to heat my chilled bones.

"Did you have fun baby?" Matt asked as he wrapped his arm around my shoulders and pulled me in close.

"So much fun. It was great Matt. I enjoyed every minute." I replied, sinking into the heat of his body.

We all laughed and joked during our huge lunch in that quiet little diner that afternoon. Everyone was happy and excited. The whole day had been carefree and joyful, just as I had always imagined family should be, during all those years I had spent alone, wishing for one of my own. There, in that diner I had my family and I loved them all. They had brought so much joy and contentment to my life, things I had never imagined I could actually have. I wasn't alone any longer. I had a man I loved with everything in me and a family to call my own. As I sat back and watched them all laughing at something Rob had said I realised every hope I had ever harboured when I was imprisoned in my family home for those awful years, had now come true for me. I had everything I had ever wanted and so much more.

***

Matt had quickly changed and headed off for work almost as soon as we'd arrived back from our day out. He was working a long night shift, but then had the rest of Christmas Eve and the next day off, so we couldn't complain. I had hated to watch him go after such a magical day together though. I never wanted the magic to end, but he had to go, so I had kissed him passionately and waved him off at the door.

I decided on a long soak in the huge jacuzzi tub Matt had fitted in the main bathroom after the night we had discussed it at Rob and Lucy's months back. I set the water running, went to gather clean pyjamas and then to the kitchen for a glass of wine. I filled a large glass with shiraz and took a minute to sit at the breakfast bar to go through my mail which Cam had brought up from the lobby with him as he took up his post before Matt left. There were some forms for me to fill out from my lawyer to complete the sale of my apartment and a Christmas card from a girl I used to work with at the unemployment office.

The last was a thick, large red envelope and I wondered if it was one of those fancy, hand-crafted Christmas cards from someone else I used to work with.

Deciding I'd open it later, I put it aside and hurried to the bathroom, just in time to shut the faucet off before the tub overflowed.

I set my playlist on my cell playing over the bluetooth speaker and then relaxed with my glass of wine in the dreamy warm water, the jets bubbling away soothingly. It was a piece of heaven, for sure.

Just when I thought I was so relaxed, I may drift off to sleep, my cell rang, startling me awake. I hurriedly dried my hands and, seeing it was lucy, hit loudspeaker.

"Hey you." I answered.

"Hi chick. I just wanted to check in. I know Matt's working." I smiled at that. It was so nice to have people who cared enough to check in on me.

"I'm good. Matt left about an hour ago, so I'm just having a soak in the tub, then I'm going to have an early night with some Mission Impossible."

"Good plan. You can't go wrong with Tom." Lucy laughed.

"My thoughts exactly."

"Ok. I won't keep you Alex. Rob and I are here so just ring if you need anything. I'll see you at Jack and Cal's party tomorrow."

"Thanks for checking in hon. See you tomorrow." We said goodbye and I felt a little emotional to know she had gone to the trouble of calling me, just because she knew I was alone. It was kindness I was so unaccustomed to, but was coming to love.

Deciding I should get out of the tub before I really did nod off and drown myself, I finished my wine and then dragged my ass out of the blissful warmth.

After drying off and slipping into sleep shorts and a matching tank top, I headed to the kitchen for some water to take to bed with me. I rinsed out my wine glass and set it upside down to dry, then grabbed a bottle of water and headed to the door to tell Cam I was going to bed for the night. I stopped as I passed the breakfast bar, noticing the Christmas card I hadn't opened before. I put the water down and slid my finger across the top of the envelope, tearing it open. I pulled out a Christmas card with a winter scene on the front. Realising there must be something inside for it to be so thick. I opened it and couldn't hold in my gasp at what fell out. It was photo's of blood, so much blood surrounding dismembered body parts. There were at least a dozen photos, all of body parts sat in pools of blood. I looked through all the pictures, unable to stop myself, just needing to know who the body or bodies belonged to. It was the very last two photos that told me what I needed to know. Each of the last two pictures were heads, cut from the bodies, laid on a tile floor looking right at me from the image. The first was my father and the second was my mother. They were dead.

I dropped the photos and looked at the card again. It had a message scrawled in it.

They are dead because of you.

You killed everyone I ever loved.

Time for me to repay the favour Alicia and then you'll return to where you belong.

Merry Christmas dear sister.

Be seeing you very soon.

I dropped the card and backed away from it all. He was threatening everyone I loved. Matt and my family could all be in danger because of me. I had to do something. I had to warn them all.

Snapping from my terror filled trance, I raced to the bathroom where my cell still sat plugged into the speaker. I pulled it free and dialled Lucy's number. She answered almost immediately.

"Hi chick. You ok?" She asked on answering.

"N-no….not really. Rob, can I speak to Rob?" I asked, my voice trembling.

"Of course hun, just a second." I sat my shaking body down on the edge of the tub as I listened to Lucy pass the phone over.

"Alex, it's me. You ok sweetheart?" Rob asked.

"I….I got a card…..f-from him. There's photo's in it. My parents….they're dead and….."

"Alex, just take some deep breaths for me." Rob instructed. "I want you to go to the front door and let Cam in. I'm coming over now. Everything will be ok."

"He….he said he'll kill everyone I love Rob. You have to warn Jack and Cal and….Matt, he's working. You can't leave Lucy either. Please, don't let him hurt anyone." I babbled.

"Alex, no one will get hurt. I'll speak to everyone on my way over and warn them and I'll get one of my guys to sit with Lucy. Everything will be alright. Just try to calm down and let Cam in, ok? Can you do that?"

"Yeah...yes. I'll do that."

"Good girl. I'm coming over now. Don;t touch the card or photos again, ok?" I agreed and Rob hung up, after again assuring me he'd be there soon. I put my cell on the windowsill in the bathroom and took a deep breath to steel myself, then moved through the lounge to the front door. I opened it and found Cam stood waiting to come in.

"Rob called. Are you alright Alex?" He asked as he laid his hands on my shoulders. I still trembled, unable to remove the images in the photos from playing on a loop in my head.

"Sure." I lied. "Rob said you should come in. The card's over there." I explained, my voice strained because of the tears that fought for release. Cam nodded and moved me from the door so he could lock it and re-set the alarm.

"Come sit down," He suggested as he wrapped an arm around me and led me to the sofa. I allowed him to lead me to the seat, feeling too shaken to form a coherent thought myself.

"Stay here. I'll be right back."Cam said, then he headed toward the kitchen where moments later I heard him cursing as he looked at the photos where I'd thrown them down on the counter. I pulled my knees up to my chest and buried my face in them as I tried to process what had happened. Had my parents been killed by whoever they or Marcus, or possibly all of them, owed money to? If so, that couldn't be my fault could it? I tried to reason whether or not I actually felt sad my parents were dead or if it was just the shock of seeing the sick way they'd been killed. It had been a violent intrusion into my happy, peaceful life with Matt and I had been ill prepared to deal with it.

I was torn from my thoughts by a hard knocking on the door of the apartment, that instantly terrified me.

"Cam!" I cried desperately and he was instantly there.

"It's ok Alex. I've got it."

"Alex, it's me hon." Cal called through the door as Cam approached it. He unset the alarm and let a very dishevelled looking Cal in. He wore scruffy joggers and a creased t-shirt and his hair stuck up wildly. I realised he must have been sleeping and just thrown something on.

"Rob called and told us what happened. Are you ok honey?" He asked as he hurried over and bent down in front of me.

"Where's Jack?" I asked as I looked across to him. "You shouldn't leave him alone. You need to stay together."

"Alex, it's ok. Rob warned us about the threat. Jack's tucked up in bed with his gun. He's working in a few hours so he needed to sleep. He can take care of himself. He'll be fine, plus Evan is out there."

"I'm so scared he'll hurt you guys." I whimpered as the tears fought their way free. I was instantly wrapped in Cal's arms as he held me tightly

"Everything will be just fine honey. Don't let him get to you." He soothed. I cried into his shoulder as I tried to make sense of it all in my head.

"Cal, is she ok?" Rob's voice cut into my thoughts a few minutes later. My head shot up and I looked around until my blurry, tear filled vision met Rob's face.

"Did you speak to Matt?" I asked urgently.

"I did. I called him at the hospital and told him what had happened. He's going to watch his back and he said to say he'll be back as soon as he can get away."

"Thank you." I whispered. "And Lucy?"

"Gareth is at my place with her. Everyone is safe Alex, I promise sweetheart." I nodded and watched as Rob walked over to the counter and pulled on a pair of blue surgical gloves, so he could go through the photos and read the card. When he'd looked at them all he turned to Cal.

"Did you look at these?" He asked.

"No, not yet." Cal replied.

"I'm so sorry you had to look at these honey." Rob said as he looked to me.

"Do you think it was the Sokolovs?" I asked, my voice weak and trembling.

"It's possible, though I think they're usually a little more discreet than this. I'll call my FBI contact and have him send someone to come and pick these up. He'll send agents to the family home to check it out."

"He said they're dead because of me. Did this happen because Yuri wanted to buy me and I got away?" I asked through the lump in my throat. Rob pulled the gloves off and stuffed them in his pocket as he rounded the sofa and crouched down in front of me.

"Sweet heart, this has nothing to do with you. Your family were greedy and this time they got mixed up in something much bigger than them, in their need for money. Whatever happened to them, they brought on themselves. Marcus is just using this as another way to torture you and I promise, I'm going to bring him down Alex. He's finished when I've done with him."

"I just want him to leave me alone. They had nothing to do with me for four years. Why come back to haunt me now?"

"They're sick Alex. They saw you as a way to settle a debt and that's why they hunted you down. Now it's all backfired. Your parents are dead and Marcus is looking for someone to blame, but he won't win Alex. We're not the only ones on his tail. The FBI wants him brought in for questioning and now, with these photos I think he will have jumped to the top of their wanted list." He smiled reassuringly as he reached behind me to the back of the sofa and pulled out the blanket that sat there. He opened it up and wrapped it around my shaking body. "We've got you Alex, I promise honey. We've all got you." He whispered. He gently kissed my forehead, then moved over to the kitchen to make a call. I sank into Cal's arms once again and let tiredness pull me under.

***

It was Jack's voice that woke me. I opened my eyes and found my head still buried in Cal's chest, my body snuggled tight into him on the sofa.

"How has she been?" Jack asked.

"She's been asleep for a couple of hours. She was really shaken up, which is no surprise. Rob showed me the photos and they were bad Jack. They turned my stomach and I did twenty years on the job, plus it was her parents in them, their bodies dismembered."

"Fucking sonofabitch! Why would he send her that? He's sick." Jack whisper shouted.

"You can say that again." Cal agreed. "You heading to work?"

"Yeah. I should be home by five tonight. You think we should still go ahead with the party?" Jack asked. They had planned to hold a Christmas eve party at Cal's gym that night, just friends and family and I had been so looking forward to it. I loved the idea of dressing up and letting my hair down with Matt and the others.

"You better." I piped up as I turned in Cal's arms and looked across to where Jack sat in an armchair.

"Hey sweet." He said with a warm smile.

"Hi Jack. Sorry, I didn't mean to eavesdrop. Just, please don't cancel the party. I'm so looking forward to it and so is Lucy."

"If you're sure honey?" Cal said hesitantly. "It's ok to not be alright after all that happened tonight."

"I know, but I am ok. They weren't really my parents were they? My mother didn't even make me and my father, well, that is literally the only thing he ever did do for me. I didn't know them except for the feel of their fists hitting me and their hands around my throat. I'm not sorry they're dead. I know how that makes me sound, but I'm really not sorry and I won't pretend to be." I admitted.

"After everything they put you through sweet, I think you're entitled to feel that way. We understand, but you still saw something horrifying tonight and you don't have to be strong for us."

"Jack, I've been the body laid in pools of blood before, luckily I wasn't dead or hacked up, , but I've woken up in huge pools of my own blood, terrified and suffering because of them and Marcus, just like those photos. I won't say the images didn't get to me, because they did. They were awful, but it's not the first time I've seen, or lived something so awful, not by a long way. At least for once it wasn't my blood. I really am ok."

Cal pulled me tighter into his chest and held me close. I knew what I'd said had hit a chord with the guys and I felt bad for bringing any of it up.

"So can we still get our party on tonight, please?" I asked, hoping to change the mood.

"As long as you go to bed and get some proper sleep. Deal?" Jack asked as he brushed my wild hair from my face and tucked it affectionately behind my ear..

"Deal. Thank you." Jack got to his feet and leant in to kiss my forehead,

"I need to get to the hospital. I'll see you tonight." He said with his trademark, million dollar smile. He leant behind me and shared a brief kiss with Cal and then left.

"Did Rob leave?" I asked Cal as I looked around and found we were the only people in the apartment.

"Yeah. He waited for the FBI tech to come and collect the card and photos, then went home to be with Lucy. He said he'd call when he got news of what's happened."

"I should get some sleep, like Jack said." I said reluctantly. I didn't want to leave the safety that Cal gave me, but he probably wanted to get to his bed too and he couldn't do that with me laid against him.

"You want me to stay until Matt gets home?" He offered and I let out the breath I was holding.

"Yes please Cal, if it's ok. I don't want to be alone tonight. I'm being a chicken I know."

"After everything that's happened recently Alex, there's nothing wrong with not wanting to be alone. Hell, I'm not sure I want to be alone either. This way we both win." He said, making me smile. I knew he'd said that for my benefit. If there was one thing I knew about the guys in my new family, it was that they did not scare easily.

"Thank you." I whispered with relief.

"Come on honey. Let's get you settled." I got to my feet and followed Cal through to the bedroom. He helped me get settled in bed, tucking me in under the thick comforter, like a child and making me feel loved and safe.

"I'll just check the door's locked and set the alarm, then I'll be right back hon." He said as he slipped from the room. I snuggled down and was just dropping off as Cal returned. He lay beside me on top of the covers and gently brushed his hand over my hair as I drifted into a settled sleep.

CAL

I had drifted off to sleep myself not long after Alex. It was the early hours of the morning and I'd had only an hour of sleep at home before Rob called to warn us there had been a threat on all of us.

Knowing how upset Alex would be I had dressed hurriedly and left Jack to sleep, so I could check on her. While she had been shaken and scared, she had done a remarkable job of holding it together and I found myself very proud of her and how strong she could be. In the short time I had known Alex, I had grown close to her. She was a tough cookie who didn't take any crap and I found myself feeling a big brotherly kind of love and responsibility toward her, wanting to be there to protect and care for her, things she had been lacking for her entire life.

Working with her at the gym and the daily physio had only cemented my protective instincts toward her, watching the way she pushed every day to improve her mobility and also the way she took a no nonsense attitude with the egotistical regulars at the gym. She constantly surprised and impressed me, making me feel every bit a proud big brother.

It was the feeling of someone in the room that had me jumping awake early the next morning. I sat up and hurriedly looked around, relieved when I saw Matt sneaking into the room looking exhausted and stressed.

"Morning mate. How has she been?" Matt whispered as he approached.

"She's slept pretty well. She was obviously shaken when we got here, but as always with Alex, she handled it well." I explained as I stood.

"Jack told me about the photos. This Marcus is so fucked up."

"It was bad Matt. The bodies were completely dismembered, but Jack and I had a chat with Alex earlier and let her know it was ok to be upset, but she was determined she was ok and to be honest, I think she is. She said it herself, she's lived worse."

"I wish to God she hadn't." Matt sighed.

"I know man, we all do. Hopefully we can put an end to it all for good now. The parents are gone. Just the brother left to deal with."

"Shame whoever it was couldn't dismember that fucker while they were at it!" Matt hissed and I felt his anger. Alex had already been through more than any one person should have to endure. The need to put a stop to it all was burning within each of us because we all cared for her so much.

"Rob called his guy at the FBI. They're looking for Marcus now to bring him in for questioning. He won't be on the streets for much longer."

"Let's hope they get him soon and find plenty to put him away. I want Alex to be able to move forward without his threats hanging over her."

"It won't be long Matt. Just keep on doing what you're doing. I really think, despite all this shit with her family, Alex is happier here with you, than she's ever been."

"The feeling's mutual." Matt said with a smile down at where Alex slept.

"I should go. I need to get a couple of hours shut eye, then start setting up for tonight. Alex wanted us to go ahead with the party so we agreed we would."

"Glad to hear it. She's really looking forward to it."

"Me too." I said with a smile. Jack and I had made a decision in the chaos of the last few weeks and we were surprising our friends with the news that night. I couldn't wait to tell everyone I cared about that in one week I would be marrying the love of my life. It would be the greatest thing that ever happened to me. I knew for sure, because Jack was the greatest thing that ever happened to me and solidifying that relationship with vows could only make it stronger.

"Thanks so much for staying with her mate."

"Anytime Matt. I'm always here for her."

"Thanks Cal. It means a lot. See you tonight?"

"Yeah, about eight at the gym. Rob's handling security so It'll be safe." Matt nodded and I turned and left with a skip in my step. One week and I would be a married man with an amazing adopted family behind me. Life really didn't get much better.

ALEX

"Baby, are you trying to kill me?" Matt groaned when I walked from our room dressed for the party that night. I had on a metallic silver dress which was short at the front, reaching the middle of my thigh, but dipped lower at the back. In the front it covered up my chest, where it tied with thin straps around my neck, but the back was completely open right down to about two inches above my ass. I had gone braless underneath and paired it with a small matching metallic silver platform shoe and purse. My hair was pinned up with just a few loose curls set free to frame my face. I had spent over an hour diligently applying makeup, including a few strategically placed false eyelashes to add to my eye makeup.

"Do I look ok?" I asked nervously, pulling on the short hem at the front.

"Alex, you look stunning baby. I just spent forty minutes getting ready and now I'm gonna have to start all over because I need a really fucking cold shower after seeing you in that dress." He said, making me giggle. He really did look very handsome himself in his charcoal suit with a pristine white shirt beneath, the top two buttons open giving off that smart casual vibe he always wore so well. His hair was waxed in place as always and I could smell his sexy as hell spicy aftershave from where I stood.

"You look pretty great yourself Dr Simmons." I purred as I walked toward him and put my hands either side of his waist. He leant in and kissed me, his masculine scent intoxicating me and sending me wild with need for him.

"So beautiful." He whispered when he pulled back and rested his forehead on mine. "We should go before I give in and rip that dress clean off you."

"I like the sound of that. Maybe we could be late."

"Jesus love. You really are trying to kill me." Matt growled. "Come on. We'll get to that, later."

"I'm holding you to that." I teased as I turned and headed for the door. I wrapped my black wool coat around my shoulders. There was no way I was going out in snowy December in that tiny dress alone. Matt pulled his overcoat on too and then wrapped an arm around my shoulders as we headed for Cam's SUV. He was our shadow for the night, driving us there and bringing us home again.

Matt gripped me tighter as we hit the street. Some of the snow had melted and turned to ice and not only was I in heels, I had decided to go without my crutch at the party knowing Matt and the others would be there to lean on when needed. Ice, I had not anticipated though.

"Just go careful love. Take your time. I've got you." Matt said as we cautiously stepped the few metres to the

SUV. Thankfully we made it to the car without incident and I jumped up and down in the car excitedly as we made the ten minute ride to the gym.

***

"Bloody hell Alex! That dress is gorgeous on you!" Lucy cried as she hurried over to us as soon as we set foot in Cal's gym.

"Me? Look at you. You look freaking awesome!" And she really did. She wore a scarlet red bodycon dress that emphasised her stunning petite figure and her generous breasts. Her beautiful dark hair cascaded down her back in loose curls and she wore stunningly sexy strappy silver heels. She looked like she walked in right off a catwalk and I saw the dreamy look on Rob's face as he watched her from a few feet back.

"Thanks chick. I feel half naked right now to be honest." She whispered to me as she attempted to pull the top of her dress up higher.

"Just be thankful you could wear a bra!" I whisper shouted back, making her giggle.

"Ladies, are you trying to upstage me at my own party?" Jack called across the room. We both turned toward him. He was approaching in his natural, god given, sexy male model way, looking hot as hell in a tailored dark navy suit that was obviously made for his body. Underneath he had a pale blue shirt and matching navy tie. He, along with all of the guys in our family, belonged on the cover of GQ. He really was an incredibly beautiful man.

"Would we do that to you handsome?" Lucy laughed as she hurried into his arms. "You look very dashing." She said as she melted into his hold. The relationship between them was so sweet, the love between them so obvious when they were together. Jack really considered Lucy his sister and it was beautiful to witness.

"And you look hot as hell! I can't believe Rob let you out looking that fine!" Jack laughed as he looked pointedly to where Rob stood scowling at any man who dared look Lucy's way.

"Like he had any say!" Lucy retorted. Jack laughed and then looked to me.

"You too, are hot to trot tonight Alex." He gushed, making me blush as he pulled me into a hug. "You doing ok sweet?" He asked.

"I'm good thanks." I replied as he held me briefly, then pulled back just in time for Cal to approach and wrap an arm around his fiance's shoulders.

"Ladies, you're both stunning." Cal commented as he reached over to kiss Lucy and I on the cheek.

"Looking pretty good yourself there, boss." I replied. He wore dark grey tailored trousers with a matching waistcoat and a form fitting black button down shirt beneath. It was open at the collar and every muscle he had was visible through the outfit. Together, he and Jack made a stunning couple.

"This place looks great." Matt said as he wrapped his arm around me returning from where he had been talking to Rob. I looked around the room and could hardly recognise it. All of the equipment had been moved into the storage room and tables were laid out around a huge dancefloor. A DJ was set up in the far corner and a bar ran down almost the entire width of the back wall. Every table was dressed with white linens and had a centrepiece glass vase filled with glittering lights. There were about fifty people mingling around, some of which I knew as regulars at the gym.

"I'd like to take the credit, but this was all Cal. He's been at it all day."

"If I knew you were going to so much trouble I'd have come in to help Cal." I said, feeling bad we had all abandoned him to do everything himself.

"It's ok honey. I brought people in to do most of it and some of the guys came in to help me shift the machines. It was all good."

"Get a drink guys. It's an open bar and there will be food shortly. We need to mingle, but I'll be expecting dances later ladies." Jack said with a wink.

Lucy and I took a seat at a table close to the dancefloor while Rob and Matt headed to the bar. I didn't miss how Cam and Alex stood a few feet away, dressed like guests, but watching over Lucy and I constantly. I took a quick look around and found Evan and Gareth also dressed as guests, but obviously also standing guard behind me.

"What's wrong?" Lucy asked as she leant forward.

"There's just so much security. Has there been another threat that I don't know about or something?" I asked.

"No chick. Don't worry. Rob just wanted to be cautious with it being such a busy party. He has guys stationed around the whole building and there's a guy at the door checking IDs against the guest list. Try to relax. It's safe here tonight." Lucy explained, making me feel a little easier about it all.

"Sorry." I whispered. "Just nervous I guess."

"It's ok. Just have a couple of drinks and we'll get on that dance floor. You'll forget all about the security when you're shaking your arse out there." She joked, making me laugh hard. There was something about the way she said 'shaking your arse' that had me in stitches.

For the first hour of the party we just all sat at the table chatting about nothing important, just laughing and joking and enjoying ourselves as the alcohol took it's grip and loosened me up. After two glasses of wine Lucy and I were on the dance floor, facing each other, shaking our 'arses' and waving our arms like crazy people to song after song. We were giggling and having the time of our lives. Any time one of the gym regulars got a bit excited and tried to dance with us one of the guys would magically appear and scare them away. Lucy and I were pretty much oblivious to it all, just enjoying ourselves in the safety of our family.

"Sorry hon. I need a rest." I called when my leg started to get shaky. Lucy pouted and I knew she didn't want to stop dancing. I looked around until I found Jack sat at the table with Matt and Rob watching. I beckoned him over and he jumped to his feet.

"You ok sweet?" He asked as he approached.

"Tired. Will you dance with Lucy while I take a break?" I asked.

"Hell yeah! I was waiting to get tagged in." He smiled, then he took my place on the dance floor while I made my way to Matt.

"Are you alright love?" Matt asked as he stood and took my hand, pulling me into him.

"Yeah, just a bit worn out. I'm taking a break for ten." I explained. Matt nodded and sat back down, pulling me into his lap where I happily sat, my arms circled around his neck.

"Lucy's a party animal once you get her going!" I joked.

"You don't do so bad yourself baby." Matt laughed.

It was almost midnight by the time Rob managed to drag Lucy off the dance floor. I had been out with her off and on and we'd danced with the guys between dancing together. It had been a fun packed night and I was buzzing with happiness and a little alcohol. Lucy was pretty merry too and as we sat slurring our words a little, I realised Matt and Rob may have been right when they tried to drag us from dancing to eat a couple of hours earlier. Of course we had refused, having way too much fun to break away, but we were feeling it now.

"Is there food left?" I asked Matt.

"I'm not sure baby. You want me to go and check?"

"No, I'll go. Come on Lucy, come with me in search of food." I ordered. Lucy laughed and stumbled in her heels. I wrapped my arm around her and steadied her not missing the movement behind me, of Rob getting prepared to catch her.

"We're good." I called as we set off for the buffet table. Most of the food had been ransacked, but there was a few nibbles and some chocolate cake left, so I gathered two plates full, one sweet and one savoury and handed them to Lucy to hold while I went to the bar for water. When I turned I saw Cal helping Lucy to the table and laughed when she stumbled and Cal pretty much carried her the rest of the way.

"A message from a friend." A guy stood next to me at the packed bar, said. I turned to him thinking maybe he knew me from the gym, but I didn't recognise him. He was short and slim, in his mid forties maybe, with greying dark hair.

"Excuse me?" I said, thinking maybe I'd misheard. He slid a piece of paper across the bar nd under my hand. "What's this?"

"A message for you." Before I could ask anything else he walked away toward the entrance of the gym. I looked behind me, but saw no one watching. I discreetly turned the piece of paper over and written on it was a cell number and a brief message.

Last chance to save your brother.

Call me or he dies.

Yuri

I crumpled the paper in my hand and turned to look for the messenger again, but he was gone. What did I do now? Did I care if Marcus died? No. In fact it would make my life a hell of a lot easier, but if he was killed would that stop Yuri wanting me, chasing me? Probably not. My guess was that Yuri Sokolov was a man who always got what he wanted. I would need to tell Rob about the note, but not that night. Everyone was having fun and no way would I let my drama ruin that.

"You ok over here honey?" I turned and found Cal beside me.

"Yeah, sure. Just getting Lucy and I some water." I replied, trying to focus on making my voice come out steady.

"You look pale. Was that guy bothering you?"

"Nothing I couldn't handle. Just a few sleazy chat up lines. I told him to take a hike and he got bored."

"Good for you hon. You go and get something to eat. I'll get some water for you."

"Thanks Cal." I whispered, suddenly exhausted. I headed over to our table, slipping the screwed up note into my purse which hung on my wrist.

"You doing ok love?" Matt asked as I sank down into his lap and cuddled into him, needing his arms around me.

"Just tired." I sighed.

"Jack and Cal are getting ready to make an announcement. As soon as they've done we'll get you home, ok?"

"Ok." I agreed. Cal brought Lucy and I a bottle of water and I sipped at it as he and Jack headed for the DJ booth.

"Ladies and gentlemen. Cal and I, first off, just wanted to say thank you for coming to our Christmas Eve party. We hope you're all having a good night." Jack said over the microphone, inciting every one to cheer and clap.

"Now, as our nearest and dearest you will all know that Cal and I met a little over a year ago. We've been engaged for six months now and due to recent events that have made us see how unpredictable life can be, we've decided it's time we tie the knot." This time there were even louder cheers and hollers.

"Thanks guys." Cal said as he took the mic and settled everyone down. "As our nearest and dearest you should also know that Jack and I don't believe in being predictable. With this in mind you should all take this as your invitation to our wedding, one week from today at the Pine Lodge Inn just outside the city. Texts will be sent with more details, but we really hope to see you all there to celebrate our big day."

"Did you know about this?" Matt asked Rob.

"No. I knew Jack was hiding something, but I didn't suspect an impromptu wedding. Good for them." Rob replied.

The whole room was once again cheering and clapping, hooting and hollering at the good news. I was so happy for them. They were so obviously meant to be together and I was excited to be there to watch them take the big leap.

"Congratulations guys." Matt said and I looked up to see Cal and Jack taking their seats at our table.

"I can't believe I didn't know what you were up to." Lucy said, sounding less slurred than earlier.

"We only decided to do it last week. Thankfully we found the venue and then everything seemed to fall into place." Cal explained.

"Matt, I fixed your shifts so you have the day of the wedding and the following day off, you too Rob. Alec has agreed to step in and run the office and he's also got Cam coordinating security for the inn while we're there. We all have rooms booked and the Inn is booked out to only us and our guests so they'll be no unknown people hovering about."

"Sounds like you've got it all figured out them." Rob said with a grin. "I'm really happy for you man." He added.

"You sure you know what you're getting into Cal? Lucy joked.

"Not really, but someone has to take him on." Cal replied as he pulled Jack in for a hug.

"Just know that Lucy and I will have a getaway car prepped for you, just in case, right up until the last minute. All you have to do is say the word and we'll go all Thelma and Louise." I laughed.

"Thanks a bunch ladies. I love you too." Jack pouted, making me and Lucy laugh harder.

"I'm only joking. You know I love you Jack." I blew him a kiss and he smiled.

"Actually ladies, we have a favour to ask. We need two witnesses to sign the marriage license and we were sort of hoping you'd do it for us and walk down the aisle with us to pretty things up." Cal said, surprising me completely.

"Yeah, can't just have our ugly mugs at the front. We need some eye candy for people to appreciate." Jack added. "Lucy, I'd like you to walk down with me and Alex, Cal wants you with him, then you'd stand at the front while we do the serious bit. What do you say?"

I looked across to Lucy who was tearing up just as I was. I was overwhelmed to be asked to be a part of their wedding such a short time after coming into their lives.

"Of course we will." Lucy cried happily.

"It'll be a real honour guys. Thank you." I added and then we were on our feet hugging the both of them.

We stayed and chatted about the wedding plans for a while. They seemed to have gone all out, hiring out a huge traditional style log cabin guest inn and bringing in a quartett, band, caterers, florists and much more. They wanted Lucy and I to go dress shopping with them to pick matching dresses and to approve their suits once Christmas was done and we were excited to hear they had a white and silver colour scheme. It sounded like they had everything planned down to the finest detail and I couldn't wait for the big day on New Year's eve. It was all exciting and uplifting and would have been the ultimate finish to a magical night, were it not for the message burning a hole through my purse. I couldn't stop thinking about it and what the hell I was supposed to do to protect the wonderful people surrounding me.

"You want to go home Alex? You look tired baby." Matt said when I had once again zoned out.

"If you don't mind Matt. I am tired and my leg aches." It wasn't a lie. My leg did ache like crazy from all the dancing and I was drained both physically and emotionally.

"Of course. I'm pretty bloody tired too. Say goodnight to everyone and I'll get Cam to bring the car round." I nodded and stood from his lap, my weak leg instantly shaking in protest to me putting weight on it. Matt held me until he was sure I was steady, then headed for Cam while I approached Jack and Cal. I hugged them and thanked them for a brilliant party. We were all eating Christmas lunch at Rob and Lucy's the next day, so I would see them all there. I hugged Lucy too and told her I'd be by an hour early the next day to help her with the finishing touches and the cooking. She too seemed exhausted and I knew they would be leaving close after us.

"See you tomorrow Rob." I said as I approached where he stood waiting for me. He wrapped me in a hug.

"Do you want to give me whatever that guy gave you, before you leave?" He said quietly into my ear.

"What?" I asked as I pulled back and looked at his face.

"I saw him Alex. I had my guys stop him at the door. He works for the sokolovs. What did he pass you?"

"I....I was going to show you. I just didn't want to ruin the night." I whispered.

"I know honey. It's ok. Just hand it to me so I can look into it. I won't mention it to the others for now if that's what you want."

"Please Rob. I'll tell Matt, but after Christmas. I don't want him stressing over it." Rob nodded so I reached into my purse and pulled out the crumpled ball of paper. Rob opened it up and quickly read it.

"Do you want me to stop him?" He asked.

"From killing Marcus?" Rob nodded again.

"No. Hell, give him a hand if you like Rob. I'm just worried about Yuri coming for me and in turn, you guys." I admitted.

"I'll deal with it sweetheart. Just try and forget about it and enjoy your Christmas with Matt. I'll let you know tomorrow if I get anywhere."

"Thank you." I whispered as I reached up to kiss his cheek. He had to bob down to meet me halfway which made me giggle.

"Ready to go love?" Matt asked as he appeared behind me. I nodded and he said goodnight to everyone before helping me out to where Cam waited in the SUV outside the door.

"Did you enjoy the party?" Matt asked on the drive home.

"Yes. It was so much fun. I loved it." I replied, in my head adding, *apart from the threats from the russian mobster.*

Wasn't that just the way my life went at that time? Lots of happiness, fun and love, tinged with just a hint of the horror of my past. I really needed to find a way to end it all from haunting me once and for all.

MATT

Alex had been completely exhausted when I got her home just after midnight. She'd taken a quick shower and curled up in my arms, falling asleep almost instantly, so I'd been shocked and pleasantly surprised when she woke me at six AM Christmas morning, giddy as hell.

"Come on Matt. Let's get up. I want to give you your gifts." She said excitedly.

"Ok baby. I'm up." I groaned, pushing down my desire to complain about the ungodly hour, not wanting to crush her excitement. I pulled on a t-shirt and shorts and followed her through to the lounge. She flicked on the christmas tree lights, casting a warm glow over the apartment which was still in darkness, the sun having not yet risen.

"Matt!" She squealed when she saw the presents under the tree. She had placed gifts for me under the tree days ago, but I had kept hers hidden and when she was asleep last night I had snuck in and put them under the tree. The completely uncensored shock and excitement on her face made it all worth it.

"I guess Santa Claus came last night." I laughed. "You must have been a good girl this year."

I was unprepared as she leapt at me and wrapped her legs tightly around my waist.

"I love you, so damned much." She whispered between peppering my face with kisses.

"I love you too Alex."

When she unwrapped herself from me I put on a christmas playlist I had prepared and made coffee, then we both sat down beside the tree while Bing Crosby sang about a white Christmas.

"This is more amazing than I ever imagined it would be." Alex said emotionally as I handed her the first gift.

"I know love. It's pretty special for me too, here with the woman I love. I never imagined I could be this happy." I reached over to wipe away a stray tear running down her cheek. "Go on, open it up."

I laughed as she very tentatively opened the tape, trying hard not to tear the paper.

"What?" She asked as I chuckled.

"Just tear it open baby. We don't need to save the paper!" I laughed.

"I want to take my time, plus the paper is so pretty."

"You're too cute Alex Harrison." I waited impatiently as she finally got it open. I had taken Lucy shopping with me for gifts so I was pretty confident Alex would like them all, but I was excited to see her reaction.

"Oh Matt, it's beautiful!" She gasped as she unfolded the two tone grey, cashmere scarf Lucy had assured me Alex would love. She wrapped it around her neck and beamed. "It's so soft. I love it, thank you!" She leant in to kiss me briefly then carefully removed the scarf and neatly folded it, gently placing it on the sofa. She rooted around under the tree and pulled out a cube shaped box.

"This one first." She said as she handed it to me. I smiled like a fool while I ripped it open the way a present should be ripped open, making Alex laugh and call me a savage. I was shocked when I got the paper off and found a Tag Heuer watch box.

"Baby, this is too much. You didn't need to spend so much." I gasped.

"Lucy said you always wanted one so I had get it. Besides, don't think I don't know how much that designer scarf cost Matt. I bet I haven't spent half as much as you have." Knowing she was right, I may have gone a little overboard, I shut my mouth and opened the box. It was a Carrera, the watch I had had my eye on for years, but never quite convinced myself to part with the money it cost.

"Alex, baby. I love it. It's the one I've been drooling over in store windows for years." I said as I leant in to kiss her and show my gratitude.

"You're welcome. I took your old watch for the measurement and they adjusted the bracelet, so it should fit."

I excitedly pulled it from the box and put it on my wrist, thrilled with how great it looked. It really was the greatest thing she could have bought me. I admired it for several minutes and then realised Alex was just sat watching me.

"I think you should open the big one after that." I said as I pulled a palm sized rectangular box from her pile of gifts and handed it to her. She once again removed the paper very carefully and looked confused when she found a small red cardboard box.

"What is it?" She asked with the wonder of a child.

"Open it up love." I encouraged, so she removed the lid and looked in at the contents.

"What….what is this Matt?" She gasped.

"We'll need to get dressed to go see it properly, but if you look down to the street from the balcony, you'll get a glimpse."

"Matt, you did not get me a car!" She almost growled.

"I leased you a car baby, because you'll need one soon, when there's no more need for security. You'll need to drive to work and it'll give you the freedom to go where you want while I'm working stupid hours."

"You said the watch was too much. This is crazy!"

"Alex, I want you to be safe. I don't want to be at work worrying about you walking the streets or taking taxis or buses. The car is one of the safest and I went on the small side since you haven't driven much since passing your test."

"Ever Matt. I haven't driven ever, since passing my test. I could never afford a car."

"Well now you have one, an Audi A3 in a beautiful silver colour. It's all yours and when you get fed up with it we can just trade it in because it's leased."

"I might not even remember how to drive. I passed my test three years ago." She said and I knew she was terrified.

"You'll remember and we can go out together in it for the first few times. Just come take a look at it. I know you'll love it." I grabbed her hand and hurriedly wrapped her pyjama clad body in a blanket as I dragged her toward the balcony.

We stepped out into the bitterly cold morning and I pointed down the street to where her shiny new car sat.

"Oh my God Matt! It's beautiful!" She squealed.

"I thought you'd like it."

"I do, I love it, but you're still crazy for getting it for me!"

"Crazy about you maybe." I agreed as I moved in toward her for a kiss. It was brief, but fiery. "Come on love, get back inside before you freeze." She nodded and stepped inside, pulling me behind her.

"Thank you for the most amazing gift and for taking care of me. It means more than you can know to me." She whispered once we were inside and once again wrapped in each others arms.

"You never have to thank me for taking care of you baby. I will always do that." I pledged.

That morning we opened the rest of the presents to each other and then cuddled back up in bed, where we inevitably ended up making love, and having a very merry Christmas.

ALEX

We arrived at Rob and Lucy's late, which considering I'd told Lucy I would be an hour early to help her, was incredibly rude. We had just been having so much fun in bed together we had lost all track of time. As a result we had both showered and dressed in record time. I had been forced to do my makeup in the car enroute and now we stood at the door of their apartment looking a little dishevelled and both feeling guilty for being so late.

"What bloody time do you call this?" Lucy demanded when she opened the door to her place.

"I'm so sorry. We lost track of time." I babbled guiltily.

"I'm joking!" She laughed. "It's fine. Dinner's not for another hour at least. Come in." She hugged us both as we walked through the door.

"Oh, the love birds finally decide to show!" Jack called as I walked in, making me blush. If Jack and Cal were there, we were really late.

"Ignore him baby. He's just jealous of your Audi!" Matt said loudly enough for Jack to hear as he wrapped a strong arm around my waist.

"Damned right I am! Can Alex even drive? That is far too sexy a car to be banged up by a new driver." Jack ranted, making me laugh.

"You're right Jack, but try telling Matt that. I've already told him if he really has to do something as insane as buy me a car, it should be a cheap heap of junk so when I inevitably have a fender bender, it won't matter so much." I explained, with a roll of my eyes for effect.

"And I told Alex that I want her to be safe, which is why I chose a new, high safety rated car for her, so if she ever does have a fender bender, which I hope to God she doesn't, but if she does, only the car will be damaged and not her." Matt retorted, looking at me the entire time he spoke, with the hint of a grin.

"Sounds fair enough to me sweet. Guess you just have to deal with it and keep the beautiful, sexy Audi." Jack laughed.

Matt was still staring at me with so much love and desire in his glare. I blushed just imagining what he was thinking about. Jees, I loved him so damned much! Everytime he looked at me I felt like the most beautiful creature on the planet. Everytime he touched me it reminded me how incredibly lucky I was to have such a spectacular man in my life.

"I guess so." I agreed with Jack as I stalked closer to where Matt stood. It had been a crazy gift he had given me that morning, but I couldn't deny his reasoning behind it, the fact all he wanted was to make sure he kept me safe even when he wasn't with me. It made me feel so cherished and wanted, things I had longed my entire life to feel.

"Thank you." I whispered as I reached up to kiss him briefly.

"For what love?"

"For just being your amazing self. I love you."

"I love you too Alex, so bloody much." Matt whispered back and we kissed again, this time deeper.

"Erm, Alex if you could tear yourself away from necking with my brother I could do with some help in the kitchen." Lucy declared midway through the kiss. I smiled as I pulled back and looked into Matt's captivating, ice blue eyes,

"Sorry darling." He said to Lucy, while keeping his eyes locked with mine. We both laughed a little at being caught kissing like horny teenagers yet again. I reached up and kissed him once more, this time on the cheek, then made my way through to the kitchen, once again riding high on the intoxication of my love for Matt.

"Ok, where do you want me?" I called as I walked into the kitchen.

"Oh God Alex, I've buggered it all up!" Lucy cried in hushed tones as soon as I approached where she stood at the counter. She had tears running down her face and she looked pale.

"What do you mean?" I asked. I was worried about how upset she looked. Just minutes before, when we had arrived, she had been smiling and now she looked devastated.

"I don't know how it happened, I'm sure I checked, but I somehow turned the oven on to the grill setting and left it and now everything in there is completely black." She was frantic and when I put my hand on her shoulder to try and reassure her, I found she was trembling badly.

"Hey, it's ok. Just try and calm down. Let's see if we can fix it, huh?" I offered. I was no great cook, that was Lucy, but for some reason she was in meltdown over some overcooked food and I just wanted to make it better for her.

She nodded, so I grabbed the mitt from her and opened the oven. It was turned off and Lucy was right, each tray of food I pulled out, including the huge turkey, was totally charred on top and raw underneath.

"See, it's totally ruined!" Lucy cried from beside me. She was crying harder and her breathing was becoming increasingly hurried. I realised as I studied her, that she was having a panic attack, probably not actually over the ruined meal, but more the remembered, terrifying consequences of such a mistake in her marriage to that motherfucker, Phil. Lucy had told me some of what she had been through with him, and I knew occasionally events could trigger panic attacks and flashbacks for her. No doubt that's what was happening at that moment.

"It's not important honey. The guys won't care what they eat. We have time to make something else," I said calmly, closing the oven to hide the disaster from her sight. I removed the oven mitt and went to pull her into my arms, but she gasped and backed away until she hit the counter. She was really freaking out, and I was pretty sure not even seeing or hearing me anymore. Knowing I was out of my depth I backed away from her slowly, not wanting to scare her further, and then hurried to the lounge. The guys were watching reruns of some sports game and laughing loudly.

"Rob?" I called, more urgently than I meant to. They all turned to look at me with concern and I took a deep breath to calm myself. I didn't want them all hurrying in scaring Lucy more. "Can you come help me with something in the oven?" I asked more calmly.

"Sure sweetheart." Rob agreed as he got to his feet.

"Are you ok baby?" Matt asked.

"Sure. Just need a hand with the technical stuff." Rob approached me with a smile and I hurried ahead of him into the kitchen, hoping Matt wouldn't follow. I knew Lucy would be devastated if everyone found out she was struggling. She would be worried she'd ruined the day.

"It's not the oven." I declared as soon as we turned the corner from the lounge. "It's Lucy. She messed up the meal and she's just freaking out. I think it's a panic attack." As soon as we walked into the kitchen Rob raced to Lucy's side and got down on his knees so he was almost eye level with her.

"Sweetheart, can you hear me?" He asked, his face a mask of calm, but his voice revealing his worry.

"I'm.....so.....sorry." She whimpered between desperate gasps for breath.

"Hey, listen to me Lucy. You have nothing to be sorry for. I don't care about dinner, nobody does. You're not back there with *him* anymore. You're here, at home with me and you're safe, always safe. Just come back to me, ok? I'm here sweetheart, just take my hand and come back to me now." He held out his hand and Lucy very slowly, very tentatively, put her own, badly trembling hand on his palm. He engulfed it in his grip and held it. He didn't touch her anywhere else and it was obvious he was used to dealing with such episodes.

Very slowly Lucy gathered herself enough to look up from where her gaze had been glued to the floor. She met Rob's eyes and he smiled gently to her.

"Hey you." He whispered.

"Hi." Lucy squeaked back. She seemed to be back in the present, though she still had tears running down her face and was visibly shaking.

"You with me again sweetheart?"

"I.....I think so. I'm sorry." She cried as she launched herself into his arms. He caught her in a huge embrace and held her close to him.

"It's ok honey. I've got you, I've always got you." Rob soothed as he gathered her up and stood with her in his arms.

"I'll take her to our room for a short rest. Can you get rid of that please? Just throw it out?" He asked as he nodded to the oven.

"Sure. Just take care of her. I have this." I agreed. I felt pretty tearful myself witnessing the shocking after effects that Lucy was still dealing with as a result of her tortuous marriage. Thank God she had Rob and the guys to be there for her when she needed them. Thank God we both did.

As soon as Rob and Lucy disappeared down the hall to their room, I pulled out garbage bags and emptied all of the trays from the oven into them. I double bagged since the food was still hot, then I grabbed both bags and headed for the trash chute in the hall.

"Here love. I'll get that." Matt offered as I passed him.

"Thanks handsome." I handed him the bags, grateful to be relieved of it. For some reason, probably all the dancing the night before, my leg hurt like a bitch that day and I was thankful to be spared the walk with the heavy bag.

Matt nodded, smiled and then headed out of the apartment with the trash.

"You need a hand in there hon?" Cal offered as I hurried back to the kitchen.

"Sure. Thanks Cal." I really did need a hand. I couldn't cook for shit and I needed to find something else to make for dinner. Sure, I could manage a decent meat and vegetable meal for two, but anything more adventurous and I was screwed. I definitely needed help.

I rushed back into the kitchen and threw the trays from the oven into the sink. I set to scrubbing like my life depended on it, wanting all evidence of what had upset Lucy gone before she returned.

"Have you been abandoned in here honey?" Cal asked as he walked in. I turned to look at him. He was smiling and rolling the sleeves of his white button down shirt to his elbows.

"Kind of. The dinner got a little messed up and Lucy got really upset. Rob's taken her to their room for a rest. I need to get all this clean and something else cooking before she comes back." I explained, not once stopping the scrubbing as I spoke quietly over my shoulder.

"Is Lucy ok?" Cal asked as he leant on the counter beside me.

"Not really, but Rob's got her."

"Good. So what are we cooking?"

"Erm....well that was kind of where you come in. I can't cook, I mean I'll make a good sous chef, but actual cooking, no way. I just....we have to fix this for her Cal. She was so upset."

"We will hon." Cal leant in, to place a kiss on top of my head, then he walked over to the fridge and started pulling out all kinds of ingredients.

I finished washing everything up and then helped Cal as he set about making several italian dishes. I chopped and prepped as he prepared a lasagne, aubergine parmigiana, steak pizzaiola and a variety of accompaniments. There wasn't ingredients to make anything like the traditional dinner Lucy had prepared, so Cal and I settled on an Italian Christmas.

***

"Guys, what are you doing?" Cal and I both looked up from where we were chopping salad a while later, and found Lucy headed into the kitchen. She looked pale and tired, but she seemed calmer. She was cuddled into Rob's side as he lead her through to us.

"Hey honey. You doing better?" Cal asked with a smile.

"Yeah, thanks." Lucy sighed. She looked completely wiped out and I wondered if we should all just leave and let her and Rob be. "You cooked another meal?" She asked as she looked around the kitchen.

"Cal did. Don't worry, I was strictly the sous chef. I haven't been allowed near any of the actual cooking." I joked.

"You didn't have to go to so much bother. Rob found a thai place in the city that's open. We were just going to order in."

"It was no bother Lucy. I'm sure it's nowhere near as good as your cooking, but it should be ok." Cal replied.

"Yeah, it's a themed Christmas now, Italian." I added.

Lucy moved from Robs hold and over to where Cal and I

stood. She wrapped an arm around each of us and we all had a group hug.

"Thank you, so much. It wouldn't really have been Christmas with take out." She said emotionally.

"Don't speak too soon honey. We haven't tried it yet. We might need the take out after all." Cal laughed as he pulled away and hurried over to the oven.

"Whatever Cal. We all know how good your Italian food is. My mouth is watering with the amazing smells in here right now." Lucy said, making me smile. That sounded more like the Lucy I knew.

The meal that afternoon really was delicious. There was no denying Cal's skills in the kitchen, but the atmosphere had been subdued, mainly because it was clear to see Lucy was tired and still struggling. Even though we hadn't actually told Jack and Matt about Lucy's panic attack, they seemed to just know. Lucy clung close to Rob throughout the meal, and barely spoke more than she had to.

After dinner we all exchanged gifts and watched a movie with drinks and a selection of desserts. Eventually Lucy dropped off in Robs arms and so we all filtered out to leave them in peace.

It had been a day of ups and downs, a wonderful morning with Matt, then a heartbreaking experience seeing Lucy crumble before me, then a special afternoon simply because we all got to celebrate together, even if Lucy's heart wasn't quite in it.

As I lay in bed beside Matt that night, snuggled close to him, feeling safe and loved, I thought to myself that, overall, my first real Christmas with the ones I loved and cared for had been pretty special and I went to sleep feeling content and happy, just hoping Lucy did too.

***

"Ta da!" Jack cried as he stepped out of the changing room at the high end tailors, two days later. He looked handsome in a black tux, crisp white shirt, and white bowtie and cumberbund. Cal came out just behind him in the same tux and shirt, but with a dark silver bowtie and cumberbund. They were both grinning and looked so damned handsome. Lucy and I were both there to help them choose suits and to get matching dresses.

"They're perfect!" Lucy declared excitedly.

"Very dashing you guys." I agreed. They did look absolutely fantastic, stood side by side like the front page of that month's GQ. Of course they did, they were very beautiful guys. They could get married in trash bags and make it work.

"You're sure sweet? You think the white is good with the white shirt?" Jack asked Lucy as she stood to straighten his tie.

"It's perfect Jack. You both look so handsome and you match the colour scheme of the wedding. The pictures will be wonderful!" Lucy was beaming and I knew she was happy for them, as we all were.

"Alex, will you be able to find something to match this honey?" Cal asked as he pointed to the silver of his bowtie. We had all decided, enroute to the store, that Lucy and I would get dresses that complemented each other, but that matched the colours the guys chose, so Lucy would have to go for white and I was looking for silver.

"Sure I will. You have to stick with that colour Cal, it's awesome on you. Lucy's right, you both look so damned handsome in those suits."

"I guess that's decision made then." Cal stated as he looked to Jack.

"Fine by me. I feel like some hollywood movie star on the red carpet in this."

Once the suits were bought we headed to the mall where we all had a quick lunch, then hit the department stores for silver and white dresses. Lucy tried three before she found the most perfect sleeveless, scoop neck, ankle length, white evening dress. It was completely open at the back and gave Lucy a stunning hourglass figure. It split up one side, to mid thigh and she was absolutely beautiful in it. We all declared it was the one, in unison, the second we saw it.

It took me longer, since silver dresses seemed to be harder to find, especially since they had to fit my curves and hide my worst scars. I tried six before I put on the right one. It was an A-line Maxi dress with a halter neck at the front and a back that dipped down about halfway, hiding the worst of my scrs which were at the bottom of my back. It was a beautifully soft satin fabric that just seemed to swath me perfectly. The dress reached my ankle, but like Lucy's, split up to my right thigh. It was the exact shade of Cal's dark silver bowtie and I knew I would match him as he had wanted, while also being similar enough to Lucy's that we fitted together at the front of the ceremony.

When we had dresses the guys insisted we get shoes and clutches to match, so the shopping continued until we were ready to drop. I was exhausted as we left the mall and so very grateful Matt had suggested I take my crutch with me that morning. My leg was exhausted and painful and I was leaning heavily on the crutch by the end.

We all hugged goodbye and went separate ways in the parking lot. Cal and Lucy headed off in Cal's truck to the gym where they were both working that afternoon.

"Nice ride." Jack said with a smile as we approached my new car in the parking lot.

"I know. I keep telling Matt he's insane getting me this for Christmas, but he won't listen." I said guiltily. I loved the car, I loved it so much and to have the freedom to drive wherever I wanted to go was wonderful, but I still felt so guilty that Matt had spent such a ridiculous amount of money on me. I had been terrified to drive it at first, but after a couple of hours driving around with Matt beside me for support, I had my confidence back and found I loved driving.

"He just wants you to be safe sweet and I agree with him. The city can be a dangerous place to be on foot sometimes. He loves you Alex, just humour his over-protective instincts." He argued good naturedly.

"I know. It's just hard after only ever counting on me. I'm trying to adapt." I opened the drivers door and climbed in.

"Bet it's easier to adapt with this beautiful Audi at your disposal." Jack joked as he too climbed in.

"It is beautiful isn't it?" I gave in with a huge smile.

"Hell yeah! I think I might have to start working on Cal to get my own after the wedding." I slapped his arm playfully and shook my head with a giggle.

"You're terrible Jack Reed." I sighed as I started the car and pulled cautiously out of the parking lot.

"I am, but luckily for Cal, he's used to it." Jack replied with a chuckle.

I drove cautiously as I navigated the traffic surrounding the mall, then relaxed a little as we hit the quieter highway, en route back into the city. Jack remained quiet, which I was grateful for since driving was still a little daunting and I needed to concentrate.

"Sweet, take a left here." Jack said ten minutes into the drive. I was confused by the route, but did as Jack asked and took the immediate left turn, heading away from the city again.

"Is this the right way?" I asked as I headed down the smaller road which was surrounded by woodland.

"No. Listen to me Alex. Someone is tailing us. I need you to keep your cool and not panic. Just keep heading down this road. I'm going to call Rob." Jack said calmly as he pulled his cell from his jeans pocket. My heart rate instantly increased and I could hear the thundering beats in my ears. I looked in my rear view mirror and found a black truck close on my tail.

"Should I put my foot down?" I asked, my voice trembling.

"Not yet sweet, just act like nothing's wrong. Hopefully Rob can get some guys to us before anything else happens." Jack said as he held his phone to his ear.

I heard him talking, telling Rob where we were and what the plate of the truck was, but I had tuned out. All I could focus on was the road in front of me and the truck behind me. I tried to see who was driving, but I couldn't make them out through the rearview mirror. It had to be Marcus. He had threatened me and everyone I cared about and now he was following us. My hands were trembling uncontrollably at the thought of what he would do if he got to us.

"Alex?" Jack called loudly, snapping me from my terror. I looked over to him quickly, then snapped my eyes back to the road. "Are you with me sweet?" He asked.

"Yeah....sorry."

"It's ok. You're doing good honey. Just keep going and keep breathing. Rob and some of his guys are headed our way. We just need to keep going like we haven't noticed."

"I'm scared Jack. It's him....it must be him."

"Alex, everything is going to be alright. I won't let him hurt you." He assured me as he gently squeezed my knee.

"He's dangerous Jack. He'll kill you if he gets chance. If anything happens then you just let him take me, ok? You get the hell away." I said firmly.

"Not gonna happen sweet."

"I can survive it Jack. I did it before, I can do it again, but not if you or anyone else is hurt because of me. Please, you have to promise me you'll just get the hell out of there if it comes to it." I cried, tears running down my face and blurring my vision.

"I'm sorry honey, but I can't do that. No way would I ever run off and leave you, and you know it. If it comes to it I will protect you from that maniac or anyone else who ever tried to hurt you. I told you you're never going back and I meant it. He may be dangerous Alex, but I'm deadly and I can deal with him. I need you to stop worrying and stay calm. Nothing is going to happen.

We're going to keep driving until the guys catch us up, then they'll stop him and hand him to the FBI. This will all be over in....." As Jack spoke calmly I once again checked the rear view and was horrified to see the truck even closer to us. As I pressed the gas a little harder the truck hit my rear end and we lurched forward with a crash.

"JACK!" I screamed with terror as I momentarily lost control of the car. Jack lurched over to my side and forcefully turned the wheel straight before we veered off the road.

"It's ok, we're ok. Speed up sweet." Jack said calmly. I nodded and clamped my hands tightly on the wheel again as I slammed the gas pedal. We shot forward at a terrifyingly fast speed, but we were moving away from the truck so it calmed me somewhat.

"Good, you're doing good honey." Jack encouraged.

"He hit us." I gasped.

"He did and he may do again Alex. Just try to stay ahead of him. Rob won't be far from us now."

"I wish you were driving." I whimpered.

"You're doing great. Just stay focused Alex. Luckily this is a fast car."

"So is his." I gasped as I checked the rear view and saw he was gaining on us. Jack looked behind us.

"Shit! Are you flooring the gas right now?" He asked more urgently.

"Yes. It won't go any faster." I cried.

"Ok. Alex, listen to me. He's going to hit us again. You need to keep a tight hold on the wheel and focus on staying in the road. If he does run us off you have to get out of the car if you can and run as fast as possible. You run and you hide until me or Rob comes for you, do you understand?"

"What about you?" I whimpered tearfully, knowing that if Marcus ran us off the road Jack was going to face him and I was beyond terrified Jack would be hurt.

"You just do as I say and don't worry about me. I'll handle Marcus if it comes to it."

"Let's just stay on the road. I like that idea much better." I said, trying to control my tears so I could see the damned road.

"Me too sweet. Let's stick with that plan." Jack said with a smile as he typed a text hurriedly into his cell. I looked in the rear view once again and almost screamed when I found the truck right upon us.

"Jack, hold on!" I yelled instead of the pathetic scream that fought for freedom from my lungs. I had to keep it together! As the truck hit us again, this time harder, I reigned in my panic and clamped my hands on the steering wheel. The car jerked to the right so I corrected it urgently and slammed the gas down again.

"Good job sweet." Jack said as he turned in the seat and looked behind us. The truck was gaining on us, this time faster. I watched it in the mirror as I sped down the straight road.

"Alex, hold the fuck on!" Jack yelled as the truck hit us again, this time a lot harder than the others. I tried to correct the wheel as it shot to the right, but the hit was too hard and I lost control. The car shot across the road and the last thing I saw was trees fast approaching as I screamed Jack's name. There was a huge crash and the deafening sound of metal crushing before darkness overcame me.

***

An annoying tapping on my cheek awoke me. I opened my eyes slowly, wondering why the hell my head was pounding so hard. There was also a butt load of pain from my left shoulder and across my chest. What on earth had happened? I cracked my eyes open and the first thing I saw was trees, hundreds of them, The next made my blood run cold. Marcus. He stood beside me, leaning into the car from the open drivers side door. It all came back to me then. The black truck hitting us. I hurriedly turned to Jack where he sat slumped forward, unconscious and bleeding a lot from somewhere on his head. The airbags had deployed and we were both covered in a fine layer of white powder.

"Rise and shine Alicia." Marcus hissed. "Places to go, people to sell you to."

"Jack!" I said as loud as I could through the pain in my chest. I needed to know he was alive. I needed him to be ok. I would block out Marcus until I knew that.

"Ah yes, the gay. I was hoping for your boyfriend, but I guess we can start with this one." Marcus sighed. I turned to him just in time to see him pulling a gun from under his jacket.

"Say bye bye Alicia." He smiled coldly and then started moving around the car to Jack's side. I started scrambling to get out of my seat, knowing he was going to shoot Jack, but my foot was trapped on something. The front of my car had hit a tree and been badly damaged and part of the mangled metal held me in place.

"Jack!" I screamed as I fought to free myself. "Jack wake up!" Marcus was already at the passenger side and fighting to open the crushed door. "JACK, WAKE UP!" I screamed at the top of my voice as I finally managed to rip my foot free of whatever held it. Pain tore through my ankle, but I ignored it and leapt out of the car. Dizziness hit me hard, but I managed to remain standing and I stumbled around to the back of the car.

"Stay the hell away from him Marcus!" I yelled as I tried to focus on him still trying to pry open the car door.

"I'm afraid not sister dearest. He's dead, along with his boyfriend and all the other losers you've latched onto. I told you you'd pay, you stupid bitch!" He raged. I saw red then. No way was I going to let that monster hurt those I cared about. No freaking way!

I screamed a war cry, powering through the pain in my ankle as I launched myself at him. He wasn't expecting it and he went down hard, landing with a thud on his back, my full weight over him. In the scuffle the gun went off, firing into the trees on my right, startling me enough that Marcus was able to flip me off of him and get to his feet.

"Stupid fucking bitch! You'll pay for that! But first..." He yelled as he pointed the gun at the window of the car. The passenger side window was cracked into hundreds of lines, so it was hard to see into, but I knew Jack was unconscious directly behind it.

"No! Marcus. Please don't. I'll go with you.....I'll go to Yuri! Please just don't!" I cried desperately.

"You're going to Yuri anyway you stupid whore." Marcus laughed as he squeezed the trigger.

"NO!" I screamed as the shot shattered the window.

"JACK!" Tears were streaming down my cheeks as I fought to get to my feet and see Jack. He couldn't be dead! He had to be ok!

"Time to go!" Marcus whispered as he grabbed my hand and dragged me to my feet. He pulled me away from the car before I could look over at Jack and I fought against him, just needing to get to the passenger side to see if the man who had become like a brother to me, had survived.

"ALEX?" Rob's booming voice echoed through the trees and made me fight harder to get away and to Jack's aid.

"ROB!" I screamed with everything I had in the direction of the road, which was about ten metres away through the woods.

"Move Alicia!" Marcus barked as he tried to drag me deeper into the woods. I stopped pulling against him and instead hurtled toward him, smashing the heel of my hand into his nose. It wasn't a great contact but enough for him to let go of my hand and shove me hard to the ground.

"ALEX?" Rob yelled again, this time closer. Marcus looked down at me on the ground with a sneer.

"One down." He laughed and then he ran into the dense woodland.

"Jack!" I cried as I fought the dizziness attacking me to get to my feet. I got up and ran for the car when strong arms encircled my waist. I screamed and began to fight, hitting and kicking out with everything I had, as I was lifted from the ground. I had to get to Jack!

"Alex, honey it's me….it's Rob. Calm down, you're ok now." Rob said into my ear. I stopped fighting and strained around so I could see him where he held me from behind.

"Rob?" I sobbed desperately.

"Yeah sweetheart, it's me."

"Oh God Rob, Jack! You need to get to Jack…..he….he shot him. Oh God, I think he shot him!" I cried as I struggled to get free again.

"Take her." Rob barked as he handed me over to another set of arms. I looked up and found Cam holding me tightly against him. I fought to get free, to get to Jack, but his hold was too strong.

"Alex. You have to stop fighting. You're hurt and you're going to make it worse. Rob will help Jack." Cam said calmly.

"He's dead….Marcus killed Jack because of me….oh God…..he's dead." I cried as I buried my face into Cam's black leather jacket and finally gave up the fight. I sobbed desperately while Cam just held me close and tried to comfort me.

"Alex, he's ok honey. He's alive and awake. Marcus missed." I heard Rob call a few minutes later. I looked up from Cam's shoulder over to the car where Rob was bent down beside the passenger door which he had managed to open. Cam released me and I stumbled on shaking legs over to the car. Rob walked toward me and steadied me for the last few feet. I grabbed the side of the car and bent to look in. Relief flooded me when I found Jack sat up, awake and alert and smiling at me.

"Hey sweet." He said, his voice a little raspy.

"Oh God…..Jack!" I sobbed as I sunk to my knees beside him.

"It's ok Alex. I'm fine, just a knock on the head. Bet you're glad Matt sprung for the high end car now, huh?" He joked.

"Jack, don't joke! I thought you were dead. I was so….so s-scared." I gasped between great gulping sobs.

"You know it'd take more than that to get rid of me sweet." Jack reached out and took my trembling hand in his.

"Where did Marcus go Alex?" Rob asked as he sunk to the floor behind me and wrapped a supportive arm around my shoulders.

"Into the woods…..th-that way." I said as I pointed the way Marcus had fled. Rob nodded to Cam and Evan and they took off the same way, running.

"Be careful….he has a gun!" I cried after them.

"They'll be ok sweetheart. They know what they're doing." Rob said calmly. Gareth and Alec appeared where Cam and Evan had been stood previously and I was so glad to know they were there, that we were safe.

"Help me out of here man. Alex is bleeding. I need to check her over." Jack said as he nodded to my leg. I looked down for the first time and saw there was a large patch of blood around a long tear in my jeans just above my ankle, obviously from where I had ripped my leg free of the mangled front of my poor car.

"I'll look at it. You stay where you are until the EMTs get here."

"Rob, I'm fine. I just hit my head on something and knocked myself out. Alex is bleeding and her breathing is laboured. I need to check her out. We don't even know how far out EMTs are." Jack said with some anger.

"I'm ok. It doesn't even hurt." I said, referring to my ankle. My chest and shoulder hurt like a bitch, but I'd had worse.

"Just stay where you are Jack. That's a nasty cut on your head and you were unconscious." Rob said firmly. "Come on honey. Let's get you sat in the car and I'll look at this cut." He added as he stood and reached his hands out to me. I took both and allowed him to pull me to my feet. He wrapped an arm around my waist and started to move. I sank into his hold, my head spinning like a merry-go-round and making me very unsteady. As we moved heat raced up my body to my head and I felt incredibly nauseous then suddenly everything started to go dark and the last thing I saw was the leaf covered ground hurtling toward me.

JACK

My head hurt like a motherfucker and Rob treating me like an invalid wasn't helping. I needed out of the car, which I had become far too close to becoming dead in. Thank fuck Alex's shit head brother couldn't shoot for shit or I'd be a goner. I watched Rob lead Alex around the car a way before I started moving my feet to free them from the wreck of the car. I was getting out, not even Rob could stop me. I was worried sick about Alex. She shouldn't be moving around with the injuries I had seen and Lord only knew if there were any we couldn't see.

"JACK!" Rob roared from the back of the car. "She's down!" I more frantically fought to release myself from the car and finally got free. I stepped out and had to steady myself for a moment as the light headedness passed. When I was sure I was steady enough to move I ran to where Rob knelt over Alex who was laid out, unconscious on the ground.

"What happened?" I asked as I knelt down beside her.

"She just blacked out and went down." Rob explained with worry.

"My backpack's in the trunk. Get it." I ordered. Rob nodded and went for the car. Cal had picked me up from work that morning and so I'd had my bag from the hospital, on me. It didn't have much in it, but there were some supplies which may help.

While Rob was gone I checked Alex's pulse and was relieved to find it steady. She was paler than usual and I moved down to the cut on her leg. I tore the rip in the jeans wider and found a deep gash a few inches long, bleeding profusely.

When rob returned I grabbed dressings from my bag and handed them to Rob, instructing him to apply pressure to stop the bleeding.

"Is she going to be ok?" Rob asked cautiously.

"I hope so." I replied as I pulled my stethoscope from my bag and moved to listen to her lungs. My biggest worry was that her shallow breathing was the result of a broken rib puncturing a lung.

"Lung sounds are good." I told Rob with relief a few minutes later.

"That's good, right?"

"Yeah, it's good. She likely has some crush injuries from the seatbelt, which are making breathing painful for her. I think the concussion likely made her black out. We need to get her to the ER. Did you call Matt?"

"I tried on the way over, but he was in surgery."

"EMTs are ten minutes out." Gareth called, having called the dispatcher.

"That's too long. Where's your car?" I asked as I started stuffing everything back into my bag.

"Not far. You sure you're ok to be moving around?"

"I'm fine Rob. We need to get her to the ER as soon as possible. I'm worried about the head injury. We don't have any choice." I slung my backpack on my shoulder and moved to lift Alex, but Rob stopped me.

"Jack, you're hurt. I've got her man. Tell Gareth to cancel the EMTs and round up Cam and Evan. That dipshit's long gone by now." He instructed as he gathered Alex up from the ground and headed for his SUV. I gave the instructions and then ran toward the road, following just behind Rob. I sat in the back with Alex and we sped away toward the city hoping like hell the woman we had all come to love as a sister in the short time we had known her, would be alright.

ALEX

The sound of the gunshot shattering the passenger side window once again, had me waking up screaming Jack's name. I was confused when my eyes shot open and I found myself in a dark room, strong with the smell of disinfectant.

"Alex, it's ok love. You're safe." Matt's voice soothed. I turned and found him leant over me. He was in navy scrubs and his hair was ruffled and messy.

"Matt? Where's Jack?" I asked fearfully.

"He's ok baby. He's in a room down the hall sleeping. He had a concussion like you and a sprained wrist. He's going to be just fine, you both are."

"Marcus?" I asked, hoping like hell Rob's guys had tracked the fucker down.

"Sorry love, he got away, but Rob's got his entire team trying to track the prick."

"He said 'one down'. He thought he'd killed Jack and he was threatening the rest of you. He'll try to hurt you all Matt.....he's insane."

"Just try to calm down for me Alex. You have a nasty concussion. Everyone is here with us along with Cam, Evan, Gareth and Alec. Everyone is safe so you don't need to get upset. You just need to rest and take it easy. They're keeping you and Jack for observation tonight and if all's well you'll both go home tomorrow, ok?"

"I need to see him Matt....I need to see Jack right now." I said firmly. I had to see for myself he really was alright.

"You're not up to moving yet baby. Just get some sleep and later we can...."

"No!" I cut him off. "I thought he was…..Marcus shot him Matt….I have to see him, I have to see with my own eyes that he's ok…..please." I begged tearfully.

"Ok beautiful. Let me see if he's awake and if he is, you can see him, ok?"

"Thank you." Matt gently kissed my forehead and then turned and left the private room I was in. Before the door to the room closed Cam slipped in and hovered across the room, standing guard.

"How are you doing over there spitfire?" He asked with a smile.

"Spitfire?"

"Me and the guys have decided that should be your nickname on account of how plucky and scrappy you are." Cam explained, making me laugh a little.

"Gee, thanks….I think."

"How's the head?"

"A little like I was hit, head on, by a train." I said honestly.

"We'll get him Alex. This will all be over before you know it."

"I hope so. He threatened them Cam, he threatened everyone I care about and Matt says I don't need to worry, but how can I not? Look what he just did to Jack and I. He was so close to taking us both out." Tears ran down my face and I had to take huge deep breaths to fight back the sobs that wanted to escape. Cam approached the bed and gently wiped the tears from my cheeks.

"Matt's right kiddo. You don't need to worry. We're all in this together, Matt, Cal, Rob and Jack along with me and Evan and Gareth and Alec. Your sicko brother has no chance of getting past one of us, let alone all of us. We'll get him, you just have to keep it together until we do, ok spitfire?" He said with a smile.

"I'll try." I said honestly.

"I know you will."

"Thank you…..for being here for me and the others."

"I owe Rob a lot. I'm just glad I can repay him a little." Cam whispered just as Matt walked back in. As he approached the bed Cam slipped back out silently and I was grateful for his kind, reassuring words. They had set me at ease somewhat, knowing what he had said was true, no one could overpower the group of amazing guys in my life.

"Is he awake Matt? Can I see him?" I asked all at once.

"He's coming to you baby. Cal will bring him in a few minutes."

"I'd have gone to him Matt. I didn't want to drag him out of bed if he's hurt. It's all my fault, he shouldn't have to suffer any more because of me. I just….I just needed to see him, know he's ok." I cried with yet more tears.

"Alex, calm down baby. For one, this is not your fault. It's all on Marcus and he'll pay for it, that's for sure. And secondly, no way was Jack going to let you trail to his room with the head injury and stitches you have. He only has a mild concussion, so he's fine to move around. Stop stressing yourself out so much, please beautiful."

"How do you expect me to do that Matt? You do understand if Marcus could actually shoot straight, Jack wouldn't be here now? He's be dead, laid in a morgue somewhere because of me!" I screamed almost hysterically. "I almost got that kind man killed today and he's coming for all of you! He'll kill you Matt, and Rob and Lucy and Cal and don't think he won't finish Jack off too! I'll get you all killed. I can't do this, I can't let that happen. I have to go….I have to get far away from all of you." I leapt out of the bed away from Matt before he could stop me, tearing the IV from my arm in one swift move.

"Alex, get back into bed baby. You're bleeding." Matt said calmly as he moved toward me.

"Stay away Matt!" I cried as I backed into the corner. "I'm sorry….I love you, but I won't get anyone else hurt. I have to leave."

"You're not going anywhere Alex. I know you're panicking and you've been through alot today, but you need to try and calm down and just take a breath. You and Jack are both going to be fine."

"This time! This time, by some miracle we made it, but I can't…..won't let it come to this again." Before Matt could say anything Jack was pushed into the room in a wheelchair by a very tired and stressed out looking Cal.

"Matt? What's wrong?" Jack asked as he looked between Matt and I. Just the sight of Jack in that wheelchair, looking pale and exhausted, a huge gash along the right side of his hairline had me filled with a sickening guilt. I had done that to him, me! My stupid past had hurt him.

"Jack…..I'm so sorry….so so sorry." I whimpered as sobs took hold of me and I crumpled back against the wall and slid into a heap on the cold vinyl floor.

"Sweet, you have nothing to be sorry for." Jack said from where he sat in front of me in the wheelchair. "You're hurt.....it's my fault....my stupid fault for ever thinking I could be normal." I cried as I slapped my hand against the side of my head just needing to get some of the pain inducing, overwhelming thoughts from my mind. "Alex, look at me!" I opened my eyes and looked up where I found Jack on his knees right in front of me. "I'm sorry." I whimpered as I moved to hit my head harder, just needing the hurt, pain and confusion to leave me.

"No, enough of that." Jack said firmly as he caught my hand midway and pulled it down into his lap where he held it in place. I looked down to the cold grey floor, embarrassed by the show I was making of myself and confused about what the hell I was supposed to do to protect the people I loved.

"Sweet, look at me now." Jack coaxed. I slowly moved my eyes up to his, trying the whole time to avoid Matt who was stood just to my right, looking worried sick. I was making such a fucking mess of everything for these kind people.

"I'm sorry." I whimpered again.

"No, no more sorries from you Alex. None of this is your fault. Marcus is a fucking lunatic and you are a victim in all of it. The only reason we both made it out of there as well as we did was because you kept your head and handled that car perfectly today. I won't let you take any guilt for what happened."

"He shot at you Jack....you could be dead right now." I sobbed.

"But I'm not sweet. I'm here, very much alive." He said with a smile, then he leant in closer and whispered, "Don't tell Cal, because I was hoping to get a few days TLC out of him, but there's nothing actually wrong with me. I was totally milking it for the bed baths." That got a half giggle, half sob from me and again Jack smiled that amazing smile he had.

"Everything will be ok Alex, I promise you sweet. No one is getting hurt and Marcus Dalton is going down. You just have to trust us."

"I'm just so scared Jack. Today, when he fired that gun and I thought.....oh God. I'd rather die than see any of you hurt."

"No one is getting hurt. Rob has all of our asses covered. I know it's overwhelming right now, because it's been a hell of a day and you've had a pretty nasty knock on the head, but if you just try to quiet those crazy thoughts and get some rest, I promise everything will be a little easier in the morning sweet."

"I kinda flipped out, huh?" I asked with embarrassment as calm returned to my mind a little.

"Yeah, a little bit, but it's ok because we're good with crazy in this family." Jack joked making me laugh through my tears.

"I'm sor...."

"Don't you dare say you're sorry again Alex Harrison." He rebuked. He reached over to a trolley which sat against the wall beside me and pulled out some white gauze pads. "Let me see that arm now sweet, it's bleeding a lot." I looked down and found blood pouring down the arm I held around my waist. I slowly moved it until Jack took hold of my hand and pressed the gauze over the cut I had made when I'd ripped my IV out. As Jack tended the cut I forced myself to look up to Matt. His face was filled with worry and his hair was even more dishevelled from his nervous habit of running his hands through it.

"I'm sorry Matt. I didn't mean to go all 'One Flew Over the Cuckoo's nest' on you." I said more calmly.

""You have nothing to apologise for baby. Like Jack said, it's been a really shitty day and you're exhausted. We all understand." He bent down beside me and placed a kiss on my cheek. "I love you Alex."

"Love you too." I whispered. Jack applied a dressing to the cut once he'd stopped the bleeding and then used some wipes to clean the blood from where it had run down my arm.

"There, all sorted sweet. Let's get you back in bed now." He said as he stood. Matt stepped forward and lifted me from the floor into his warm arms. He lay me back in the middle of the hard hospital bed and tucked me in tightly with the blanket.

"Get some rest now sweet. I promise everyone is safe and they're gonna stay that way." Jack whispered as he leant over me and gently kissed the top of my head. "I'll be in my room just down the hall so just let me know if you need anything."

"Thank you Jack." He nodded and moved over to where Matt stood in the doorway. They were whispering to each other, probably about my break down.

"Jack's right hon, just rest now and stop worrying. Everything is going to be all good, I know it."

"Take care of him Cal. I know he says he ok, but he was in a bad way when I climbed out of that car."

"Don't worry sweetie, I've got him." He said, then with a kiss on my forehead he turned and helped Jack back into the wheelchair, then they left my room.

"You need anything baby?" Matt asked as he took the seat beside my bed.

"You." I admitted. Matt nodded, knowing what I meant, and climbed onto the bed beside me. It was a tight squeeze, but with his arms around me, keeping me safe and calm I finally felt like I could breathe.

"Sleep now love. I'll be right here with you the whole time. I promise." And that was all I needed to relax enough for sleep to take me, just the knowledge that he was there, keeping me safe.

MATT

I laid with Alex all night, afraid what may happen if I left her. Her breakdown earlier in the night had been terrifying and I was so relieved when Jack had gotten through to her. I had felt so useless, stood silently at the side, but I knew it needed to be Jack. Alex has gone through the hell of thinking he'd been killed and she needed to be reassured by him that everything was ok. She had slept fitfully, tossing and turning throughout the night and she woke up screaming twice from terrible nightmares. Thankfully I had been able to calm her both times and settle her back to sleep. I woke myself from a very light sleep at seven the next morning, exhausted having not let myself sleep properly in case she needed me and in agony from fighting to stay on the narrow bed all night. My neck and shoulders were stiff and aching so I quietly got to my feet and tried to stretch them out to relieve the tension.

"Matt?" Alex cried a few minutes after I left her side. She turned hurriedly in the bed and I knew she was panicking.

"It's ok love, I'm here." I soothed as I approached and leant in to gently kiss her.

"Is it morning?" She asked.

"Seven o'clock, How are you feeling?"

"Pretty rough, but my head's not pounding quite so hard."

"That's good baby. You look to have some colour back."

"Is Jack still ok?"

"I don't know, I was in here with you all night. You want me to go check?" I offered.

"Yes please and do you think you could get me some coffee?"

"No problem. I'll be back in a few minutes." I kissed her once again and then hurried from the room and across the hall to the waiting room where I knew Rob and Lucy had spent the night, refusing to go home until we all did. Cam and Evan were stationed outside Alex and Jack's rooms and seemed, as always, on high alert. As I approached the waiting room I found Gareth outside the door.

"Morning mate." I greeted him.

"How's she doing?" He asked with genuine concern.

"A little better this morning I think."

"Glad to hear it." He said with a smile as he opened the door to the waiting room for me. I walked in and found Lucy and Rob sat chatting in the corner, Lucy curled into Rob's side.

"Oh Matt! How is she?" Lucy cried as she leapt up.

"A little better I think. She had a rough night though. She wants me to check on Jack and get her some coffee. Would you mind sitting with her while I'm gone please darling?"

"Of course not. I'll go now." Lucy replied. She quickly kissed Rob, then hurried from the room.

"How is she really doing?" Rob asked once she was gone.

"It was a very long night, but she does have some colour back this morning."

"Jack told me what happened last night, in her room."

"Yeah, it was rough Rob. I think she was just so overwhelmed by everything and the very real fear that Jack could have been killed. Plus she has a concussion on top of her brain injury. She does seem more with it today though."

"She's done well to hold it together to this point Matt. She's lived through hell, survived being thrown down a flight of stairs and escaped to make herself a better life. Having it all come back to haunt her again must be terrifying. I think she was due a melt down."

"I agree. We just need to end this shit. Any news on Marcus?"

"Nothing yet. His truck was still in the road when the guys returned to the scene. They checked it for info on where he's staying, but came up empty. It was completely clean, a rental from the airport. Don't worry though. My entire team is hunting his ass down, along with half the FBI. We'll get the sonofabitch."

"We have to. I can't let him put her through anything else Rob. I really don't know how much more she can take right now."

"We'll keep her safe. He won't get near her again. I've increased her security detail and they'll be with you guys at all times."

"Thanks mate. I appreciate you looking out for her."

"She's family Matt. Go on, go check on Jack. I'll check in on Alex and Lucy." We parted ways at the waiting room and I headed for Jack's room, hoping like hell he was still doing ok. I really didn't want to take Alex any bad news back.

I knocked on the door to Jack's side room, then walked in. Relief washed over me when I found him fully dressed, tying his boots.

"Hey Matt." Cal greeted from where he sat in the corner. He looked exhausted, as we all did.

"Hi guys. How you feeling Jack?" I asked as I perched on the bed beside him.

"Good to go. The headache is minimal now and my wrist has been strapped up for a few days. It should be fine by the wedding." Jack replied in his usual upbeat tone. "How's Alex?"

"Worried about you mainly. She sent me to check on you. She had a tough night."

"Nightmares?" Cal asked.

"Yep and plenty of them."

"I've been released so that should set her at ease. I'll call in to see her before I head home. Is she going to be released today do you think?"

"I hope so. I don't think it's doing her any good being in the hospital. They seem to terrify her."

"We're not working from now until the wedding, so you can count on us if you need help to get her home any quicker."

"Thanks mate, I appreciate that, but you two have a wedding to plan."

"The wedding's all planned. We don't have anything left to sort." Jack replied.

"Jack's right. We don't need to be anywhere except where you and Alex need us Matt." Cal agreed.

"Thank you, both of you. I am so grateful for the way you've taken Alex under your wing since you met her." I said, feeling uncharacteristically choked up. It really was amazing the way she had instantly been accepted into the family fold and meant so very much to me.

"She's a part of our family now. We've all fallen in love with her, just the way we all fell for Lucy. She's special Matt and she has earned the love and respect of every one of us." Jack slapped me on the shoulder to cement his words, then got to his feet and shrugged on his coat.

"Come on, let's check in on her." Cal said as he wrapped an arm around Jacks shoulders and led him from the room.

I left them heading to Alex's room, while I went in search of a decent cup of coffee for her, happy in the knowledge my entire family were sat with her, taking care of her and keeping her safe.

ALEX

The second Lucy walked into my room and closed the door behind her, the floodgates opened again. Just the sight of her comforted me and gave me the confidence to crumble just a little.

"Oh Alex, it's ok chick." She said as she rushed over and climbed onto the bed beside me. She wrapped her arms around me and we leant on each other as I sobbed, over which part of the whole awful episode, I couldn't quite pinpoint.

"Have you seen Jack, is he ok?" I asked between sobs.

"Matt was going to check on him, but I'm sure he's fine. He only had a mild concussion. That man's got a head like a rhino, I'm telling you." Lucy replied with a laugh.

"Marcus tried to shoot him....I thought he had Lucy."

"I know hun. I can't even imagine how terrifying that was, but Jack's really ok. Everyone's ok. You have to stop torturing yourself."

"My life isn't worth yours, or any of the guys Lucy. I'm nobody. Before you guys not one person on this earth had ever even cared about me, let alone loved me. I have nothing, I've done nothing. If anyone has to die because of Marcus Dalton it should be me....I want it to be me." I explained as tears ran down my cheeks. Lucy sat back and pushed me up so I faced her.

"Stop talking like that right now Alex, do you hear me? You are somebody, you're the love of Matt's life, you're my best friend and you're Cal, Jack and Rob's, unruly, very scrappy, adopted little sister. Four of Rob's guys are outside this room, not because they're being paid, but because they care about you and about keeping you safe. They're your friends too Alex and we're your family. Nobody is dying because of Marcus Dalton because Rob and the guys won't let that happen so I don't want to hear you talking about sacrificing yourself, or any other daft talk like that, again. Am I clear? You are where you belong now, with us and that's where you're staying." I slumped forward into her arms again, tired of trying to work out what I should do for the best when my head pounded so hard it made me want to throw up. I couldn't think straight anymore. Lucy just held me and let me cry for a while and I appreciated her comfort and the silence.

"Alex, honey are you ok?" Rob's voice startled me and Lucy, causing us both to look up at the same time, to see him walk into the room looking tired and concerned.

"Have you seen Jack this morning? I asked tearfully.

"Not this morning, but Matt's gone to check on him. I'm sure he's fine though."

"Can you take me to s-see him….please Rob? I need to know he's ok….please?" I begged.

"Let's just give Matt a few minutes to come back to us and if he doesn't I'll go and check on Jack myself, ok? I don't think you should be up and about yet sweetheart."

"No one's seen him yet this morning. What if something happened over night? He had a head injury, that's really serious. I freaking know, I live with it every damned day!" I cried with fear. The longer I waited to hear Jack was ok, the more I convinced myself he'd had major complications through the night.

"Alex, just breathe sweetheart. You're getting all worked up over nothing. I'm sure Jack's fine and driving the nurses and Cal crazy as we speak." Rob joked, but I didn't smile. I couldn't seem to do anything but cry and get myself in a state. I just couldn't seem to organise my thoughts past panic and horror.

"I just want to see him for myself Rob….please, I have to see him, right now!" I pleaded going between hysterics and desperate sobs. When Rob looked between me and Lucy with hesitation I gave up begging and started to move my legs off the edge of the ned. I'd go alone to Jack's room if I had to!

"Alex, where are you going?" Lucy asked as she scrambled down from the bed and to my side.

"Something's happened, I know it has. You're all keeping it from me because I'm crazy, but I have to know. I have to see him." I cried hysterically.

"Alex, get back into bed." Rob said sternly as he stood right in front of me, where I had managed to get to my feet, very unsteadily.

"We're not keeping anything from you hun, we just haven't checked in with Jack yet," Lucy said.

"Get back into bed and I'll run to his room right now sweetheart, please. You're shaking and you've gone completely pale. Please just lie back down." Rob said as he reached out to steady me as I started to waver on shaky legs.

"What's happening in here then?" Jack's voice was like music to my ears. I turned to look at him and completely lost my balance. Rob caught me quickly and made short work of lifting me back into the bed.

"You ok honey?" He asked as he pulled the blanket over my trembling body.

"I'm sorry Rob." I whispered, embarrassed once again by my behaviour. I just couldn't seem to control myself. I knew it was the result of yet another knock to my already damaged brain.

"What happened?" Jack asked as he approached the bed and started checking my pulse and studying my face.

"Jack! Thank God!" I gasped breathlessly, exhausted from the tiny amount of exertion.

"Sweet, I know I'm hot, but don't swoon every time I enter the room. Matt will kick my ass." Jack joked, making me smile. He was dressed in jeans and a Navy Polo with his grey overcoat and he looked great except for the line of stitches just below his hairline.

"You're ok?" I asked.

"Of course he's ok sweetie. Were you worried?" Cal asked from where he stood beside Jack.

"I just….you got a head injury Jack….because of me. I know how bad a head injury could be. I just thought…..I was worried something had gone wrong." I admitted feebly.

"Alex, you have to stop this. I banged my head, a little. I wasn't hurt anywhere near as bad as you were and I am absolutely fine this morning. I've been released. You have to stop blaming yourself for what happened and you really have to stop upsetting yourself so much." Jack gently chided.

"I'm sorry. I don't know what's wrong with me. I can't seem to get myself together….my thoughts are just so jumbled."

"You have a concussion honey. It's understandable." Rob cut in as he patted my hand reassuringly.

"Have you had your usual meds?" Jack asked and then, of course, it clicked.

"No, they were in my purse, in the car." Jack nodded.

"I'll speak to your doctor on my way out sweet. I'm sure things will settle down after you get those and a little more rest."

"You're going home?" I asked.

"You'll be right behind us Alex. Matt already says he's going to try and get you out of here today." Cal answered.

"But you'll be careful, won't you?" I looked around at all of the people I had come to love more than I ever thought possible, and panic set in again. "All of you? You have to watch out for him. He told me…...he said 'one down'. He wants to get to me, through you guys."

"Alex, it's all taken care of honey. Everyone has security tailing them. Jack and I are armed. You have Cam and Evan or Gareth and Alec with you and Matt at all times and there are other guys with the rest of us. Everyone will be safe until this is over. I promise you." Rob said firmly, so much certainty to his words that it was hard not to believe him. I just hoped, more than I had ever wanted anything before, that he was right, because nothing could happen to any of them because of my fucked up history. I would never survive knowing I got any of them hurt or worse.

As Matt signed me out of the hospital later that afternoon and drove me home, I debated again, for the millionth time since waking in the hospital, what I should do for the best. My fight or flight instincts told me to run, to flee far away from everyone I cared about to lure Marcus away from all of them. He'd catch up with me, especially if I was alone, but I didn't care. If it meant everyone I loved and cared for was safe, he could have my life. I'd do anything to save each and every one of them, even go back to hell.

But I didn't run, didn't flee. I let Matt lead me up to our apartment where I collapsed into bed and snuggled into him, because I was selfish. For the first time in my entire life I was loved and cared for. I felt safe and secure with Matt and it was a feeling I couldn't bare to lose. I loved him and the thought of leaving him was too much to bare, so I chose to believe when they all told me everyone would be safe. I chose the cowards way and stayed where I felt I belonged, which, I was assured again and again, was the best place for me to be. I chose love and safety. I should have known better.

MATT

"Alex, you ready love?" I called from the small lounge area of our hotel suite. We had arrived that afternoon for Jack and Cal's wedding, at the beautiful lodge style inn they had hired out for the weekend. We were on the outskirts of one of the most beautiful national parks in the area and it really was a special location for the occasion. The guys had chosen well.

"Two minutes, sexy!" Alex called back making me smile. I was relieved she seemed to have come back to herself in the last day or so. It had been a stressful time after the crash she and Jack had suffered, because the resulting concussion seemed to exacerbate her existing brain injury and she had been erratic, emotional and pretty muddled and confused for a couple of days. Thankfully it had all settled down and she had been back to her usual chirpy, upbeat self since the previous day. She still had extensive bruising across her chest and pain in her shoulder, but she was definitely on the mend.

"I hate to rush you baby, but we're already late." I said as I walked through to the bedroom to hurry her up, adjusting my cufflinks as I went. Jack and Cal were holding a meal, for the guests staying in the lodge that night, mainly family.

As I walked into the bedroom Alex came shooting out of the en-suite, her shoes in one hand and purse in the other.

"Don't say another word Matt! I'm almost ready. I just need to re-do my lipstick. I smudged it." She barked playfully as she ran past me to the dressing table. She grabbed her lipstick and then ran back past me to the bathroom again.

"Maybe slow down a bit love. We won't make it all if you take a spill." I cautioned.

"I really didn't want to be late tonight Matt."

"Do you really expect Jack and Cal will be on time? Don't worry so much. I know for a fact we'll be there before them." I assured her as I shrugged on the jacket to my charcoal, three piece suit. I had paired it with a crisp white shirt, open collar since it wasn't a formal dinner and I bloody hated ties.

"I guess you're right." Alex agreed as she stepped more calmly into the bedroom. "Do I look ok?"

I almost swallowed my tongue when I finally got a proper look at her. She was stunning in a black dress that hugged every spectacular curve of her body. It ran to just below her knee, but split up the right side to mid thigh. It was low cut in the front and had tiny little straps over her shoulders. Her beautiful blond hair hung down her back, in long, loose curls. She smiled nervously at me and I had never felt more like I was punching above my weight with this stunning woman.

"Breathtaking Alex....I can't speak baby. You're too beautiful." I whispered, causing her to smile more.

"It's not too fancy?" She asked.

"It's perfect." I stalked closer to her and ensnared her in my arms. She squealed a little as I pulled her swiftly into my front. "You're perfect." I whispered as I moved in for a kiss. I kept it light, not wanting to ruin the makeup she had spent great effort applying, but I had to at least get a little taste, something to cling to until I could do what I really wanted to do later in the evening, tear that sexy dress off and touch every inch of her intoxicating body.

"I love you." She said as we pulled apart reluctantly.

"Love you too baby."

***

"You're late!" Jack called mockingly as we descended the staircase to the main lobby of the hotel. I looked behind me and found him and Cal running down the stairs behind us, Cal buttoning the waistcoat he wore and Jack only half way through tying his tie.

"Not as late as you two by the look of it." I laughed.

"What were you guys doing? How can you be late for a meal you're hosting?" Alex asked, stifling a laugh herself.

"We got side tracked." Cal replied with a wink to Jack.

"This will not be happening tomorrow. Lucy and I will get you two down that aisle on time if it kills us!" She said firmly as she pointed to them both with an accusing finger.

"As if we'd be late for our own wedding sweet." Jack said innocently as we reached the lobby and all hurried towards the lodge's five star restaurant.

"Just get in there!" Alex barked with an eye roll as she shoved them both through the door with a push in the back.

"Jackson Reed, you're late!" Jack's mum barked as soon as he was through the door. We followed them in and stopped abruptly behind where Jack was getting his telling off.

"Sorry mom. You know timekeeping never was my best skill." Jack replied, making me laugh. He really was a mummy's boy.

"It was my fault Mrs Reed." Cal said.

"Cal, how many times do I have to tell you, please call me Helen. We're family." She scolded, putting both guys in their place, both of whom were at least a foot and a half taller than her. Alex and I looked at each other with a giggle. "And you can stop Laughing Matthew. You're late too!" She added. I stopped laughing and looked to the tiny woman.

She really was beautiful, a tiny female version of Jack with the same sandy blonde hair, hers cut into a neat little bob that framed her face. She had bright blue eyes, just like Jacks, only hers didn't seem to miss a bloody thing. She was a very slight, petite woman, dressed impeccably in a pale blue trouser suit with a floral top underneath. Her matching pale blue stilettos gave her a few extra inches of height, but she still looked tiny, barely taller than Alex's five foot, even in the shoes.

"That would be my fault." Alex said nervously. She clutched my hand tightly and I felt her anxiety. Mother's had never been a good experience for Alex, thus far.

"Was it really young lady?" Helen asked with the mock sternness I knew well from her.

"I'm so sorry. I didn't mean to.....I just.....we...." Alex floundered with true fear.

"Sweet, it's ok. She was just joking." Jack said hurriedly, calming her terror laced apology.

"Oh, ok." He placed a reassuring hand on her shoulder and she smiled, still looking somewhat pained.

"Get over here and give me a hug Matt!" Helen said, not seeming to notice Alex's melt down. "It's been too long since I've seen you sweet boy." Helen gushed as she crushed me in a typical mum hug. She really was a lovely woman. I had been lucky enough to spend quite a bit of time with her in the time I had lived in Chicago.

She never failed to make me smile and think of my own, wonderful mother.

"You're looking beautiful as always." I hugged her briefly, wanting to get back to Alex, knowing she was struggling with the stranger in front of her and the room full, all around us.

"And you're still a shameless flatterer!" Helen laughed as I released her.

"Helen, I'd like you to meet my girlfriend, Alex." I wrapped my arm tightly around Alex's waist and squeezed a little, hoping to reassure her she was safe.

"Alex! I've heard a lot about you from my boy. It's lovely to meet you." Helen gushed and then before anyone could react, she grabbed Alex's arm and yanked her into a huge hug. Alex squeaked a little as she was wrenched from my grip and I looked hurriedly to Jack with concern.

"Mom, just go easy." Jack barked as Cal and I both took a step toward Alex, both I think waiting for the freak out, but luckily Alex kept it together. She was blatantly stiff in Helen's arms, but she maintained her calm.

"Helen, great to see you!" Lucy's loud cry was enough to break the hold Helen had on Alex and I was beyond relieved when Alex scurried back over to me and curled into my side. She was trembling slightly, and her breathing was fast, but she forced a smile my way. Thank Christ Lucy had intervened.

"You ok sweet? I'm sorry, she's a hugger. I should have warned you." Jack said hurriedly as Helen and Lucy chatted a few feet away.

"I'm ok Jack. It's fine." Alex laughed, but I knew she was putting a brave face on when she cuddled into me, burying her face in my shirt..

Jack and Cal both looked to me over Alex's head with concern, but I just smiled and nodded, assuring them she was ok.

"Let's find our seats." Cal suggested as he ushered everyone over to the top table where Alex and I were sat with Rob and Lucy, Cal's Dad - Martin, Helen and of course Jack and Cal. Other tables were filled with Jack and Cal's more distant family and all of their friends from the hospital and the gym.

"Alex, this is my Dad, Martin. Dad, this is Alex." Cal introduced. I was grateful he had waited until we were all sat down, so hugs were unlikely.

"Ah, the famous Alex. I've heard a lot about you dear." Martin chuckled as he extended his hand across the table to Alex. She took it and looked shocked when Martin placed a kiss on the back of her hand.

He was an old charmer. He had to be in his seventies, but he didn't look a day over fifty, more like Cal's older brother than his dad. He had dark hair, greying slightly at the sides the dark mediterranean colouring that Cal had obviously inherited. He was as tall and broad as his son and obviously spent a lot of time at the gym since retiring as one of New York's finest. I had only met him once before, but instantly took a liking to the ladies man.

"All good things, I'm sure." Alex joked nervously.

"Of course it was all good hon." Cal cut in.

"Like he'd dare say anything against you Alex! He's seen you knee at least two guys in the nuts!" Lucy roared, making us all laugh, except Martin and Helen who looked confused.

"Alex is a bit of a scrapper." Jack told his mother with a chuckle.

"Really?" Helen asked as she looked to Alex speculatively.

"Only in self defense. You make me sound like I go looking for trouble." Alex cried with embarrassment.

"Boys! Why is Alex having to defend herself at all? You all should be taking care of her!" Helen barked.

"It's ok Helen. They do take good care of both of us, there's no denying that." Lucy said quickly as she smiled at Rob with so much love and affection.

"Lucy's right. The poor guys are run ragged with the trouble Lucy and I seem to have following us. No, we were on a girls night out a while back and things got a bit scary. I kneed the guy and he ran off. Thankfully the guys got to us and everything was ok." Alex explained quickly.

"What kind of trouble?" Martin asked with a cop voice.

"Oh….erm, nothing really. I shouldn't have brought it up. I just wanted to assure Helen the guys really do take the most amazing care of me and Lucy." Alex said hurriedly, obviously not wanting to discuss it further.

"I've noticed all the security you have around this place. Is there something going on? I can help if there is." Martin offered. Alex looked helplessly to Cal for help.

"Dad. It's all under control. You can turn your bat signal off for this weekend." He joked, but Martin looked far from convinced.

"How's retirement treating you Martin?" Rob asked and I saw Alex visibly relax at the subject change. The conversation moved on and me and the other guys did all we could to steer topics away from Alex's past and Martin's curiosity over the additional security surrounding the lodge that weekend.

A couple of hours in and the meal was over and the dancing had begun. Alex and Lucy were both pretty tipsy and were 'shaking their arses' as Lucy so nicely coined it, on the dancefloor with Jack. Cal and Martin were sat at a table a few over chatting with some cousins who had flown in from Canada. Rob and I remained at our table, both as awkward as ever at those kinds of occasions, chatting with Helen. She also, wasn't a fan of busy places, likely the result of her abusive marriage with Jack's dad years back, so she had stayed where she felt safe, with 'her boys' as she had labelled the four of us.

"You are two lucky SOBs boys, they are two beautiful girls you've gotten yourselves." She said as we all watched Lucy, Alex and Jack dancing.

"I know. Trust me Helen, I count my blessings every damned day for Lucy being in my life." Rob said, very candidly.

"How long have you and Alex been together Matt?" She asked.

"A little over three months." I replied.

"I would have thought longer by the way you are together. You love her, correct?"

"Very much."

"Has she told you about whatever's haunting her yet?" Helen asked, startling me. Had Jack told her something? I couldn't imagine him doing that, not without asking Alex's permission first. I looked to her with confusion and she smiled softly. "Don't worry. Nobody has said anything. I just see it, in her. I see the fear and wariness she carries beneath that beautiful smile. I see her pain, the same way as I can see Lucy's. They've suffered, both of them, more than anyone ever should." Rob and I shared a look of anger at the thought of what they had both been through.

"Yes, she's told me." I finally replied.

"And this history, it's the reason for the bruise on her chest and the increased security?"

"Yes, but I have it all in hand Helen." Rob answered this time.

"I have no doubt you do Rob. I won't pretend to know the full extent of the skills you and Jack have acquired over the years, but I do know you two, along with Matt and Cal are the best people on earth to protect that precious girl.

"All I want to say is, be careful Matt. Alex seems like a happy, positive soul, but underneath she is cracked, deeply. One more hit and she may just shatter. Someone with that many pieces will be very difficult to ever get back together the way they once were. If you love her, as I know you do, you have to do all you can to hold those pieces together for her. Don't let her shatter, not again." Helen advised. Her words hit me hard. I knew she was right, Alex was cracked, maybe more deeply than anyone realised. She had been through a hell most people couldn't even imagine, but she was strong and she had come out of the other end of it. She had escaped and found a way to piece a life for herself. Now everyone saw her smiles and strength and assumed she was whole, but I knew she wasn't. I'd witnessed the nightmares and flashbacks again and again. Helen was so right. I loved Alex and I would do all I could to hold her together. I wouldn't let her shatter, I couldn't. I needed her in my life, she completed it and no way was I going to let anything happen to her.

"I've got her Helen, I swear I have," I said firmly.

"We all have." Rob added. Helen nodded, what I took as, her approval and so we all turned back to the dancefloor as Alex screamed excitedly. I laughed as I watched Cal sneak up behind her, grab her hand and spin her into his body. She laughed as she sank into his hold and danced with him to the slower song that had just commenced.

She continued to beam as she danced with him and she looked so joyous. I swore there and then, not for the first time, to do whatever it took to keep her safe and happy for as long as we got together.

ALEX

"Cal, this may be your wedding day, but I will kick your butt if you don't hurry the hell up!" I called through the door, into the bedroom of the suite where Cal was getting dressed. I had left him half an hour ago with his suit. All he had to do was put it on and style his hair, yet every time I asked if he was ready he said 'no'. How long could it take? We were due down in the great hall for the wedding in ten minutes!.

This was a terrible idea. I may kill him before he walks down the aisle. How you doing? Xx

I sent the quick text to Lucy, hoping she was faring better then turned back to the closed bedroom door.

"That's it. This is your warning Cal, I'm coming in!" I yelled before I stormed into the room where I found Cal, sat on the end of the bed. His tux was all in place, except for the dark silver bow tie. He had his head in his hands and I was instantly worried. I had never seen him look so unanimated.

"Cal, what's wrong?" I asked as I sank to my knees in front of him. He lifted his head enough to look at me and I saw worry in his eyes. "What is it?"

"Am I doing the right thing Alex?" He asked and my heart pounded at the thought of me having to tell Jack Cal had changed his mind.

"What? What do you mean? You love Jack, don't you?" I asked with fear.

"Jesus yes! Of course I do. I love him more than I have ever loved anybody." He said vehemently, calming my frayed nerves a little, at least.

"Then what are you unsure about?"

"Am I really good enough for him Alex? I mean look at him, he's straight off the cover of some fancy magazine. He's funny and so damned smart. He has this great future ahead of him.

"I'm just me. I'm almost a decade older, a fuck ton uglier and I have no real prospects to give him. I've had my career, and it's over now. Am I just going to bring that amazing man down by tying myself to him?"

"Cal, that may be the biggest load of horse shit I ever heard anyone spout." I snapped firmly, realising he needed a very swift reality check. "Yes, I agree, Jack is a beautiful, very smart, ridiculously funny guy, but the rest is crap. You are also an amazingly handsome and very sexy man. You are just as, if not more funny and likable as Jack and as for prospects, you have so much to give Cal. You have, your own, thriving business which nets you a small fortune. You have 20 plus years cop experience which is invaluable in the disasters this family seems to attract. But, most importantly, you really get Jack. You have never tried to change him, you take him as he is. You accept he's a massive flirt, who loves to play the fool and who has a serious OCD streak. You accept his past and the issues that has brought him. You accept his crazy career and the insane shifts he works. You accept him, as he is and that's all he needs. I didn't know Jack before you Cal, but I can tell you for damn sure, his life is whole with you in it. Together I know you two will go forward and do great things, live extraordinary lives and I am just so honoured that I'll get be there with you along the way.

"So please Cal, stop doubting how amazing you are because I won't hear it anymore. I know what a wonderful man you are because you have proven it to me every single day since the one I met you. Jack is a really lucky guy to get you, just as you are, to get him. You two belong together. It's as simple as that."

"You're pretty damned special yourself Alex." Cal said as he took my hands and stood, pulling me to my feet and into a tight embrace.

"So are we doing this then?" I asked hopefully.

"Damn right we are. Thanks for talking me off the ledge honey."

"Anytime. I'm always here for you Cal."

"Likewise sweetie. Come on, help me with this tie." I stepped back and tied his bowtie neatly for him.

"There, all done." I declared when it was done.

"Will I do?" He asked as he held out his arms so I could get a good look at him.

"You look perfect Cal. Let's go get you married!" I declared as I took his arm and we headed out together, We were halfway down the staircase when my phone beeped with an incoming text. I hurriedly pulled it from the clutch I had under my arm and laughed at the text from Lucy.

Tell Cal it's off. I've already murdered Jack and buried him in the woods! 40 minutes to style his hair!! What bloody hair?? ETA 2 mins xx

"I take it Lucy's having fun with Mr perfectionist?" Cal asked with a chuckle as I put my phone away and took his arm again.

"He may be being a little precious about his hair. Lucy says ETA 2 minutes." I explained as we stopped outside the doors of the great room where the ceremony was being held. The remaining guests, who hadn't stayed at the inn, had arrived by coach a short while before and the room on the other side of the doors sounded packed. It was enough to send my heart racing. The thought of all those eyes on or around me as I walked down the aisle with Cal was terrifying.

"Alex honey, breathe. It's all going to be fine." Cal said soothingly, snapping me from my panic.

"Oh....I know. I'm ok Cal." I said hurriedly, not wanting him to worry about me on his special day.

"You're not, you're trembling and breathing way too fast. Is this going to be too much for you sweetie, because if it is I can go and get Matt and you can sit with him. I'll be fine on my own."

"No! No way Cal. You're right, I'm nervous, but I can do this. I want to do this, for you. I want to be by your side today, just like you've been by mine for months. I'm ok." I said firmly. He nodded and then cupped the back of my head as he pulled me close enough to place a kiss on my forehead.

"I'm proud of you honey." He whispered, taking my breath away. No one had ever said those words to me before and they meant so very much. In the short time I had known them, all of the men in Matt's family had become the loving brothers I had wished so many times for, protective, caring big brothers who I knew would always be there for me as I would be for them.

I was fighting back some serious emotions when Jack and Lucy appeared behind us at the doorway. Jack looked wonderfully handsome in his tux, which matched Cal's except he wore a white bowtie and cumberbundt, where Cal wore a dark silver. They smiled at each other and no words were needed because the love they held for each other was plain to see in their eyes and their expressions.

"Cal, you look great." Lucy declared excitedly.

"Yep, she's right. You both scrub up pretty well." I joked with a smile.

"Cheeky!" Jack laughed. "You ready to do this babe?" We all looked to Cal who looked proud as punch of his groom.

"Born ready. Let's make this official." Cal agreed. They shared a brief kiss and then Jack and Lucy set off into the room and down the aisle arm in arm.

"Deep breath honey." Cal whispered as we linked arms ready to follow.

"You too." He nodded and took a deep breath as we set off down the centre of the great room. There must have been around a hundred guests all seated in neat rows on both sides of the room. It was beautifully dressed with greenery and winter flowers. Candles were lit in tall, antique looking candelabras on each window ledge and at the front on the table where the wedding officiant waited. It was the most romantic, intimate wedding venue I had ever seen and I had never felt more desperate to be near Matt.

I looked across to him as we neared the end of the aisle. He was sat in the front row with Rob, Helen and Martin and he looked so damn sexy in his tux- my very own 007. I smiled at him and he returned it with a look that said he was eager to get to me too.

When we finally reached the end and met Jack, Cal led me over to the side where Lucy stood and held me for a moment as he placed a kiss on my cheek.

"Love you." I whispered in his ear.

"Love you too sweetie." With those words he turned and took his place beside Jack and they shared the most beautiful look of love and excitement to be marrying each other. It brought tears to my eyes and I hurried to calm them before I was a sobbing mess. Lucy tapped me and I was glad when I turned and found tears in her eyes too. She handed me a kleenex and we both stood dabbing our eyes.

The ceremony really was the most wonderful and romantic affair. Jack and Cal had written their own vows and of course, there were some laughs from them, but at the heart of it all, was simply love, an amazing, unquestioning love that they shared for one another which shone through the entire occasion. Lucy and I had quietly sobbed throughout, clutching a hand between us, and dabbing our tears with a kleenex in the other. I think we were both relieved when it was done and we could get ourselves together a little as we all sat down to sign the marriage certificate.

"You ok ladies?" Jack asked with a grin as we sat.

"Don't you start Jack! It was so bloody romantic and heartfelt. I told you I'd end up blubbering." Lucy whimpered as she pulled another tissue from her purse.

"It really was beautiful. You guys are perfect together." I added after a deep, cleansing breath.

Jack and Cal signed first, then Lucy and I followed and that was it complete. We all stood and Cal and Jack stepped forward as the officiant declared them 'Mr and Mr Warren-Reed'.

Loud cheers, hooting and hollering erupted as they set off down the aisle hand in hand and my heart seemed to spark into defense mode at the loud sounds around me. I took a deep breath and tried to calm myself as adrenaline hit and my legs trembled. I stood still, gripping Lucy's hand as I told myself in my head, over and over, *it's ok, it's a happy day. It's safe.* I chanted it silently, over and over as I took deep, calm breaths.

"Alex, it's ok." I heard Lucy whisper to me. I snapped from my chant and looked to her. She was smiling nervously and squeezing my hand.

"I'm ok." I whispered as I moved to start walking down the aisle.

"No. Just wait here for the guys. No one's looking at us now, they're all leaving. We can wait here." She said calmly. So we stood and watched as everyone left, and as they did, it got quieter and I got calmer. Matt and Rob were chatting to Helen and Martin, but I didn't miss the way they kept a watch on us out of the corner of their eyes. Once the room was pretty much empty Helen and Martin got up and walked out too and finally Matt was walking toward me.

"How you doing love?" He asked as he wrapped me in a huge hug. I sank into him and finally let out the breath I'd been holding.

"I had a moment with all the noise, but I'm ok now." I admitted.

"You look so bloody beautiful. It almost killed me to stay away from you throughout the whole thing."

"You're looking very handsome yourself in that tux. I was thinking we might have a little James Bond role play tonight." I purred as I stepped back and ran my hands over his hard chest.

"We have an hour right now love before the meal." Matt grinned that sexy damned grin that always got him what he wanted.

"Oh no you don't, you two!" Lucy barked, snapping Matt and I from our lust fuelled conversation. I turned to where Lucy stood with her hands on her hips, glaring at her brother.

"No sloping off today. I'm not explaining to Helen where you've disappeared to. Get your backsides out there and behave."

"Yes mum." Matt laughed as he took my hand. We followed Rob and Lucy out to the lobby where champagne and canapes were being served and found Jack and Cal to congratulate them properly.

"Alex, I need to speak to you a minute!" Lucy whispered in my ear about ten minutes later. I had been stood chatting to CJ, the manager at the gym and Lucy had run up to me so fast she almost barrelled me over.

"What's going on?" I asked, worried by the fear I saw in her face.

"Not here. Come with me." She said as she pulled on my hand and dragged me across the room. I hurriedly apologised to CJ and then scurried after her and into a disabled toilet that sat off in the corner of the room.

"Lucy, what's wrong?" I asked as she shoved me in and closed and locked the door behind us.

"I'm sorry, but I have to speak to you now. That's why I stopped you and Matt....you know." She said nervously.

"Hon, it doesn't matter. Whatever it is, just tell me and we'll deal with it." She looked at me with nothing but utter terror and then she pulled her purse from under her arm and started rifling through it.

"I don't know what I'm going to do." She cried as she pulled out a white paper bag and handed it to me. I looked from her pale face and down to the bag. I took it from her trembling hand and opened it to peek inside.

"Oh my God! Are you….?" I asked as I looked in at a pregnancy test.

"Yeah, that was the fifth test. It's conclusive. I only found out last night…..I wasn't…..we didn't….oh Jesus Alex. I'm on the pill. Rob and I, we haven't even discussed kids properly yet. How has this happened?"

"I think you know the how honey." I laughed, but stopped when Lucy just looked distraught.

"Alex, I'm in melt down. What if Rob doesn't want this?"

"Lucy, forget about Rob and plans and all of that shit. Do you want this baby? Are you happy about it?" I asked as I placed my hands on her shoulders to stop her pacing back and forth.

"I'm shocked. I guess I do want kids, I just….I wasn't planning on it happening yet."

"So it wasn't planned. The best things never are. If you are happy and you want this baby then I'm sure Rob will too. He loves you Lucy and babies would have come along eventually. He'll probably be surprised and a little terrified, but I'll bet he'll be the most excited damn father to be there has ever been. Stop stressing yourself out and embrace this brilliant news. You're going to be a mom!" I said excitedly.

"And you're going to be an Auntie." Lucy added with a smile I was so damn relieved to see.

"Cool Auntie Ali, I like it."

"Do you really think Rob will be ok with this?" She asked.

"Yes I do. I think he'll be over the freaking moon, but there's only one way to know for sure."

"I can't tell him today. This is Jack and Cal's day. I'm not hijacking it. Can we just keep this between us for today please? I'll tell him when we get home tomorrow, so he has privacy to process the news."

"Ok hon. Just between us for now, but just so you know, I'm happy for you and I can't wait to be an Aunt!" I cried as I hugged her tight.

"Thankyou. I knew you'd calm me down."

"Any time hon. Just take it easy and no drinking. Rob's gonna keep you in a protective bubble when he finds out!" I laughed as I thought of how overprotective he already was when it was just Lucy. Lord help her when Rob found out she was carrying their child.

"Don't! I should just not tell him until the week before the due date!" Lucy whined, making me laugh more.

"Yeah, good luck with that hon." I handed her back the bag containing the pregnancy test and she stuffed in her purse. We quickly straightened up, fixed our makeup and washed our hands, then headed back out to the party.

We were both startled when we stepped out and were stopped dead by Rob and Matt jumping in front of us.

"What's wrong?" Rob demanded at the same time Matt asked, "Are you ok love?" I looked to Lucy who was once again pale and looked like a deer in headlights.

"Sorry guys." I said quickly. "It's the crowd, you know. I got a little panicked and just needed a minute. I'm ok now."

"You should have found me baby." Matt sighed as he pulled me into his arms.

"It's ok Matt. Lucy was there and I'm feeling better now." I hated lying to him, but for Lucy I would.

"Come on, let's get a drink and see if we can find a seat for you ladies." Rob commanded. Lucy turned to me with a quick smile and I nodded to her. I had her back, I would always have her back as I knew she would have mine.

***

"It was a really amazing day you guys." I slurred, feeling a little the worse for wear as the six of us sat in the middle of the great room, which only an hour earlier had been in full party flow. It was almost three AM and everyone had either left or gone to their rooms, everyone but us six who were sat around a table having a nightcap, having had too much fun to call it a night. Lucy was fast asleep on Rob's Lap, nestled into his front and looking perfectly content. I had also made myself comfortable on Matt's lap and I had my arms wrapped around his neck. He was pretty merry himself and kept smiling at me like a fool. Jack and Cal were wasted and leant against each other, sideways as they swayed in their seats. The only one of us who was any use was Rob, who had barely touched alcohol all night, maintaining vigilance at all times, always on alert. That was Rob

"It was, wasn't it?" Cal almost shouted.

"Yes…..Mr Warren-Reed. You are correct…..it really was." Jack declared with a giggle.

"Ok guys. I'm cutting you all off." Rob declared in his usual bossy tone. "Come on, up to your rooms." He stood, adjusting Lucy a little in his arms so he wouldn't wake her and then just waited for us all to follow.

Matt stood with me in his arms before I knew what was going on and I squealed as he stumbled back a little. Rob, fast as lightning, grabbed Matt's arm with his free arm and steadied him.

"Matt, maybe Alex should walk." Rob said with a small chuckle.

"Nah, it's ok. I've got her now." Matt replied as he stepped away from Rob's grasp and steadied himself.

Jack and Cal stood and led the way. They were swaying a little too and definitely holding each other up with the arm they had across each other's shoulders.

I laughed as they began to stagger up the stairs and then hung on with everything in me as Matt did the same. Rob was right behind us, holding Lucy with one hand and his other on Matt's shoulder, keeping him upright.

"You should have had more to drink tonight Rob….I feel bad." I said over Matt's shoulder, suddenly realising the reason he had not drunk and stayed on alert was me and my history.

"You have nothing to feel bad about sweetheart. I had a good time tonight without drinking and I got to keep my family safe, which is all I care about and all I need to be happy." He replied with a soft smile.

"You're such a nice guy Rob. Th-thank you for looking out for me....for all of us."

"Don't tell any of the security guys that. You'll ruin my tough guy image." He laughed.

"Whatever Rob. You know, they all already know how s-soft you are really!" Jack yelled down the stairs, causing Lucy to stir and then wake with a start.

"Rob?" She cried and I looked down at her over Matt's shoulder.

"It's ok sweetheart. We're all headed to bed."

"While discussing how nice Rob is!" I added, giggling.

"Right then." Lucy whispered with confusion.

"Guys, this is us!" Cal declared when we stopped halfway down the corridor at the honeymoon suite.

"Thank you all for being here with us today. You all made it the best day of our whole lives." He gushed, sounding very intoxicated, but genuine with it. Rob put Lucy down and she hurried to hug them both. Matt did the same and I stumbled into Cal's arms.

"Thank you for being my rock today." He whispered.

"I'll be your rock whenever you need me Cal. Love you," I replied as I squeezed my arms around his waist.

"Love you too sweetie." When Cal released me I was passed over to Jack who held me tightly, making me feel so cherished.

"You did us proud today sweet. Thank you for being a part of this special day." He said, choking me up.

"No Jack...thank you for letting me be part of it. It was so beautiful." I whimpered through the huge lump in my throat.

"Love ya sweet. I'm so glad you're here, with us, where you belong."

"Me too. Love you too Jack." I reached up and gently kissed his cheek, then stepped back into Matt's arms. He pulled me back against his firm body, my back to his front, and wrapped his arms protectively around me.

"We still on for that run tomorrow guys?" Rob asked.

"Definitely" Jack and Cal said at the same time.

"Probably." Matt grumbled, making the others laugh.

"0600 hours, out front?" Rob asked.

"Guys, that's in less than three hours." I cried drunkenly.

"It's not often we get chance to run somewhere as perfect as this. I'm not passing that up." Rob replied.

"And you two? It's your wedding night?" Lucy asked as she pointed to the newlyweds.

"We've got a whole week together with no work. Don;t you worry about us missing out sweet" Jack purred with a cheeky lift of his eyebrows.

"Ewww!" Lucy and I both cried at the same time. "TMI Jack!" I added.

"Rob's right. It really is a beautiful place. We should make the most out of it." Cal offered.

"Fine, as long as you all know you're nuts!" I concluded.

"Meet you all out front at 0600. We'll get 20 kilometres in and then head to breakfast. They all agreed and we said goodnight, then headed to our own rooms.

Rob and Lucy were just one door down from Jack and Cal, but Matt and I were right at the end of the corridor, a strategic position for safety apparently. When we stopped to get the key from my purse, Cam appeared and helped me find it and unlock the door.

"I'll be out here all night if you need anything." He explained with a smile.

"Thanks Cam. Good night." I said in my best non-drunk voice before shutting the door. I put my purse on the console table near the door and kicked off my heels as I headed through the lounge area and into the bedroom. Matt walked in from the bathroom, his tie hanging open around his collar, stalking toward me like a predator approaching prey.

"What are you up to?" I laughed.

"Name's Bond, James Bond." He said in his fanciest British accent.

"Oh really Mr Bond? You going to show me your weapon?"

"I certainly am!" Matt growled as he grabbed me and pulled me into his arms. It took only seconds for the both of us to be completely naked and rolling around on the bed in fits of giggles. It was the perfect ending to the perfect night and I had never, ever been happier in my life.

***

Matt and I had made love for hours that night so I had been gobsmacked when Matt got up after maybe forty minutes of sleep and got ready for the run. I was exhausted and barely woke enough to kiss him goodbye before he left. I woke a couple of hours later, still exhausted, but knowing I had to get up and showered, ready to head to breakfast when Matt got back, which would be soon.

I stepped into the shower, my head pounding and my stomach churning. It was the hangover from hell and I was wondering why the hell I had felt the need to drink quite so much as the water pummeled down on my sore head.

By the time I got out of the shower and dried my hair, I was feeling a little more human. I dressed in skinny jeans and a pretty green chiffon blouse I had bought for the occasion. I applied a little makeup to hide my pale face and bags, then settled on the bed with a coffee and my kindle to wait for Matt. I was right near the end of a brilliant mystery romance and I was hoping to finish it in the peace of the inn before Matt got back and we had to head to breakfast. Just as I got settled my cell beeped, so I picked it up and found a text from Lucy. I opened it, laughing to myself assuming it would be her having another mini-meltdown about the pregnancy, but it wasn't. As I stared at the screen, my heart began to pound, the sound deafening in my ears. My hands shook uncontrollably and nausea hit, forcing me to bolt to the bathroom, where I threw up repeatedly, until there was nothing left in my stomach. When the heaving stopped I collapsed back on the cold bathroom floor and looked at my cell again. There on the screen, was a photo of Lucy, tied up and cowering in a dark corner. She was crying and in just her underwear. It was attached to a message with what looked like a residential address, followed by;

You have 20 mins to get here or I have some fun and kill the bitch. Come alone and ditch your cell or she's dead.

That was all it said and I was terrified at the thought of Marcus hurting her. I debated what I should do. Rob had his cell on him. I could call him and we could all go to the address together to get Lucy back, but Marcus had said I was to go alone. What if he saw us all arrive and killed her before we had a chance to get near? I couldn't risk Lucy's life like that. Marcus was a monster and I knew he'd take pleasure in hurting and possibly raping Lucy for as long as he had alone with her. It wasn't just Lucy's life at stake either. She was pregnant. I had to get to her before Marcus did something to hurt that precious life.

How the hell had he even gotten to her? There was security all over the lodge and Lucy must have been in the room when Rob left only a couple of hours earlier. I couldn't think straight. All i knew was he had her and I had to get her out. I couldn't keep wasting time knowing that. I had no choice, I had to go and get her, whatever it took. He'd take me, but I didn't care as long as I could get Lucy and her child out and away from him.

I ran to the desk and wrote Matt a very hurried note, telling him what happened and giving the address, with any luck they'd catch up before Marcus got away with me. I left it on the bed where I was sure Matt would see it, then pulled on my boots and coat and grabbed Matt's car keys. I knew Cam was outside the room door, so there was no way I could go that way. Instead I went to the window and looked out. We were in a room at the back, so there was no one around and it was only about six feet from the ground. I pocketed my cell and the keys, then opened the window and climbed out. I scaled down the side of the lodge very carefully and jumped the last few feet to the ground. I landed with a thud and set off running before anyone spotted me. I made it to Matt's Range Rover and adjusted the seat so I could reach the pedals, then punched the address into the navigation system. It was a ten minute drive and I knew I'd have to floor it if I was going to make it in Marcus's allotted time.

The whole drive I fought for control of my emotions. There wasn't time to fall apart. I had to get Lucy away from Marcus. He could do what he wanted with me as long as she got away unharmed. I couldn't bare to think of her suffering again after everything she'd been through already. She was carrying a baby and I would not let Marcus take that from her. He had ruined enough lives, it stopped then and there. I wouldn't let him break Lucy too.

As I drove I formulated a plan. I needed to be clever about approaching the situation or Marcus would simply take both of us. I had to be smart and make sure that didn't happen.

I slowed when I reached the street Marcus had led me to. It was very run down and several of the houses were abandoned. When I found the one I was looking for I reversed the car into the driveway, as close to the house as I could possibly get it, then I left my cell on the seat with Rob's number pulled up and ready to call. I opened the door wide and left the car running, with the keys in the ignition. I pulled off my coat and left it on the passenger seat, knowing Lucy was in only her underwear and would need to cover up. When I was sure everything was ready, I walked up the few steps to the house and opened the door, which sat unlocked. I guessed from the photo, Lucy was in a basement and I also knew Marcus would be having far too much fun torturing her, to not be down there too.

I walked through the house, which, thankfully, was completely empty of any furniture. If there had been any, I'd have cleared it from the path to the door, but it wasn't necessary. I moved through to the kitchen where the door to the basement sat open and I could hear Lucy crying out. It was all I needed to spur me on. I took a breath and hurried down the stairs.

"Alex, get the hell out of here!" Lucy yelled. I stopped halfway down the rickety wooden staircase and looked across at her. I fought tears at the sight of her bleeding face and beaten body. I bolted down the remaining stairs and stopped a few feet from where Marcus roughly held her by the arm.

"Ah, goody. Alicia's here." Marcus sneered as he shoved Lucy across the room toward me. I grabbed her and pulled her close. She was frozen and trembling, her hair wild around her bruised and bleeding face.

"You have to go." She panted.

"Matt's car is outside with the engine running. You run, get in it and drive the hell away. Don't hesitate, just go. Do you understand? Get to the guys." I whispered frantically. Marcus was watching us, but couldn't hear what I was saying.

"I can't...." She started, but I cut her off.

"You can and you will. You have to protect that baby. You get the fuck out of here and to the guys. I love you Lucy."

"I love you." Lucy whimpered back.

"Tell Matt I love him. Now, go!" I said as I shoved her toward the stairs and launched myself at Marcus as a distraction. If we had both run, Marcus would easily have caught us. The only way to get Lucy out was to keep him busy while she ran. It all happened so quickly, Marcus had no idea what was going on. I jumped at him, knocking him to the ground before he could anticipate or counter it in any way.

"Alex!" Lucy cried.

"Just go, now Lucy!" I yelled back and I was relieved moments later, to hear her footsteps pounding over head, followed by the squeaking of tires as Matt's car tore off. I was on top of Marcus, hitting and scratching at any part I made contact with. Eventually he got hold of me and threw me off to the side. He stood and backhanded me across the face hard.

"Stupid fucking whore. You'll be sorry for that!" He yelled.

"I'll never be sorry for that." I gasped. I would never regret the fact everyone I loved was safe, no matter what happened to me.

"We'll see." Marcus hissed and then his fist met my face and everything went dark.

LUCY

"Oh God! Oh God! Oh God!" I chanted through my chattering teeth as I tried to maneuver Matt's beast of a car a safe distance from that house and the monster in it.

I was completely frozen, in nothing but my underwear, and surging with adrenaline. My body was battered and bruised from the beating I'd taken, but I'd had much worse. It was the tears that were really hindering me. I'd run away and left Alex with that evil piece of shit and I felt so unbelievably guilty, but we'd never have overpowered that monster alone. I knew that, so I ran in the hope I could get the guys to Alex before It was too late.

I fought for control of my scattered thoughts. What the hell had even happened? Rob had left early that morning and I had got up at the same time, unable to sleep with the anxiety of having to tell Rob my news later that day. I'd been in the shower when I heard a noise in the bedroom. Thinking it would be Alex, or possibly one of the security guys I'd dried off quickly and pulled on my underwear and a dressing gown. I walked out to the bedroom, expecting to find Alex laid out on the bed, but there had been no one there, then something had hit my head and all had gone dark. I woke up in the basement of that house with that psycho. I had no idea how he had gotten into our room, past the security and then gotten me out again, but he had.

Alex's brother really was a true psycho. I knew one when I saw one and there was no denying, Marcus had a serious screw loose. He had been talking to himself and ranting and raving the whole time he had held me in that basement. Nothing he said seemed to make any sense and every so often he would get himself more worked up and slap me around. He had hit me and kicked me, but not as hard as Phil used to. I just curled up and protected my stomach as much as possible, doing all I could to keep the tiny life inside me, safe. Then Alex had appeared and I had been devastated. Much as I wanted to survive and protect my baby, I never wanted it to be at the cost of Alex. She couldn't and shouldn't ever have to go back to the depths of hell she had escaped from. I was so mad she had sacrificed herself for me, but I should have known really. Alex would do anything to protect others, she had proven that over and over, and as she shoved me toward those stairs, she made the ultimate sacrifice.

"Oh Alex." I sobbed as I thought of what Marcus could already be subjecting her to. I drove for a few minutes until I came to a superstore. I parked up terribly, unable to manoeuvre Matt's monster car, in a crowded area of the car park and pulled on Alex's coat so people stopped staring at me, then grabbed her mobile from the seat beside me, Thankfully I knew her passcode, we both knew each others because it was Matt's birthday. Rob's contact was already on the screen and I burst into more tears as I realised how clever she had been preparing everything for my escape. I had to get her back before her brother did something terrible. I had to get the guys. They'd save her, like they saved me from Phil. I knew they could, couldn't they?

MATT
The run had been great, out in the open countryside on a beautiful sunny morning. It reminded me of the beautiful Yorkshire town I had grown up in, and almost

made me wish I didn't live the in such a crowded city. Rob and I were running together, with Jack and Cal chatting non stop behind us.

"They're like fucking old women!" Rob groaned.

"You only just noticed mate?" I laughed as we rounded the last corner and the inn came into view.

"I just thought they'd get worn out eventually, but apparently not." He grumbled. I looked ahead to the inn, my mind running overtime with ideas for what I would do with Alex for our last couple of hours in the room before we had to head back, but as I dreamed and stared ahead something struck me and I stopped dead. Jack, obviously not paying attention ran into the back of me.

"Woah man, sorry." He called as he backed up. "What's up?"

"My car.....it's not there." I said as I continued running through my mind where I had parked it.

"What?" Rob asked as he stopped running and walked back toward me.

"My car. It was parked in the back corner. I saw it when we set off, but it's gone." I looked up to Rob, but he was already on his cell.

"It's me. Where's Alex?" He barked. "Go in and check, right now!"

"Where is she?" I asked with worry.

"Cam said she hasn't left your room. No one has been in or out. He's checking on her." I set off running then. Something wasn't right. No way anyone came all of the way out there to steal cars. I was almost to the inn when Rob called from behind me.

"Matt! She's not there. The window was wide open and there's a note." I stopped and turned to him, instantly feeling nauseous at the look on his face.

"The fucker took Lucy as leverage. Alex went to get her back. She left an address he told her to go to."

"Fuck!" I raged at the top of my voice. Marcus had both women I loved in his grasp and there was a chance I'd lose them both. "We need to go now, to the address. There's a chance they'll still be there, isn't there?" I asked desperately, knowing more than anything I needed to keep my cool.

"There's a chance, but we don't know what time Alex left. It could have been hours ago." Rob said and I knew he was as terrified as I was. The love of his life had been taken from him for the second time.

"We just have to hope she only just left. Come on, let's move!" Jack barked as he and Cal bolted ahead to Rob's SUV. Cam flew out and threw Rob's keys at him.

"Check CCTV. I want to know how that fucker got to Lucy! And how much head start he'd got on us." Rob raged at Cam.

"On it boss." Cam nodded and disappeared back inside the inn.

We all jumped in and set off racing to the address Jack punched into the navigation system from Rob's phone. A few minutes in, Rob's cell started ringing and we all turned to it hopefully, just desperately needing it to be the ladies, saying they were safe.

"It's Alex!" Jack said as he answered the call and put it on speaker.

"Alex?" I yelled frantically.

"Matt, It's Lucy."

"Sweetheart, where are you? Is Alex with you?" Rob asked hurriedly.

"He has Alex. She got me out. You need to go back for her Rob. I left her....I fucking left her!" Lucy cried, her voice raspy and trembling. She was clearly in pieces.

"Where Lucy? At the house he took you to?" Jack asked.

"Yeah, she attacked him....in the basement. I got out maybe five minutes ago. They could still be there."

"We're almost there Lucy. Where are you? Are you safe?"

"Yeah, I'm parked in a supermarket. Just get Alex. I'll stay here until you have her. Just......please Rob, get her back." She whimpered.

"We will sweetheart. Sit tight. I'll call you back." With that Jack hung up and reached under his seat. He pulled out two handguns and checked they were loaded.

"Rob and I go in first, armed. You guys watch the front and back of the house in case the fucker tries to make a run for it. We'll clear the house and get to the basement. If Marcus is there we take him down, then we get to Alex. You come down as soon as we give the all clear, got it?" Jack ordered. We all agreed, knowing there was no time to debate the plan because we were pulling into the address. Rob parked on the street and we all jumped out. Jack handed Rob the gun and they went in, while Cal covered the back and I the front, just in case Marcus somehow got past Jack and Rob. I was buzzing with adrenaline, just needing to know Marcus was dead and to have Alex safe in my arms again.

It seemed an eternity before Rob called the all clear and I was able to run into the long since abandoned house. I scoured the down stairs rooms as I ran through, but they were all completely empty and caked in a thick layer of dust. Cal had come through a back door and met me in the kitchen. We both headed for the door down to the basement immediately,

"She's not here," Jack said as he appeared at the foot of the basement steps. I ran faster needing to see for myself, hoping that they had missed something and the woman I loved was there.

"Matt, he's already cleared out man. I'm sorry." Jack said firmly as he stopped me with his hands on my shoulders.

"We'll find her Matt. I've already got my tech checking traffic cams in the area and digging into Marcus' financials for possible locations he could take her."

"How long though Rob?" I growled, consumed with anger and terror for what Alex would have to suffer. "How much of his abuse is she going to have to go through before we find her? Will he have already passed her to that Russian fucking sadist bastard so she can suffer some more before we get to her Rob? How fucking much will she have to suffer because we fucked up and left her?" I was laying into Rob knowing it wasn't his fault as the words left my mouth, but I was losing it. Alex was in the hands of her abusers once again and I was terrified I would lose the woman I loved forever if they broke her again, just like Helen had warned me.

"I will get her back Matt," Rob pledged as he slapped his hands down on my shoulders. "Keep it together man.

She's going to need you." With that he walked past me and raced up the stairs. He was already barking orders into his mobile as he went.

"Come on. We need to get to Lucy. There's blood on the floor down here and I'm worried it's hers." Jack said, making me feel physically sick once again. I nodded and followed Jack up to the kitchen and out to the SUV. Rob already had the engine running and Lucy on loudspeaker. I jumped in the back with Cal, while Jack got in the passenger seat.

"Tell me you found Alex." Lucy whimpered. She was crying and short of breath.

"We were too late sweetheart. I'm so sorry." Rob replied, his voice tight and pained.

"Oh God!" Lucy wailed. "I shouldn't have left her. This is all my fault." I couldn't stand to hear the pain and anguish in her voice. Despite everything happening, my first instinct was to soothe my sister and take the pain away.

"Darling, don't say that. I know Alex went to that house with one objective, to get you out. She would never have forgiven herself if she had failed. Knowing you got away will be helping her stay strong now."

"But if I'd just stayed and helped her…."

"Then that psycho would have both of you now." Cal said and I heard the rage in his voice when he spat the words. I knew he had grown extremely close to Alex since meeting her, taking her on as a little sister of sorts, as they all had.

"Sweetheart, just tell me where you are. We're coming for you now."

Lucy gave Rob the name of the superstore car park she sat in, in between sobs and frantic breaths. She was distraught and I was desperate to get to her and hold her.

Minutes later Rob swerved into the car park Lucy had directed us to, like a madman. He leapt out of his SUV without even shutting off the engine and ran the few feet to where my Range Rover was badly parked at the end of a row.

We all got out behind him and watched on as he threw the door open and Lucy leapt into his arms. She was wearing Alex's long black wool coat, but her legs and feet were bare. I looked across to Jack and tried to swallow past the lump forming in my throat. Jack gave me a look that said he was thinking the same horrifying thought. Where were her clothes and why had they been removed?

"Oh Rob. He's a monster.....and he has her. You have to find her.....you have to." Lucy was wailing between sobs. As I got closer I saw her lip was split and several bruises were darkening on her face. Rage washed over me as I thought of what she had been through in a short time with that bastard and what the hell Alex would be forced to endure before we tracked her down.

"Sssh, it's ok sweetheart. We'll find her. We'll get her back. You need to try and calm down now and breathe, ok?" Rob soothed.

"Matt.....I'm so sorry. She told me to run....I didn't know what to do. I'm sorry." She cried when she looked over at me. I walked to her and brushed her hair from her tear stained face.

"Rob's right darling. We will get her back. It's not your fault, you did the right thing getting out of there. Do as Rob says now and take some deep breaths." I said, showing a calm I did not feel.

"I didn't want to leave her….I would have stayed, helped her batter that fucking prick, but…." Lucy stopped her rambling and looked to Rob with fear.

"What is it sweetheart?" Rob asked as he placed a reassuring hand on her arm.

"I….I didn't want to tell you like this but…..I...I'm pregnant Rob. I only found out yesterday and I told Alex because I was freaking out. She told me to run….she told me to protect the baby and I did…..I left her and now she's gone."

"Lucy, you're pregnant?" Rob gasped with shock.

"Yeah." She whispered nervously. "I know we didn't plan it, I don't even know how it happened. I never miss my pill, but….well, it did. Are you mad?"

"Mad? No I'm not mad!" Rob growled. "It's great sweetheart, brilliant, amazing news. So what if we didn't plan it? I don't care. We're gonna have a baby." Rob cried excitedly as he pulled Lucy in for a hug.

"Don't get too excited yet Rob. It's very early days and well….I tried to protect my stomach but I took some hits. It could already be over for us." Lucy whimpered.

"Jesus Darling, don;t say that." I said emotionally.

"Jack?" Rob snapped with worry.

"Do you have any cramp type pains right now sweet?" Jack asked. Lucy shook her head as tears flowed. Rob was clutching her tight, as if terrified to let her go.

"Let's get her back to the inn so I can check her over and clean up the cuts." Jack suggested. Rob nodded, gathered Lucy into his arms and headed back to his SUV where he climbed in the back and sat with her on his lap.

"You good to drive your car Matt?" Jack asked. I nodded and went to climb in. I shut the door and just lay my head back on the headrest, forcing myself to breathe. What a fucking nightmare! Alex was missing and in the hands of a lunatic. My sister had been beaten and may be about to lose her child and we had no clue where to even begin fixing it all. I roared with anger as I punched my hands down on the steering wheel repeatedly, then stopped myself and took another deep breath. I needed to find a way to keep my head because Rob was right, Alex would need me when I found her and I would be there for her every step of the way, no matter what.

ALEX

I came around from a thick darkness, what felt like, hours later. It was the sense of being shaken that woke me, but I couldn't see where I was. It was pitch dark. I tried to focus through the fog in my head and remembered what had happened. Marcus. Driving to that crappy house and getting Lucy out and me being knocked out. I reached up to feel my head, which throbbed and found a sticky, very sensitive spot on my temple. *Great, another fucking blow to my already broken brain!*

Further jostling had me snapping further into awareness and after a moment of thought I realised I was in a trunk, again! This trunk was bigger than the last, so I began to feel around the space hopefully for that magic leaver that would pop it open. Again I came up empty. Why the hell hadn't I googled that after last time? Oh right, I didn't think I'd find myself trapped in a trunk ever again! I felt around frantically for anything I could use as a weapon once the trunk was opened, but there was nothing in there other than me.

Frustrated, frozen and in pain I did the only thing I could do and got comfortable. There was no way I was escaping from there, so the best thing I could do was conserve energy and fight when the opportunity arose.

"Matt." I whispered as I tried to picture his handsome face and that sexy smile. Tears ran down my cheeks at the realisation I may never see him again. The image of his face was the last thought I had before I drifted into an exhausted sleep.

***

I lay in the trunk, waking occasionally, for what felt like days. I was pretty sure Marcus was drugging me because there was no way I would sleep so much in such a terrifying situation otherwise, plus I had a very painful mark on the side of my neck where I thought the sonofabitch may have injected me with something a few times.

When I did actually fully awake it felt like weeks could have passed and I wouldn't have known. I was relieved to find I was out of the trunk of the car, but where I lay, on a cold concrete floor wasn't much of an upgrade. I sat up and looked around. The space was small, the walls seemingly made up of ramshackle wood slats. It was like a shed or an outhouse. There were no windows and just one heavy wood door. The only light source was the small gaps in the structure that allowed small slivers of light in. It was freezing, due to the draft whistling through all of the gaps and the fact the structure was definitely outside. Also I was stripped down to my bra and panties, just like Lucy had been.

I jumped to my feet and tried the door, knowing it would be locked, but chancing it anyway. When the handle didn't budge I tried shouldering it a few times and then set to kicking it as hard as I could, but I did more damage to myself than to the door. I was furious by the time I gave in. How dare that monster do this to me again! He had taken enough from me, he had destroyed me once, completely. Wasn't that enough?

"MARCUS!" I yelled as loud as I possibly could, over and over again. I wanted answers form the fucker! I was done fearing that piece of crap! Finally when my throat was raw from yelling, I heard rattling at the door and I readied myself for a fight.

"Good. You're awake Alicia." He said as he stepped in. As always he looked immaculate in black slacks and a dark red button down shirt, never a hair out of place with this sonofabitch!

"Where the hell are we?" I demanded.

"Somewhere you can scream all you like. No one will hear you out here." He sneered.

"Why are you doing this? What the fuck do you want from me?"

"Me? I'd like a little revenge for what you did to my parents."

"I didn't do anything to *your* parents!" I yelled, emphasising the 'your'. I certainly had no desire to call them mine.

"You, you stupid fucking whore, got them killed!" Marcus raged as he leapt forward, his face so close to mine I felt his venomous breath in my face. "It was all set up. Yuri would take you in exchange for the debt, but you had to fuck it all up, you stupid bitch! Yuri got sick of waiting and sent a message….with two bullets through my parents heads, then he left parts of them spread through the house for me to find."

"Oh you poor thing. My heart just bleeds for you." I spat sarcastically. "You got into bed with the fucking Russians Marcus! This is all on you! What did you think would happen?" Marcus grabbed me at my throat and slammed me hard against the rough wood wall. My head bounced and things became a little blurred in my vision.

"You are the child of a cheap whore! You had one purpose to this family, the only thing you were ever good for! That nasty little body of yours could have saved them, had you not been under the illusion you were anything other than the grubby little whore you were raised as! I'm gonna remind you where you belong, you little bitch and when I'm done with you, Yuri will come to collect!" He slammed me hard into the wall again, then dropped me and I slumped to the ground, shaking and fighting hard not to cry.

"You'll never break me again Marcus. Never." I gasped, assuring myself I was stronger. I could face whatever came because I wasn't the scared girl I used to be. I had changed. I had lived a real life, free of the evil that had raised me. I had loved and been loved and I had been welcomed into the strongest group of people I had ever met. I knew they would come for me and I was determined I would hold on. There was no way I would never see Matt again, I wouldn't let it happen.

"We'll see Alicia" He sneered, then he lunged forward and grabbed my left ankle. He ripped me from the tiny wooden shack by it and across rough ground to a clearing in front of a small wood cabin. I looked around hurriedly, trying to ignore the pain of the every stone and branch that had cut and scraped me on the way.

The cabin sat in front of a lake, which in any other situation I would have said was beautiful. I couldn't see any other cabins around, in fact all that seemed to surround it was woods and one rough track, on which sat a rusted up old car.

"Strip." Marcus demanded.

"Fuck you!" I spat back as I clambored to my feet. There was no way I was going down easily. I'd fight him at every turn.

"I see you really have forgotten your place. We'll soon rectify that." He sneered as he began to unfasten the black leather belt he wore on his slacks. I didn't wait to see what he would do. I ran at him and punched him as hard as I could in his face. There was a sickening crunch and his nose seemed to explode with blood. He reared back in shock, and I moved again, this time kicking him hard in the shin. It hurt my bare foot, but not as much as it hurt him, judging by the way he cried out. "Fucking bitch!" He roared. "You'll regret that!" He lunged at me and shoved me hard to the floor. I landed with a thud and before I could right myself he had his belt loose and was hitting me with it, each hit landing with a harsh snap against my bare skin. He hit me about a dozen times with the full length of the belt, then when he grew tired, he folded it over and hit me with it doubled. He lay hits on every inch of my body except my face and the burning pain became more and more agonising. My body shook with the agony and the urge to scream out, but I clamped my mouth shut and never let anything except the odd whimper escape. I was determined not to give him the satisfaction he was looking for.

Eventually, when I was at the point where I thought I may lose consciousness, Marcus became exhausted and stopped. His nose was still pouring with blood and he kept on choking on it because of how heavily he breathed with the exertion of beating me.

I was only on the edge of awareness when he stalked over to me and cut away my underwear. I tried to protest, but I had nothing but the all consuming pain left within me.

"Still think I won't break you?" He sneered as he literally kicked my battered body across the clearing and back into the shed. He left me laid out, on my front, on the freezing concrete floor and locked the door again, then stomped away.

"You can't break me again." I whispered, more to myself.

Beaten and bloodied, I faded away into a peaceful darkness chanting over and over again, *Don't let him break you. Matt will come. Don't let him break you. Matt will come.*

MATT

Two days! Two fucking days that psycho had held Alex and we were no closer to finding her. We were back in the city, camped out at Rob's apartment.

Lucy had taken a nasty beating and had bruised ribs and a ton of cuts and bruises, but that was all thank God! He hadn't touched her sexually as we had all initially feared. Overall, she was doing well physically and the baby was fine. Jack had booked her in for an early scan the previous day and all had been well. The pregnancy was only about seven weeks along so it was early days, but for the time being, all was as it should be. Rob and Lucy had been overjoyed that their baby was doing well, but the whole thing was overshadowed by the fear we all felt for Alex. Lucy was struggling the most. Mentally she couldn't get over the thought they may have been able to overpower Marcus if she hadn't run from the basement. We all tried to tell her that wasn't true. They were both fighters, Alex and my sister, but neither of them was much over five foot, they weighed nothing and Lucy was pregnant. They'd never have overpowered that monster and we all knew it, except Lucy.

Rob had done everything in his power to track Marcus down. He'd sent men to every property Marcus owned, but they'd all been empty. He had turned the bastard's life upside down in the hope it would produce a lead, but so far nothing.

The FBI had found the Daltons bodies in the family home after the night Alex received the photos several days ago, but forensics had turned up no leads. Marcus was wanted for questioning on the matter, but the feds were no closer to finding the fucker than we were.

We were aware that Marcus was likely to pass Alex off to Yuri Sokolov to settle his debt with the Russians, so Rob had Yuri under surveillance too, in the hope he may lead us to Alex, but he was a slippery fucker and he kept on evading the tail.

I was at the end of my tether. Marcus had held Alex for over forty eight hours and I could only imagine the hell he could be putting her through. It turned my stomach constantly and I felt totally useless just sitting back and waiting. I needed to do something to get Alex back. I needed her to be safe with me once again.

"Matt, please try and eat something." Lucy coaxed. I was sat at the kitchen table, nursing the sandwich Lucy had made for me an hour ago. I couldn't eat, couldn't sleep, I felt as though I could barely even breathe knowing Alex was in evil's clutches.

"Not hungry." I replied as I pushed the plate away.

"Alex will kill me when she gets back and sees the state of you."

"If she gets back." I sighed hopelessly.

"Matthew Simmons! Don't you dare give up on her! She is, by a mile, the toughest woman I have ever known. I know, no matter what, she will be holding on and waiting for you guys to find her. Don't you start doubting that now!" Lucy ranted.

"I'm just so scared for her." I admitted, my voice cracking as tears threatened.

"I know Matt." Lucy whispered as she bent down and wrapped her arms around my neck. "But Alex doesn't need you to be scared for her. She needs you to be strong and determined to get her back. Don't give up. Hold it together for her."

"I'll try darling." I replied, knowing she was right.

"Matt? Where's Jack?" Rob asked as he walked into the kitchen looking just as tired and stressed as I felt.

"He got called into the ER and since I'm out he had no choice, he had to go in. They were short staffed." I explained. Jack had taken as many of my shifts as he could over the last two days, since there was no way my head was straight enough to perform surgery, and in between he had been working with all of us on picking apart Marcus Dalton's existence. He was the most exhausted of all of us, but he never complained or gave up the hope we would get Alex back. He was always the eternal optimist and somehow that kept us all going.

Cal had flown to LA with Rob's guys to search the family home and any other properties the family held. Rob wanted one of us there in case she was found, so she would have someone she trusted. I had wanted to go, but Rob said it was more likely Alex would be found on this side of the country, so I'd stayed wanting to be where I was most likely, closest to her.

"How long is he going to be?" Rob asked.

"A couple more hours probably, why?"

"Cal found holiday photos of Marcus as a kid. There's a beach house in Malibu and a lakeside cabin, neither of which were listed in the financials for the family. Cal's headed to the beach house with my team now, but I'm thinking they could be at the cabin. I want us to go in ASAP."

"Where is it?" I asked.

"Oregon, near Medford. It's a day and a half drive from here. Seems possible he took her there."

"I'll call Jack now. How are we getting there?" I asked, feeling my first real bit of hope in days.

"I have a favour I'm calling in. We'll be there by tonight." Rob said, then turned and disappeared again.

"That sounds hopeful." Lucy said.

"Let's bloody hope so darling." I agreed as I hurriedly dialled the hospital. She had to be there. *Please let her be there and please let her be alive.* Anything else I could handle and help her through, as long as she was alive.

ALEX

I came around again to be hit by a solid wall of pain. My entire body was so cold I could barely move my limbs and there were angry red welts on every inch of me. I was shaking uncontrollably, though I had no idea if it was because of pain or the cold. I took some very deep, fortifying breaths as I tried to think clearly for a moment. Marcus had said Yuri was coming for me and I knew him getting his hands on me would be even worse than Marcus. Yuri was a really sick sonofabitch who loved to see women suffer before he raped them. I had dozens of first hand experiences of how depraved he was.

I knew I needed to find a way to escape, but at that moment I was unable to even move my hand to my chapped, sore lips. I realised it must have been days since I drank anything and I was really starting to feel the dehydration. Worse than that I realised it had been days since I took my pills and I knew soon the seizures would start. Once that happened there was no way I'd have the strength to escape.

I fought to move, but froze in terror when, moments later, I heard the locks being removed from the door again. Fear fought for a grip on me, but I fought it back. I had to be strong and make sure I didn't let the sonofabitch break me. I couldn't let that happen again. *Don't let him break you. Matt will come.*

"Wakey, wakey bitch!" Marcus yelled. I focused my eyes on his face and was pleased to see he had two huge black eyes and his nose was swollen and crooked looking. At least I got him good.

"I'd hoped to play a little more today, but it seems Yuri is ahead of schedule and is en route as we speak. It's a shame really, but I know he will make up for my missed opportunity. I used to love the way that man could make you scream and beg for mercy." He laughed.

"Anyway, time to get you cleaned up." He sneered and then he was dragging me by my foot again, across the rough ground and then up three steps into the cabin. I cried out as my back and head bounced up the solid steps, but he ignored me and there was nothing I could do to soften the blows which hurt ten times more to my frozen, tingling body.

He dragged me inside a filthy, dilapidated looking cabin. There was furniture covered with dust sheets and the floor was an inch thick with filth.

He stopped dragging me when we reached a small bathroom off of a dark hallway. Without a word he lifted me from the floor and dropped me into the tub which was filled to the brim. I landed with a huge splash, my entire body sinking to the bottom. I opened my mouth to scream as the pain of the ice cold water hit me, but instead just took in water. I fought to the surface and took huge gasps of air in my panic, coughing and spitting water in between.

It was only when I caught my breath that the real pain kicked in. There was something in the water that was burning the welts and cuts on my skin. It smelt like bleach and some sort of disinfectant and I started to clamber out, my skin burning so much I worried it was causing chemical burns. As soon as I managed to lift myself out a little, Marcus pushed me back under and held my head beneath the water until I was almost unconscious. After three attempts to escape and three near drownings, I stopped fighting and just tried to battle through the agony until he let me out.

"Yuri requested you be ready to get straight to work with him, so we better get you clean, hadn't we little whore?" Marcus sneered as he lifted a filthy looking rag from the water and started rubbing my entire body roughly with it. I gritted my teeth and just bared it as he ran over my back, shoulders, stomach and breasts, but as his hand ventured between my legs I started to hit out in blind panic. He easily subdued my weak fight and shoved my head under the water again. He held it under as, with his other hand, he roughly touched between my legs. When I thought I really was going to die in that bath he finally yanked me up out of the water by my hair. He pulled me completely to my feet as I gasped desperately for air for my starved lungs.

"You never learn, do you Alicia? I always win." He hissed as he dragged me by my hair from the bathroom and into a bedroom containing only a bare mattress on a wooden bed frame. He threw me onto the bed and started tying my hands to ropes he had already tied to the bed frame. I hit and kicked out, but I was so weak, it was fruitless and within minutes he had me tied, spread eagle on the bed. I tried hard to stop my tears from escaping, but they went rogue and managed to get free, trickling down my cheeks.

Just as Marcus crawled over me we heard a car pull up right outside the window and the slamming of doors.

"Right on time." Marcus said as he stood and ran from the bedroom. I sat, just hoping it was Matt and the guys, but that hope was dashed when I heard one of the voices that had plagued my nightmares for the last four years, Yuri.

"I got her ready for you, as you requested." Marcus snivelled as they both walked into the room. Yuri Sokolov had aged quite a bit in four years. He was a big guy, but compared to Rob and Jack, not so big. His once heavily muscled body had thinned down and his jet black hair was peppered with grey. His face still held that stone cold killer look and he had a new, long ragged scar down his right cheek.

"Da, Very good." He said in his heavily accented English. "Still a pretty bitch I see?" My stomach revolted as he leered down at my naked body.

"So Yuri, we're even now right? All debts paid?" Marcus asked and for the first time I saw what a snivelling little weasel he was. Years ago, as my captor, Marcus had incited nothing but terror from me. I'd seen him as the big bad monster who I cowered beneath. There, in that moment, I realised how truly weak and cowardly he actually was and I wondered how I had ever been pathetic enough to let him control me in any way.

"Not quite." Yuri laughed coldly and before I realised what was going on, he pulled a gun from a holster at his hip and shot Marcus clean through the head. I should have looked away, I knew I should, but as Marcus' body slumped to the ground and blood poured from the large hole in his head, I couldn't stop staring. He was dead, my biggest tormentor was dead, my whole sick birth family were dead and all I felt about that realisation was relief.

"Now for some fun." Yuri hissed as he stepped over marcus' dead body to close the bedroom door.

"Just kill me too Yuri!" I yelled, but he just laughed as he started to remove the suit he wore piece by piece.

"I do not think so *cyka*. We have much fun ahead first."

MATT

"Rob, that was a gunshot!" I gasped as we trudged through the woods closer to the cabin which Rob had linked to Marcus' late uncle. In the time it had taken Rob to make that link Jack had returned from the hospital. Rob had called in his favour and thirty minutes later we were boarding a private charter plane to Medford. It had been an agonisingly long six hour flight, but we had used the time to clean and load weapons and I had double checked the bag of medical supplies I had brought, ensuring I had everything I could possibly need, not knowing what state I'd find Alex in.

At the airport a contact of Rob's was waiting with a large SUV, which we had all piled into and made the forty minute drive to the cabin.

Now we were walking the last half mile, through dense woodland up to the cabin, having left the car hidden on the edge of the woods about half a mile back, to keep our approach stealthy. We were all dressed in black tactical gear and wore bullet proof vests. Rob and Jack were armed with their handguns and wore belts loaded with bullets and knives and all manner of weapons they had loaded up with from the armoury at Shepard Security. I had my glock in my hand, just incase, but the plan was clear. Rob and Jack would clear my path and all I had to do was get to Alex.

"Keep moving. Stay out of sight until we get eyes on the cabin." Rob ordered after we all heard the gunshot. He and Jack shared some strange hand signals and I watched as Jack branched off a few feet over from us. I stayed beside Rob, trying to step where he stepped, not wanting to be the one who gave us away and messed everything up.

As we got within a few metres of the back of the cabin, Jack re-joined us, sneaking up behind us in complete silence and scaring the hell out of me.

"Two vehicles. There's a guard at the door with a .40 calibre. Guessing the Russians are here." Jack explained hurriedly in a whisper. Yuri Sokolov had slipped the tail Rob had put on him late the previous night and now we knew why they hadn't yet caught back up with him. He was there, in Oregon.

"Any idea how many?" Rob asked.

"There's only two cars. One must be Marcus, so can't be many."

"We need a number. Stay here. I'll do a quick recon." And before anyone could react Rob had disappeared into the woods like a hunting jungle cat.

"These Russians are serious Matt, You shoot first, ask questions later, got it?" Jack whispered as we watched the cabin.

"Got it." There was no arguments from me. I'd kill anyone who came between me and Alex, no questions, no hesitation.

"We need to move." Rob said as he appeared behind us. "Just one guard and Sokolov has Alex in the back bedroom."

"Is she alive?" I asked, terrified of the answer.

"Yeah, but she's in bad shape."

"Marcus?" Jack asked.

"Dead." Rob grunted.

"Good." I said with relief. That was one less person for Alex to worry about. "Let's go and get Alex then" I demanded.

"Stay behind us. Let us take them both out first, then you get to Alex, clear?" Rob ordered. I nodded and followed behind them both as they approached the cabin and pressed their backs against the side of it. I hung back as Rob slipped around the front and moments later a single shot sounded. Jack flew around and they both smashed through the wooden door into the cabin. They started moving through it room by room, clearing each space as they went. I stood back as they'd told me to, but the waiting was killing me. Rob said Alex was in the back bedroom.

Realising she could be suffering while I stood waiting, I refused to stand about any longer. I checked the safety was off of my gun and started for the back hallway of the shabby old cabin. As soon as I got into the hallway I heard Alex scream and it was all I needed to spur me on. I heard Jack quietly saying my name, but it didn't register as I stormed forward and planted my boot in the centre of the door, sending it flying open with one hard kick .

"MATT!" Alex screamed. She was tied, naked to a bed frame and Yuri Sokolov stood over her, stark naked, with some kind of whip in his hand. There were bright red lines across Alex's torso and breasts and I knew he'd put them there and done fuck knows what else to her.

Sokolov looked to me with shock, then bent to pick something up from his pile of clothes at his feet. I reacted without any real thought, shooting the sick bastard right in the chest. He dropped to the floor just as Jack burst into the room.

"You good?" He asked as he scanned the room. I nodded, my heart pounding, and Jack lowered his weapon and stepped over one body and approached the man bleeding out on the floor. Happy Jack had him secured I tucked my gun at the small of my back, stepped over Marcus' body, relieved to see the bastard dead, and hurried to Alex.

"Matt.....I knew you'd come." She sobbed. I looked her over, assessing her condition. She was in a bad way. Her body was covered, from her neck down, in huge angry welts and cuts and she was clearly in a lot of pain and violently trembling.

"I'm here baby." I whispered as I reached down to kiss he forehead, afraid to touch anywhere else in case I hurt her.

Rob ran in and froze in the doorway. He surveyed the scene, then sprang into action, pulling a small knife from his pocket and starting work on the ropes holding Alex. I hurried to remove my shirt from beneath the bullet proof vest and lay it gently over her naked body. I resecured the vest over my bare chest and then bent to hold the hand Rob had already freed.

"Hey honey, I'll have you free in just a minute." Rob said softly.

"Is....is he dead Jack?" Alex asked, her voice hoarse and shaking. Jack stood from where he'd been checking Yuri for a pulse and nodded.

"They're both dead sweet, It's over." Jack assured her. Rob finally cut through the last rope holding Alex to the bed and pulled the remains of it from her bleeding wrist. "Let's get you out of here love, ok?" I said as I hurriedly pulled my shirt over Alex's head, It fell to her mid thigh and would cover her enough for now. I knew it would anger the wounds across her body, but also knew she would rather be covered.

"Yes please." She whimpered tearfully. I slid my hands beneath her and lifted her into my arms, feeling calmer for the first time in days. She was alive and safe. The rest we could deal with.

"I'm so tired Matt." She whispered as I carried her from the room and into the kitchen of the disgusting cabin.

"It's ok baby. I have you now. You can rest. No one will ever hurt you again."

"I love you Matt. I knew you'd find me…..I knew it." She whispered.

"I love you too. I'll always find you baby." I promised. She smiled a little and then lost consciousness in my arms.

"She out Matt?" Jack asked as he stepped up beside me.

"Yeah. She passed out. We need to get her to an emergency room. Her breathing is shallow and these cuts and welts are deep "

"I'm going to get the car now. Rob's talking to his FBI contact and local PD. He's going to stay and deal with them while we take care of Alex." I nodded and watched as he hurried out of the door, to get the car we had come in. I held Alex as close as I dare, not wanting to cause her any more pain, but needing to feel her against me, needing to find a way to believe she was once again safe in my arms.

ALEX

A very irritating, repetitive beeping woke me from a deep sleep. Pain hit me hard and I tried to recall what the hell had happened. It came back to me in flashes, Lucy, beaten by Marcus, then I woke up in that shack and the beating with the belt. I remembered almost drowning in that tub and then Yuri Sokolov was there. He shot Marcus and Matt arrived and shot him.

Just the thought of Matt had me fighting my fatigue to open my heavy eyes. It was no small feat, but eventually I got them open and blinked as I adjusted to the bright room I lay in.

"Alex? Can you hear me baby?" I heard Matt ask, then he was there, leant over me, his face pale and covered in scruffy growth.

"You have a beard?" I whispered, my voice quiet and raspy. Matt laughed as he ran a hand over his cheeks down to his chin.

"Not a fan of facial hair love?" He asked making me smile.

"I….I'm a fan of anything on you." I replied honestly. "Where are we?"

"Medford. You've been in and out of consciousness for the last twenty four hours."

"Am I….will I be ok?" I asked.

"Of course you will. You're on bucket loads of antibiotics because you had a lot of open wounds, but they'll all heal baby. You have some stitches here and there where the cuts were deep, a concussion and you were also severely dehydrated, but nothing to worry about. Jack's out there now, terrifying all the staff, making sure you have the best care." I laughed, but it quickly morphed into a sob.

"I was so scared I'd never see any of you again." I admitted.

"It's all over now love. You made it through. You just need to take time to recover and you'll have your whole crazy adopted family to help you do that."

"Yuri killed Marcus. He shot him through the head."

"We figured that much. Rob is handling the police, but you will need to make a statement when you're up to it. Cal's on his way to be with you when the time comes."

"When can we go home?" I asked.

"Soon, I promise. We just need to make sure you get plenty of antibiotics through this IV first, He said as he pointed to the needle in my arm, hooked up to a bag of fluid on a hook.

"Will you stay with me?"

"I'm not going anywhere baby. Just rest. I'll be right here with you." I smiled, soothed by Matt's words and his presence. It was over. Marcus and Yuri were dead. For the first time in my life I truly was free.

***

I slipped into a nightmare after a period of peaceful sleep. It wasn't my usual nightmares of my time spent in hell at the Dalton family home. In this nightmare I was back in the basement of that house Marcus had lured me to. I did everything as before, left the car running and the door open ready for Lucy, but as I descended the rotting stairs to the basement I heard Lucy screaming and when I got to the bottom she was laid on the floor, naked with Marcus on top of her. She was sobbing and screaming for me to help her as Marcus raped her with a gun to her head.

"Marcus! I came, let her go!" I screamed as I ran toward them.

"One more step and she's dead." Marcus hissed.

"Alex! Help me!" Lucy screamed, but there was nothing I could do. I knew he would kill her if I moved.

"Marcus, please. It's me you want." I sobbed. He looked up at me, his cold eyes boring into me.

"You're right Alicia." He said and then he pulled the trigger while I watched on as my best friend was killed.

"LUCY!" I screamed, startling myself awake. I looked around frantically, trying to workout where I was and what was going on. I was gasping for breath and sweat poured from me.

"Alex, it's ok. It was just a nightmare. You're safe." Matt soothed as he leant over me.

"Lucy?" I gasped frantically.

"She's fine baby. She was here earlier, but Rob took her to the hotel to rest for a while. She's safe Alex. Everyone's ok." At that moment the door into the room opened startling me, but I instantly calmed when I saw Jack walk in looking exactly the way he always did, calm and smiling.

"Hey sweet. You having a little trouble there?" He asked softly.

"She had a nightmare." Matt explained. Jack approached the side of the bed, opposite Matt. He reached for something behind my bed and then gently lowered a mask over my nose and mouth,

"Deep breaths now sweet." He instructed as he brushed wild strands of hair from where they stuck to my clammy face. I turned back to Matt and focused on his face as I tried to do as Jack had said.

"That's it baby." Matt encouraged as my panic began to subside and fatigue took hold of me instead. "Don't fight it love. Get some rest. I'll stay right beside you.

**

The next time I opened my eyes I was so relieved to find Lucy sat holding my hand. Rob was fast asleep in the chair beside her, snoring quietly.

"Hi chick." She whispered with a half smile.

"Hey. I'm so glad to see you. Are you alright? Is the baby?" I asked as I took in the bruises on her face.

"I'm fine Alex. It was only a few bruises. I've taken much worse beatings than what that wanker was capable of and the baby is doing fine. We had a scan the other day. I'm only just over seven weeks along. How are you feeling?"

"Sore and tired, but ok. Did you tell Rob?"

"Yep, I told everyone. Rob was happy, you were right." She said with a smile.

"Of course I was." I joked, then winced in pain at the slight smile I had attempted.

"I convinced Matt to go to the hotel and get a shower and shave. I can ring him to come back though?"

"No, it's ok. He needed a shave. He was starting to look like Grizzly Adams." I joked making her smile.

"They're all looking a little mountain man right now." Lucy said, nodding to Rob who also sported some serious stubble.

"Thank god they came when they did." I whispered, thinking of what Yuri had told me he had planned for me in that room, before he took me to the prison he had set up for me in his home.

"I'm so sorry about what they did to you Alex. I feel so responsible. If I hadn't have left you in that basement."

"Lucy, I wanted you as far away from those monsters as possible. I survived them once. I knew I could again. I wasn't willing to subject you to any of it and I wasn't willing to risk the life of my niece or nephew. You did what I asked you to and trust me when I tell you, it was the best thing you could have done for you and the baby. None of it was your fault honey. Please don't take Marcus' guilt on yourself."

"I'm still so sorry for everything you had to go through. I'm here for you hun, whatever you need to get over this."

"I know. Thank you," I whispered through the pain shooting up my back. I wiggled to try and settle it, but found my limbs to be heavy and stiff.

"Are you ok?" Lucy asked.

"My back….it's hurting a bit. I'll survive." I said, not wanting to worry her too much.

"Jack's right outside. Shall I get him?" She asked nervously.

"Yes." I gasped as the pain increased. "Please Lucy."

She nodded and hurried to the door, returning moments later with not just Jack, but Cal too. Lucy was right, they were all sporting varying lengths of beard. Rob shot awake at the sound of footsteps in the room, but relaxed when he realised who it was.

"Hey sweet. Lucy says you have some pain?" Jack asked as Cal stood back looking anxious.

"My back....it's like a shooting pain.....it's really sharp." I tried to explain.

"You have some really bad bruising back there sweet. I'll get some pain meds brought in. Just hang in there for a minute for me, ok?" I nodded and watched as Jack left the room. Tears started to pour down my face as the pain intensified and I fought to hold in great big baby sobs.

"Come here honey." Cal whispered as he wrapped his arms around my shoulders and held me tightly. I gripped his soft t-shirt and clung to him desperately, just needing the comfort he offered. Jack returned with a nurse, who administered a painkiller into my IV. I remained clinging to Cal the entire time, not ready to let him go yet.

"It's getting better." I whispered to Cal as the pain began to lessen.Cal moved to pull away, but I panicked and gripped him tighter. "Please don't go Cal." I whimpered, knowing how pathetic I sounded, but not ready to feel alone again. I was close to all three of the guys in the room with me. They had become like big brothers to me and I loved every one of them, but I was closest to Cal and I felt safe with him near. I needed that safety in Matt's absence.

"Ok honey. I'm here. I'm not going anywhere." Cal soothed as he perched on the bed and held me tighter. Seconds later I felt Lucy's small hand running through my hair and Jack at my right foot, while Rob grabbed my left and squeezed reassuringly over the blanket.

"We're all here with you Alex." Rob said, giving me the peace I needed to let sleep sweep me off into peaceful darkness once again.

MATT

Alex spent a total of four days in the hospital, then another two recuperating in the local hotel we had all checked into. Physically, her wounds were healing quickly and the bruises were getting a lot less painful for her. Overall she was doing well, but it wasn't her physical state that worried me. It was the emotional effect it had all taken that scared me. She wouldn't talk about what had happened, not even to the police when they tried to take a statement. If I asked her, she just clammed up and burst into tears. She was having terrifying nightmares that had her waking up screaming for her life every time she closed her eyes and panic attacks were happening at almost every turn. The strong feisty woman I had been so drawn to seemed to have disappeared and in her place was a nervous, tearful little girl.

I understood, of course I did. She had been through hell. We weren't even sure exactly what they had done to her. She had been examined by a gynecologist on being admitted at the hospital who had found some heavy bruising on Alex's thighs and signs of some abuse between her legs, but she assured us it was unlikely Alex had been fully violated judging by the injuries. I knew from the marks on her body she had been beaten from the tips of her toes, to her neck with a belt or strap of some kind and I'd walked in on her body being whipped by Sokolov.

I knew she had every right to deal with things the way she was. It must seem so much easier to just shut everyone and their questioning glances out. I was being patient, trying to give her the space she needed while at the same time letting her know I was there for her when she was ready.

When Lucy or one of the guys came by to see how she was she'd smile and play the part, but it was obvious to everyone she wasn't herself and as soon as they left she would shrink back into herself and hide in bed.

I had hoped that getting her back to the safety of home would improve things, but after a week back at our apartment she was still laid in bed pretending to sleep anytime I entered the room. I was terrified I had lost the Alex I had fallen for, completely. Not that it made me love her any less. She still was, and always would be, my Alex and I would be there for her no matter what, but it tore me apart to see her struggling so much.

By the afternoon of our seventh day at home I was desperate to get through to her somehow. I had tried everything to get through to her, but she seemed completely lost. I needed her to open up to me, even if only a little. I needed her to understand I was there to help her bare the burden of it all. She simply wasn't strong enough to handle it all alone and she didn't need to.

I walked into our room and found her pretending to sleep again. I knew she wasn't really sleeping because her breathing was too fast and she wasn't tossing and turning as she constantly did when she really slept.

"Baby, come on. Time to get up now." I said as I pulled back the blanket.

"I'm tired Matt." She whined as she reached for the blanket to cover herself again.

"Alex, you're not tired. You're depressed and laying here won't change that. You need to get up, wash and get real clothes on, then eat something. You'll feel so much better when you do that baby." I said firmly.

"Just leave me alone." She groaned as she got a hold on the blanket and pulled it back over herself.

"No love. Not today I'm afraid." I reached down and lifted her from the bed before she could struggle. I was determined to get through to her.

"Matt, put me down right now!" She yelled as she kicked her feet.

"No. I'm doing this for your own good Alex." I told her as I headed to the bathroom where I had filled the bath with steaming hot water and her favourite bubble bath, just how she liked it. As I prepared to put her down so I could help her take her clothes off, she looked at the filled bath and completely freaked out. She started screaming and hitting out at me anywhere she could make contact. I lowered her to the floor, not wanting her to hurt herself and she fled to the corner of the bathroom where she curled up in a ball and screamed over and over at the top of her lungs for me to stay away.

I stood near the door, trying to work out what I had done wrong. She hadn't been happy when I lifted her from the bed, but she wasn't screaming about it. I realised it was when she saw the water that she had really lost it. The water had scared her. I hurried to pull the plug and drain the bath as quickly as possible while she continued to scream hysterically.

I wasn't surprised when there was pounding on my door moments later. Cal was home and the bathroom wall was on the other side of their lounge. Before I had to move to answer it there was a jingling of keys and Cal's booming voice erupted through my apartment.

"In here Cal." I called as I remained across the room from Alex.

"What the hell's happened?" He asked as he looked at where Alex now sat sobbing, her voice hoarse from screaming.

"I ran her a bath and carried her in here. I just wanted to get through to her…..she freaked Cal. I think it was the water." I tried to explain through my shock at what had happened. "She won't let me go anywhere near her."

"Go and have some water Matt. You look pale. Let me try and calm her, ok?" Cal said calmly. I nodded, knowing my presence was doing nothing to calm her, then turned and left hoping Cal could make her understand I would never, ever hurt her.

ALEX

I curled up in the corner of that bathroom, knowing I was losing my mind. I had known I was with Matt as we came into the bathroom and even as I screamed and cried hysterically part of me knew where I was, but a larger part of me had seen the water in that tub and convinced my mind I was back in that cabin, back in that bath of bleach and other chemicals burning my skin and filling my lungs as my head was held under.

The sound of Cal and Matt talking had been enough to ease me from screaming hysterically and then I just sat, crying, knowing I really had lost my mind and scared the hell out of the only man I had ever loved, the only man crazy enough to ever love me.

"Alex?" I looked up at the sound of Cal's voice. He was knelt on the floor, a few feet in front of me, his face wrinkled with concern.

"I'm sorry." I sobbed. "I don't know what's wrong with me. I think I'm losing it Cal."

"No sweetie, you're not. You've just been through a very traumatic experience and your brain is still trying to handle it all."

"I was screaming at Matt.....he left Cal. I scared him."

"He only went for a breather. He's right out in the kitchen. You're right, you did scare him, but only because he wanted to help you and he couldn't. He loves you Alex and he's not going anywhere. He knows what you're going through. You just have to let him in."

"I can't. I can't go back there again." I gasped.

"Honey, until you find a way to let your mind process what's happened these kind of freak outs are going to keep happening. I know it will be hard to discuss what happened, but you need to process it with someone. It doesn't have to be Matt, it could be Lucy or one of us, or we could look into finding a trauma counsellor you could talk to."

"No, no strangers!" I snapped. No way was I unravelling the craziness in my mind with someone I didn't know.

"Ok. It's completely up to you. No one is ever going to make you do something you don't want to do."

"I just want to be me again." Tears were flowing at full force now and my body began to shake with the deep hacking sobs that started to escape.

"You will be hon, I promise. You just have to give it time."

"I-I…...I'm so scared I'll lose him Cal." I sobbed.

"That man out there is head over heels in love with you. When you were missing he was the one losing it. There is no way in hell you will lose him. He's yours Alex, whatever you throw at him, but try to open up to him sweetie. He's a tough guy and he can handle whatever you need to tell him. He did it once with Lucy and he can do it now for you. Trust him and stop trying to protect him from the truth." Cal said vehemently. "Whatever you tell him will likely be nowhere near as bad as what he's imagining you went through." That hit a chord with me. I had spent days not telling Matt what happened because I wanted to protect him, but by doing that I had probably left him to picture things much worse than they were.

"You're right, I'll try to talk to him Cal. Thank you."

"You never need to thank me for being here." Cal whispered as he held out a hand to me. I took it and he pulled me to my feet. I felt lightheaded and nauseous and knew it was likely because I hadn't eaten for days. Cal pulled me into a hug and placed a gentle kiss on top of my head. "You want me to help you back to bed?" He offered.

"No. Matt was right about that. I need to get my ass out of bed and start functioning. I'm gonna take a shower and put some clean clothes on."

"Glad to hear it." Cal said with a grin. "I'm going to get Matt to come and help you, ok? You're really unsteady on your feet and I don't think you should be in here alone right now." I thought about his words and I knew he was right. My legs were trembling and Cal was pretty much holding me up.

"Ok." I agreed.

"Good girl. How about I run to Papa Gino's and get some pizza for when you're done. You look like you're wasting away."

"Pizza sounds good Cal, thank you."

"No problem. Shall we call Matt in now?" He asked and I nodded. I was terrified as I heard Matt approach as soon as Cal called his name. What if he was angry at me because of the way I behaved, or hated me and wanted out? Matt was so honest, however he felt would be all over his face and I dared not look up from where I buried my face in Cal's shirt.

"Everything ok?" He asked, his voice tense.

"Better." Cal replied. "Alex wants to take a shower and get clean clothes on, but I think she's gonna need your help. She's a little like newborn Bambi right now." I laughed, I couldn't help it, his description was too accurate.

"Thanks Cal!" I said as I lifted my head to glare at him and smacked his arm playfully.

"There's our spitfire." Cal whispered, making me smile. I took a deep breath and forced myself to turn and look at Matt where he stood tentatively in the doorway. He instantly smiled and it melted all of my fears away. It was obvious he was nervous about how I was going to react to him. after flipping out on him, but his face showed nothing but love and concern, as always. He wasn't angry or hurt, just worried and that I could find a way to tackle.

"I'm really sorry." I squeaked as my bottom lip started to tremble with the threat of tears again.

"Oh baby. You have nothing to be sorry for." Matt said as he rushed towards me. I left the comfort of Cal's arms and leapt into Matt's. He gripped me tight and lifted me clean off the ground. I wrapped my legs around his middle and rested my head on his shoulder and the tears flowed. "It was my fault Alex. I shouldn't have pushed."

"It wasn't that. It wasn't you at all. It was the tub. I'll tell you Matt, I....I just need to get things straight in here first." I said as I tapped my head. "Just....no more tubs, or maybe any bodies of water for a while, ok?"

"Ok love."

"Right. I'm going for pizza to feed her up. I'll be about forty minutes. Call if you need anything." Cal said as he turned to leave the bathroom.

"Thanks mate." Matt said, and I knew he was thanking him for a lot more than going for pizza.

Matt carried me over to the bathroom door and pushed it shut, then moved over to the huge shower and turned on the waterfall shower head that was near the ceiling.

"This ok baby?" He asked and I nodded. He sat me on the vanity unit and started unbuttoning the flannel pyjama shirt I wore. He stopped when he had the buttons all unfastened and pulled his own T-shirt over his head, revealing his ripped body.

"What are you doing?" I asked with a smile.

"Coming in the shower with my Bambi, if that's ok with you?"

"It's ok Matt, but….." I didn't have to finish.

"I'm just going to help you love. I promise, just a shower. We're not going to do anything in that regard until you are totally sure you're ready, no matter how long that takes, ok?"

"Ok." I agreed emotionally. How had I ever been lucky enough to meet a man as good as the one stood before me. Matt bent to remove his socks and then his jeans. He kept his boxers in place and turned to me again.

"Are you going to be ok with me getting you undressed?" He asked.

"Yes. I trust you Matt. That hasn't changed. It's just some things may set me off. I'll try to tell you before I lose it next time though."

"Lose it as many times as you need to baby. You'll always find me here waiting for you to come back to me. I love you so much Alex."

"I love you too Matt, more than I ever thought it could be possible to love." I reached up and softly kissed his lips. He caught my face in his hands and peppered my forehead and cheeks with gentle kisses in return.

"Come on. Let's get in and get you warm." Matt said as he pulled back and started removing my rather ripe pyjamas. I really hadn't been looking after myself and in turn I had tortured Matt. It was time to make an effort for myself and for the people who were crazy enough to love me.

When I was naked, Matt removed his boxers and then lifted me into the shower. He pressed my back to his front and supported me there as the blissful warm water cascaded over us.

"Hold the wall love." Matt directed and I did as he said and braced my hands on the wall for support. Moments later Matt ran a soapy washcloth over my body and at first it felt good, but as he moved to my front and down my chest the cloth felt too similar to what had happened in that damned cabin.

"Stop!" I cried, both to Matt and to the images that were trying to play in my mind.

"What is it baby?" Matt asked as he took a step away from me.

"The cloth....I can't." I tried to explain.

"Do you want me to step out and give you some space?"

"No Matt. Don't leave.....just....the cloth, throw it out, please. Your hands Matt, I need to feel your hands on me." I was still staring at the wall, too afraid to see the look on his face at my lunacy.

I heard the wet cloth being thrown across the room and landing with a splash in the sink, then Matt's hands were on my shoulders, turning me to face him. I looked straight at his chest, still too nervous to meet his eyes. "Alex, can you look at me love?" He asked. I took a deep breath and slowly looked up into his face, filled with worry.

"I'm sorry." I whimpered.

"No more sorries from you now baby. You have nothing to be sorry for. Now tell me honestly what you need. You want me to go?"

"No!" I cried as I buried my face into his chest. "Do what you were doing Matt, but with your hands. I need to feel your touch on me and not what happened, please." I begged.

"Ok, but keep your eyes on mine Alex. I need to know if it's getting too much for you, ok?" I nodded and wrapped my arms around his neck to hold on as he released me and poured my vanilla shower gel into his hands. He rubbed tham together until they were soapy, then he slowly started rubbing my arms, one at a time. It felt amazing, like the first step in Matt making me his again, making me 'his Alex'. He never looked away from my eyes as he moved over my body, from my shoulders, down my chest and over my breasts, then down to my stomach. I was relieved he skipped the area I was worried would freak me out and instead bent and started at my thighs. I put my hands on his shoulders to steady myself and kept my eyes locked on his as he'd requested. He moved down my legs, then moved me so I leant on the wall while he moved down the back of my body. When he was finished he released my hair from the band it was screwed up into and started washing it, massaging my scalp like a professional. By the time he was done I was completely relaxed and had momentarily forgotten about Marcus and what happened, consumed by nothing but Matt. There was just me and the man I loved in a magic bubble of safety and love.

"Are you still with me love?" Matt asked as he wrapped his arms around me again, my back to his front.

"No…..I'm far far away, somewhere very peaceful." I whispered dreamily. "That was exactly what I needed Matt, thank you." I added as I leant back into him, placing my head back on his shoulder. I felt more like myself than I had since the day I had been taken and it felt good. After a few blissful moments of silence I took a deep breath and let a little of what happened out while I felt safe in his arms.

"He put me in a tub Matt…..I think it was full of bleach or something….it hurt and h-he touched me." I blurted, trying to explain to Matt why I had freaked out. "That's why the tub and th….the cloth…..they freaked me out." I was talking so quietly, scared that if I said it out too loud I would be inviting the flashbacks in. For a minute I wasn't even sure if Matt had heard me over the shower, but when he tightened his hold on me and placed gentle kisses on the side of my face I knew he'd heard me. His actions were the perfect comfort to keep me in that moment, there with him, rather than drifting back into the horror of my mind. I was relieved he didn't say anything, didn't tell me he was sorry, or try to make it better. There was no making it better and it wasn't why I had told him. I just wanted him to understand at least some of what I was trying to deal with, to help him understand where my head was at.

"Come on baby. Let's get you dried off before you freeze." He said after holding me for several minutes. I nodded and Matt shut off the shower, then stepped out and wrapped a towel hurriedly around his waist. He laid another large towel across his arms and then held his arms out to me. I stepped into them and he lifted me into his embrace. I curled into him, too drained physically and emotionally to try and feign any strength.

Matt helped me dry off then helped me into clean underwear and a thick pair of lounge pants and one of his huge hooded sweaters. He left me sat on the bed while he slipped on his own underwear and sweats, then he climbed on the bed and sat behind me, his legs either side of me, my back leant into his front. He picked up the towel from the bed and very gently towel dried my wet hair.

"You look exhausted again now Alex." He said softly as he rubbed down to the ends of my long hair.

"I'm ok. I think maybe I'll feel better if I eat something."

"Well, I know I'll feel better when you eat something." He said with a smile and I knew even though he'd meant it as a joke, there was a lot of truth in it. He had been trying to get me to eat for days and I'd pretty much refused every time.

"I'm sorry I've worried you so much Matt." I sighed with guilt.

"You don't need to be sorry love. I have no idea how you've stayed as strong as you have. I'm just glad you finally let me in a little. I just felt so useless to you."

"Matt, having you near is the only reason I haven't just imploded. Knowing you're with me makes me feel safe and gives me strength. I just needed some time to process everything and get my head in order. I'm really going to try and open up a little more and do what it takes to get back to where I was before this happened."

"Just take things slow baby. There's no hurry. No one is expecting you to just wake up tomorrow and be ok. You're allowed to process what happened however you need to. I just need you to know I am here for you, no matter what. Whatever you need, you only have to tell me and I'll do it. The others too, they all want you to know they are always there at the end of the phone if you need them. You're not on your own any more Alex. We're all here, so lean on us, ok?"

"I'd like to say, 'it's ok, I'm fine', but I'm really not. I think I'm going to need all the help I can get for a while." I admitted tearfully.

"Then you'll have it baby. I've already taken a month's leave from the hospital and I'll take more if you need me. I'm going to be here for you the whole time. I promise." I sank back against his strong body and relaxed. He had said what I needed to hear, that he would be with me. I wasn't ready to be alone, not yet. As long as Matt was with me I could face what was to come, no matter how hard it may be.

***

A week later and we were in the elevator up to Rob and Lucy's apartment for dinner. It had been a tough week. All manner of things caused debilitating flashbacks for me, including standing in my underwear, being cold, Matt leaning over me in any way, Matt removing his belt from his trousers and of course the tub and many other things that were so innocuous normally, but had instantly set me off into anything from my usual, sweating, short of breath panic attack to a full blown, screaming, cowering in a corner episode. Matt had been forced to deal with it all and I knew the poor guy was afraid of doing anything anywhere near me, for fear of setting me off. He had handled my meltdowns well, learning when to back off and give me a little space and when I needed him to approach and hold me while I cried. There were nightmares too, to deal with. I woke up a few times at least, every night screaming, sweating and usually fighting Matt off as he tried to calm me. He just did whatever it took to calm me each time and then held me until I slept again. I knew he had barely been able to sleep a wink all week and he was exhausted, but despite that, his patience knew no bounds. He never got angry or annoyed with me, he just showed an amazing amount of love and compassion that managed to soothe me in the end, no matter what had set me off initially. As we stood in the elevator under the bright lights and I studied his face I felt terrible. He was pale and there were very dark rings under his eyes. I knew he was stressed out and more than that, completely exhausted and I was worried about him. I knew it was my fault, but I was trying to get it together, it just wasn't happening.

Two nights ago I had drank two large glasses of wine and then sat and told Matt every single detail of what had happened from the moment Marcus had text me that morning. I was hoping the therapy of letting it all out would help me, and also that Matt knowing everything would help him to know what my many triggers were, but so far it hadn't done anything to help my emotional state and if anything I thought it had just made Matt more anxious about what he dare do, or not do, near me. Just that morning he had taken his pile of clean clothes into the bathroom and dressed in there. He had never done that before, always having dressed in the bedroom, in front of me since the first night we spent together, and I knew it was because he was worried me seeing him undress would set me off. It wouldn't have, but that was the way it had become. Matt was literally scared to move when he was anywhere near me and I hated it. I was really starting to worry we may not make it through the whole mess together and that was the most terrifying thought of all.

"Are you sure about this, baby? We can still back out and go home?" Matt asked as we exited the elevator and walked down the hall hand in hand. It would be the first time since the hospital we would all be together again. I had refused all such dinners up to that point because I was worried about freaking out in front of all of them, but when Lucy called and offered the previous day I had agreed because I knew Matt needed the break and the chance to unwind. I would just have to try not to break down for the upcoming few hours. At least if it did happen Matt wouldn't have to handle it all alone for once.

"I'm sure Matt. It'll be good to see them all." I replied as upbeat as I could force.

"Ok, but as soon as it becomes too much, you let me know, promise?"

"I promise. Just please...try and relax a little Matt." I pleaded. "I'm worried about you."

"You don't need to worry about me love. I'm just fine." Even his eyes didn't believe that lie, but I let it go and knocked on the door to Rob and Lucy's.

"Oh, I'm so glad you're here!" Lucy gushed as she opened the door. She was dressed up in black slim fit capris and a pretty pink sweater. Her long hair was pinned up on her head and she looked beautiful, as always.

"Hey hun." I greeted. She smiled as she looked over me, then to Matt. I watched as her smile faltered momentarily after taking both of us in, then she slapped it back in place. Yep, we both looked like crap.

"Hi darling." Matt said as he pulled his sister into a one armed hug then ushered her and me inside, kicking the door closed behind him.

"Are you both ok?" Lucy asked as we stood in the doorway removing our coats and boots. I turned to her first and shook my head. She was the only person I had discussed what I was going through with, other than Matt, and Cal that one evening. She knew about the mess I was and the state Matt was in as a result.

"We are darling. Are you?" Matt said as he hung our coats on the coat stand.

"Fine." Lucy replied as she threw me a sympathetic look.

"Hey guys." Rob greeted as he walked into the room, also dressed up in black tailored trousers and a pale blue button down shirt. He smiled at me reassuringly, but I didn't miss the fact he stayed a few feet back instead of walking up to hug me as he usually did. I realised Matt must have warned him to tread carefully and I hated it. Deciding I needed to prove to Matt I could still deal with some normal things I strode up to Rob and hugged him as I always had since the first week of meeting him.

"Hey Rob." I said as he finally returned my brief hug.

"How you doing sweetheart?" He asked with a more genuine smile.

"Not great, but I'm ok." I said honestly.

"You're looking stronger. That's good."

"That'll be Matt. He's been feeding me up." I laughed as I looked to him.

"Oh Jesus! Please tell me he hasn't been cooking!" Lucy cried. "No one deserves that form of torture."

"Hey, I make an excellent slice of toast actually." Matt joked, with the first full smile I had seen from him in days.

"It's ok. We've been keeping every eatery that does take out in our vicinity, in business this week. No cooking."

"You should have said. I'd have sent some meals over. I think even Matt can manage to reheat." Lucy said with a cheeky smile at her brother.

"It's ok. We've been fine and I'll get back in the kitchen soon."

"Can I get anyone a drink?" Rob offered.

"Beer please mate." Matt said very quickly.

"I have red and white Alex. You might as well drink it because I bloody can't." Lucy pouted, making me smile.

"I'll have whichever wine you come to first thanks Rob." Rob nodded and disappeared into the kitchen as Matt walked over and flopped into a huge armchair.

"I need to check on dinner, coming?" Lucy asked me. I looked to Matt who was staring into space and then back to Lucy.

"Sure." I agreed, thinking it would give Matt some breathing space, but as soon as I walked into the kitchen I regretted it. Mat hadn't left my side for almost two weeks since he stormed into that bedroom and saved me. Being just a room from him suddenly made me feel very anxious.

"Here chick. Come sit down." Lucy said as she placed a glass of red wine at the breakfast bar. I tried to take a deep breath, through my rapidly tightening chest, and then moved to sit down. *Come on Ali, he's in the next room! Get it together you loser!*

"You ok honey?" Rob asked as he walked from the refrigerator with two beers in hand.

I nodded, but he just studied me harder. "You look pale." I looked to Lucy pleadingly and thankfully she stood in front of me.

"Rob, she's fine. Stop harassing her and go and entertain my brother while we sort the food out!" She ordered.

"Sorry sweetheart." He said with a kiss to her lips, then he turned and left. As soon as he was in the lounge Lucy turned to me and held both of my hands.

"Squeeze both of my hands tight Alex and don't think about anything except doing that." She instructed. I did as she said and after a couple of minutes my breathing seemed to come easier. "It's ok. You're safe here, everything's ok." She whispered as I calmed.

"I'm sorry." I said between short breaths. "It's the first time Matt hasn't been closeby."

"Oh hun, you should have said. I'll get him." She started to pull away, but I gripped her harder.

"No!" I snapped. "He needs a break."

"He'd want to be with you if you need him Alex."

"No. You've seen him Lucy.....he's a mess. I came here tonight to give him a break from this!" I whisper shouted as I pointed to my chest. "I'm so worried about him.....I don't think he's slept for more than an hour a night for weeks."

"That means you haven't either." Lucy admonished.

"I sleep more than he does because he stays awake to watch over me. I'm a mess too Lucy, but Matt's worse. Please help me to let him relax tonight....please." I begged.

"Do you want me to talk to him?" She offered.

"And say what? I'm so fucked up right now. I don't know how to fix my brain. I just...." My voice broke as tears began to escape. "...I just want to be better for me and for him, but nothing helps and I'm so scared he'll give up on me."

"Alex, Matt will never give up on you. He knows how hard you're trying. He told me on the phone the other day he's amazed how well you're doing."

"Well he lied because I'm a wreck….and I'm dragging your brother down with me."

"Alex, stop it! What you're going through is normal. I went through it after Phil and Matt was with me then. He got me through and he'll get you through too."

"How? How did you get through it Lucy? I have to close my eyes when I walk in the bathroom in case I see the tub. I had to ask Matt not to wear a belt. I can't even let him use peroxide to clean! I freak out at everything and the nightmares…..I'm scared to sleep." I admitted tearfully.

"I know it's hard Alex, but you need to open up. Talk about the nightmares or flashbacks after they happen. Talk to Matt or us about how you're feeling. If you're upset don't hide it, call me or anyone and let it out. It hurts to do it, but little by little it helps until one day you have more good days than bad."

"They got off easy." I sobbed.

"Who?"

"Marcus and Yuri. They did this to me and then they got to just die, while I'm stuck here, living with the whole thing on repeat. They got off so fucking easy."

"Oh Alex. I know that's how it feels, but it will pass, mostly. One day, not too long from now you'll be happier than you've ever been and all of this will be tucked away where it belongs. I'd like to say it will be gone, but you already know, it never goes completely. We just have to find a way to deal with it, then a dark corner where whatever still lingers can be filed away out of sight most days. You're strong Alex. I know you can get through this and I'm here for you, whatever you need"

"What about Matt?" I asked as I tried to pull my sobs back.

"He's tougher than you think. Don't worry about him. The guys will keep a close watch on him and they'll step in if they think they need to."

"I'm scared Lucy. I found out who I was when I escaped the first time. What if I can't get back to that person again? What if Matt doesn't want what's left of me?"

"Firstly I know, without a doubt that you will get back to who you were, you're already getting there. Think how you were last week, you couldn't get out of bed, now you're here with all of us. You will overcome it all. And secondly, I can guarantee, no matter how you come out of this or any other situation, no matter what you do or how you may change Matt will always want you. He loves you unconditionally Alex. You will never lose him chick."

"Alex?" We both turned at the sound of Matt's voice. He was stood in the doorway staring at me, his face back to the expression I had seen all week, worry. "What's wrong baby? You should have called for me." He said as he approached me.

"I'm fine Matt." I hurriedly turned away from him and tried to wipe the tears from my cheeks.

"You're not. I knew it was too soon. I'm sorry love. Come on, we can go home."

"No, I'm ok Matt, really. I want to stay." I argued as he walked around to face me over the counter.

"What happened?" Matt asked. I looked to Lucy again for help and again she came to my rescue.

"She's ok Matt. We were just having a little heart to heart. Just let us be and go have some guy time.....talk about sport or something." She said flippantly. Matt moved his stare from me to his sister and I knew by his facial expressions they were having some kind of silent conversation.

"You sure you're ok love?" He asked when he looked back to me. I felt the urge to crawl into his arms and cry as I had all week, but I was determined to give him a break so I took a deep breath and pulled on my big girl panties.

"I'm good, just girl talk, like Lucy said." I lied through my teeth.

"Ok, but call me if you need me, promise?" I nodded and he leant down to place a soft kiss on my tear stained cheek. "Love you Alex."

"Love you too." I whispered and then he left the room and I let out the breath I'd been holding.

"More wine?" Lucy asked with a smile. I threw back what I had left in the glass and handed her my glass. She walked around the counter and re-filled my glass, then sat beside me at the counter.

"Have you thought about maybe talking to someone?" She asked.

"Like a counsellor?" She nodded. "Cal mentioned it and Matt has too, but I just don't see how talking to a complete stranger about every fucked up thing that's happened to me is ever going to help. I know it works for millions of people, but I went the first twenty two years of my life with everyone around me being a stranger. I think the thing that will get me through this, if anything does, is you guys, is feeling loved and supported for the first time in my life by people who actually know and understand me."

"I understand that. I felt a similar thing after Phil. I had the guys, I didn't need a stranger to unload on. It worked out ok for me I suppose."

"I'm going to try and do as you said earlier, just open up more and speak to someone when I'm getting anxious. Maybe it will help and I know it would help Matt. He might stop looking at me like a ticking time bomb if I give him some warnings."

"See how it goes chick. I'm always here for you if you need someone to talk to, or if you just want to cry, I don't mind. Last year, I spent hours on the phone to Rob, not saying a word, just sobbing and listening to his voice. It got me through."

"Thanks Lucy. I love you, you know that right?" I said as I leant in to hug her tight.

"I do and I love you too. Me and you hun, two crazy cows for life." She joked and I couldn't hold in the laugh that escaped. It burst out of me like it had been trapped.

"Crazy cows?" I laughed and once the giggling started I couldn't stop it. It took over me, obviously spurred on by the two huge glasses of wine I'd chugged, but hell, it felt good to laugh. I was doubled over, tears running down my face and Lucy was laughing pretty hard too.

"Sweetheart?" We both looked up and found Rob in the kitchen behind us, Matt peeking in behind him.

"Everything ok?" He asked.

"Yep. Just a couple of crazy cows losing it." She howled before laughing again. The guys looked confused and I understood, It really wasn't that funny, but after the heavy talk we'd had I think we both just needed to let rip and that comment had done it and the guys confusion just made it even funnier.

"Huh?" Rob asked, but Lucy just shooed him away.

"I think we scared them in a whole new way." I said as I tried to get control of myself.

"Good. I like to keep him on his toes." Lucy replied with a giggle.

"Thanks for that hun. I really needed it." I said.

"Me too." And for just a few minutes I remembered what it was like to laugh stupidly with my best friend. It felt so damned good and I knew I needed to fight to do that more, and less crying, whatever it took.

MATT

"Are they ok?" Cal asked from where he and Jack sat on the sofa. They'd arrived a few minutes earlier, late as always.

"Yeah, they were laughing….really laughing." Rob replied as he took the armchair again.

"More like in hysterics. I don't know what Lucy did, but that's the first time I've seen Alex laugh like that since….." I didn't say it. I didn't need to. They all knew.

"She still having the nightmares Matt? You look dead on your feet man." Jack pointed out. I was, if I was honest. I tried to stay awake to keep an eye on her in the hope I could soothe her before the nightmares really took hold. Sometimes it worked, other times she ended up screaming a few minutes later and fighting me away as I tried to calm her. I was sleeping for ten minutes here and there, but nothing more and I was feeling it. As a surgeon I was used to long periods without sleep, but that week was pushing it to the extreme.

"Yeah, the nightmares are really bad, at least three a night. The other night she woke up screaming for her life five times!"

"It was the same with Lucy, remember? Still is occasionally." Rob said.

"I know. It was just different with Lucy though. She was never scared of me. She woke up upset and wanted me to hold her. Alex hits at me like I'm the one hurting her and when she wakes up it can take ages for her to let me get close. And the flashbacks and panic attacks are even worse. On Monday I was getting undressed for bed and pulled my belt from jeans and she just went into meltdown. She was screaming, begging me not to hit her. I didn't know what to do. Every time I went near her she screamed more. It took nearly an hour to get through to her and now I can't even get a belt out of the drawer."

"She must have been through hell Matt." Cal said solemnly.

"She told me, the other night. She told me everything and you're right. That bastard tortured her and near killed her more than once. I was glad she told me, it helps me with triggers and the panic attacks, but it was hard listening to it. I just wanted to go back and kill the fucker again and again,"

"What can we do Matt? You need help man. You can't run yourself into the ground like you have been." Jack said and I knew he was right, but the thought of not being with Alex when she needed me made me feel ill. "I'm ok. We're managing. I just wish there was some way I could make it all go away for her. She's suffered so much in her life. She shouldn't have to go through all of this too."

"She's tough Matt. She has been given a shit hand, no denying that. But if anyone can handle it and come out on top, it's her." Cal interjected.

"He's right and so is Jack. You need to share the burden a little Matt. You need to at least get some breaks to sleep. We're here for her. Let us help." I took a deep breath and considered what Rob said. I hated the thought of passing Alex off to someone else for selfish reasons, but the truth was I was running on empty and I really didn't know how much longer I would be any good to her if it carried on.

"Maybe you're right. If I could just get a few hours sleep, it would help."

"So we'll work a schedule then. One of us will come and take her out or stay at yours with her and you can go to our place and sleep. We're hardly there during the day and you can use the guest room." Jack offered.

"I need to speak to Alex first. I won't leave her if she doesn't want me to." I said stubbornly.

"She'll agree. She's worried about you. I can see it in her face." Rob said. "Besides, she knows she's safe with us. She'll be fine."

"I'll talk to her tonight. It would be good if she could get back to some physio Cal. She was doing so well. I don't want her to take a step back."

"Is she ready for that?" Cal asked.

"Physically, yes. She's pretty much healed up now. It's just whether she can be convinced to go out in public. This is the first time she's left the apartment since we flew back from Oregon and she was anxious the whole drive over."

"We'll go slow. Maybe get her to places she's familiar with, like the gym and short walks in the neighbourhood. We've done this before Matt, with Lucy. We know how to handle things. Just lean on us a bit more. It's what family's for." Rob said firmly and I knew he was right. I was drowning, trying to do everything for Alex alone. If Alex agreed I would just let her spend some time with the others so I could sleep for a couple of hours a day. It would be all I needed to get me through everything else.

"What are you guys whispering about?" All four heads turned to see Alex walking into the lounge. She was smiling with a glass of wine in hand. If it weren't for the dark circles around her exhausted eyes I could almost forget everything that had happened and was happening and just see my Alex from before it all. "In fact, don't answer that. I can guess." She added. For a second I thought she was mad, but she remained smiling as she approached Jack and Cal.

"About time you guys got here. Do you even have clocks in your apartment?" She giggled and I knew she was obviously a little tipsy. Maybe it would help her relax. It seemed to be working so far.

"Sweet, you know us. We run on our own time." Jack replied. She flopped down on the sofa between them and sighed.

"You're looking better today hon." Cal remarked.

"Lucy's had me peeing my pants in there. She's so freaking funny and she doesn't even realise it."

"Well, it's good to see you smile again." Cal added with a quick nod my way. He was right, it was good to see her smile, but I knew she was putting her bravest face on for their benefit. I could still see how tense her body was and the way her eyes periodically flicked around the room. She was anxious beneath the smile she had painted on.

"The guys at the gym have all been asking after you. They said to say 'hi' and to let you know they're there for you if you need anything. To be honest I think they're sick of seeing only my ugly mug when Lucy's off. They miss you brightening the place up."

"Tell them thanks." Alex replied and her smile dropped. "I don't know how long before I can come back Cal. Maybe you should just replace me."

"Not happening. I love having you and Lucy working with me. I don't want to hire some stranger, I'll wait honey. That is your job and it'll be waiting for you whenever you're ready."

"And what if I'm never ready?"

"You will be. I know you Alex, you'll be back to ordering me around my own business before I know it. I have faith in you."

"We all do sweet." Jack added. Alex shot a glance across to me and I nodded my agreement with what they were saying. They were right. She would learn to live with what had happened and get back to her life. It was just going to be one hell of a journey.

The meal that night was more subdued than usual. Jack and Cal worked hard to keep it lively, but Lucy seemed upset, Alex and I were exhausted and Rob was his usual quiet, watchful self. It was nice to all be together, but in a way it just emphasised how much things had changed in the previous few weeks and as the evening wore on I noticed Alex's facade slipping more and more. She had stopped drinking after a few glasses of wine, which I agreed was probably for the best. I had no idea how alcohol could affect her panic attacks or nightmares, but I was pretty sure it would deepen them and I wasn't sure I could handle any more than we'd already been dealing with.

It tore me apart every time I saw the fear in her eyes, or heard the pain in her screams with every nightmare or panic attack. I so wanted to just wrap my arms around her and take it all away, but I couldn't. It took everything I had to convince her it was me and for her to let me near her. I was trying so hard to be what she needed to get through, but I was terrified that with every episode that passed I was losing her piece by piece.

ALEX

I had been watching Matt for the last hour. He was sat in the biggest armchair opposite me and as we all chatted he had been drifting off to sleep and then jumping awake. Finally he had fallen asleep and not jumped awake again. He was out, even snoring now. I was so relieved. More than anything he needed to sleep. I knew that and I had tried hard for days to convince him to just leave me and get some sleep. Every time he had refused. Now, finally he slept.

"He finally gave in then?" Jack asked from where he sat beside me.

"Yeah. I think he's out cold now, thank God. He's exhausted." I replied guiltily. It was my fault he was running himself into the ground and I felt like crap about it.

"Wake him sweet and we'll give you guys a ride. He's too tired to be driving."

"No, we can't wake him. He'll just get back to ours and sit awake all night. He needs to sleep Jack. Just let him sleep there. He's comfortable enough."

"She's right Jack. Let him sleep. Alex can sleep in the guest room tonight." Lucy pitched in.

"Thanks Lucy, but I'll get a ride home with Jack and Cal if that's ok?" I looked to Jack and he nodded. "He'll hear me wake up screaming if I stay here and he won't rest. I'll go home and sleep there. I'll be fine." I lied. I wouldn't be fine. I'd be terrified alone in the apartment, but I needed to do what was best for Matt and that was to stay away from him and let him get at least one good night's sleep.

"We'll stay with you honey." Cal said with a reassuring squeeze of my hand.

"You don't have to." The thought of someone else being witness to my hysteria after a nightmare was pretty daunting. Matt was used to it by that point. Jack and Cal wouldn't know what to do when I woke up freaking out.

"You're not ready to be alone yet sweet. We'll stay with you tonight and let Matt sleep. No arguments. " Jack said in a stern voice I had never heard him use before. It brokered no argument.

"Ok. Thank you. But I'm warning you, get ready for some crazy." I said it like a joke, but it was no joke. They were about to witness some serious crazy!

"Trust me chick, there's nothing these guys didn't have to put up with from me after what happened with Phil. They can handle crazy." Lucy assured me, making me feel a little better about them staying with me. I just hoped she was right, because I was pretty sure my first night without Matt was going to be a really tough one.

JACK

It took less than five minutes from leaving Rob and Lucy's for us to see Alex's first full blown panic attack. We walked down to the underground parking lot where we'd left my new Mercedes C Class parked. The car was my prized possession, a wedding gift from my amazing husband. It still felt so strange to call him that, but in the best possible way.

When we reached my car, Cal walked just ahead and opened the trunk to throw his jacket in as he always did because he hated to be cramped in a car with it on. Before he even got his Jacket off Alex had stopped walking and started backing away from the car and me.

"No no no no!" She cried as she held her hands out in front of her.

"Alex, what's wrong sweet?" I asked as I slowly edged closer to her.

"Please.....don't.....please." She whimpered. She was visibly shaking and tears were flooding down her cheeks. Wherever she had gone, she didn't see us there with her anymore.

"What's wrong?" Cal called. I looked up to him and tried to work out what had happened to trigger her. The only thing that had happened was the trunk opening.

"Close the trunk!" I yelled and he did so quickly, then I turned my attention back to Alex who had crumpled to a heap on the cold ground. I bent down a few feet away from her, not wanting to startle her.

"Alex, look at me now." I said calmly. She continued to sob, her face hidden in her hands.

"Alex, look at me." I said more firmly. It was the only way I was getting through to her I realised. Her head snapped up and her terror filled eyes met mine. "Good girl. Now focus on me, on my voice. Say my name. Who am I?"

"J-Jack." She whispered.

"That's right sweet. It's just you, me and Cal. We're safe. Nothing bad is happening. You're protected now. You're safe." She looked up from me, to Cal who stood behind me and then nervously to my car.

"The.....trunk."She gasped.

"It's closed. We won't open it again. Everything's ok. Do you think you can get in the car?" I asked. She nodded and moved to stand. She was trembling uncontrollably and her breathing was rapid. Cal was instantly at her side, helping her to her feet.

"I'm sorry." She whispered.

"Nothing to be sorry for honey. Come on, you're freezing." Cal soothed as he wrapped his arm around her shoulders and led her to the back seat of the car. She climbed in and Cal jumped in beside her. I closed the door and took a deep breath as I rounded the car to the driver's side. It was definitely going to be a long night. No wonder Matt was exhausted. She was suffering a lot more than any of us had realised if that was her reaction to a trunk opening. It was painful to watch just that panic attack, to see how much she tore herself apart internally. How the fuck had Matt handled it all for almost two weeks, all alone?

***

"STOP. PLEASE NO!" Alex's screaming startled me awake. I hadn't meant to fall asleep, but it was four AM and I'd worked a ten hour shift the previous day. I was bone tired. I'd slept for a couple of hours when Alex first fell asleep, while Cal sat with her, then we'd switched out. Now Cal was laid on the sofa in the lounge while I sat in an armchair beside Alex's bed. I doubted Cal was getting much sleep. I hadn't when I'd laid there. Alex's nightmares were one after the other and she was waking up almost hourly screaming and flailing in terror.
"Alex, sweet. Wake up now." I said as I shook her a little. She instantly hit out catching the right side of my temple with a really fucking hard punch. I reeled back a little and wondered for about the hundredth time that night, how the hell Matt had coped.
"Alex, it's Jack. Wake up. It's just a bad dream. You're safe." I said from a safe distance back.

"No, please…..Noooo!" She cried as she started digging her fingernails into her neck, clawing at it like she was trying to rip the skin away. I sat on the bed beside her and pulled her hands away before she hurt herself. She fought me and flailed around, but I kept a tight hold on her wrists.

"Alex, wake up!" I called, louder than I should have, but I really had no idea how to get through to her. She was completely terrified and really fighting to breathe between screams.

"Jack?" I looked up as Cal walked into the dimmed room, looking as emotionally drained as I felt.

"Quick, come help me before she hurts herself." I said and he hurried over. He stepped up beside the bed and tried to hold her kicking legs still as she fought.

"Alex!" He called in his booming voice and suddenly she stopped fighting and her eyes flew open. She studied us holding her in place, her eyes darting between us and the rest of the room. She was like a wild animal, penned in by a predator. She was more scared than anyone I'd ever witnessed and it tore me up.

"Don't touch me!" She gasped. Cal and I instantly let go of her and she scrambled back across the bed, away from us. She fell off the other side and as I ran around to check she was alright. She was crawling to the back corner of the room, where she curled up into a ball and started to really sob.

"This is so much worse than Lucy ever was." Cal whispered. "How the hell has Matt managed?"

"No clue. No wonder he looks like shit. He can't carry on doing this. She needs some real help, or some medication or something. I need to talk to him when he gets home." There was no way in hell what Alex was going through could be handled with just some extra care and attention. She was suffering one of the worst cases of PTSD I had ever seen, probably worsened by the brain injury she had, which made emotions complicated in the first place. She needed medication to ease the symptoms and some counselling would help too. I needed to talk it over with Matt as soon as possible. Until then I was done watching her suffer.

"Keep an eye on her. I'll be two minutes." I said to Cal, then I headed next door to get my sleeping pills. They had been prescribed to me for the bad nights I suffered with sometimes. Night's when I couldn't get the images of my two team mates and brothers, Tom and Gage, screaming for help as they slowly bled out, blown to pieces by that fucking IED, from my mind. It was rare I took them now. It had helped having Cal beside me, comforting me on the occasions the nightmares would strike, but I kept the pills as a lifeline and I was glad I did that night.

Alex was where I had left her when I returned with the pills and a glass of water. Cal was knelt on the floor a few feet from her, whispering softly to her, assuring her she was at home and safe. He looked up at me and I held up the pill bottle. He nodded and turned back to her.

"Honey, Jack has some pills to help you sleep. Do you think you can take them for us?" He asked. Finally she looked up and she was deathly pale.

"Pills?" She whispered.

"They're mine sweet. Sleeping pills. They'll help keep back the nightmares for a while so you can rest." I explained.

"I don't like taking pills." Her voice was weak and shaky.

"Just for tonight sweet. You can't keep on fighting these nightmares, you're beyond exhausted. You have to get some rest."

"I don't know. I don't like to take strong meds." She hesitated.

"Just trust me, please Alex? They're not very strong, just enough to knock you out." That was a lie, they were strong, but she needed the reprieve from the hell she seemed trapped in and I'd say whatever it took to give her that.

"Ok." She gave in. Cal scooped her exhausted body up from the carpet and gently placed her back into the centre of the bed. I handed her two capsules and the glass of water. She hesitated for a moment, studying the pills, then took them with a sip of water.

"Thank you." She whispered as I took back the glass and set it beside the bed.

"Sleep now sweet. Don't fight it. The nightmares won't get in now you've taken those pills." I assured her as she shuffled down the bed and pulled the comforter up to her chin.

"I miss Matt." She admitted.

"He'll be here soon honey." Cal offered from where he stood behind me. "Get some sleep and I'll bet he's back when you open your eyes again."

"I warned you guys." She said sleepily. "A whole lot of crazy, huh? I warned you."

"That you did sweet. Rest now." I ordered as I gently pushed her wild hair from her face and tucked it behind her ear. Within minutes she was asleep and I knew instantly she was more settled than she had been all night because she wasn't fidgeting as she had continuously since she climbed into bed hours ago.

"She'll be out for hours now." I whispered to Cal. "Those tablets are strong."

"Thank fuck for that. I don't know how Matt does it. I think I'm liable to break in two if I have to see her suffer one more fucking nightmare."

"She has PTSD for sure and mixed with her brain injury, it's extreme. Matt needs to get her on some new meds. I'll talk to him when he gets back. She can't go on like this." I explained. I just hoped Matt had gotten a good sleep because he sure as hell needed it after what he'd been dealing with. Alex had absolutely done the right thing giving him a night off. Like Cal said, I had no idea how he'd managed as long as he had.

MATT

I woke with a start. *Fuck, I'd dropped off again!* I looked to my right, where Alex usually laid on the bed beside me, but I wasn't in bed, I was in a chair, in Rob and Lucy's living room. A blanket had been thrown over me. I sat up and looked around. The sun was just beginning to rise and the rest of the room was empty. I stood and threw the blanket on the seat behind me. I'd slept all bloody night and jesus, did it feel good. I felt more alive than I had in days. Then it hit me, Alex! Where had she slept? I hadn't heard her screaming with nightmares. Had she slept through too? I raced to the guest bedroom and went to open the door, assuming she'd be in there, but Rob's voice stopped me.

"She's not in there." He said as he appeared behind me in lounge pants and a t-shirt.

"What? Where is she?" I demanded.

"She wanted you to sleep. Cal and Jack stayed at your place with her for the night."

"Fuck Rob! You shouldn't have let that happen. You should have woken me up. Jack and Cal have no idea how to handle her right now." I raged angrily. They thought that they knew what she was going through, they all thought it was like the panic attacks and nightmares we had all dealt with after Phil, with Lucy, but it wasn't like that. Alex's panic attacks and nightmares were much, much worse and it had taken a lot of effort to learn how best to handle them. There was no way Jack and Cal had been prepared for the terror Alex awoke with each time.

"I'm sure they managed just fine. If they couldn't they'd have called." Rob said.

"I have to go!" I left the apartment, annoyed and angry before Rob could say another word. I had to get home to her. I had to know she was alright and apologise for leaving her. She wasn't ready for that and if I was honest neither was I. It was hard, being with her, seeing her suffer with every flashback or nightmare, but it was harder still not to have her close to me. After everything that had happened I wasn't ready to be seperated from her. I needed her near me, where I was sure she was safe.

***

It was just after seven AM when I stormed into my apartment, even more worked up and anxious than I had been when I left Rob's. Jack was asleep on my sofa and leapt up at the sound of me opening the front door.
"How is she?" I asked, panicked.
"Matt, breathe man. She's asleep, Cal's with her." I took a breath and tried to calm myself a little. She was asleep, that was good.
"How's she been?" I asked. Jack looked at me, sympathy filling his face as he shook his head.
"Why didn't you tell us how bad she is?" He asked. I took a deep breath and sat down opposite him with a long exhale.
"We were getting by. I thought she was getting better, but now I've actually slept and I can think straight, I'm not sure I'm not just deluding myself." I admitted.
"She has terrible PTSD Matt. She's been awake screaming every hour at least and she had two full blown panic attacks before we even got her back here. She needs help."
"She has me, We manage."
"Matt, come on man. You're an MD. You did a psych rotation. You know she needs more help than you or anyone can give her right now."
"I know." I admitted. "She doesn't want to talk to strangers about what happened though Jack. After what her family did to her she finds it so hard to trust people and I get that. I'm not willing to force her to get therapy if

she doesn't want it. She's been forced too much against her will in her life. I won't do that to her."

"Then she needs to be medicated Matt. PTSD and her brain injury are a bad mix. It's why her panic attacks, nightmares and anxiety are so extreme, you know this." He rebuked and he was right. I did know that. I had just been burying my head into the sand, hoping I could get her through without pushing her into anything she didn't want.

"She hates taking those kinds of pills. She was pumped full of drugs after the fall that caused her injury and she was terrified and alone. She's scared of strong drugs now."

"Then you have to talk it through with her, assure her she won't be taking anything that will affect her the way she's scared of. You have to make her see the meds can help her get better. She can't go on like this Matt. She won't survive it."

"I can't lose her Jack." I whispered, tears threatening.

"But you are losing her Matt. Every time she endures one of those episodes she loses a little piece of herself and you lose it too. Do something man. Screw your head on and get her in for a consult. There's only so much you being here for her, can do. She needs anti-depressants and sleeping pills, for a while at least. I can step in if you need me to. I can arrange a consult and talk to her, but it would be better coming from you."

"I know. You're right Jack. I'll make some calls and talk to Alex." I gave in. He was right. It was my responsibility to do what was best for her, no matter how it might scare her. I would just have to do all I could to reassure her, as Jack suggested.

"Just let me know if I can help with anything." He offered.

"I will mate, thank you. I should go to her."

"She's out Matt. I had to give her two Temazepam around four AM."

"Fucking fantastic Jack!" I raged, my previous calm instantaneously gone. "One fucking night with her and you've drugged her!"

"It wasn't like that and you know it. I didn't slip something in her drink Matt! She was exhausted. She woken up screaming at least six times and she couldn't do it again. I explained what she was taking. She was unsure, but when I explained that they would help, she took them."

"Why the hell didn't you ring me? She needed me. She doesn't have that many nightmares when I'm with her."

"Because you were like a zombie last night Matt! We all saw it, even Alex. She wanted you to stay there and get some sleep and we knew she was right. We did what we thought was best for both of you, you miserable asshole!" Jack barked back, making me realise he was right. I was being a dick with him when he'd only tried to help.

"Sorry mate." I said with regret. "I shouldn't have said any of that. I'm just fucking this whole thing up. Alex needs me and I can't seem to do anything right for her."

"Don't do that Matt. You are doing amazing with her. She missed you last night and I'm sure if you'd been here she'd have been better than she was, but you're not a robot. You have to take care of yourself too. Just keep doing what you've been doing man, but get her on some meds. It will benefit both of you."

"I will Jack." I agreed. He was right. It was time to pull my head out of my arse and get Alex the help she needed. It was the best thing I could do for her and she deserved that and so much more.

ALEX

I was terrified, not that that was anything new lately, but this was a new fear. We were at the hospital, my hand clamped tightly in Matt's as we headed to see a doctor he had convinced me to see. A psychiatrist. That word had instantly made me think of mental health facilities and straight jackets. I cried when he suggested the visit, thinking that Matt had finally realised I really had lost my mind and was having me committed, but he assured me it was nothing like that. He wanted me to see the psychiatrist because he was concerned about the way my brain injury was messing with the PTSD I was apparently suffering with and he wanted an expert to discuss medication options with me. That was another idea that worried me, medications. I had spent two months out of my mind on drugs after Marcus pushed me down the stairs. The doctor my parents had appointed, was on their payroll and had kept me heavily drugged for as long as possible at their command. It was partly why I refused to take any pain meds for my TBI symptoms. I refused to ever be drugged out of my mind again. It had taken a lot of convincing from Matt that he would never let any drugs like that, drugs that could alter my alertness, be given to me. I trusted him of course, but not this new doctor we were on our way to see.

"It's going to be ok baby." Matt whispered as we walked through the fancy corridors of the private practice hospital just outside the city. Matt had researched and found that the doctor we had an appointment with, Dr Lia Sanders, was the best in the state. I was guessing by the fancy building we were walking through, she had a hefty price tag for the appointment too, but Matt wouldn't even let me mention cost. I didn't have health insurance and even if I did, it wouldn't have covered that appointment. He had told me not to worry about any of that, he had it covered apparently and since that was all he'd say on the matter, there wasn't much I could do.

"You won't…" I stopped my words almost as soon as they started. I knew I was being ridiculous, but I was so damned scared. Matt stopped and pulled me to the side. He stooped a little so his eyes were almost level with mine.

"What is it love? Talk to me." He said softly.

"You won't let her take me away will you?" I asked hesitantly. "Like the crazy house or a psych ward or anything?"

"Alex, baby, we talked about this." He whispered as he pulled me into his arms.

"I know. I'm just scared."

"There's nothing to be scared of. She won't even touch you. We'll go in together. I'll be right there with you. We'll all talk about what you've been struggling with and she'll give you some treatment options. None of those options will involve taking you anywhere, You're staying with me baby. I promise. Forever." It was the first time he'd said it since the day he found me in that cabin and it reassured me. I took a breath to calm myself and looked up into his face.

"Forever." I said back and he smiled too. "Come on. Let's go and get it over with." Matt nodded and took my hand again. With him by my side I knew I was safe. That was the only thought that was getting me through at that time, day in day out. It had been hell, but each time I came out of the latest meltdown and found Matt beside me, I knew I was safe.

***

"Well. you've had quite the time of it my dear." Dr Sanders declared after I gave her the cliff notes version of my twisted life. She wasn't at all what I had expected. She was in her mid forties maybe, with a neat blonde bob that sat on her shoulders. She was dressed impeccably in a red shift dress with Louboutin heels, the famous red sole pointing up slightly as she sat cross legged in front of me. She had a soft voice and a kind smile and I had found her pretty easy to chat to as I recounted everything that had happened, gripping Matt's hand throughout.

"Have you thought about some counselling, or maybe some cognitive therapy? It really is the most effective treatment for PTSD." She suggested.

"Matt and our friends have spoken to me about it, but it's not really something I want to do. I have strong support in that way. My friends have all experienced a similar situation before with Matt's sister and they're good at being there to talk things through when I need it. I don't see how talking to a stranger would be better than talking to people that I trust and who care about me." I tried to explain,

"Sometimes it's easier to open up fully with someone you have no personal attachment to."

"Not for me." I said, maybe a little rudely, but I wanted to be clear. I didn't want counselling and it was not what I had gone there to discuss.

"And cognitive therapy. Do you understand how that works?" She asked.

"I do and I don't want anyone messing in my head. I've had enough of that for one lifetime." I said curtly. "Look, I'm sorry if I seem rude, but my boyfriend and one of our friends are both doctors and I've had them suggesting the exact same options for weeks. It's not what I want. If there was any way I could handle what's happening to me with no intervention at all, I would, but we've been trying and it's not working, so I'm here hoping like hell you can offer me something to help me even a little, but nothing that involves people poking round in my thoughts….please. I had my mind messed with by my family for over twenty years and I can't let anyone in there again."

"I do understand Alex. The only real option we have left then is medication. You already take an antidepressant, correct?"

"Yes. My doctor suggested it when I found I was struggling with controlling my emotions and concentration on tasks about a year after the TBI was confirmed. He said it would help ease those symptoms of my brain injury, which it did, until this."

"Well we could try moving you onto a new antidepressant, which would help and I'd also like to prescribe you some sleeping tablets, short term, just to help settle you at night until things settle down."

I looked to Matt and was encouraged by his smile. We had discussed the fact the doctor would most likely want to up my meds, so I was prepared to give it a try although, not a hundred percent happy to need to do so.

"If that's what you think best then I'll give it a try." I replied. I had little choice really. If I wasn't willing to give any of the therapy a go, meds were my only choice and Christ knew, I needed something to help with the mess I had become.

MATT

It had been three weeks since our visit to Dr Sanders and I was relieved things seemed to have improved for Alex. She was sleeping much more soundly, making it through to the early hours of the morning before the nightmares found their way in. We were both getting a decent night's sleep for the first time in weeks and it made a huge difference to our mood during the day. I wasn't frazzled, as I had been, and so I had a lot more patience and awareness to deal with Alex's panic attacks when they struck, which also wasn't quite so often as it had been before. The drugs seemed to help ease her anxiety levels, which in turn helped her to be able to stop or at least lessen the effects of the attacks when they did happen.

Lucy and the guys had been great at rallying around us over those weeks. Lucy had persuaded Alex to go to lunch with her and Rob, at a closeby italian restaurant and they had also spent a few evenings together watching films at our place with takeaway food and masses of ice cream and junk food. I knew those times with Lucy really helped her feel like she had felt before the kidnapping, more like herself. Lucy seemed to have the ability to make Alex feel stronger and she also always managed to put a smile on Alex's face. It was a joy to see, the two women who meant most in the world to me, getting along perfectly.

Jack and Cal had also been great, calling around to check in whenever they could and sitting with Alex on the few occasions I had been forced to go into the hospital to deal with one of my patients. Alex had been to the gym with Cal several mornings over the last week, to resume her physio sessions. Returning to those sessions had made the biggest impact on her. When I picked her up afterwards she was always smiling and full of positivity. The physio seemed to give her a confidence boost which she desperately needed and I was just relieved to see all of the changes taking place within her. I had been so afraid that I would lose her after what she had been through, but with the adjustments to her meds and the support of our wonderful family, she really seemed to be getting stronger and more like herself with each day that passed.

"Hi love. Good session?" I asked as Alex approached the front desk where I waited for her in Cal's gym after her fourth physio session that week.

"It was great Matt. We're already caught back up to where we were before….well, everything. Cal thinks I'll be completely rid of this crutch in the next few months if we keep going."

"That's brilliant baby." I replied as she finally got close enough for me to wrap her in my arms. Ever since the kidnapping I hated being apart from her. I was always desperate to have her back by my side where I could be completely sure she was safe.

"Also, I've talked it over with Cal and I'm coming back to work tomorrow." She blurted from where her face was buried into my chest.

"Are you sure you're ready for that? I'm sure Cal wouldn't mind if you took a little longer." I dreaded the idea of being seperated from her for hours at a time as we would be if she returned to work.

"I know. That's exactly what Cal said, but I'm ready Matt. I need to keep on moving forward and the next logical step is to get back to work. Cal was unsure too so we've agreed I'll just come in for four hour shifts to start with and build it up from there." I nodded, preferring the idea of her being out for four hours at a time, rather than the usual eight or nine she worked.

"Sounds like a good plan. I suppose that means I should make the most of today then, my last full day with you to myself for the week."

"I suppose so." She laughed. I took her hand and led her out to my car. The entire way I was silently thanking my lucky stars that Alex seemed to be getting stronger day by day. When I had found her tied to that bed in that disgusting cabin just weeks before, I had thought for sure I would never get her back whole. The weeks between, weeks of nightmares, panic attacks and pain had only solidified that fear for me, but there she was in that moment as we drove home together, smiling and positive and seeming so much more healed than I ever thought possible. It wasn't over, of course. Alex still had bad times when the dark thoughts would consume her, but they were becoming less and less and I had high hopes that those bad times would become fewer and further between as time passed.

I should never have doubted her. She had led a life of pure misery, fear and torment and yet she had come through it. I should have known she would find a way to come back from her latest trauma. She was too strong not to. I was so lucky to have such a truly spectacular woman in my life and I would never ever forget that fact.

ALEX

"Hey Lex! I'm headed out. You change your mind about that date yet?" One of the regulars, Troy, called behind him as he passed me at the reception desk.

"In your dreams Casanova!" I laughed back. It was the usual banter I took from the regulars at the gym. They flirted with me and with Lucy and we both abruptly shot them down. It was a game we all played and I had to admit it was fun and all totally harmless.

It had been almost two months since the horror at the cabin and I really did feel as though I had once again found my feet. The meds were the biggest help in that happening. As Matt had promised, they hadn't affected me badly, they simply seemed to help me balance my thoughts and take control when the darkness came as it often did. My flashbacks were rare and the nightmares, though still regular, were less intense and I was sleeping much better.

Matt had been amazing with me, supporting me throughout all of the craziness and through my very long recovery. He had been patient and caring and I knew without him I would never have gotten through. He had stayed with me for over a month, taking time from work and just being there for whatever I needed. The rest of the family too, had been there for both of us and had spent time with me when Matt couldn't until I felt strong enough to be alone.

It had taken time. At first, every time I found myself alone, the darkness would consume me and convince me Marcus was coming for me once again. Over time I had found ways to overcome those fears and learned to feel safe in our home alone.

Being out in public, alone, had been much harder to overcome and it was still an issue I was struggling with, but I was getting there. For the last week I had driven myself to and from the gym in the car Matt had gotten for me as a replacement for the one Marcus forced off the road so many months ago. I had even been to the grocery store on my own, twice that week, but I was very jumpy and nervous the entire time. I forged on though, determined I would find a way to get back to being a normal person. Being at the gym helped. I felt braver there, more like my old self. Cal didn't crowd me, he simply stepped back and let me find my feet, safe in the knowledge he was always close by to step in if I needed him. He left me to deal with the cocky assholes who worked out there, which, at first, had been hard for me, but over time had given me back the confidence I had lost.

All in all, I was more the Alex Harrison I had been before the cabin. I wasn't back completely and the darkness still tried to take me when I let it sneak in, but I was getting better at blocking it out and finding the confidence to live my life.

"Trust me sugar, you're always in my dreams!" Troy called back as he exited the building backwards while blowing me a kiss.

"Cocky asshole." I muttered to myself with a laugh as I turned back to the desk and checked my cell. I couldn't hold in my smile as I opened a text from Matt. The excitement at hearing from him never faded.

How's your day Baby? Mine is dull as dishwater! xxx

I laughed at another of his strange sayings. He was full of them and some hilarious British words too.

My day's been good. Managed most of it without my crutch! Sorry your day sucks. Maybe I can liven it up a little for you when you get home? xxx

I text him back and had to clench my thighs together at the thought of what we could get up to when he got home that night. It had taken time for us to become intimate again. It had triggered flashbacks for me at first and Matt had been terrified of scaring me, but we moved very slowly and eventually got our lovemaking back to what it had been, loving and spectacular.

At that point it took all of my willpower to keep my hands off of my amazingly sexy man each time I saw him. My addiction to the pleasure he could bring me was back with a vengeance!

Thanks love! Now the last of my shift will be livened up by me trying to hide my hard on! Xxx

I laughed out loud at the image in my head and looked up to see Cal and the two guys at the free weights looking at me like I was crazy. I smiled to reassure them I hadn't lost my mind then looked back to my phone.

Only seems fair since I've been turned on all damned day! Hurry home handsome! I love you xxx

Matt replied less than a minute later telling me he'd be home in record time and that he loved me too. I couldn't hold in my stupidly happy smile as I put my cell aside and set about tidying the desk. My shift was almost up and I liked to leave things tidy for Lucy who worked the next day.

"You ok honey?" Cal asked as he approached.

"I'm good. Just straightening up for Lucy tomorrow. Are you working the late shift?"

"Yeah. CJ had a date tonight, and since Jack's working all night, I didn't mind him taking the night off."

"CJ on a date? Poor woman!" I laughed as I thought of how torturous it would be to date that man. He had the biggest damn ego I had ever encountered. He was a pretty decent guy at heart, but in love with himself far too much!

"If she's agreed to a date with him, she's probably just as bad!" Cal remarked with a smile.

"I sure hope so, for her sake." I started to gather up my things and pack them into my purse.

"Go grab your coat hon and I'll walk you to your car. Is Matt working?"

"He's off in a couple of hours. I'm going home to make a meal for when he gets home." I replied.

"Ugh, don't talk about food! I'm half starved over here!" He cried dramatically.

"You want me to run to the diner for you before I head home?" I offered.

"Thanks sweetie, but I ordered in. It'll be here soon. You get home before it gets dark," I nodded and hurried to the kitchen to get my coat. Cal walked me to my car and watched me as I drove off, making me promise to text him when I was safely locked in the apartment. It was nice, the way they all looked out for me. Some days I wondered how the hell I had ever survived any of my life without them.

Hey hun. How was work? You fancy dinner with us tomorrow? xxx

Lucy's text arrived as I stepped into the elevator from the parking garage in our apartment building and again I was smiling. Matt was working all night the next day and those were the worst times for me. I hated being alone at night and I knew Lucy knew that. It was why she had invited me over and I was immensely grateful.

I stepped out of the elevator on our floor and as I walked down the corridor, I text Lucy back. That's why I didn't see them until I was almost at our apartment. I looked up briefly to see if I was near the door and was met with the ice cold, grey eyes of Dmitri Sokolov. He was flanked by two burly men I hadn't had the misfortune of being tortured by in the past, but Dmitri, I knew well. His pleasure had been found in slicing the huge cuts on my abdomen and witnessing the pain he caused before he would brutally force himself on me.

I turned, every intention of fleeing, but found another gun toting thug behind me. I was trapped. I took another step forward and thought about screaming. If Jack and Cal were home they'd hear me, but they weren't home. Cal was where I'd left him at the gym and Jack was working, Cal had told me that only minutes earlier.

"Pleasure to see you again Alicia." Dmitri said, in his thickly accented English, his face filled with the twisted enjoyment I had seen many times before, enjoyment at witnessing my fear.

"What do you want?" I asked, trying to not let him see my hands desperately shaking.

"Straight down to business huh? I like that. No fucking around like your brother."

"I think we both know I'm nothing like Marcus."

"Da. He was stupid. You will not be so stupid, will you Alicia?" He stepped closer and ran a rough finger down my right cheek, making my skin crawl.

"Maybe if you tell me why you're here we can actually get something settled." I said firmly, taking a step back out of his reach, hoping it wasn't glaringly obvious how terrified of him I was.

"Very well. Open the door. We don't discuss business in hallways." He ordered. I fought to gain control of my breathing. I would not lose it infront of this monster. I needed my wits about me. I took a deep breath and considered my options. I couldn't fight, there were four of them. I couldn't exactly just call on my cell for help and there was no option to run. Dmitri could simply grab me and carry me away if he so wanted, but he hadn't. I decided my best option was to take them inside. Once the door was closed they could do as they pleased with me and I'd be screwed, but upon entering, when I had to shut off the alarm I could enter the code Rob had taught me. It was a different code to the al one, a code which would signal to the alarm company and Rob's security company, that I was under duress and in danger, without alerting the bad guys to what I'd done. It would get help to me eventually. I just hoped they would come before Dmitri did any real damage.

While I stood debating my decision Dmitri produced a gun and pressed it into my side.

"Open the door, now *cyka!*" The sound of that Russian word, the name he had hissed at me over and over when he had hurt me years ago, instantly set my mind reeling to the past and had me sweating and panting. As I stepped toward the door of the apartment, he walked with me, keeping the gun pressed hard into my hip. I took deep breaths as I berated myself, in my head, for allowing flashbacks to come at that moment. I unlocked the door slowly, giving myself the time I needed to get it together.

As soon as the door was open the alarm started beeping as it always did. I looked to Dmitri and he shoved me forward into the room.

"Shut it off and if you try anything, I kill you!" He barked. I nodded and hurried over to the alarm panel. I fought to concentrate through the hell invading my brain and mentally checked I knew the emergency code before I punched it in. I did not want to get it wrong. When I was sure I knew what I was doing I punched in the four digit code Rob had drilled into me. The alarm stopped and the light on the top corner flashed green, just like it always did. For a minute I worried I had done it wrong and just put the regular code in to disarm it, but when I thought for a second I knew I hadn't. I had done as Rob had taught me and he would now know something was wrong. I just hoped he came quickly. There was only so much time I could buy, trapped with such a monster.

MATT

I sat down to a very late lunch, midway through my shift. It had been a hectic day with emergency surgeries following a five car pile up earlier in the day. I was exhausted and desperate to eat something and call Alex to hear her voice before I got called back in again. I had been texting her not more than thirty minutes before, but I needed to hear her beautiful voice to assure myself she was alright and to power me through the last of my shift.

I was only midway through the soup I was eating when my mobile started ringing. I pulled it from my pocket quickly, hoping it would be Alex, but instead it was Rob. "Hi mate." I greeted upon answering. I continued eating, determined to get finished before my next page hit.

"Matt, are you working?" He asked.

"Yeah, twelve hour shift. Why?"

"I just got an emergency signal from your place. Alex just entered the alarm code to say she's in danger."

"What?" I barked, knocking my spoon flying as I leapt to my feet and set off running.

"I called her cell, but she's not answering. I have a tech pulling surveillance footage from your building and I'm en route there with Cam and Gareth now."

"I'm on my way too. Should I grab Jack? Is it the Russians?" I asked all at once.

"It's possible, though my sources said the remaining Sokolovs weren't interested in the Dalton debt. That's why I was happy to pull Alex's security detail. Grab Jack if he's free. If it is the Russians we may need all hands on deck."

"How far away are you?"I asked. I was frantic. If Alex was taken or hurt again, neither she nor I would survive it.

"Seven minutes. Just get your ass there. I need to hang up and call my tech." With that Rob hung up and I almost ripped the lockers from the wall in my rage and haste to open mine and get my car keys. I grabbed them and set off running towards the ER where I hoped I would find Jack. If he wasn't there I was going without him. There wasn't time. I needed to get to Alex.

"JACK!" I yelled when I saw him at the nurses station up ahead. All heads turned to me, but I ignored them.

"What's up man?" He asked with concern.

"It's Alex. We have to go, now!" I barked as I continued running for the exit. Jack stared at me for a monect, then ran behind me.

"What's going on?" He asked as we neared my car.

"Alex is in trouble. She triggered the home alarm with that emergency code. Rob's on his way. He said to grab you too."

"Russians?"

"I really fucking hope not!"

ALEX

"Move! Sit!" Dmitri barked as he grabbed my arm and dragged me from where I had stood frozen by the door. He shoved me across the room and I just caught myself from falling on my ass. I stepped back behind the coffee table, feeling safer with a barrier between me and the monster. I stood and crossed my arms over my chest, refusing to sit as he'd demanded. I continued my battle to appear strong.

"Come on then Dmitri. We're in the fucking apartment. Spit it out. What the fuck do you want?" I demanded, my voice surprisingly low and calm. He was flanked by all three of his goons and I tried not to let them intimidate me, which was ridiculous. The four of them would intimidate anyone, but I, at least, refused to let them see they scared me.

"You better watch that mouth *cyka* or I'll be forced to give you lessons in manners, like old times. Remember Alicia?" He sneered. Oh I remembered. I spent large portions of my life wishing I didn't, but I did.

"Da! She remembers!" He laughed as he took a step forward. I stepped further around the table away from him.

"What do you want?" I growled angrily. I was sick of games.

"My brother is dead. Word is you are responsible for that."

"I think you mean Marcus is responsible for that. At the time your brother was shot through the heart, I was tied to the bed." I lied. No way was I telling the Russians Matt killed one of their own.

"Really? I did not think he would have the balls for such a play." He almost laughed in his thick Russian accent.

"He was a fucking psycho. He killed your brother and the guy with him. Luckily for you Marcus was killed during my rescue so that loose end has been neatly tied for you." I said calmly.

"Not quite. There still is the debt he owed my family. Since your family have all met such…. tragic ends, that debt now falls to you."

"What debt? How much?" I asked dumbly, hoping to buy time.

"Your family try to screw us on a deal. They owe us $100,000. If they just paid, all of this trouble would have been unnecessary. My fucking idiot brother was so desperate to have you he gave them extension after extension. Now he's dead, it's my debt and I am offering no extension. I want my money, now or you come with me. I know a nice trafficker who will pay big money for you *cyka*!" He said, making me tremble even more. No more dragging this mess out. It wasn't my debt. I had nothing to do with the Dalton's shady dealings or the Sokolovs, but I was the last Dalton standing, by blood anyway, and if I wanted an end to this mess there was only one way.

"If I pay, this will be the last I hear from you or your family, correct?" I demanded.

"If you pay." He nodded. I took that as his agreement and walked to the kitchen where my laptop sat on the dining table. The Sokolovs were criminals and murderers, but they lived by their word so I trusted that with one payment I could be rid of them for good. Dmitri followed me, his men close behind him. I opened the laptop and pressed my hands on the table beside it in an effort to still the shaking, as it fired up. Thankfully it booted up quickly and I opened my banking app, moving the screen from Dmitri's view. No way was he seeing all the money I had received from the sale of my Chicago apartment and the sale of the Dalton family home, which had automatically come to me, the last surviving family member, after Marcus' death. I knew he'd be demanding more if he knew what I had amassed over recent weeks. I quickly set up the transfer from my account with the amount. I knew there would be IRS repercussions, transferring a large amount of money to a known mobster, but Rob would help me figure that out later. I just wanted them away from me.

"Bank account." I said as I looked up to into the face of one of the demons of my nightmares. He pulled a piece of paper from his pocket with neatly typed account details on it. I hurriedly typed them in and watched as the transfer was made. When It was complete I turned the screen to him, but never released my laptop.

"I knew you would be smarter than your stupid family Alicia." He said with that sick smile.

"You have what you came for now." I maintained my false cool as I got to my feet and walked toward him a little. "Time you left." He looked down at me with that damn terrifying smile, then before I could react he had hold of my arm and ripped me forward into his body.

"What, no fun today? For old times sake *cyka*?" He whispered into my ear.

"You will never lay a hand on me again you sick sonofabitch!" I yelled in a panic, as I fought to escape his hold.

"Take your fucking hands off her, right now dickhead!" Matt's voice boomed through the apartment. I looked up to find not only him, but Rob, Jack, Cam and Gareth backing him up, all with guns drawn and aimed at Dmitri.

"Woah, calm down cowboys. Just having a little fun, aren't we Alicia?" Dmitri said as he let go of my arm. I stepped away from him a little, but didn't retreat. I wouldn't let him know how he affected me.

"Just go Dmitri. You have what you wanted. It's settled."

"Da. Shame you paid up. You always were a good little *cyka*!" He spat as he turned to leave.

"You have two seconds to get out of this apartment fucker. I see you in Chicago again and we're gonna have problems. Got it?" Rob roared in a voice that scared the crap out of me. It was a voice I had never heard him use and I was sure, as I watched the Russians slightly hurry their pace through the apartment, it had gotten to them too.

"Our business here is settled, for now." Dmitri dared to say.

"For fucking ever if you know what's good for you dickwad!" Rob raged as he aimed his gun right at Dmitri's head.

"Enough. Come on! We have other matters to attend." Dmitri snapped to his men. They all turned and were out of the apartment in a matter of seconds.

"Alex? You ok sweet?" Jack asked as Gareth walked to the door behind them and watched down the corridor. Rob nodded to Cam and Gareth and they walked out of the apartment without a word, presumably to make sure Dmitri and his guys left.

"Alex?" Matt was in front of me now, bent a little, his eyes level with mine.

"I....I'm ok." I whispered, my voice failing me.

"Did he hurt you?" Matt asked as he looked up and down my body.

"No."

"What's settled Alex? What did he want?" Rob asked as he and Jack stepped closer to me.

"Money of course." I was still staring at Matt, feeling completely overwhelmed by what had happened. "I paid the debt Marcus left, the hundred thousand."

"Motherfucker! That wasn't your debt to pay Alex!" Rob said with anger. "I'll get it back for you."

"No! Just leave it now. It's paid. It came from the money I got for that damned house in LA, money I never wanted anyway. They'll go back to LA and I'll be done with that damn criminal family for good. It was a small price to pay for this hell to finally all be ended. I don't want any more trouble Rob, please." Rob looked from me to Matt, who nodded.

"Fine. If it's what you want." Rob relented.

"Come sit down baby." Matt wrapped his arm around me and led me to the sofa in the lounge. I was still shaking, but feeling much stronger at the realisation that what I'd just said to Rob was true, it was finally over. The Dalton's and Yuri were dead and the rest of the Sokolovs had the money they wanted.

"You did good sweet, putting the alarm code in and holding them off. You should be proud of yourself." Jack said as he sat on the coffee table opposite and held my shaking hand.

"It's over. That's all that matters. It's all, finally, over." I whispered with relief. After over a quarter century of living through hell, inflicted on me by my own flesh and blood and truly dangerous criminals, it was all over and I was surrounded by people I loved and trusted. I was stronger and braver and more ready than I had ever been to see what my future held.

***

Four months later....

"Where have you been love? I was about to send out the search party?" Matt asked as I walked into our apartment, sweating and out of breath.

"Sorry, I got carried away. It's a really beautiful morning." I replied with a smile. Matt was sat at the breakfast bar in the kitchen, drinking tea and working on his laptop. He looked sexy as all get out in low riding shorts, his sculpted chest bare. His hair was still stuck up from sleep, untamed and so damned cute.

"Just go easy baby. You don't want to rush things." Matt cautioned. He was right, Cal kept on telling me the same thing, but I was finally free of my crutch and the limitations of my injury. Thanks to Cal's physio sessions and a rigorous exercise regime I had been sticking to, my left side was pretty strong again. My limp was barely noticable and my crutch had long since been abandoned. I could work out as I wanted and I loved to run, as I had that morning. I still dealt with some pain in my leg and my left hand was still, and likely always would be, weak, but compared to the way I had struggled when I met Matt, I was doing great.

I still dealt with the mental side effects of my brain injury, I was overly emotional and concentration would never be my greatest skill, but with meds those symptoms were managed, as were the odd flashback or nightmare I sometimes struggled with in the aftermath of everything that had happened. Matt was always there to help me through those times. He was my rock and throughout everything we had been through, our love for each other had only grown.

"I'm good Matt. I came back as soon as my leg started to hurt. I know what my limits are." I replied as I approached him and placed a kiss on his cheek, not wanting to touch him more until I showered, but he had

other ideas and snagged me with an arm around my
waist. He pulled me into his lap in one move.

"Don't Matt! I'm all sweaty and gross!" I cried.

"Don't care." He stilled my fight to be released with one
arm around my back, then his other hand lifted my chin
until my eyes met his. "I missed you." He whispered.

"I was like an hour at most," I replied with a roll of my
eyes. Matt smiled, that amazing smile that instantly had
me melting into a pile of goo. When he moved in to kiss
me I leant in and my lips were on his instantly. We
tangled in a fiery, intense, burning kiss that could lead to
only one thing. Reluctantly, I pulled away. We had
somewhere to be that morning. We didn't have time for
that one thing, no matter how much I wanted it.

"We have to be at Jack and Cal's in thirty minutes." I
reminded him when he looked devastated I had halted
the raging inferno between us.

"It's next door!" He whined, making me laugh.

"I have to shower and get ready though, and we can't be
late."

"They're always late, why can't we be?" I couldn't hold in
my laugh as I climbed down from his lap. He sounded
like a petulant five year old and I loved it.

"This is too important to be late and you know it Matthew
Simmons!" I scolded playfully. He snagged me again,
this time by the hand and pulled me in for another,
briefer, but no less passionate, kiss.

"Later?" He asked hopefully.

"You know it handsome." I kissed him once more and
then hurried to get ready. I was just as eager as Matt to
return to bed with him, but it was an important day for

Jack and Cal and there was no way we would miss it, despite Matt's protests.

***

Thirty minutes later Matt and I stood outside Jack and Cal's apartment. I had showered, changed into a bright sundress and hurriedly dried and styled my hair. Matt looked handsome, as always, in khaki cargo shorts and a white polo t-shirt. I held the bright pink gift bag with the present Matt and I had spent almost an hour agonising over in the city's largest toy store.

"Hey guys!" Cal greeted as he opened the door. "Come on in." He was beaming, a state he seemed to have been in for the last two weeks. Both he and Jack were happier than I had ever seen them, and considering they had always seemed to be happy before, that was astonishing.

"Hi Cal." Matt greeted as we walked into their place which had been lost to an explosion of pink decorations. Helium balloons filled the ceiling and there were banners and streamers on every wall. The dining table had been set for a tea party, covered in a bright pink tablecloth and laden with platters of food and pink paper cups and plates. In the very centre sat a huge glittery unicorn cake adorned with four candles.

"Jees Cal. It's a princess paradise in here!" I gasped.

"It's amazing isn't it? I'm so jealous!" Lucy cried from where she sat beside Rob at the table. She was glowing as as she stood to greet us with her huge, ever growing baby bump. She was radiant. Rob on the other hand, had become even more overprotective of his fiance and seemed more stressed than ever. The pregnancy had been an unexpected surprise for them, but they were both extremely excited about it, even if it had turned Rob into a nervous wreck!

"Hi Darling. How are you feeling?" Matt asked as he swept her up into a hug. He was desperate to meet his new niece or nephew and he didn't have long to wait. Lucy's due date was less than a month away.

"Pretty good except for the back ache, but I think I'm getting off pretty lightly so far so no complaints." Lucy laughed. She had been lucky in that she had escaped any morning sickness and had seemed to sail through the whole thing thus far.

"Don't go jinxing it now." I joked as I walked over to hug her.

"You sound like Rob!" Lucy giggled.

"Take a seat guys. Jack will be out in a minute." Cal said as he ushered us all to sit at the party table. I sat between Matt and Lucy and placed our present beside the huge pile of brightly wrapped packages at the far end of the table.

"Sure you have enough gifts man?" Rob asked as he sat beside Lucy and wrapped a protective arm around her shoulders.

"I know. We couldn't help it. She deserves to be spoiled. This is her first real birthday celebration from what we've been told." Cal said in hushed tones. I felt the pain of that statement. I knew how that kind of life felt. "I just hope we won't overwhelm her." He added with concern.

"She'll love it Cal. She's so lucky to have you guys." I said through the huge lump in my throat. Tears were threatening at the thought that I knew what she had lived through and at the joy of knowing she now had two of the most amazing people I knew to fight for her. Matt grabbed my hand and squeezed reassuringly. He always knew just what I needed and I was so grateful to have him in my life, fighting for and with me.

"Ok guys!" Jack's voice called from down the hall. "Are you all ready for the beautiful birthday girl?" As he finished the words he appeared before us, a tiny hand in his own. Bright blue, wide eyes looked around the pink paradise before her with wonder.

"Happy birthday sweetie!" Cal said as he approached them.

"Is....is this for me?" She asked, unsure and excited.

"Yes Em, it's your birthday party, all for you." Cal replied. Emily beamed and started jumping up and down excitedly as she continued to cling to Jack's hand. She really was the most beautiful little girl, with golden blonde curls and the cutest smile. She was small for her age and too slim, though Jack and Cal were working on that day by day.

Jack had first met Emily when he treated her in the ER a few months back. She had narrowly escaped a fire at the crappy apartment she had been living in with her drug addict mother. She had clearly been beaten on a regular basis, and was severely undernourished. Somehow her situation had been overlooked by family services and she had suffered for over three years at the hands of her incompetent, evil mother. She had formed an attachment with Jack in the ER, and Jack, having lived through and witnessed so much abuse in his own young life, didn't have the heart to detach himself. He had taken care of her for the week she had spent at the hospital because of some minor burns and smoke inhalation. Her mother had died in the fire and no other family could be located. The father wasn't even listed on her birth certificate.

When Emily was released from the hospital and taken to a group home, Jack had taken Cal to meet her and he had instantly become attached, just as Jack had. They started the process to adopt her that day. It had taken time and been frustrating for them both, but eventually the adoption was granted and Emily had arrived at their place two weeks ago.

It hadn't been plain sailing for them all. Emily had night terrors from her previous life and also a lot of deep rooted issues, but Cal and Jack had taken it all in their stride and with a lot of care and patience Emily was becoming more and more comfortable with them. They both doted on her and were determined to do whatever was needed to give her the life she deserved, including a spectacular fourth birthday party.

"It's all pink!" She squealed.

"It sure is, pink for our princess." Jack said with a huge smile. Every single thing the guys had offered Emily, she always opted for pink. She loved princesses and unicorns and all the typical girly characters. She had chosen pink paint for the walls in her room, pink unicorn bedding and almost every outfit she wore was pink, including the adorable floral sundress and matching hair band she wore that day.

"Let's go say hello to everyone Em." Cal took her other hand and they both led their beautiful daughter over to us.

"Uncle Matt!" She cried as soon as she saw him. She pulled her hands free and ran to Matt who she adored. He had visited her regularly during her hospital stay and they had formed the cutest bond.

"Come here birthday girl!" Matt laughed as he got to his feet and swept her up into his arms. He had never looked more handsome to me than he did at that moment with a child in his arms. I couldn't wait until he stood with our child in his arms one day.

Emily squealed excitedly as Matt spun around quickly with her in his arms. She was so filled with joy and life. The first time I had met her she hadn't been that way. She had been shy, unsure and so quiet. I saw a lot of my own miserable childhood in her pain filled eyes and I had been so afraid for her. Seeing her that morning, smiling and laughing and looking so much like the four year old she was, I was no longer afraid for her. I knew Jack and Cal and the rest of the family she had inherited in all of us, would help give her her childhood back. She had been saved, as I had wished to be so many times. She had a great life ahead of her with Jack and Cal and it lightened my dark heart to witness it.

"Hey little dot, there's a ton of presents over there. Any idea who they're for?" Matt asked as he stopped spinning and sat back down beside me with Emily on his lap.

Jack and Cal took their seats and started pouring juice and wine in the glasses around the table.

"Presents?" Emily repeated as she looked at the mountain of gifts beside her. Her eyes bulged and she looked to Jack and Cal with confusion. "Who's are those for?" She asked.

"They're for you princess, they're your birthday gifts." Cal replied with a reassuring smile.

"Here sweetheart." Rob said as he got to his feet and leant over the table. "Open this one. It's from me and Aunt Lucy." He placed a huge box before her, wrapped in purple and pink striped paper.

"You bought me a present Uncle Rob?" She asked with uncertainty.

"We sure did honey. It's your birthday. Everyone gets presents on their birthday." Emily started to squirm down from Matt's lap and I was worried for a minute it was all too much and she was going to run away and hide, but she didn't. As soon as Matt placed her down she ran to Rob and scrambled onto his lap. She wrapped her arms as far around his huge neck as she could and hugged him tight.

"Thank you Uncle Rob. It's so pretty." She whispered. I looked to Lucy and was relieved to see I wasn't the only one moved to tears.

"You're welcome honey, but that's just the paper. You need to tear it off and see what's inside." Rob replied with a chuckle. Matt handed the gift back over to Rob and together he and Emily tore away the paper to reveal a princess castle complete with all the figures and furniture to play inside.

"A princess castle!" She cried ecstatically. "Look Jack, it's a castle!"

"I see sweet. That's great." Jack replied.

"Aunt Alex, did you see?" She asked as she looked up at me. I hurried to wipe away the tears that ran down my cheeks, but I wasn't quick enough. "Why are you crying?" She demanded with concern.

"They're happy tears Emily. I'm just so happy to be here with everyone." I replied.

"Oh, ok." She relented instantly. "You want to look at my castle?"

"I sure do honey." I replied as I looked to the man I loved for the strength to swallow past the emotions fighting for power within me. Being with Emily, seeing how happy she was, swirled up a tidal wave of my own history and emotions I wasn't quite sure I was ready to deal with. Matt reached over and gently kissed the top of my head. "Love you baby." He whispered and it was all I needed to get myself together and remember what mattered, that moment. How happy we all were and how much I loved that man.

"Love you too."

"Come on Aunt Alex! Cal's gonna help us put it together!" Emily called as she grabbed my hand and dragged me over to the middle of the lounge where Cal already sat pulling out the contents of the box.

"Wait until she realises she has all those other presents left to open yet!" Matt laughed as I walked away.

***

By late evening that day we were all exhausted. Emily had made each of us play with her and her new toys every time she opened a gift. She'd been like a whirlwind of excitement and happiness all afternoon, spurred on by each new and exciting toy she revealed. She had finally crashed in Jack's arms around seven pm and he had carried her through to her room to sleep. Now we all sat in the lounge drinking coffee and chatting quietly as we tried to recover from the wonderful, wild afternoon.

"I don't know how you guys keep up with her! I'm beat!" Rob declared. He was in the biggest armchair, his head back and his eyes closed, Lucy curled up in his lap.

"She's not normally quite that excitable" Cal sighed. "I think we let her have too much cake. She was all hopped up on sugar!"

"You better get used to it Rob. You'll have your own to contend with before you know it." Jack laughed.

"I can't wait." Rob said as he opened his eyes and looked to Jack with a huge grin.

"We'll see man. You're so screwed. If it's a boy it'll be a mini you and you know no one's ready to deal with that little terror and if it's a girl it'll be a mini Lucy and you won't dare take your eyes off of her!"

"Fuck you Jack!" Rob whispered shouted with a laugh, maling us all laugh, mainly because we knew Jack was right. Rob was so screwed.

The sound of Rob's cell seemed so loud in the hushed apartment and we all looked to him as he scrambled to answer it before it woke Emily, who was a very light sleeper thanks to her past. Again, that was an experience I shared with her, the fear of sleeping too deeply and missing some impending danger.

"Sorry." Rob said as he finally answered and stopped the ringing. Lucy climbed from his lap and he stalked through to the kitchen to take the call.

"I'll just check on Em." Cal said as he too stood and disappeared.

"She seems so happy Jack. You guys are doing great with her." I remarked as we all watched Cal walk away.

"It's all her. She's a tough little thing. She just takes everything as it comes and handles it with a smile."

"She knows she's safe with you guys. That's what makes her strong." I said, squeezing Matt's hand in my own, telling him silently what he already knew, he was my safety.

"WHAT THE FUCK?!" Rob's voice raged from the kitchen. Jack was instantly on his feet and rushing to him, Lucy right behind. Matt and I followed a minute later, in case there was something we could help with. When we entered the kitchen Lucy was pressed to Rob's side, her arms clamped around his waist and he stood, red faced and looking more enraged than I had ever seen him. If I didn't know better, I'd have been scared of him.

"What's going on?" Matt asked.

"It was Ethan, Amy's best friend." Jack answered. Rob was taking rapid breaths and looked ready to kill something.

"Amy? Rob's sister?" Matt said.

"Yeah. She's in hospital. Ethan found her at some motel, beaten and bleeding. She'd been on a date and he thinks maybe she was...." Jack didn't finish the sentence, he didn't need to.

"Oh God!" I gasped as tears stung my eyes. That poor girl.

"How is she?" Matt asked as he pulled me tighter into his side.

"Ethan didn't say much. He wanted to get back to her, but she was unconscious for a while. They think she was drugged."

"Rob, mate. What can we do?" Matt asked as he looked over to where Rob stood, frozen and gripping Lucy tight.

"I have to go to her." He growled. "Lucy's not flying with the pregnancy. Can she stay with you guys?" He was talking, but he wasn't in the room. He seemed to have mentally checked out.

"Of course she can" Matt replied at the same time Lucy piped up.

"No way Rob! I'm coming with you!" She cried.

"No sweetheart, you're not. I don't want you flying while you're carrying our baby. I don't even think you can fly as far on as you are."

"But I want to come with you. I want to be there for you and for.....for Amy." Lucy whimpered through her tears.

"I don't want you stressing yourself out either Lucy. You know what seeing Amy in that state will do. You'll have nightmares, maybe even panic attacks. It's no good for our baby."

"He's right sweet." Jack cut in before Lucy could argue. "You need to try and keep calm and stress free through this pregnancy. I'll go with Rob. Everything will be ok."

"What about Emily?" Lucy asked.

"She has Cal and you guys. I'll only be gone a few days."

"You don't need to come either Jack." Rob barked. "I don;t need a fucking babysitter!"

"No, you don't, but you do need someone to make sure you don't do anything bloody stupid Robert Shepard!" Lucy cried, hands on her hips, face filled with determination before Jack could utter a word. "If you won't let me go, then Jack goes. End of discussion!" Rob looked down to where she stood glaring at him angrily and took a deep breath.

"Fine. Jack comes with me. Now stop getting yourself all worked up and go sit back down. You look so tired." Rob said, the anger momentarily gone from his voice and replaced with the usual calm he portrayed.

"Just.... please don't do anything stupid Rob. I know someone hurt your sister and they deserve whatever they have coming, but just remember we need you, me and your baby here. We need you at home, not in prison."

"I'm not going to do anything that stops me from coming home to you, to both of you. I promise sweetheart." Rob held her tightly again and Jack, Matt and I stepped aside to give them a moment.

"I'll get your shifts covered at the hospital and help Cal with Emily." Matt assured Jack in hushed tones.

"And I'll cover the gym for Cal. Don't worry about things here." I added.

"Thanks guys, but it's Rob I'm worried about."

"He'll be ok mate. Just keep a close watch on him."

"How old is Amy?" I asked.

"Almost twenty three." Jack answered. "Rob's so protective with her. This will kill him."

"If she needs more support, then you just call me Jack. I'll fly over there for her. I know what she's going through. I might be able to help if she needs it." I offered.

"Thanks sweet. We might take you up on that."

"Jack, you good to get going?" Rob barked as Lucy walked towards us. Matt wrapped a supportive arm around her. Rob had been right, she looked exhausted.

"I need to pack a bag and talk to Cal." Jack replied.

"Fine. I'm going home to get stuff for me and Lucy. I'll be fifteen tops. That good with you?"

"I'll be ready." Jack replied. Rob nodded and walked over to kiss Lucy briefly.

"I'll call at Matt's with your suitcase before I go sweetheart." He explained, then he turned and left in a rush.

"Come on darling. Let's get you to ours so you can rest." Matt suggested to Lucy. She nodded her agreement.

"Take it easy sweet." Jack whispered as he hugged Lucy goodbye.

"I will. Just take care of him for me Jack….please look after him." Lucy whimpered through her tears which were once again running freely.

"I always do. He'll be fine Lucy. I promise. You know I've always got his back." Jack placed a kiss on the top of her head and then handed her back into Matt's waiting arms. I briefly hugged Jack goodbye and once again told him to call me if they needed me, then we all left. It had been a brutal ending to a wonderful afternoon and evening. My thoughts were with Rob's sister Amy. She was so young and had probably just experienced the worst night of her life. I hoped she could find a way to get through it.

***

Lucy was finally asleep in our guest bedroom. She had been tearful until Rob returned with her packed suitcase, then after she had said an emotional goodbye to him, she had been inconsolable. Both Matt and I had tried hard to convince her Rob would be fine and that Jack would look out for him, but she was just so worried about him reacting stupidly to what had happened. I understood her concern. Rob had been stood with nothing but murder in his eyes after he took that call. Eventually I just laid beside her quietly, comforting her as I allowed her to cry it all out, until finally, she fell asleep and seemed more settled. When I was sure she was fast asleep, I crept out of the room and quietly closed the door behind me. Matt was sat in the lounge, on the sofa in sweats and a t-shirt, a large tumbler of whiskey in his hand.

"Is she ok?" He asked as he turned to study me over the back of the sofa.

"She's asleep. I think she's calmer than she was. Are you ok?" I asked. It wasn't often I found Matt drinking hard liquor.

"It just brings it all back. Thinking about what Amy is going through makes me think about what happened to Lucy and to you. It's hard going back to all of that. I feel terrible for Rob right now. I know exactly what he's facing" Matt said sadly. I walked around the sofa and climbed into his lap where I curled up against his chest.

"He's strong. Amy's lucky to have him. He'll get her through this." I whispered as I took the glass from Matt's hand and took a drink. It burned as it went down and I relished the warmth it provided almost as much as the warmth Matt provided with his firm body surrounding me.

"I don't know what I'd have done if I lost you baby." He said, his voice hoarse and rough.

"But you didn't I'm here and I'm stronger and happier than I have ever been. Lucy too. We both made it through and we have good futures ahead. You don't need to worry so much anymore." I assured him.

"I'll always worry love. You mean too much to me. There will always be a fear within me that I could lose you some day and jesus Alex, I don't know how I'd survive without you."

"You'll never need to know Matt." I whispered as I placed the glass on the table behind me, then wrapped my arms around the back of his neck and clung on. "I'm here and I'm not going anywhere. I'm yours. Forever."

"Marry me?" Matt blurted out. I looked at him and smiled.

"What?" I asked, not daring to believe what I'd heard him say.

"I love you Alex, so bloody much. Nothing is going to change that. Please baby, marry me and be mine legally, forever?"

"Yes!" I cried. "Yes Matt, I'll marry you! I love you too."

"Yes? You said yes?" Matt asked with shock.

"Did you think I'd say no?" I laughed.

"You said yes! God Alex, I swear I'm going to spend everyday of our life together proving how bloody much you mean to me." He said as he gathered me into his arms and leapt to his feet. He spun me around excitedly and I was giggling uncontrollably, happier than I had ever been in my life.

It was hard to take in all of the ways that my life had changed in the last nine months. I had gone from a scared, lonely, deeply scarred girl and grown into a strong, confident, happy woman, surrounded by love, family and friends. I had everything I had ever dreamed of, including my very own knight in shining armour. He had rescued me from hell, more than once and cared for me and protected me as I found the strength that was buried deep inside of me. He had stood beside me while I slayed the evil I could face and had slayed those I could not. Matt had taught me to trust, and how to love and be loved. He had shown me the beauty those gifts brought into my life and had surrounded me by the family I had always longed for. He had made me a whole instead of the million shattered pieces I had been in when I met him. Together he and my new family had shown me what it was to live a happy, contented life. With them I had discovered that there really was more to life than darkness and misery. They had pulled me into the light and given me everything I needed to believe there really was more to life, that I truly could have a future involving something other than pain. Finally, I had my happily ever after.

Don't Miss the next in the Shepard Security Series!
Coming soon! Amy's story- **Something Other than Darkness**
Find out how the story of Rob's little sister, Amy, unfolds and catch up with Matt and Alex, Jack and Cal and Rob and Lucy along the way.

Shepard Security series reading order:
Something Other Than Fear - Lucy's story
Something Other Than Pain - Matt's story

Something Other Than Darkness - Amy's story
(Coming Soon)

Printed in Great Britain
by Amazon